# THE
# EVOLUTION
# OF THE
# GOSPELETTES

# THE EVOLUTION OF THE GOSPELETTES

## A NOVEL

### TAMMY OBERHAUSEN

FIRESIDE
INDUSTRIES

Published by Fireside Industries
An imprint of The University Press of Kentucky

*Editorial and Sales Offices:* The University Press of Kentucky
663 South Limestone Street, Lexington, Kentucky 40508-4008
www.kentuckypress.com

This is a work of fiction. The characters, places, and events are either drawn from the author's imagination or used fictitiously. Any resemblance of fictional characters to actual living persons is entirely coincidental.

Library of Congress Cataloging-in-Publication Data

Names: Oberhausen, Tammy 1966- author.
Title: The evolution of the Gospelettes : a novel / Tammy Oberhausen.
Description: Lexington, Kentucky : Fireside Industries, 2024.
Identifiers: LCCN 2024018196 | ISBN 9781950564446 (hardcover ; acid-free
    paper) | ISBN 9781950564453 (paperback ; acid-free paper) | ISBN
    9781950564460 (pdf) | ISBN 9781950564477 (epub)
Subjects: LCGFT: Novels.
Classification: LCC PS3615.B473 E96 2024 | DDC 813/.6—dc23/eng/20240429
LC record available at https://lccn.loc.gov/2024018196

This book is printed on acid-free paper meeting
the requirements of the American National Standard
for Permanence in Paper for Printed Library Materials.

Manufactured in the United States of America

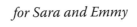

*for Sara and Emmy*

# ANGEL BAND

The Holliman girls could sing like angels. They could hit a note dead center, perfect pitch, make their harmonies soar, croon comforting words like a mother singing love to her baby. They could sing a prodigal home. They could bring the hardest man to tears in his pew and compel a woman who had long ago been saved, sanctified, and baptized in the river and in the Holy Ghost to come forward and rededicate everything she'd already dedicated, just to be sure.

Before there were the Holliman girls, though, before they were the Gospelettes, it was just Jeannie and Junior, swimming in the womb together before the world began.

They must have heard a hundred times, a thousand times, about the angel visitation that their daddy, Garland Holliman, had after they were born. He had gone home to sleep after seeing them in the hospital, and a tall, shining man with wings and no shoes appeared at the foot of his bed and told him that his son would perform a great work and be known in the land far and wide.

There was no mention of the other twin—the firstborn, Jeannie—or the two girls, Debbie and Patty, who would follow soon after to round out the group that would sing the glory down.

Over the years, the vision became more elaborate and detailed in Garland's recitation until it was prophesied that Junior's gift would be to become the minister of a large congregation. Multitudes would come from all around, even outside the county. He would proclaim God's word from the mountaintop. His would be the voice crying out in the wilderness, preparing the way for Christ's return.

The angel may not have mentioned it, but the Holliman sisters had a gift too. Everybody said they had the best voices anywhere around Bethel, Kentucky.

The little town of Bethel, all low rooftops and high steeples, the place their father thought would be the same yesterday, today, and forever.

On the edge of town, across the river where they were baptized, near a grove of whispering trees, a white tent stands.

The clouds part, and that cold, distant moon glows pale blue.

Sweet hay from a nearby field and smoke rising from a barn filled with curing tobacco scent the air.

Voices in harmony vibrate through time and space.

# THE 1970S

# The Family of God

This is how it started, according to Garland Holliman: He was sitting in his chair watching Walter Cronkite on the evening news in July 1972 when he heard his girls singing in the kitchen while they washed the supper dishes. He opened his mouth to yell at them to hush, but then they struck a chord so lovely it shivered down his neck and stung his eyes. He missed the news about the Common Market, a crucial sign of the end times, because all he could hear was how his daughters were holding that chord, crescendoing, and then dropping, all of them together. How did they learn to do that? He sat in disbelief, not because they sang so beautifully—they sang all the time around the house—but because he had never thought about it before. An idea rose up in him, not from his brain but from his chest. They were going to be a family gospel group. The Gospelettes, to play up the three singing sisters aspect. It came to him, just like that.

He ran into the kitchen as the girls were finishing their song. Patty, the youngest, was fanning Jeannie and Debbie with two Rogers Funeral Home fans, one in each hand, while they washed and dried at the sink. The air was sticky hot. They wore their long, straight hair—three shades of straw—pulled back in ponytails, pinned up high with barrettes to stay off their necks. The kitchen window was open, but no breeze blew through, just still, hot air that the electric fan stirred around a little.

Funny that the idea of starting a family group hadn't come up before, considering Garland's collection of gospel albums—the Speer Family, the Blackwood Brothers, the Florida Boys, the Sego Brothers and Naomi—and considering that he had been in a gospel quartet himself, along with his preacher cousin, Brother Clarence Weekes.

They'd been popular in the area for a few years but hadn't taken it seriously enough for Garland.

"Junebug! Big Jean!" Garland called. "Get in here!" He had broken into a sweat.

Junior appeared in the doorway and raised one eyebrow at his sisters.

"Get your bass out, Junebug," Garland said, clapping, almost dancing in his jerky way.

His wife, Jean, whom he had named "Big Jean" after Little Jeannie was born, had gone to lie down on her bed with a sick headache after scrubbing the stovetop. She roused, bleary-eyed but with her majestic black beehive intact, to see what the commotion was about.

"I want you to hear these girls sing!" Garland said. The girls all looked up and at each other. "Let me hear y'all again. Sing 'Keep On the Sunny Side.'" They did—in close harmony, finding their parts naturally as they went along, with voices so similar they seemed to blend into one vibrating sound.

"You better start practicing on that piano again, Big Jean," Garland said, pulling a handkerchief from the back pocket of his trousers and wiping the sweat erupting on his forehead from all the excitement. "Looks like we got us a gospel group."

Jeannie's heart did a flip when he said those words, like when they were kids and Garland would quiz them, make them recite Bible verses on command, and she knew how to please him. Her parents might have expected her to be a little version of her mother and Junior to be a little version of Garland, but she knew *she* was the one who was like her daddy. She had sat at his feet listening to him read the Bible since she was old enough to sit up, while Junior ran around acting a fool. "Acts 2:2," Garland would say, out of the blue, and while Junior sat blank, Jeannie would sit up tall, because she knew it: "And suddenly there came a sound from heaven as of a rushing mighty wind . . ."

She hadn't known what to do with herself since she'd graduated from high school the month before. At graduation, as Mr. Berry, the high school principal, was calling out the names of seniors who won awards and having them come up on stage, Jeannie was applauding each winner, half-listening, when she heard him say, "The William Reed Pickett Scholarship for Outstanding Achievement in Music goes to Jeannie Holliman." Her friend Lisa, sitting to her left, had to elbow her twice to rouse her from her stupor so she could get up and walk across the stage to accept the envelope. She spotted Mr. Cecil Warren, her choir teacher, as she walked back to her seat and gave him a thank-you smile. He always told her she was his best singer, and she sometimes accompanied the choir on piano, playing by ear, like Big Jean did. She knew he was the one who had arranged for her to get the scholarship, despite the fact that she hadn't applied to any colleges.

Back in her seat, she stared at the envelope for the rest of the ceremony, running her fingers over the letters of her name and not listening to the speeches. She slid one finger under the flap, quietly opened the envelope, and peered inside at the $500 check, made out to her. That moment was as if a flock of wildly colored birds flew out, fluttering from her hands and whirling above her head and through the auditorium. She had to catch her breath and hold it. She had been considering which local businesses she might apply for jobs with— the laundromat, the Bethel Dipper, one of the town's three grocery stores—but now she was wondering where she might go to college, where she might perform or teach music, possibilities she hadn't dared to consider before.

Then "Pomp and Circumstance" played, and she followed the line out to the school lobby. She found her family near the exit. Junior was talking to Ray Hankins, one of the boys in her and Junior's class (until Junior had failed a grade), teasing Ray about his graduation gown. Patty played with the tassel hanging from Ray's cap, flirting. Debbie was wedged between their parents by the front door. But when Jeannie rushed over to them and held up the envelope, Garland refused to look at it.

"Give it back," he said.

She stared at him, not sure she'd heard him right. "But—it's a check!" She held the envelope open so he could see inside.

"I know what it is. You're not going to use it. Give it back." He turned toward the door, one hand on the push bar.

"But, Daddy—" She'd never gotten a check before in her life, and now she had one that would cover the cost of a year of college tuition. She pulled it out of the envelope to show him.

"Go on. Give it back." His face—eyes narrowed, lips tight—let her know he meant it. He pushed the door hard and walked out.

She looked at Big Jean. Cigarette smoke from the crowd drifted between them, and a crease developed between her mother's eyes. "I'm going to have to go lay down," Big Jean said. "That smoke is giving me the headache." She turned and followed Garland out the door.

Junior, Debbie, and Patty made a half circle around Jeannie, all watching Garland's back as he walked out.

"Well!" Patty said, arms crossed. "Happy graduation to *you!*" Junior shook his head, looking at the floor. Debbie grabbed Jeannie's hand and squeezed.

Jeannie stared out the big window at him striding toward the parking lot. "I am *not* giving it back," she said, stomping after Big Jean, with Junior, Debbie, and Patty behind her, all of them like a line of ducklings following Garland. She caught up to him before he reached the car. He frowned at the envelope still in her hand.

"Do you know what happens to girls in college?" he demanded.

"They learn things?" Patty, standing behind Jeannie, muttered.

"That's what he's scared of," Junior muttered back.

"You're not going!" Garland yelled, jabbing a finger at the envelope. Other graduates and their families walked around them, staring.

"Daddy—"

"Hush your mouth! You're *not going*! You hear?" His whole body shook with rage, his arms jerking as if he'd touched a live electric wire.

"But—"

He grabbed the envelope from her hand, ripped it in half, and threw the pieces to the ground.

Jeannie gasped, then bent and picked them up. For a few seconds, she stood holding the pieces in her hands tenderly, like a stillborn baby.

She looked up at him, but he had already turned and walked to the car. Big Jean shaped her mouth around a word that never came out. Junior and her sisters stared at Jeannie, wide-eyed, wondering what she'd do next. This was the closest she'd ever come to defying her father, and the set of his jaw told her that one step more would be too far, that he could withhold his favor forever. She couldn't bear the thought of it. Pleasing him always held supremacy.

She walked back into the lobby and found Mr. Warren leaning against the wall, talking to some other teachers.

"I can't use it." She held the torn pieces out to him, not trusting herself to make eye contact.

When he didn't speak, she eventually had to look up, blinking back tears. He kept his arms crossed in front of him and studied her over the top of his half-glasses for several seconds. Finally, he said, "I'll tell the committee you've turned it down and they can give it to the runner-up," but he made no move to take the pieces from her outstretched hand. He seemed sad or disgusted, and she figured he knew that her father had torn up the check. She sensed his pity, and she hated it. She wanted to explain to him about Garland, how much he loved her and wanted to protect her, that he wasn't some ignorant rube who hated education. She remembered her grandfather Papaw Virgil telling them once about what a good student Garland had been: "Miss Doss said he was brilliant. She said, 'Garland is the most brilliant student I've ever had.' But Chester was gone off to war and I needed his help on the farm, so I made him quit." Maybe Garland didn't want her to get her hopes up about something that wasn't in the divine plan. How could Jeannie explain all this to Mr. Warren, standing there with the other teachers, exchanging glances, their minds made up about the Hollimans?

She tucked the torn check into her bra as she walked away. She wanted to turn around and tell Mr. Warren she'd changed her mind, that she really did want to go to college, to go *anywhere*. Could they cut her another check? She even did a little jerk-step, almost turning back to ask him. But on that day, she wanted her father's blessing more.

And that was the thing—the beautiful, unbelievable, miraculous thing—about this idea of Garland's. Jeannie wanted to do something great, something that would please God and Garland. She wanted a gift. And now she had it. She was the lead singer of the Gospelettes, and she decided it was her job—her calling—to make them gospel stars.

# Will the Circle Be Unbroken?

It may have taken a while for Garland to realize that he had a band right under his own roof, but once he did, he wasted no time. The kids had watched with some amusement as he got his old Telecaster out of his closet, then climbed the pull-down ladder into the attic and retrieved his amp. They'd had no idea that their father had ever been hip enough to be plugged in. He had one of his old quartet buddies come over and tune Big Jean's piano, and they were set.

They practiced at least two hours every day, starting as soon as Garland got in from working at the sewing factory. There was no sitting down to play guitar or sing. They stood, as if on stage, or sometimes, Garland had the girls lie on their backs on the hard floor and sing, to challenge them and build vocal power.

At the end of the first month of daily practice, after Garland had made them sing "There's a Light at the River" for what seemed like the hundredth time, Patty complained about the lyrics. "Why a light at the river? What are you doing at the river after dark anyway?" she demanded after Garland went to the bathroom, out of earshot. She slumped onto the couch and sighed loudly.

Jeannie couldn't understand this attitude. She felt these songs in her soul. She felt the music, of course. Even if the songs had been in a different language, she would have felt them. Each chord had its own emotion, its own story. But then, with just the right words, a song was something powerful moving through her body, a wonder. Surely Patty must have felt that. "Think about it," Jeannie said. "If it's dark and you don't know your way, think how lovely and comforting it would be to have a light at the river—just for you!"

Debbie, always the worrier, nodded. "If it's dark at the river, you might step on a water moccasin or trip over a tree root or slide down a mud bank—"

"OK, stop," Patty said, closing her eyes and chopping the air with one upraised hand. "Just stop."

Junior tuned his guitar and sang the chorus of "One Toke over the Line," thumping out the bass line. "I think we ought to do that one," he said.

Jeannie laughed. "I'm sure Daddy would go for that."

"Why not? It has 'sweet Jesus' in it." Junior smirked. Always the comedian.

"What are you doing, sitting down?" Garland demanded when he stomped back into the living room, adjusting his belt. "We ain't done yet!" He loomed over Patty, hands planted on his hips, and glared.

Patty exhaled loudly, and Junior gave her a hand, pulling her up from the couch.

They'd just finished another round of "There's a Light at the River" when they heard a knock at the front door. Jeannie let in their neighbors, Leonard and Imogene Moody, who had been listening from out in their yard. "Something about being kin makes your voices go together so good," Imogene said.

"Blood can harmonize," Leonard agreed.

It was easy to see that the kids were kin. They were "all Holliman," Big Jean said, but Jeannie wasn't so sure of that assessment. Junior, for instance, despite being named after Garland, didn't have their daddy's serious bent and studious nature. He was back in school that August even though he was supposed to have graduated with Jeannie. He'd only made it that far by copying her homework. He had excelled only at shop, where the teacher let him spend most of his time tinkering with motorcycles. He got around Garland's anti-hippie rules by wearing his hair short in back but with sideburns and long bangs, which he flipped out of his eyes with a toss of the head. He enjoyed coming up with nicknames for everyone, joking around, keeping the mood up wherever he was. Where did this trait come from? Certainly not from their parents, with their apocalyptic gloom.

Debbie had come along just eighteen months after Junior and Jeannie and was used to fading into the background. Maybe that was why she was such a good backup singer. She never competed with Jeannie for the melody line.

Patty, born less than two years after Debbie, was the spitfire of the family. Tiny and light as a rag doll. Neighbors, church friends, and perfect strangers were all fooled by her size and high voice into thinking she was sweet. She had always been handled against her will, picked up, squeezed, and patted. She'd spent her childhood squirming and struggling to get loose and take off running. Once, when Patty was four years old, Sister Bertie Collier at church swooped her up into her clammy, padded embrace, and Patty told her, "You smell bad, and I hate you." Big Jean shushed her, and when they got home, Garland whipped her with his belt. Jeannie was sure it hadn't done a bit of good. She would absolutely say it again under the same circumstances.

"Do y'all know 'Will the Circle Be Unbroken?'" Imogene asked.

"Why, yeah," Garland said.

"Would you sing that one before we go?" she asked. "I might cry now. It makes me think about my mother and daddy and all my brothers and sisters. I was one of eleven, and there's just three of us left." Jeannie tried to imagine Imogene crying. She was a bony woman, just barely five feet tall, dry and hard as a piece of gravel, with a smoker's rasp, black cat's-eye glasses, and a sharp beak of a nose, nothing soft about her.

Garland played the opening on his harmonica, and then Jeannie sang the first verse, backed up by Big Jean on the piano and Junior on bass. Then Debbie, Patty, and Junior joined in on the chorus. Four different parts. Jeannie's voice had a little vibrato on this song. She glanced over at the Moodys and saw Leonard's eyes get shiny-wet, though not a tear fell, and saw Imogene dab hers.

A kind of energy took over when the Gospelettes sang sometimes, like electricity surging through their limbs, almost lifting them off the floor. Jeannie loved that song too. It was a little different. A question. That's what made it interesting. Most of their songs were statements. *There's a light at the river. I will meet you in the morning. I'll have a new body, I'll have a new life. I know who holds tomorrow.* But this song asked, not quite certain, *Will the circle be unbroken, by and by, Lord, by and by?* Then came the answer: *There's a better home a-waitin' in the sky, Lord, in the sky.*

Jeannie looked around at the Gospelettes, making eye contact with each member of her family, one by one, the air electrified by their communion, as they held that final *sky*, raising it up to heaven, lowering it back down to earth, letting it die.

# God's Not Dead

Garland pushed them hard, and in two months of daily singing practice under his critical tutelage, Jeannie went from a high, thin soprano to a strong lead. She could hear the difference in Junior, Debbie, and Patty too. They had always had a natural talent for finding harmonies, but Garland had fine-tuned each part in each song and adjusted the volume of each note to perfection. Now, over breakfast on a Sunday before church, he was giving final instructions for their debut.

He held a biscuit in his left hand and a fork in his right, to scoop up bits of runny fried egg. "Listen here. Gospel singers *cannot* act like just any kind of performer. Do you get what I'm saying?"

They all nodded. Jeannie glanced at the wall clock.

"Every expression on your face, every move you make, every piece of clothing you wear on that stage is a reflection on your faith," he warned.

Jeannie frowned at Patty, who had finished eating and put one elbow on the table and propped her head on her hand, eyes rolled up to something above Garland's head.

"Listen now," he said. "They're gonna know whether you're doing it for God's glory or your own. You better believe it."

Junior poured himself another glass of milk. "Remember the Dixie Inspirations?" They had come to their church to perform, and one of the singers, a woman in a splashy orange-and-yellow dress, had displeased Garland with her showmanship and "opera singing," as he called it. The way she waved her arms, the way she held the high notes long after everyone else had let their notes go, the way that bright dress drew every eye right to it whether you wanted to look there or not. Garland had complained about them for days.

"I seen it all," Garland said, referring to his gospel-singing days in the early 1950s. "Ungodly behavior. Things you would not believe."

"Like what?" Patty wanted to know, but he refused to elaborate, probably not wanting to give them any ideas.

Now, Brother Clarence Weekes had asked the Gospelettes to sing at church, and they were all at various points on the scale from nervous to excited. Jeannie rounded up the girls to get ready, with Garland still rattling off instructions.

After Debbie had been in the bathroom for far too long, Jeannie knocked on the door. She could hear sobbing inside. "Debbie? What's wrong with you?" She put an ear to the door and heard a choked sob. "Debbie! Open the door!" Jeannie banged on it, harder now. "We've got to leave in ten minutes. What are you doing?" As Debbie unlocked the door, Jeannie pushed her way in. Debbie, red-faced and tear-streaked, was dressed in a stretchy, ribbed, brown body suit that covered her from neck to wrists to toes. Jeannie yanked the plaid jumper dress from the hook by the door. "Why aren't you dressed?"

Debbie was hunched over the commode, hugging herself. "I can't—" she gagged, midsentence.

Jeannie felt a rising panic. "You can't? What do you mean you can't?"

Debbie looked down at her shaking hands as if they belonged to someone else. "I can't get up there and sing, Jeannie. I can't!"

For a moment, Jeannie stood over her, holding the jumper dress, waiting, without speaking. She was listening to their perfect harmonies in her head, minus Debbie's part. It physically hurt her to imagine the loss. They'd been working for months to perfect their sound. To change it now, to lose Debbie's harmony line, would be unbearable. When Jeannie spoke again, her voice was low, a forced calm. "Debbie. We can do this without you, but you know it wouldn't be the same. The harmonies wouldn't be complete." The idea of all of them up front performing while Debbie sat in a pew made her feel like crying. "You're one of us!"

Debbie tore off a strip of toilet paper and blew her nose. "I know I'm one of us, but I'm also . . . me."

Jeannie cleared her throat, twice, stifling the raised voice that threatened to erupt. "This is our debut," she said slowly, controlled, "and you're ruining it for all of us."

Debbie dry-heaved into the commode.

There was a knock at the door. "Are you almost done?" Patty's voice came through the crack in the door. "I've got to pee."

"Just a minute." Debbie's voice broke. She sat on the fuzzy pink bathmat and laid her cheek against the cool bathtub.

"We've sung these songs at least a hundred times," Jeannie said. "You know them inside and out, backwards and forwards, could sing them in your sleep. And if Daddy says your singing is good enough— well, it must be. He doesn't go around dropping compliments for nothing."

Debbie lay down on the bathmat, her head resting on one arm, tears rolling into the forest of pink fuzz.

There was another knock. "What's going on?" Patty asked from outside.

Debbie closed her eyes. "I'm . . . I don't know. I'm nervous," she called out.

Garland was outside the door now, having a discussion with Patty. "She says she's nervous," Patty told him.

"You ain't nervous!" Garland yelled at the closed door. Jeannie could imagine him turning red, sweating through his dress shirt. "Now get out of there and straighten up before I give you something to be nervous *about*!"

"Well, that should fix it," Patty said.

Jeannie opened the door a crack. "I've got it under control, Daddy," she assured him. "We'll be out in a minute."

Garland scowled and stomped away.

"Gotta pee," Patty said.

Jeannie pulled her inside. Patty looked down at her sister on the floor, dressed in the brown body suit, and laughed. "You look like a mud turtle that lost its shell."

"I can't do it, Jeannie! I can't sing—" Debbie gagged on the word *sing* like a finger in her throat. "—in front of all those people."

"Why not? They're just our church family." Jeannie patted her shoulder mechanically. "They're people we've known our whole lives." Jeannie hadn't had a single moment of doubt since the day they'd started the Gospelettes that this was the thing she was supposed to do with her life. It was as if Debbie had said, "I can't breathe in front of all those people." It made no sense at all.

Debbie stood at the sink and wiped her face with a wet rag. "Why is he making us do this anyway? I don't want to be a singer. I've never wanted to be a singer."

"Me neither," Patty said. "I've got to pee, so hurry up."

Jeannie felt as if her sisters held her heart in their hands and just dropped it. "But y'all are so good!" She handed Debbie her dress. "You have beautiful voices!"

"I didn't say I *can't* sing," Patty said. "I said I don't want to."

Jeannie looked at Patty and then back at Debbie, dumbfounded. "Do you mean to tell me that God has given you this gift and this *calling*, and you intend to turn it down because you *don't want to* sing?"

"I can't get up in front of people," Debbie said. She leaned into the mirror and looked at her eyes, bloodshot from crying.

"Nervousness, I can understand," Jeannie said. "I'm nervous, too. But not wanting to sing? Not even wanting to try? Just sinking into whatever Bethel, Kentucky, has to offer us without taking a shot at anything? No. That, I don't understand." She grasped Debbie's upper arms and turned her around. "We have the opportunity of a lifetime to do something great! To be gospel singers!" She took the dress from Debbie's hands, pulled it over her head, forced her arms through the holes, and zipped it in back. "I'm not going to let you throw this away. You're going to get up there and sing for the Lord."

Debbie lifted one hand to her throat and squeezed. "What if nothing comes out? Can I just stand there and move my mouth and pretend like I'm singing?"

"Oh, good grief, Debbie! We've been working on these songs for months. Don't ruin it for us." Jeannie whirled around and frowned at Patty. "And what's *your* problem? You don't want to be a singer? What is it you want to do?"

Patty examined herself in the mirror, running her fingers through her hair. "I just want to be free."

Jeannie grabbed a brush and pulled it through Debbie's hair. "You want to be free," she muttered. "You and Bobby McGee."

"I just want to be a wife and mother," Debbie said, sniffling. "Like Mama."

As the oldest sister, Jeannie had had many moments of irritation over the years, but this took the prize. "You can be a wife and mother," she told Debbie. "And you can be free," she told Patty. "But you're also going to be Gospelettes. And we're going to get up there and sing," she said, jabbing the hairbrush at them both, practically gritting her teeth. "And we're going to make records and be on the radio. And then you'll thank me for making you do this, and I'll say, 'I told you so.' You wait and see."

Jeannie could see it. She just needed them to open their eyes and see it too. An angel had appeared at the foot of Garland's bed and told him that Junior would perform a great work. Jeannie imagined that angel coming back for one more visit and telling them all, "*And* you're going to do the Lord's work as a famous gospel group!" Surely there was more to the story than just Junior.

By the time they got to the church, even Jeannie's stomach was in knots and her throat clenched tight. She kept one eye on Debbie, who, though not exactly overflowing with happiness, at least remained upright. Garland was barking orders, telling everyone what equipment to pick up, how to carry it and how not to, where to walk and how and at what speed. They set up and shook hands and hugged necks on the way to their seats. Garland glared at Debbie, who was wringing her hands, and at Patty, who was yawning, before settling on Jeannie with a hard look that said he was depending on her to lead her sisters.

Brother Jenks Smith, who served as an emcee of sorts for all the services at the Bethel Independent Church of the Pentecost, announced that the church had a new group—the Gospelettes!

Jeannie marched up on the stage with her family and pulled the microphone from its stand. It was the large metallic kind, big as a man's fist. She had considered leaving it there but decided that holding it might steady her. Debbie crowded her on the left, close enough to touch the hem of her dress. Patty stood a few steps to the right and pulled up her knee socks. Junior planted himself in a rock-and-roll pose farther off to the right, guitar strap slung over his shoulder. Jeannie looked out at the expectant faces of people she'd known all her life, people who were like family or *were* family, kin to them one way or another. She felt a pressure behind her eyes, a sweet tenderness for these people, old, young, and in-between. Men with calloused hands and sun-reddened faces who worked on farms and in factories all week and then put on starched shirts and ties and hair pomade to come sit in the house of the Lord. Women whose only dress-up occasions were Sundays, powdered and perfumed and panty-hosed. She could see them all before her: Brother Clarence and Sister Lucy, Brother Jenks and Sister Ruth, Sister Nannie Johnson, Sister Bertie Collier, Brother Roy Lee, Sister Carol Harper—all the giants of her childhood. She tried to take a deep breath, but her lungs seemed to have shriveled. She imagined that Debbie must be about to pass out and felt a sudden rush of sympathy. She reached over and gave her sweaty hand a squeeze.

Big Jean played the first notes of "God's Not Dead," a rocking little number the audience could clap their hands and pat their feet to. Jeannie sang the lead, with her family repeating lines behind her, slipping into the groove that those hours of practice had formed.

Suddenly, Garland unlatched his guitar strap, dropped the guitar into its stand, and danced in the spirit, across the stage, down the steps, out into the congregation. His eyes were closed, and sweat plastered his thinning gray-brown hair to his head and dripped down the collar of his beige shirt. He removed his clip-on tie and undid the first button of his shirt, never stopping his dance.

Big Jean banged out the tune, her fingers flying across the keys, her great beehive bobbing. Junior thumped out the bass line. The girls swayed like identical grasses in a breeze.

Garland bent forward, still stepping, straightened, shook. He was average in height and weight, but he seemed taller and bigger as Jeannie watched him. Drops of sweat flew from his body, sprinkling the altar as he made his way back up to the stage. And then he cried out, more high-pitched than his normal voice, startling and sending a jolt through her. Some of the ladies in the church cried out in response, "Thank you, Jesus!"

Jeannie's eyes followed him up and down the aisles. It was amazing, this glimpse of something behind the material form. He was this sack of bones and blood and skin and organs, but then she could see there was something else. Something animating the whole thing. Joy animating a bag of blood and bones called Garland Holliman. Seeing him this way, how could anyone not believe?

Halfway through their first performance, the Gospelettes had the congregation on their feet singing along and clapping their hands. Old Brother Don Calvert circled the sanctuary half a dozen times, half-walking, half-dancing, like some long-legged, crazy, endearing bird. All around them were joy and love, embodied, as if those fragile, fleeting emotions burst to life, loud and in brilliant color, on faces tilted upward, raised hands waving, shouts and whoops, middle-aged and older bodies jumping and dancing like children.

"We're not the show, God is," Garland said that day and would repeat at other singings when the spirit was moving. Big Jean softened the piano, and Junior alternated two chords in the background. "It's not me playing this guitar!" Garland declared, wiping his red face with his handkerchief. "Amen? The Lord's moving my fingers!" He raised his arms and wiggled his fingers in the air.

Everybody said amen.

"And these girls, they have beautiful voices, don't they?"

"Amen!"

"But it's not their glory," Garland said. "It's the Lord's. If he wanted to, he could make them rocks out yonder cry out. They could sing these songs just as well as we can, if the Lord wants it that way, hallelujah."

Jeannie imagined this: a smooth, gray rock on the side of the road, singing with her voice. Herself, Debbie, and Patty, all trapped inside rocks like genies in bottles.

Brother Jenks invited them back up to sing during the altar call. Jeannie stood holding the microphone, her wide-open eyes turned upward to keep the tears in as they sang "What a Day That Will Be." They had made it. Even Debbie. Garland was pleased. A rare calm had settled over his face. Church usually let out at noon, and the congregation would rush out to eat dinner. But this time they stuck around until nearly two o'clock, until everybody got taken care of. Brother Clarence told them to welcome two new brothers, and the congregation cheered. Several rededicated, others came up to pray about one thing or another—a sickness, marriage troubles, a wayward family member. Sister Nannie got up and testified for a good fifteen minutes, as she was wont to do when the spirit was moving. When she paused to take a breath, Garland started "Sheltered in the Arms of God." A few people sneaked out to go have Sunday dinner, but most stayed. Finally, they sang the last verse for the fourth time, and Brother Clarence dismissed them all.

When the doors opened, cool October air reminded them of the world outside the church walls. Jeannie felt emptied, transformed, as she walked out beneath the clearest and bluest of skies, carrying the equipment to the car. Everything was different now. People kept stopping the Gospelettes to shake their hands or hug their necks or tell them how beautiful they sounded and how the Lord was using them. Sister Nannie grabbed Jeannie by her arms and shook her. "The Lord is going to use that voice!" she declared.

"Amen!" Sister Bertie, standing beside Sister Nannie, shouted, waving the damp tissue she kept clutched in her fist.

"I have given thee the voice of an angel," Sister Nannie continued. "Lift up thy voice, thus saith the Lord!"

Jeannie thanked her and followed her family to the car. She could hardly look the other churchgoers in the eyes, not sure what to do with the feelings of gratitude and embarrassment and excitement all tangled up together. She felt powerful, taller somehow. This surely beat sitting in a college classroom, listening to a professor drone. She felt she must be glowing. How could they go home, turn on the TV, and have their usual spats now, now that they were like little gods?

# The Old Country Church

The 1964 Chevrolet Impala station wagon carrying the Gospelettes to their singing engagement was the slowest vehicle on the road. Every car passed them at nearly twice their speed, but Garland's speedometer needle stayed firmly planted between forty-five and fifty. Jeannie felt it would take forever to get there, but Garland knew the statistics on traffic deaths caused by speeding.

Garland was always on guard against the dangers of interstate highways, elevators, hippies, motel rooms, drugs, water fountains, airplanes, caves, tornadoes, electrical outlets, universities, restaurant food, and public toilets.

Jeannie, sitting in the back seat between Junior and Debbie, checked her watch and sighed, but she knew better than to urge her father to speed up. Sometimes she wondered what had made him so afraid. As far as she could tell, he had led a fairly safe and sheltered life for the times he lived in. His older brother had been killed in World War II, but he'd never been in the military himself. Nor had he, to her knowledge, ever been in a car crash or been attacked by a hippie or suffered any electrical shocks. If he had, he surely would have told them all about it, repeatedly. Big Jean had said once that his mother had petted him too much and he didn't know how to act without her. It seemed to Jeannie that Big Jean had just picked up where her mother-in-law left off.

The kids had never known Garland's mother, who had died before they were born, but they knew that she, not Papaw Virgil, had been the source of his faith. She must have also been the source of his fears. The two were so mixed together in their church. The Book of Revelation seemed to be on a constant loop in Garland's speeches.

Disaster was always imminent, and the devil was always out to destroy whatever you thought you had.

Big Jean had packed dinner for them: fried chicken, ham sandwiches, deviled eggs, and fried apple pies, with iced tea in thermos jugs. They had that same meal on nearly every trip, sometimes both ways, dinner and supper, except when the church where they were singing held a potluck or a church member invited them home for a meal. They usually pulled over at a roadside picnic table to eat, but it was too cold on this day, so they ate in the car at a rest stop. Garland wouldn't eat while he drove. He kept both hands on the wheel.

Jeannie watched the passing frozen fields and bare trees. Everything was still and cold outside—the sky, the land, the nearly deserted road. Even inside, wedged between Junior and Debbie, she was chilly. The heater was barely functioning. Garland worried that they'd freeze if the car quit.

Junior was itching to drive. "I don't understand why you don't want somebody to help you on these long trips, Daddy," he complained from the back seat. "Most guys my age have their own cars already. I'm getting one this year with my tobacco money, so you ought to just go on and let me get some practice."

"You still have some observing to do, Junie," Garland said, gripping the steering wheel as if he feared Junior might yank it away. "Watch how I handle certain problems that come up. You never know what kind of situation you might find yourself in on the road when you're dealing with other drivers." He looked over at the car passing in the other lane as if to say, *See there!* "It's not just you on the road. You have to get some experience in observing first before you just jump behind a wheel and take off."

Junior leaned over Jeannie, draping his arms over the front seat between Garland and Patty, who was stuck against her will between their parents. "Watch, observe, watch, observe! There comes a time you got to do something, Daddy," Junior insisted. "I'm a man of action."

Patty turned around and gave Jeannie and Debbie a smirk, and they all laughed.

"When the time is right, I'll let you," Garland said.

"You'll let me," Junior mumbled. He sat back and cracked the window to cool himself off even though it was close to freezing outside.

"I already know how anyway. I've been driving my buddies' cars for two years," he said to Jeannie under his breath.

"What about me?" Jeannie asked Garland. "I've already graduated. Are you going to teach *me* to drive?" She'd been thinking that having a driver's license might come in handy now that she was doing promotions and scheduling for the group.

Garland said their husbands would drive the girls.

"What if we don't get married?" Patty asked. "Look at Debbie. She won't even talk to a boy. She's probably going to be an old maid. And what if I become a women's libber?"

For once, Garland didn't seem to think he needed to reply. He kept driving—forty-eight miles per hour on the interstate.

Big Jean didn't have a driver's license. Garland took her to the grocery store and to church. He paid the utilities and did the banking. They lived right in town, so they could walk if they wanted to go to the beauty shop or go shopping or just look around. Since she'd graduated from high school, Jeannie walked four blocks to work at Ogles Market every day. It wasn't too bad. Mr. Ogles let her have weekends off so she was free to go to singings. When business was slow, she had time to plan ways to promote the group. Sometimes she even wrote songs in her head while she sat there waiting for customers. The songs just poured out, came right through her, without any effort at all, really. She'd open her mouth, and a new song would come out, something the world had never heard before. She had a notebook full of songs she'd written and plans she was making—churches they might perform at, recording studios between Bethel and Nashville, radio programs they might be able to do a live show for. This had all naturally fallen to her, as the lead singer of the Gospelettes and the oldest and most responsible of the Holliman kids.

They passed a sign for Mammoth Cave. None of the Holliman kids had been allowed to go with their classes on field trips to the cave. "Wonder how big Mammoth Cave is?" Jeannie mused.

"Mammoth," Junior said.

"Lisa Page told me that when she went on the school trip, a guide took them deep inside and then turned off all the lights and it was so dark she couldn't see her hand in front of her face," Jeannie said. "He told them there were blind fish in there. They had eyes—or remnants of eyes—but they'd been in absolute darkness for so long that they didn't need them anymore, so they'd lost their vision."

Garland drove by the sign.

"Reckon how come they got eyes if they can't see with them?" Junior asked.

"Because God made them that way," Garland said.

"Seems kind of petty," Patty said.

"But they *used* to have eyes," Jeannie said. "That's what the guide told them. They still had the eye—what do you call it?—the apparatus back there, but where the eyes should be, it's just covered up, like scales just grew right over where the eyes used to be."

"The Lord has his own reasons," Garland said. "We don't have to know why."

"Why don't we go in there, Daddy?" Junior asked.

Every time they drove up I-65, Junior asked if they could stop and take a tour through the cave, and every time Garland told them about a girl who had gotten lost in there and was never found. "She was with her group, and then one of them looked around and said, 'Where's so-and-so?' and they couldn't find her anywhere. They went back the way they came in, they called for her, they showed lights all over, but they never found her. It's pitch black in there, you know. No light whatsoever, except what people bring in. She must've starved to death."

They all sat in silence for a while. Jeannie imagined the poor girl lost in the cave, all alone, cold and hungry, calling out but no one answering, just the echo of her own voice. She thought that would be the loneliest death in the world.

"How long do you think it took her to die?" Debbie asked in a reverent whisper.

"Oh, about a week, maybe," Garland said.

"I'd yell real loud until they come and got me," Patty said.

"They wouldn't hear you in there, if you got lost on some of them side passageways," Garland said. "There's passageways all over the place down there, miles and miles of them. And drop-offs. She probably fell in some drop-off, hundreds of miles down, and drowned in one of them underground rivers."

"Jeff Davis went last summer, and his *grandmother* went on the tour with them," Junior said. "His *grandmother*."

"I wonder if you can see those blind fish," Jeannie mused. She wanted to see them for herself, these creatures with eyes that couldn't see, as if seeing them would help her understand God.

"By the time *we* get to go in there, *we'll* be the ones that's blind," Patty said, crossing her arms. "From old age."

Their singing that night was to be at Beaver Creek Pentecostal Church in the eastern part of the state. They'd never been there before, so Jeannie navigated with Garland's worn map of Kentucky. As the roads grew darker, narrower, and curvier, the mood in the car turned apprehensive.

"How in the world did you hear about this place?" Patty asked Jeannie.

"Shhh!" Garland said. "I'm trying to see!"

Patty turned around and gave Jeannie a look.

Finally, they came upon a gas station, and Garland pulled in, took out his wallet, and began counting his money.

A weathered, white-haired man in gray coveralls limped over. "Fill her up?"

Garland drew a deep breath. "I reckon. Yeah." He turned to Big Jean. "Did you bring any money?"

"Why, no." She didn't need to carry cash since Garland accompanied her just about everywhere.

He turned around to face Junior, Jeannie, and Debbie in the back seat. "Anybody bring any money?"

They shook their heads.

"Oh, Lord!" Patty looked out the windows at the gas station and the empty road ahead. "Don't tell me we're stuck *here*!"

"Hush! We ain't stuck here," Garland said. "We might have enough. We got another forty or fifty miles to the church anyway." He told the gas station attendant to put in five dollars' worth. He studied the gas gauge and said, "We can probably make it back home."

Jeannie scribbled calculations in a notebook she carried with her everywhere. "Two hundred and thirty miles to the church and then back home," she said. "What's the gas mileage for this car, Daddy?"

"Eight miles per gallon," Junior said.

"Naw!" In the rearview mirror, Jeannie could see the crease between Garland's brows. "Ten, twelve," he said.

"*Maybe* ten," Junior said.

Jeannie calculated in her head. "If we got back as far as Bowling Green, we could call somebody from church to come get us."

Patty dropped her head back against the top of the front seat as if shot.

Even though they had been performing at churches for months, they hadn't yet made money from it, beyond the occasional small collection plate offering. Jeannie didn't want to charge a fee for fear the churches would withdraw their invitations. She insisted they had to get established first.

"So what do those big-time famous gospel groups do in this situation?" Patty asked the light above her head.

"Well, for one thing, they probably make money from record sales," Jeannie said. "I need to find out how to cut an album. And . . . we should probably start charging a fee for performances."

"You reckon?" Patty asked, raising her hands.

"Yeah, *maybe* we could start with charging enough money for gas to get home," Junior suggested.

Debbie, sitting to Jeannie's right, patted her hand and whispered, "You're doing a good job."

Outside, the church looked like most of the others they had sung in over the past few months—a simple faded-white building with a modest steeple. Even inside, at first glance, it was familiar, with the smooth, worn wooden pews Jeannie loved to run her hands over, with crackly old wallpaper and that musty hymnal smell and a wooden Sunday School Register with changeable attendance numbers hanging on the wall. But this community seemed poorer than most they'd seen. Old men and women sat motionless, looking weary beyond desperation. Even the middle-aged and many of the young had the hollow eyes of the aged. The whole place had a haunted look, to Jeannie's mind. Garland always said ghosts weren't real because they weren't in the Bible, but Jeannie knew of quite a few things that had been left out.

"Where do you reckon they keep the rattlesnakes?" Patty whispered as they set up.

"I don't know, but you can have mine." Junior draped his amp cord over Debbie's shoulder.

"Y'all hush," Jeannie said. They didn't spend months practicing and hours driving just to make fun of these people. Sometimes it seemed like her siblings couldn't understand the most basic things about what they were doing.

From the raised platform, she looked out at pale, undernourished faces and the clashing patterns of out-of-style, homemade clothing, the worn once-red carpet, and the bare bulbs dangling from the ceiling. To her right, a cold wind whistled through a broken window. To her left, a plywood cross leaned, empty except for a crown of thorns dripping with red paint.

"We sure are blessed to see you here, and we hope ever' one of y'all'll be blessed to hear us," Garland said. "We're just here to sing old-time gospel music and have a good time in the Lord."

They opened with "Blood Washed Band," not a favorite of Jeannie's, with its military beat and warrior stance, but Junior liked it, and she was eager to keep her siblings happy, to keep the group going. They slid into "I'm Standing on the Solid Rock," a song she liked better, that acknowledged disappointments, discontentment, even depression, things she felt pretty sure this audience—most of their audiences—could identify with better than marching, drenched in blood, to battle against Satan. In this one, her high notes rang out and echoed off the walls and ceiling of the sanctuary. Jeannie could feel it right away. The spirit. That vibration that seemed to lift everyone in the room and hold them, suspended, for the duration of the performance. The Gospelettes had gotten so in sync that one of them could do something different—hold a note longer, repeat a line, add a new riff—and the rest of the group would fall right in without missing a beat, as if they'd become parts of one body.

After their performance that evening, as they loaded up the car, the preacher, a scarecrow-thin man in high-water pants, handed Garland a well-stuffed envelope. The church had taken up a collection during the service. Garland had Big Jean count the money once they got out on the highway.

"A hundred and twenty-eight dollars," Big Jean said in a quavering voice. Junior clamored over the front seat, wanting to see, but Garland told him he didn't need to handle it, money being just covered with germs. Jeannie thought of the poor people in that church and how willing they were to give what little they had. She would have been tempted to turn around and give it right back to them had the Gospelettes not needed the money for gas.

"The Lord has provided a way," Garland said, pulling into a gas station to fill up their tank.

On the long drive home, Jeannie wrote a new song in her notebook and then hummed it to herself. *I know you're here, though I can't see you. I know you're here, for I can feel you. I feel your presence here in my heart.* Everyone else was sleeping except Garland, who leaned forward, squinting into the road illuminated by his headlights. She wanted to sing her new song to him and tell him the song list she was planning for their first album, but she knew he couldn't stand chatter while he was driving.

At two o'clock in the morning, they finally made it home and dragged themselves to their beds. In a few hours, almost before they had a chance to get their eyes good and closed, they had to get up and go to work and school. They were doing this nearly every weekend by then, sometimes two or three days in a row, usually for a lot less than $128. They did it for nothing. Or, rather, they did it for the Lord, according to Garland, and for Jeannie, his saying it made it so.

# Shine On Me

Sister Nannie Johnson's hair had turned solid white overnight years ago, before she was forty years old, after a prophetic vision. (Garland had told Jeannie this story when she was a child, and she was never quite sure how to feel about it. Impressed by the power of her gift? Hopeful that she never got one like it?) Since then, Sister Nannie had prophetic visions on a regular basis. These usually occurred, she said, between six and nine in the morning, while she was in her prayer closet (which was actually her bathroom), fixing breakfast, or getting her grandchild off to school. One of her visions concerned the Gospelettes. When they finished singing "Hallelujah Square" one Sunday morning, she stood up and gave them a word.

"The Lord showed me a stadium filled with people jumping and cheering, and I thought it must be a rock music concert," she said, "but then I noticed that people were crying out, 'Praise the Lord! Praise his name!' And I saw thousands falling to their knees and coming to the Lord." She shut her eyes tight in concentration as she talked. "And I saw this family on the stage in bright gold garments," she said. "And there was a darkness there, a dark fog all over the arena, but as they sang, it drifted away, and the bright gold garments shone like the sun."

When she finished, Brother Clarence stood up and said that called for a hallelujah.

They didn't get gold garments, but Jeannie bought several yards of red gingham and, with Big Jean's help, sewed up matching outfits for them to wear on stage. She wanted them to look like real professional gospel singers, not just a family in their regular church clothes. Big Jean and the girls wore red-checked dresses with butterfly sleeves, trimmed in rickrack. Garland and Junior wore red-checked shirts stitched in a western style, with white leisure suits. Junior suggested that they could all go down to the Copper Kettle and cover the tables. But Garland was proud of their new outfits, so Jeannie arranged to have their picture made professionally, something they could use in promotional materials.

She submitted that picture to be used in a full-page newspaper ad for a big camp meeting and gospel singing. The Gospelettes, after just ten months of performing, were the headliners. She cut out the ad and hung it on the wall of the bedroom she shared with Debbie and Patty. They were all smiling, looking full of the joy of the Lord. She wanted to climb into that picture and live there instead of in the real world.

Junior, however, did not appreciate the attention. "I don't know why we had to go and put that picture in the paper," he said at supper one night. "Don't y'all know I got to go to school and face people?"

Garland set down his iced tea and scowled at him. "'Blessed are ye, when men shall revile you, and persecute you, and shall say all manner of evil against you falsely, for my sake.'" He picked up his fork and continued eating.

*Matthew 5:11*, Jeannie said to herself.

Junior insisted that he wasn't being persecuted for Jesus, he was getting laughed at for looking like a dope in the newspaper.

When Jeannie taped a poster for that camp meeting and gospel singing on the door of Ogles Market, where she was still working, her intention was to spread the word in song, as Garland always said. But as it turned out, that was how she met Wick Whitaker.

She saw him as soon as he walked in, and as much as she wanted to, she couldn't stop looking. He wasn't someone you half noticed. She'd never seen someone move with such grace, so at ease in his body. His skin glowed, as if he'd absorbed the sun and was releasing the rays now, into the drab little world that was Ogles Market.

"Are you one of them gospel singers?" he asked, hitching his thumb at the poster. He smiled and gazed at her with his pale blue eyes, so light they didn't seem to belong in this world. She had to look away.

She told him that she was.

"I believe I know you." He looked at her carefully. "I've seen you somewhere around here." He had a few days' growth of a gold-tinged beard, lighter than his curly brown hair, which hung to his shoulders.

She knew who he was. Everyone in town knew the Whitaker boys. In the listings of court records in the newspaper, there was always a Whitaker charged with something. His daddy was their dry town's best-known bootlegger, and Wick and his two older brothers had expanded the business into drug dealing. He'd also fought in Vietnam, and not a one of the boys Jeannie knew who had gone had come back unscathed.

He was leaning on the counter in front of the cash register, smiling. His teeth were amazingly white for someone who had probably never been to a dentist. Probably never been to a doctor either, unless he was on his deathbed. Probably never even been inside a church. Jeannie figured his family couldn't be any more different from hers and still live in the same town.

"Are you at least going to tell me your name?" he asked.

She wished she could be the breezy type of girl who felt comfortable talking to anyone anywhere, but that was not the case. She was more confident than Debbie, though less outspoken than Patty. When she stood in front of an audience, now that she was used to it, she could sing with hardly a flutter. But singing was one thing and speaking to Wick Whitaker was another. She finally found her tongue and croaked out, "Jeannie Holliman." Something about him made her feel like she had taken off her clothes instead of just saying her name. It wasn't that he was leering but that his expression was open, naked, without the usual masks that people wear. Like he'd never been taught to hide his motives or put on Sunday clothes.

"Wick Whitaker." Still smiling, he extended his hand and shook hers. He squinted at her. "You're Junebug Holliman's sister."

She nodded. "Twin sister. He's right there with me on the poster."

He walked back to the door and examined the picture. "Yeah. I was looking at his good-looking sister. Didn't even notice him." He returned to the cash register and winked, making heat rise from her neck to her hairline. "Junior's a good guy," he said. "I didn't know he was a gospel singer though." He laughed, as if she had told a good one. She wondered how Wick knew Junior so well. Had Junior been running around with a known drug dealer? Garland would have a fit.

Wick lit a cigarette with his head tilted down, his sky eyes still on her. "So how do you like working at Ogles Market, Jeannie Holliman?"

"It's all right. I like it." She wiped off the counter with a damp rag, just to be doing something. "I like it fine."

He leaned back against the wooden counter, smoking thoughtfully. "Well, what do you like to do when you're *not* working at Ogles Market?"

She straightened the pens beside the cash register, not breathing. She wasn't sure she could speak. She wasn't sure she *should* speak to him, knowing his reputation. Was it better for a Christian young lady to keep her distance or share her testimony when faced with an attractive heathen? Her mind did a quick scan of the many sermons she'd heard in her life and came up short. "I stay pretty busy, going to singings on weekends," she said finally.

Wick turned toward her, leaning one hip against the counter. "So that's it? You work in here all week, and then you spend your weekends in church singing?"

She shrugged. "Mostly." And suddenly it did seem that there ought to be more to life, even though five minutes before, singing in churches every weekend had been plenty, had been a dream come true, actually.

"Do you know this song—how did it go?" He flicked ash on the smooth concrete floor and looked into the distance. "What a friend we have in Jesus, da da da-da-da-da-da!" he sang.

"All our sins and griefs to bear," she sang back to him. Her voice rolled up from deep and husky to high and bright, and she saw his back straighten and his eyes flash with pleasure.

"Yeah. That's it." He smiled wider. "My mama used to sing it around the house. How does it go again?"

She didn't know what possessed her—the Holy Spirit, she hoped, or maybe Aretha Franklin's rendition on the album she'd recently bought—but she sang the whole song, standing right there in Ogles Market.

Wick stood completely motionless until she sang a line that seemed to catch on something behind his eyes. He jerked suddenly like a fish on a hook, then ran his hand over his hair and quickly down his face. Were his eyes wet? She couldn't say for sure. They stood in silence for a minute. "Damn, girl." He looked around. "How's this place still standing?" He blew a stream of smoke at the light overhead. "Yeah. I hadn't heard that in years and years."

She smiled and turned back to the cash register, wiping off imaginary dust with her fingertips. "Why haven't you heard it in years and years? Your mother doesn't sing it anymore?" she asked finally.

He sighed. "I haven't seen the woman since I was ten years old," he said, and then he strolled toward the rack of Nabs and peanuts. She watched the top of his wild, curly head as he made his way around the store. He disappeared down the canned goods aisle, and then he came back around, like the sun rising, and set his purchases on the counter—a carton of Cokes, a couple of Moon Pies, and several cans of Vienna sausages.

"Don't tell me this is supper," she said, feeling that the whole world was about to shift as the words came out of her mouth.

Wick leaned close, gave her a slow, sleepy-eyed smile. "Can you cook as good as you sing, Jeannie Holliman?"

Wick Whitaker was everything her daddy hated: a long-haired hippie, a druggie, a heathen, a representative of all that was wrong with the world in 1973. He was beautiful.

That night, she lay in bed replaying their meeting in her mind from the moment he walked in until he left, lingering over the way he looked at her and the touch of his hand when he shook hers. She hadn't been this wide-awake excited since that night she'd planned the entire future of the Gospelettes. She lay in the dark, listening to her sisters' deep-sleep breathing, wondering whether Wick was sleeping or awake thinking of her—imagining her—too.

# The Streets of Gold

On a sunny Saturday in June 1973, the kind of day made for being a teenager, Jeannie sat on the front porch looking at bikinis in the Sears catalog. Junior passed by on his way to work at the gas station. "Whatcha looking at?" he asked, laughing.

"Nothing." She flipped to another page.

"You off today?" he asked.

"Yep."

"Don't go too crazy," he said, as he got in his blue Duster.

He had finally graduated high school, a year after Jeannie did. "By the skin of my teeth," he had said. In fact, Jeannie suspected some of his teachers had passed him out of sympathy, probably because he was a nice kid who always said "sir" and "ma'am" and was lively in class discussions, even if he knew nothing about the subject at hand. He missed the draft by the skin of his teeth too. One boy in Jeannie's class just the year before had been sent to Vietnam. But the country was pulling out of the war during Junior's senior year, so Garland and Big Jean's fear about him being called up never materialized. They had worried, fretted, and prayed about it all through Junior's high school years. God might be in charge, but he apparently needed their help in the form of constant vigilance. Sometimes Big Jean had tried to see the bright side. "One good thing—at least the army keeps them boys off the dope," she said. "We're losing all our youth to the dope."

Besides working at the gas station, Junior helped Garland grow a couple of acres of tobacco every year on the old family farm for extra money. The farm had passed to Garland and his two sisters after their father's death five years before. By the time they split the inheritance and his sisters sold off their part, Garland was left with the old farmhouse he'd grown up in and forty-seven acres. There had been hard words, and now he and his sisters barely spoke. They'd married Baptists and went to a different church, so their families didn't see each other now that Virgil was gone. Garland moaned over the land he'd lost, though he had no intention of leaving his foreman job at the sewing factory and going back to farming full time. But the little tobacco patch and a vegetable garden had kept his family at the homeplace most Saturdays and Sundays from the time he and Big Jean married until the singings took over.

Before they started the group, Jeannie, Debbie, and Patty had wanted to help with the tobacco to make some money, but Garland, always protective, said it was too hard for them. If he was feeling generous, he would pay them five cents a jar to snap beans. Otherwise, the girls spent weekend days lounging under the shade trees in front of the old house, or, after they were older, lying in the sun in the side yard, braiding each other's hair, and snooping through the house in search of fancy old hats and letters, which they were disappointed to find were mostly about the ailments of old people rather than love and romance.

Jeannie loved the old house and the buttercups and irises that arose every year, before the peonies and hydrangeas bloomed, all planted by the grandmother she'd never met who had died when Garland was a young man. Most of all, she loved the huge old oaks out front that shaded the mossy lawn and housed generations of squirrels and birds. Though Garland and Big Jean said it wasn't safe, she loved to walk to the back of the property and wade the river with Debbie and Patty, their skirts pulled up to their hips. Their parents had always forbidden swimsuits. But Jeannie had recently discovered that Patty had one, a bikini no less. She had been hiding it beneath the underwear in her drawer and wearing it under her clothes when she went to her friend Cecile's to lie out in the sun. Jeannie found it when she was putting away laundry. She had rehearsed the lecture she would give Patty: she'd remind her of the scripture about how women should adorn themselves in modest apparel.

But now, Jeannie leaned against the rough post beside the front steps, imagining herself in the yellow Sears bikini at the lake, with Wick. She could see him, shirtless and tan, his face turned up to the sun, laughing, then pushing his sunglasses to the top of his head of wild curls and admiring her. She could feel him take her in his arms, his shoulders hot from the sun.

How many lies would she have to tell to get past Garland and all the way to Kentucky Lake with Wick Whitaker? She pondered this dilemma a while. Not that she would ever do such a thing. He wasn't the type of guy that a good church girl—a gospel singer at that—would ever get involved with. She wasn't even sure why she kept thinking about him. She hadn't been looking for a date. Most of the space in her head was dedicated to the Gospelettes—planning performances, scheduling dates, mapping routes, making contacts, writing songs. There wasn't room for a boyfriend. She figured that, when the time was right, she'd meet someone at a singing or church service, maybe another gospel singer or some young preacher, someone who would fit with her life.

Debbie came outside through the screen door, closing it carefully so as not to disturb Garland. She sat on the step and flicked paint peels from Jeannie's shirt.

"Where's Patty?" Jeannie asked.

"At Cecile's," Debbie said. "Or so she says."

The day was almost too bright and beautiful to bear. Jeannie felt as if it would be an insult to the sun for her to sit on the porch any longer. "Let's walk down to Meyers' and look at the bathing suits," she said in a low voice. Debbie followed her without a word.

They walked the four blocks to the department store. Jeannie's plans to lecture Patty when she got home from her friend's house faded. Who was she to rein Patty in? Let Garland do that job. Something had happened to her when she'd met Wick at the store. All she'd been thinking about was the Gospelettes, but his appearance somehow threw everything off.

Barefoot on the shaded sidewalk, she felt young and free. She rolled up her shorts and tied her shirt to show her stomach, and Debbie followed suit, once they were a half block from their house. Their hair swung at their waists. Boys sped down the street in hot rods, slowing down and calling out when they were even with them, then speeding up again when they saw that they were going to ignore them.

The sidewalk ended at Calvert Street, so Jeannie and Debbie walked on the side of the road. Jeannie heard a rumble behind her and edged over to let the motorcycle pass, but it stayed behind them, so close she could feel the heat of the engine on her legs.

Debbie glanced back. "Who in the world is that with the long hair?"

Jeannie turned and saw Wick Whitaker, with no shirt or helmet, on a low-slung motorcycle. She hadn't seen him since that day he'd come into the store a few weeks before, though she watched for him every day with hope and dread. She had wanted to see him again, wanted to watch him swagger in like he owned the place, but she was afraid he would ask her out, and then what? She couldn't go out with Wick Whitaker. She knew what Garland would say.

Wick pulled up even with them and coasted along at their speed. The hot air vibrated around them, and despite her determination to stay cool, Jeannie felt her heart speed up. "Let's see—who are these fine ladies walking down the street?" He grinned. "What do you know! Junebug Holliman's sisters!"

Debbie moved closer to Jeannie. "How does he know us?"

"Jeannie Holliman, how would you like to attend a party at my house tonight as my personal guest of honor?"

He'd remembered her name. She suppressed the smile that wanted to surface. They continued walking, the heat of the pavement rising and lapping at their legs like flames. "Well," Jeannie said. "I don't know."

"It's going to be a big time."

They reached Main Street, where they would turn toward Meyers'. "Tonight?" she asked.

"Yeah! I give the best parties in town. You'll see." His smile grew wider. His curls clung to his glistening face. She wanted to touch them, smooth them back. She wanted to climb up on the back of his motorcycle and ride away.

Debbie bumped against her, pulled at her arm.

"Sorry. I can't," Jeannie said.

"Aw, come on. Don't be a drag." He was an overwhelming vision of tanned skin, muscles, sweat, wild hair, relaxed smile. She had to look away.

"We've got a singing tonight at Oak Grove Baptist," she said. But then she had a vision of Wick scrubbed and suited, in a pew, watching her perform. It was a stretch but surely not impossible, and it was the only way she could see that she might get to have both the things she wanted, a gospel music career and Wick. "You're welcome to come out and hear us." She crossed the street in front of him, Debbie on her heels. Then she looked back. "It starts at six."

"That's all right." He smiled again. "You can come over after. I don't start till ten." He told her where he lived, winked at Debbie, and took off.

Jeannie stood in his golden dust and watched him ride away, full of a longing as strong as any she'd felt in her nineteen years, as strong as her desire to be a singer for God, as strong as her desire to make Garland proud of her.

"That's one of the Whitakers. You can't go to a party over there." A crease formed between Debbie's eyebrows. "They'll be drinking and doing drugs."

Jeannie walked ahead of her, irritated. She didn't need her little sister to tell her right from wrong. "I didn't say I was going."

"But you're talking to Wick Whitaker out here on the street like you know him, and he's asking you to a party—"

Jeannie stopped on the sidewalk in front of Meyers' and grabbed Debbie's arm. She wanted to shake her. She hated how Debbie's whining was like her own thoughts and fears, spoken out loud. "I said I'm not going to his party, OK?" She released Debbie's arm. "I'm not going anywhere." She glanced at the Meyers' department store window display. Three 1950s-era mannequins wearing wigs at crazy angles and pastel polyester dresses looked ready for a church picnic. "I don't need a stupid bathing suit." And she turned back toward home.

# A Voice from on High

"Now don't none of you eat or drink anything," Garland said as he pulled their station wagon into the parking lot slowly, a captain easing a barge up to the dock. They'd driven a couple of counties away to a city park where a "Musical Extravaganza" was taking place, but all the Gospelettes saw, everywhere they looked, were hippies. This was a relatively new phenomenon in Kentucky, and Garland was uneasy about it.

A bearded guy shuffled in front of the car, flashing a peace sign. "Look at that," Big Jean said. "No shoes. He's going to step on a piece of glass, and then he'll be sorry."

Garland's head took on a twitching motion—left, right, straight ahead, right again—his eyes bouncing from one long-haired, shirtless heathen to another and finding no acceptable place to rest. "Are you sure we're in the right place?" he asked.

Jeannie checked her notebook. "This is it." She looked around, her heart racing. "Must be more than just a gospel event, but I'm sure we'll find our people." It would be just like Garland to turn around and drive home just because he saw a few "kooks."

"Now don't none of you eat or drink anything," he said, again. He pulled out a handkerchief and patted his forehead, tucked it back in his pocket, surveyed the crowd again. "There's all kinds here, and somebody could slip drugs in your Coke or something, and you'd never know what hit you."

"There's the Heavenly Harmoneers' van," Debbie said, pointing to the far end of the parking lot. The Gospelettes had met them before at a singing at the Harmoneers' home church. They were nice people, two heavyset brothers, their wives, and a friend. One of the brothers had invited them to his house after the singing. His wife, a petite woman with a tall pile of blond hair sculpted on her head like the icing on a fancy cake, had served slabs of salty country ham and biscuits drowned in thick white gravy.

They recognized the van belonging to the Glory Girls, another group with three sisters. Jeannie had thought they'd have a lot in common, but when they met, the Glory Girls had turned out to be stuck-up, though the basis of their sense of superiority was unclear. (Certainly not talent.) Next to the Glory Girls' van was one belonging to the Kentucky Kingsmen, a quartet of good-looking guys in their twenties. Jeannie and Debbie had admired them from a distance, and Patty had gone so far as to flirt with two of them after a singing.

But none of the gospel singers were nearby, and Garland didn't like the looks of the young people lounging around the pavilion. He scowled at them from behind the windshield. The Gospelettes sat in the hot car with the windows rolled up and looked around.

"Let's just go ahead and eat now," he said, "before y'all touch anything." He got out of the car, opened the tailgate, and brought the cooler to the passenger-side door, never taking his glaring eyes off a particularly dirty man leaning against the car next to them.

"You like what you see, old man?" the hippie asked.

"I wish I could just die." Patty turned her head so the hippie couldn't see her face.

Garland got back in the car and locked his door. "And whatever you do, don't go to the bathroom here."

"But we've got another two hours before we go on," Junior reminded him.

"You can go in them woods over there, but don't go in the restrooms," Garland said.

"Yeah, that seems safer," Patty said, rolling her eyes.

Big Jean opened the cooler and passed out sandwiches. Junior convinced Garland to let them open the windows halfway while they ate, and they listened to a guy seated on a picnic table a few feet away playing a guitar and singing a dark rendition of "Little Sadie."

When they finished eating, Jeannie begged Garland to let them walk around the park while he and Big Jean threw out the trash and packed up the leftovers. "I'm sure there are more pavilions over yonder," Jeannie said, pointing toward a rise. "Maybe the gospel singers are over there."

"Y'all stay together!" Garland warned.

"We will," she promised. The girls ventured out slowly in their red gingham granny dresses, like new kittens coming out of the shed and into the light for the first time. Junior ambled off in his white leisure suit and red gingham shirt.

"When I get grown, I'm going to go in every public restroom I see," Patty said as they walked. "I swear. And I'm going to sit right down on the seat. Right smack down on my bare bee-hind!" She picked up a handful of rocks and began stoning a tree stump.

"Where is he going?" Debbie asked, gesturing toward Junior, who was approaching a group of teenagers sitting under some trees a few yards away smoking a joint.

"I think he's going to ask for a hit," Patty said.

"A what?" Debbie asked.

"A hit, you moron," Patty said.

Jeannie turned toward Patty. "What do *you* know about that stuff?"

"More than you, I reckon."

They stood watching Junior from afar. He had squatted next to the teenagers and started talking. He said something that made them laugh. He flipped the hair from his eyes. One of the guys passed him a joint and patted the ground, urging him to sit with them, but Junior said something and spread out his arms as if showing off his suit. Jeannie guessed he was making a joke about his clothes and telling them he couldn't get dirty. They seemed to like him.

Patty lifted her skirt as if she were going to step over the rope that divided the parking lot from the grass and follow him, but Jeannie pulled her back. "Nope. We're going to find the gospel singers."

They walked up the rise, following the sound of music. Debbie started crying over Junior, worried about something she'd heard about a girl who jumped out a window after doing drugs. Patty walked along several feet to their left, as if she weren't with them, which was, of course, ridiculous, as they were wearing identical dresses, white platform sandals, and hairdos.

Soon they came upon a pavilion with lawn chairs set up around it. The Kentucky Kingsmen were singing "Will the Circle Be Unbroken?"

to a good-sized crowd. "Here it is," Jeannie said. She scanned the park, which stretched out among trees and more pavilions in the distance. The Kingsmen concluded their song with a flourish of arms and four-part harmony on "in the sky-iiiiiiii!"

In the moment of quiet following the crowd's applause, Jeannie heard a woman's voice in the distance hit a high note that gave her chills, followed by a river of voices that rolled down the hill like a flood, sweeping her up. She looked over at the crowd gathered there, and then she jogged toward the sound, followed by Debbie and Patty. The pavilion was surrounded by Black listeners, and she wound her way through the crowd to get as close as she could to the stage.

"It reaches to the high-ighest mou-ountain!"

The singer, a woman about Jeannie's age and about Patty's size, held the audience as if suspended in midair for another seven minutes. When she finished, the crowd stood and cheered. Patty leaned toward Jeannie's ear and said, "Damn. She's even better than you."

Jeannie knew this was true, and it didn't bother her to hear it. Nor was she concerned, for once, about Patty's bad language. She turned to a man standing nearby and asked, "Who was that?"

"The Benton Family Singers," he said.

Jeannie watched them leave the stage and ran over to meet the lead singer. She stuck out her hand at her. "I'm Jeannie Holliman."

"Hey, Jeannie." The woman, looking slightly amused, shook her hand. "Marcella Benton."

Jeannie didn't know what to say, so she just said what she was thinking. "I thought I was the best singer around here until I just heard you."

Marcella's laugh was as rich and beautiful as her singing voice. "Well, then, I want to hear the second-best singer around here." She bent forward laughing, one hand on Jeannie's arm.

"We sing at two o'clock over there." Jeannie pointed down the hill at the other gospel pavilion. "The Gospelettes."

"All right, girl!"

Other audience members were crowding in to talk to Marcella, so Jeannie backed away, waving goodbye, and then walked with her sisters back toward their car, still under the spell of Marcella's voice.

Garland trotted up to them, out of breath. "Did you find where we're supposed to go?"

"Yeah." Jeannie pointed back from where they'd come. "Have you heard of the Benton Family Singers?"

"Benton?" Garland frowned. "Naw."

"They're Black. Really good. Like, unbelievable." She picked up her pace to walk with him toward the car. "Why don't we ever have singings with Black gospel groups?"

He looked at her quizzically. "I mean, they have their churches, and we have ours."

"I know, but why? We've had singings with other groups."

He lowered the tailgate and started pulling out equipment. "I don't know. They're welcome to come to our church any time. People just generally like to be with their own kind, I reckon." He looked around. "Where's Junior? He needs to help carry this stuff."

"I'll go find him," Jeannie said, frowning, mulling over what Garland said. She walked over to the grassy area where she'd left Junior. He was still there. He'd taken off his jacket and sat on it, with the inside facing down, and was helping his new friends finish off a joint. She yelled at him, and he looked up, handed off the joint, grabbed his jacket, and walked toward her. Leaning one hand on a post, he jumped over the rope and back into the parking lot.

"I can't believe you did that!" she said, sniffing him. "We're going on stage here in another hour. Is this how you're going to represent Jesus?" She wondered if he'd picked up this behavior hanging out with Wick Whitaker. Maybe it was a good thing she hadn't seen Wick around in a while, as much as she'd wished to. "Daddy's going to smell it on you," she said. "I know he will."

"I'm cool, Little Jean." Junior laughed. "He won't even know what he's smelling."

"And stop calling me that!" She crossed her arms and followed him, limping from the platform sandals that pinched her toes and rubbed the skin on the back of her heels raw.

At the car, Garland handed each of them something to carry. They had to walk right past the hippies in the nearby pavilion to get to their own. The hippies watched them file past in their matching gingham outfits, carrying their guitars and amps, Junior leading the way in a strut. They were laughing, and one of them called out, "What are you, man?"

Junior turned toward them, walking backward. He waved one hand in the air and shouted, "I am a Gospelette, brother!"

At their pavilion, the Gospelettes set up and sang "Put Your Hand in the Hand," a number the kids had had to push Garland to let them cover since its presence on pop radio made him suspicious. Junior wanted to add drums to the band, especially for this song, but Garland had drawn the line there. Big Jean started with a riff on the piano. Jeannie sang the first two lines and saw a ripple of attention go through the crowd. Junior harmonized with her on the next line, followed by her sisters. Soon, the audience was clapping along, heads bobbing, some standing and waving at the sky. And then Jeannie watched the hippies from the pavilion below climb the rise toward them and encircle the lawn chairs, dancing. Junior smiled at her and mouthed, "Right on!" But the best moment was when she looked down and to her right and saw Marcella pointing at her and singing along.

# Dearest Friend

On the way to a singing one Sunday, Jeannie watched Junior from the corner of her eye. His arm was propped on the open window, hair twisting in the summer wind, head resting in his hand. His look was far away, maybe back in their driveway, where the Camaro he'd recently bought was parked. He was still living at home, still in the group, still working at the gas station, but Jeannie could see he was restless. After work, he usually cruised around town, listening to Led Zeppelin and the Allman Brothers, rarely returning home before midnight. He was living two lives, in a way—the home and church life and the party life—a split he was able to get away with, apparently, as a boy. She wondered if things were about to change, despite all her efforts to hold the group together.

She also wondered if he was running around with Wick, but she didn't dare mention his name. She couldn't let Junior see even the little spark of interest she *might* have.

On the way home that night, after they'd performed and Junior had gotten all the brooding out of his system, he nudged her: "Oh, I forgot to tell you! Somebody was asking about you the other night, Little Jean." He winked and made kissy faces.

"Who?" she mouthed so that Garland, in the front seat, wouldn't hear.

"Initials dub-ya dub-ya mean anything to you?" Junior smirked.

She pretended not to know what he was talking about.

He shrugged. "I guess he's heard about your singing. He seemed real interested, but I didn't think he'd be your type."

So he *was* hanging out with Wick. He was partying every night, drinking, she assumed. She'd already seen him smoke pot once, and who knew what other drugs he might be doing. She was worried about him but wasn't sure what to do. If she told Garland, he and Junior would get into it, and Junior would probably end up leaving the group. What would happen to the Gospelettes then? Would Garland decide to end the group? If not, who would play bass? She couldn't imagine Garland bringing in an outsider to play. He'd probably rather end the group than let another man in, especially a young man who might be of interest to his daughters. So she kept her eye on Junior and did her best to cover his tracks so that Garland didn't find out what he was up to. Somehow, Junior still managed to put on his leisure suits—Jeannie and Big Jean had added a powder-blue matching set to their performance clothes—and join the family at singings, no matter how late or how intoxicated he'd come in the night before.

Late one Friday night, Jeannie was writing a song on the floor in Junior's room, leaned back against the side of his bed, when she heard him come home and stumble up the stairs. She sometimes read books or wrote songs or listened to records in his room late at night if he was out so that the light and noise didn't bother Debbie and Patty as they slept. Sometimes she and Junior would talk when he came in, but often he was in no condition for meaningful conversation. This night he staggered past her as if she were invisible and collapsed on his bed, a stinking mess. She pulled off his shoes, covered him with a blanket, and turned off the light.

She had begun to realize there were limits to Garland's power, at least when it came to Junior, who was a full-grown man. And even though they were the same age, she knew she couldn't expect the same freedom in their house. She couldn't get away with coming home in the middle of the night drunk—not that she wanted to. But she couldn't get away with, say, going out with Wick. And she knew she shouldn't want to. It was better not to think about him.

She paused at Junior's door and turned back. "Junior?" she whispered.

"Eyah?" he answered, too loudly.

She looked down the stairs and back at Junior and whispered, "Did you see Wick?"

"Mm?"

"Were you with Wick tonight?"

Junior grunted.

"Does he ever ask about me?" She waited in the dark for Junior to answer, holding her breath. "Wick Whitaker. Does he ever ask about me?"

Junior's snoring let her know the conversation was over. She walked to her room and climbed into bed in the dark. She relived the day Wick came into the store and talked to her, trying to remember everything he'd said and how he'd looked when she sang to him. Then she went through the same play-by-play of the conversation they'd had when she saw him in town on his motorcycle. When day broke, she'd barely slept at all.

A few days later, Jeannie was at work at Ogles Market, feeling bored and restless. Normally, it wasn't too bad. When business was slow, she had time to make plans for the group or write snippets of songs that came to her. She kept a spiral notebook and pen under the cash register to jot down notes and lyrics. But on this day, she'd had only three customers and couldn't focus on the Gospelettes at all. She was trying, again, not to think of Wick when he sauntered into the store in the flesh. He smiled as if he knew she'd been thinking about him, just a little twist of his mouth barely visible in a full beard. He was wearing jeans and sandals—no shirt—and she kept glancing back and forth between the soft-looking fur of his chest and his sandaled feet. She hadn't ever seen many men in sandals. They made her think of the Bible characters the teacher stuck on the felt board in Sunday school when she was a child. Still, it wasn't a look that would carry over to churchgoing. As attractive as he was in his natural state, she knew he'd have a better chance of getting Garland's approval if he cleaned up and got a church suit.

He got a Coke out of the cooler, then walked over to the counter and leaned toward her. "Have you ever gone out to Lake Elmore on a clear moonlight night?" His shoulders, chest, and back were burned brown, and she felt the heat he radiated.

She smiled and rang up the Coke.

"Do you know what's out there?" he whispered.

She shook her head no.

He looked around, as if to check for spies, and leaned in close enough that his breath moved her hair. "Snipes," he whispered. "They dance around the lake and then run back into the woods when a car drives up."

"Did you see the sign?" she asked, pressing the Coke into his hand. "No shirt, no shoes, no service." She was proud of herself for finding the nerve to tease him back.

"No, I must have missed that. I was looking at a poster with a sexy gospel singer in a Hee Haw dress." He stretched and smiled. "So what do you say?"

Now her nerve was gone. "I better not," she said. She could imagine what Garland would have to say about her at the lake with Wick Whitaker. She also felt sure there'd be no witnessing at Lake Elmore, and, during her long, sleepless night the week before, she'd made up her mind that, if she ever saw Wick, she was going to work on getting him to one of their singings and from there to a real Sunday church service.

He seemed not to be used to girls saying no to his offers. He blinked twice.

"But we can go over to the Bethel Dipper for a cone," she said. "I get off in forty-five minutes."

When she walked out, he was waiting on his motorcycle, wearing an easy smile. She climbed on the back of his bike and held on to him, amazed by how right it felt, how her body fit with his perfectly. She'd never been so close to a guy. She leaned against his broad, warm back, her cheek resting on his shoulder, her heart pounding against him, as they rode faster than she would have liked, the wind blowing his hair in her face. She scanned every car they passed, hoping Garland wasn't out and able somehow to recognize her.

She wanted to keep going, but he stopped at the Bethel Dipper and bought her a cone of soft-serve vanilla, which she couldn't even finish because she was too excited to eat. She straddled the bike seat, licking the cone now and then but mostly letting melted vanilla stream down onto her hand. Wick leaned against his buddy's Mustang, smoking and smiling at her.

"When's your next singing?" he asked.

"Saturday night."

"You're the best singer I've ever heard, you know that? In person or on the radio."

She shook her head, smiling, looking down at the cone and her sticky hand.

"No lie." He took a deep drag. "You got any Sunday school jokers after you?"

She pursed her lips, trying not to smile. "No. Not really."

He grinned and tossed his cigarette butt to the street. "Oh, come on."

"No. I really don't."

"Just me, huh?" He crossed his arms. "So you don't go out and have a big time on the weekends at all? I know some of them church people do because I see 'em. Junior, for one."

Jeannie sighed, sorry to be reminded of that worry. "I'm afraid Junior is backsliding."

Wick laughed. "What about you? Ever thought about backsliding a little?"

Jeannie shook her head. She didn't like the direction this was taking. "Me and Junior may be twins, but we're very different. We have different dreams."

"What are your dreams?" He stepped forward and took the melting cone from her hand. "You done?"

"Yes." She laughed.

He put the soggy remains of the cone in his mouth and chewed. He made a rolling motion with his hand. "Go on," he said around the half-eaten cone. "Your dreams . . ."

"Well." She took a deep breath. "I want to be a gospel singer."

He swallowed and grinned at her. "You *are* a gospel singer. And a damn good one, from what I heard at Ogles."

"You can hear more if you come to church with me," she said.

"I can hear more if you come to my house and sing, too." He leaned forward as if he might kiss her but then backed up. "You were telling me about your dreams."

"Yes. I want—" She rolled her eyes. "I guess I want to be a gospel star." She felt uncomfortable saying it out loud, but he had asked. Not many people did. "I want to make the Gospelettes . . . I don't know. Famous. Successful. You know, *real* gospel singers."

"Full time," he said. "Not just a hobby?"

"Yes! And successful like the Blackwoods and the Happy Goodman Family. Not just money-wise. I don't really care about money. I mean, I want to touch people like they do."

"I'd say you already do that," Wick said. "You sure touched me."

"I don't mean like *that*," she said. "I mean touch their hearts."

"What did you think I meant?" He grinned. "You sure didn't touch anything else." He leaned back against the car again.

She traced the edges of the motorcycle seat with her fingers. "I guess what I'm trying to say is . . . I want to do God's work. That's how I see my singing. Not just entertaining people and making money. I want to make them feel something." She put her hands over her heart. "Here. You know? I want them to feel that . . . *power* that I feel when I sing. I can see it sometimes—" She suddenly felt self-conscious, but when she looked at Wick, he wasn't making fun of her, like most people would, just listening, so she went on. "I can see something lift off people when we sing. Like there's a cloud in the room—a spirit maybe—and then it lifts off them, and they come alive. You can see something change in their eyes, and you can *feel* it, sort of this . . ." She groped for the right word to describe what she felt performing. "This . . . buzz . . ."

Wick's serious face cracked then. "Yeah, I know exactly what you're talking about," he laughed. "That buzz. You and me are in the same business, sweetheart."

Her mouth flew open, and she felt herself blushing. "No! Not like that! That's not what I mean!"

"That's not what you mean, but that's what it is."

He got on the bike, and they rode through town. She was less excited this time, thinking about what he was suggesting. He took her to the end of her street, safe from her parents' eyes, and let her off so she could walk the rest of the way home. She was still thinking about their conversation on the walk home. *Buzz* had been a poor word choice. *Vibration* maybe? That sounded like hippie talk. What *did* she mean, anyway? Whatever it was, she didn't like the idea of equating the spiritual feelings that the Gospelettes' music evoked with *getting high*. That was blasphemy, plain and simple.

Even so, she didn't want to stop seeing Wick. He started picking her up every day that she worked and taking her riding on his motorcycle. He even bought her a helmet, though he continued to ride without. She never stayed out late enough to make her parents ask questions. They would ride around a few times and then end up back at the Bethel Dipper for an ice cream cone, after which she'd walk home so Garland and Big Jean wouldn't see Wick and demand to know who he was.

"Am I your little secret?" he asked her one evening when she'd dismounted his bike. He removed her helmet and smoothed her hair back from her face, sending a chill down her spine with his touch.

In the third week of riding around, she walked out of the store to find him waiting for her in his El Camino instead of his motorcycle. Each time she saw him there, her heart jumped. She always looked for him, expecting that he wouldn't be there this time. She couldn't figure out what he saw in her. She was so shy and awkward, and he was just the opposite. Everything about him was loose and free, his curly, shoulder-length hair, his worn hip-hugger jeans, the way he laid his right arm on the seat behind her and backed out of the lot, steering with just his left hand. "I've got an idea," he said.

"What's that?"

He leaned over and whispered into her hair, "Let's go to my house and get high."

She crossed her arms in front of her and looked away, afraid. Afraid of ungodliness and afraid of losing his attention, and not at all sure which would be worse. "I don't do drugs, Wick."

"It's not drugs," he said. "Just grass."

"No, let's just go over to the Bethel Dipper for a while."

"I'm gonna turn into a damn ice cream cone," he said, turning toward the Dipper.

She waited in the car while he walked up and placed their orders at the window. He leaned against the window counter casually, cutting up with the women who worked inside, waving at people in other cars. He lit a cigarette, blew a stream of smoke straight up, and flashed a peace sign at one of his buddies as he drove by. Three girls in a Mustang honked and yelled enthusiastic greetings at him.

As he walked back to the car, another carload of girls honked at him. Jeannie turned and watched a girl with long black hair and seductive eyes lean out the window and yell something that sounded like a suggestive inside joke. He laughed and got back in the El Camino. Jeannie sat stiffly, as close to her door as she could get. And when he went back up to the window to pick up their orders, a freckled redhead leaned out the passenger-side window of a blue Chevy, about to fall out of her tube top, and called out to him. He waved.

"Maybe she'd like to join us," Jeannie said when he returned to the car.

He handed her a cone of chocolate soft-serve. "You sound more like a jealous girlfriend than anybody ought to who's just eating ice cream with a man," he said. "Hell, I've had more physical contact with my granny."

She turned her head, not wanting him to see how possessive she'd become. Junior had told her that Wick could "play him under the table" on guitar. She fantasized about marrying Wick and having him join the Gospelettes. She could see him playing guitar, singing duets with her on the same microphone. They could ride to all the singings in a separate car from the rest of the family, talking and laughing the whole way. But first she had to get him to church.

"American Pie" came on the radio, and he turned it up, along with several other cars that were parked around the Bethel Dipper. Jeannie cocked her head and smiled. It was so beautiful the way each car radio rose up like a voice and joined in until the air vibrated with the sound. Everybody in all those different cars listening to the same song on the radio and singing together, almost like singing at church.

As Don McLean sang about the book of love, the two girls in the blue Chevy to their right got out and danced. They swung their long hair and shook their skinny hips. Jeannie knew they'd go get high with Wick in a heartbeat. They probably had already, maybe lots of times.

He could have been with those wild girls instead of hanging around Ogles and the Bethel Dipper with her every day, and she couldn't imagine why he wasn't. She watched him out of the corner of her eye, singing along. He had a sexy, gruff voice that she could almost feel on her skin.

A guy she'd seen around, called Headlight, for reasons unknown to her, pulled up on their left and cut the engine. "Who's your friend, Wick?" he called out, teasing.

And Wick turned down the radio and yelled back, so anybody could hear, "She's my favorite!"

# Steppin' on the Clouds

Gospel singers always had to be on guard against pride. Jeannie knew it would be easy to get the big head, when people were constantly telling them how great they were and particularly what an exceptional singer *she* was. Even if they didn't say a word, she *knew*. She could see it on their faces when she sang. She could feel something in the room change. And when her sisters' and Junior's harmonies were layered over her voice, the sound was otherworldly.

But, on the other hand, if she didn't feel some pride in her God-given talent, would she even bother to use it? It seemed to her that a little bit of pride was necessary to get the Gospelettes anywhere, and she definitely wanted to get them *somewhere*. After a year, they were in demand and had performed in churches all over Kentucky and Tennessee—even into Indiana, Alabama, and Georgia—but somehow they always made just enough money to break even. They'd talked to members of other gospel groups and realized that that was typical. Gospel singers did it for the love of the music and for the Lord, they all said. These were Jeannie's main reasons too, but she had to admit she wanted more. It wasn't even about money. She had enough to meet her needs. But something in her longed for greatness. Maybe it was ridiculous, but it was true.

She had asked some other gospel singers about how to cut an album and arranged for the Gospelettes to record at a little studio near Music Row in Nashville. It was a small, brick building, with paneled walls and shag carpeting inside, nothing fancy, but they were awed by it all as if it were the White House. At the end of their sessions, the producer, always serious and hidden behind huge gold aviator glasses, played back their best cuts. They sat in the tiny control room, completely silent, listening to their own voices soar and fill the room.

Garland stood with his back to them, not moving. Jeannie watched him and held her breath, hoping it was good enough, feeling that it was, but you just never knew.

Finally, he turned around. "That's good," he said.

The girls all exhaled and smiled at each other. The producer pushed his glasses to the top of his head, rubbed his eyes, and nodded. "Wow. That's all I can say."

Jeannie asked the photographer of the *Bethel Standard* to take a picture for the album cover. The girls and Big Jean wore their matching dresses, and Garland and Junior wore their matching leisure suits, all homemade from the same powder-blue double-knit polyester fabric.

It was happening. Their first album.

The day the first box of albums arrived, Jeannie tore it open with her bare hands and held the top album like a holy relic. There they were on the cover, posed in a field near the river at the Holliman farm. The three sisters stood in front, same height, same hair, same dresses. Only the looks on their faces suggested that they might be different people: Jeannie's expression was pure joy, Debbie's hesitant smile said she'd do this if she had to, Patty's squint dared the photographer to make her stand there for one more minute. Behind them and slightly elevated were Garland (out-of-style black horn-rimmed glasses, sideburns and pompadour the color of tree bark), Big Jean (her hair closer to heaven than ever before), and Junior (a hint of a smirk, one hand at his hip, thumb hitched to his waistband).

Jeannie pulled the album out of its sleeve and held it by the edge, careful not to get a single fingerprint on it. She placed it on the turntable, her hands trembling. And then the needle dropped, the first notes of Garland's guitar rang out, and a shiver ran down her back as she heard her own voice sing the opening line of "This Is Just What Heaven Means to Me" and then the rest of the family join in, from five different planes, on the chorus. The sound was almost a physical presence coming from the speakers, filling the room, making it seem to swell to a cathedral, to the whole beautiful world, to heaven. She imagined all the angels must be shushing each other, cocking an ear to hear the Gospelettes.

Halfway through the first side, Big Jean came in from hanging clothes on the line and sat down to listen with her. Near the end, Debbie and Patty walked in from school.

"It's here!" Debbie squealed.

Patty picked up the album cover lying on the floor beside Jeannie and made a disgusted face. "I hate that picture."

They played the whole thing again when Junior and Garland came home from work. After the last song, Junior nodded and said, "Right on!"

Jeannie looked over at Garland. He removed his glasses, wiped them on a handkerchief he kept in his pocket, and put them back on. He picked up the album cover and looked at it as if he'd never seen his own family before. It was strange for him not to have anything to say. A little smile, so rare for him, came over his face.

"We can take copies to radio stations and ask them to play them," she said, "and the rest we can sell at singings."

"People at church have been asking when they can get an album," Big Jean said.

Junior held up the album and started imitating each person's pose and facial expression, and the girls collapsed onto each other laughing. Jeannie felt tingly from the excitement of being a real gospel singer with an album. She could see the whole thing, that unlikely but still longed-for goal of being gospel stars. Albums, tours, packed venues, their songs on the radio, TV appearances.

She didn't want to think about the obstacles, but they were there, all around her. She couldn't control what her siblings did. They weren't as committed to this dream as she was. That was obvious. It was a lark for Junior, an obligation for Debbie, an annoyance for Patty. And then there was Wick Whitaker. How could she fit him, if what she'd heard about him was true, into this life? She knew the answer. She couldn't.

The next day, Wick came by Ogles Market to take Jeannie for a ride. She declined that day and the next, and he didn't come back.

Walking home from work the next Friday evening, she took the long way, past the Bethel Dipper—no Wick—and through Creekside

Shopping Center, where the teenagers and single twenty-somethings in town often hung out, listening to music on their car radios, passing joints or bottles in paper bags, sitting and talking on car hoods or making out in back seats. She didn't see Wick there either, but she spotted Patty standing in front of a blue Cutlass, pressed against some tall, long-haired boy, her hands in his back pockets and his in hers. The curly ends of her long hair danced on her butt, which was decorated with embroidered designs—a rose, a smiley face, "LOVE" with a heart for the O. She had on her "Keep on Truckin'" T-shirt that Garland never let her wear because he didn't know what it meant but was sure it was something bad. The boy was kissing her, his shoulders stooped over to reach her. She was barefoot and on tiptoes. Jeannie, peeking out from behind a telephone pole, held her breath, imagining Wick bending to kiss her like that, her standing on tiptoe to reach him. The bottoms of Patty's feet were black from the pavement as if she'd walked a long way to get to him.

# I'll Fly Away

The dull, white sky was spitting snow, just enough to dust the front yard. Jeannie was turned backward on the couch to stare out the living room picture window, listening to the clock tick. The house felt small and stifling. The wall heaters made the air inside stale and too warm. Other than the plans she made for the group, which brought her some pleasure, winter had been almost unbearable. Big Jean, when she wasn't in bed with the headache, padded around the edges of rooms, silent and ghostly, while Garland filled the center with his Bible readings and TV news and tirades against principalities and powers, mainly in Washington, DC. Junior had almost disappeared from the family. He worked, came home only to eat dinner, followed by practice. Then he'd go out with his friends, coming home to sleep sometime in the night after the rest of the family had gone to bed. Debbie flopped around, pale and listless, or else drove Jeannie crazy with her whining. Patty seemed to be slipping away, finding excuses to go to her friend Cecile's house for sleepovers.

Jeannie missed the traveling they'd done in the warmer months. Requests had slacked off in the winter. It was a good time to make contacts, write songs, plan their next album, but she was preoccupied with a longing for Wick that she tried to talk herself out of daily. He hadn't been by Ogles Market to see her in months. It was what she had wanted when she declined his invitations, and yet she was heartbroken. He had picked her up and taken her riding around almost every day during the summer and fall, never pushing her to do more, just enjoying her company, and then, just as easy as he started, he quit. Apparently, there was only so much ice cream socializing that a man like Wick could endure. He didn't even try to change her mind. Was she that easy to forget? She wondered if he wanted her to come looking—begging—for him. Or had he just forgotten about her completely, replaced her with a girl more willing to let loose and have fun?

Garland traded in the station wagon for a used van with thick, gold shag carpeting and had "The Gospelettes / Bethel, Ky. / Proclaiming the Word in Song" painted on the outside in purple and white letters. Jeannie was thrilled. It felt like something a real gospel group would do. Having more room to stretch out on their drives and more storage room for their gear was great, but Jeannie was disappointed that having their own travel van didn't seem to inspire her siblings. They used to sing together in the station wagon on the way to performances—not really practicing, just doing it for the joy of it. They had worked on their harmonies until they were as tight and perfect as anything she'd ever heard, at church, on the radio, anywhere. But now, when Jeannie started up "Turn Your Radio On" in the van, everyone just sighed and looked out the windows at nothing. About the only thing Junior would sing was "If We Make It Through December," when it came on the radio, doing a fine Merle Haggard imitation. It seemed to Jeannie that they might not make it through December, much less the rest of the winter.

Before spring could arrive and deliver them all from the winter blues, Junior packed his things in an army duffel bag that Wick had given him and drove away. When Jeannie got home from work, she found Big Jean crying over the stove and got the whole story. He'd taken his guitar, amp, and clothes to his car, kissed his mother goodbye, and told her he was moving into a friend's trailer off Gilbertsville Road.

"Did he quit the band?" Jeannie asked, hand over her mouth.

Big Jean wiped her eyes on her apron and shrugged. "I didn't think to ask him that, I was so upset about him running off. But I don't expect he wants to come around and argue with Daddy."

Jeannie sat at the kitchen table and buried her face in her hands. She was planning a new album, and now their bass player and bass vocalist was gone. All her plans, all her hard work to get them somewhere, meant nothing to him. Hadn't this always been the way, though? She cared, he didn't. She studied the Bible, prayed, listened to Garland's endless home sermons, and Junior didn't. Yet Garland held on to that angel visitation—the Junior prophecy—as if that was all that mattered.

When Garland came home from work that day, the girls were gathered around the table, staring at the salt and pepper shakers. Big Jean told him that Junior had left, and he walked all over the house looking for him, as if he didn't believe her. Junior had asked Big Jean not to tell Garland where he'd gone, but she did anyway. Garland ran out to his car to go find him and bring him home.

Big Jean sighed, shaking her head. "He's wasting his time."

When Garland returned two hours later, he stomped past them as they sat at the table eating.

"I'll fix you a plate," Big Jean said, rising.

He drank milk of magnesia straight from the bottle and replaced the cap. "Do you think I can eat?" he asked, the line between his brows pointing down at his nose like an arrow. "I can't eat! How y'all can eat is beyond my understanding!"

Jeannie barely slept that night. She hadn't questioned Garland about where this left the Gospelettes, even though that was her biggest concern. She knew her parents were more worried about Junior's living arrangements and who he might be associating with. By morning, she had resolved to go plead with Junior to come back.

After work, she asked Lisa, her one friend from high school that she had stayed in touch with, for a ride to Junior's. Lisa worked at the library, drove a Bug, and was engaged to her high school boyfriend. Jeannie didn't have much in common with her anymore, but she appreciated that she was willing to help her out. "So this is it," Lisa said, pulling into the driveway, which was just a flattened-out path in the dead weeds.

Jeannie saw Junior bent under the hood of his Camaro in the driveway. "I reckon it is." She thanked Lisa for the ride.

"Don't be a stranger," Lisa said out the window as she waved and drove away. Jeannie knew that was exactly what she was being to Lisa and everybody else outside her family. The Gospelettes were really all she had time for.

She walked over to Junior. Led Zeppelin blasted from another car parked next to his. She looked around but didn't see any of Wick's vehicles. She was disappointed, and she was annoyed with herself for being disappointed.

"Do you know what you're doing? You're going to tear that thing up!" she yelled.

Junior popped out from under the hood and grinned at her. "Hey! I didn't hear you come up. How'd you get here?"

"Lisa dropped me off," she said. "Come here and let me hug your neck." She squeezed him, patted his back. It felt unreal, going to visit her twin at another house, being separated for the first time in their lives.

He wiped something on the engine with an old T-shirt and turned down the stereo. "How is everybody?"

"All right. How are you?"

"Doing good."

They stared at each other, nodding. "You're really going to do this?" she asked, finally.

"We're almost twenty years old," he said. "Every little bird's got to fly away."

"I know, but what about the group, Junie? You don't have to leave the group." She was pleading now. "The Gospelettes need you."

"Y'all will be just fine. Come over sometime, and I'll give you some bass lessons. You'll pick it up like that," he said, snapping his fingers.

"I don't know about that."

"You'll get it. I promise."

"But Junior, we've gotten so good! Our harmonies won't be the same without you. And I want you to be on the new album!"

"I'm doing my own thing," he said. "The boys I live with are starting a band."

A pale, thin guy, like a dried stalk, came out of the trailer, and as he got closer, Jeannie recognized him as Wick's buddy, Headlight. "I think I've seen this young lady before," he said, grinning.

"This is my sister, Jeannie," Junior said. "That's Headlight."

"Yeah! You were Wick's woman, right?" Headlight asked.

Junior raised his eyebrows at her.

"I was not *his woman*." Jeannie made a weak smile. "We just rode around some."

Junior cut his eyes at her. "I ain't heard about this."

"Uh-oh. I done it now," Headlight said and ambled back inside.

"Wick hadn't told me nothing about this," Junior said.

Jeannie sighed. "That's because there's nothing to tell. He used to come by and talk to me at work, but I haven't seen him in a long time." She looked down, dug into the dust with the toe of her shoe. "Do you ever see him?"

"All the time. He's in our band."

Her heart sped up, and she covered it with one hand, as if it might show.

"He'll probably come over later tonight to jam with us." Junior lit up a cigarette—a habit she hadn't been aware he had. "You want to stick around? I'll give you your first bass lesson."

She wanted to see Wick, despite everything she'd been telling herself over the past few months. But the Gospelettes were more important. The wind was getting chilly, and she pulled her jacket tighter and rubbed her arms. "Please, just think about coming back, all right? You don't have to move back in, but think about coming back to the group, Junie. Because this is God's work we're doing. We've been called to spread the Gospel in song. Just think and pray about it."

"I've done done all the thinking and praying I can do." He gave her a playful push. "You need a ride home?"

He borrowed Headlight's Dodge Charger and drove her through town, past all the hangouts, but nobody was out in the cold weather. Junior dropped her off up the street from home, like Wick used to do, to avoid Garland.

Jeannie got out, wondering if this was it, if the Gospelettes were over. She couldn't bear it. What else did she have? She bent down to look in the open door at Junior, who peered into the distance, as if expecting Garland to come up and snatch him out of the car. "Hey," she said.

He looked up.

"Tell Wick I said hey, all right?"

He winked at her. "That I'll do."

# I Feel Like Traveling On

Junior taught Jeannie to play bass, as promised. It wasn't difficult for her—she had a natural talent for music and played piano by ear—but, still, it made her sad that Junior wanted to leave the Gospelettes. She couldn't understand it, no matter how she tried. What could be better than playing music and serving the Lord? She'd been going to Junior's trailer for lessons and didn't like what she saw there one bit. He was backsliding, for sure.

A couple of times while she was there, Wick had dropped by. She worked hard at not looking at him for too long, just gave him a nod and a curt "hey." The first time, he'd walked in holding an acoustic Fender by the neck. His hair was longer than the last time she'd seen him. He sat in a chair in the living room and watched, sipping on a beer, but she refused to make further eye contact or acknowledge him in any way. Junior could throw away his calling and hang out with a bunch of no-counts if that's what he really wanted, but she wasn't about to. The next time Wick walked in on a lesson, he went on through to the kitchen and talked to Headlight. It was all Jeannie could do to focus on the bass and not strain to hear what Wick and Headlight were talking about. She was pretty sure she heard the name Sheila. She turned up the volume on her amp.

Since then, she'd taken over bass guitar at their singings. It was unusual to have a lead singer—and a girl, at that—playing bass, but Garland couldn't find fault with her performance. They were still in demand at churches, and their album was getting airplay on several AM radio stations in the region. They missed Junior's vocals and his banter with the audience, but his absence didn't slow them down.

In fact, Jeannie was making more bookings than ever, and Patty wasn't happy about it. "Someday I'm getting out of here," Patty said one afternoon as they put on their matching granny gowns for a performance. "I swear. I'm going to live in Australia." She was angry that Jeannie had scheduled another Saturday night singing engagement, for the fourth week in a row. "I never get to go out like normal teenagers."

"We're not normal teenagers," Jeannie reminded her. "'You are a chosen generation, a royal priesthood, a holy nation, a peculiar people.'" This was a Bible verse she'd been quoting to herself a lot lately, every time she thought about Wick and felt her desire for him rise up.

Patty gave her a disgusted look. "Well, you'd better not last-minute schedule anything for next Saturday because this peculiar person ain't going nowhere unless we can be back here by seven."

The next Sunday, after church, the family rode in the Gospelettes van to Junior's trailer. Garland had given Junior some time on his own to get the rebellion out of his system, but now he wanted to know when he was planning on coming to church. Staying out of the group, well, that was his choice, Garland said, but staying out of church was *unheard of.* "Our family helped found that church!" Garland said as he pulled into the driveway, as if this argument should send Junior scurrying back. He parked, opened his door, turned to the girls in the back, who sat frozen. "What are y'all waiting for?"

"Do we have to go in?" Debbie asked.

"What do you mean do you have to go in? He's your brother!" Garland shouted.

"We need to see him and love on him," Big Jean said, dabbing her eyes with a tissue.

"They're gonna love seeing us," Patty said, rolling her eyes.

"It don't matter if they want to see us or not. You think I care about that?" Garland slammed the door.

"Come on, y'all," Jeannie said, opening the back door. She still wanted Junior back in the group. He hadn't seen the family all together since he left home. Maybe it was worth a try.

Garland banged on the trailer door, rousing Junior's roommate, Hatcher, from bed. Hatcher let them in, then went back down the hall to his bedroom, banging on Junior's bedroom door on the way, and called out, "You've got company!" Empty beer bottles littered the living room's shag carpet. Jeannie wondered if Wick had been at the party they'd apparently had the night before.

Junior appeared in a pair of dirty jeans, looking mashed, blinking.

Big Jean, apparently having forgotten that he needed to be loved on, stood near the front door, hugging her pocketbook, as if afraid to sit on the soiled and tattered furniture. "Everybody at church is asking about you," she said.

Junior rubbed his face and mumbled that he had a lot of things he needed to work through.

"There ain't nothing you can work through without the Lord," Garland told him. He paced the living room, fists on his hips.

"Anyhow, I might not be here long," Junior said, falling onto the couch. "I might be going to Florida. There's some guys I know down there, and they say it's a good place to live."

Garland and Big Jean stared at him, waiting for him to finish, waiting for some explanation that made sense. "You're going to *where*?" Garland finally asked.

"Florida. You know, live on the beach?"

"*Beach*?" Big Jean repeated, as though hearing the word for the first time. "Why, honey, they have hurricanes down there, and the sun is so strong, it'll burn you in a minute."

"You ain't going to Florida," Garland said.

"I reckon I am," Junior replied, hands locked behind his head, leaning back on the arm of the couch, trying to look casual.

"You go get your things right now," Garland said, pointing toward the bedrooms. "You're going home."

Debbie moved behind Jeannie and Patty, where they stood near the door.

Junior looked around. "I hate to tell you this, Daddy, but I *am* home!" He held his arms out toward the dingy walls and crumpled beer cans. "This is it, until I decide to move."

Just as Garland opened his mouth to dispute Junior's claims, there was a rattle at the front door and Jeannie turned to see Wick Whitaker walk in. If he'd been drinking all night like Junior and Hatcher, he showed no adverse effects. His long, loose curls were tousled. He was bearded and wearing an open denim shirt. He was breathtaking.

"Hello, Gospelettes!" he called out. He smiled, admiring Jeannie's dress as he brushed past her.

"Who are *you*?" Garland demanded.

Wick kept his eyes on Jeannie, and she returned his gaze, unable to look away.

"Who is this, Junior?" Garland asked.

"That's Wick Whitaker. He's in my band," Junior said.

"Whitaker?" Garland seemed to calculate the likely proximity of this Whitaker to the bootlegger and put himself between Jeannie and Wick. "Are you behind this Florida nonsense?"

"No, sir," Wick said. "I'm staying right here in Kentucky." He walked across the room, back into Jeannie's view, and winked at her. "Where the horses are beautiful and the women are fast."

Patty laughed until Garland turned and ordered the girls outside. Out in the yard, they peered at the closed door of the trailer.

"What was all that about?" Patty poked Jeannie.

"What?" Jeannie turned her head, feeling her cheeks getting hot.

"All that winking and smiling in there," Patty said. "And all the—" She batted her eyes, covered her mouth with her hand, and giggled.

"Believe me, there's nothing going on," Jeannie said.

Patty frowned. "Why not? I can tell he digs you."

"I don't care what he *digs*," Jeannie told her. "He is not good Christian dating material."

"That's what I was trying to tell you that day we saw him in town," Debbie said.

Patty watched Jeannie for a minute, hands on her hips. "So you wouldn't care if somebody else goes out with him? It wouldn't bother you?"

The front door of the trailer opened, and Garland stomped out, with Big Jean on his heels.

"Like who?" Jeannie asked Patty under her breath. Garland ordered them into the van before she could answer.

At the end of the summer, Junior left for Florida. Debbie, who had graduated that spring, got a job keeping books at Glenn Richards's hardware store downtown. Patty, not quite sixteen, moved into Junior's vacant bedroom without asking anyone's permission, just moved her clothes, her albums, and her stuffed animals into his room and shut the door.

Jeannie was still working at Ogles Market and planning the Gospelettes' takeover of the gospel music world. They had an important gig in Springfield, Tennessee, coming up the next Saturday evening. An actual Nashville music executive, the brother-in-law of a friend of a friend from church, had agreed to be there just to hear them.

Late Saturday morning, Jeannie peeked in Junior's old room, wondering why Patty wasn't up yet, and saw her bed was untouched. A sense of dread flooded her body. Had Patty stayed out all night? She knew they were going to rehearse that morning and needed to leave early. It was a big opportunity for them. She ran downstairs, where Garland sat scowling at the newspaper while Debbie dusted around him, and Big Jean sat at the sewing machine in the corner, working on new stage clothes. "Have y'all seen Patty?" Jeannie asked, trying to tamp down the panic in her voice. Nobody had seen her since the evening before.

Jeannie got out the phone book and called Cecile's house, but her mother said Cecile was still in bed and Patty wasn't there.

Big Jean was up and circling the room, twisting a piece of fabric. "Oh, Lord. What if she's been kidnapped? I think we'd better call the police."

"Why would anybody want to kidnap Patty?" Jeannie asked.

"Well, there's all kinds of crazy people in this world!" Big Jean burst into tears. "Look at what happened to that Patty Hearst!"

Garland walked out to the street and paced the sidewalk in front of the house, stopping from time to time, hands on his hips, to glare in one direction or the other.

"Listen, Mama, knowing Patty, she went off somewhere on her own," Jeannie said. She figured that Patty had stayed out all night with some boy—maybe the one Jeannie had seen her kissing at Creekside months before—and that she'd come creeping in soon with some sorry excuse.

But as the time for them to go to their performance neared, Patty still wasn't home. Garland was out driving around looking for her, Big Jean was lying on the couch with a cool washrag over her eyes, Debbie stared out the living room window like a sentry, and Jeannie sat nearby, head in her hands, worried—not that Patty was in any kind of danger but that she was going to miss the Springfield gig and ruin this chance for the Gospelettes.

"Maybe she's gone down to Florida too," Big Jean said. Junior had called them once from Daytona Beach, but he had no phone, so they had no way of reaching him to find out if Patty had joined him. "I wish he had a phone." Big Jean had been crying all day, and now she was starting again. "Two of my babies!"

Garland returned, having had no luck, and chased a BC Powder with a dose of milk of magnesia. Jeannie decided to go out herself and see what she could find out. She figured she could go to Creekside Shopping Center and catch the early Saturday night crowd before the Gospelettes were supposed to leave for their singing, which her parents were threatening to cancel. She took off walking.

Nearly a dozen cars were already lined up on the Grayson Shoes and Albright Jewelers side of the parking lot. Kids in bell-bottom jeans and bare feet leaned against the cars or sat on the hoods. Heat rose from the pavement, but it felt good in the shade of the stores where the cars were parked. Jeannie circled the lot, scanning car after car, covered with teenagers, smoking, taking drinks from bottles in paper bags, looking for familiar faces. Finally, she approached two girls sitting on top of a green Chevy. She recognized them from Patty's class. The black Ford Cobra next to them was blasting "Stuck in the Middle with You," so Jeannie had to yell. "Y'all know my sister, Patty Holliman?"

They said they did.

"Have you seen her lately?"

"Last night," said the dark-haired girl with heavy blue eyeliner.

Jeannie's heartbeat accelerated. "What was she doing? Who was she with?"

The girls looked at each other. "She come by to say goodbye," said the strawberry blonde.

Jeannie felt the picture in her head crack, the Gospelettes going from six to five to four, just her and Debbie and their parents. They wouldn't even be the Gospelettes anymore, without the three singing sisters. They would be something sad and reduced. She couldn't bear it. She let out the breath she'd been holding. "Do you know where she was going?"

"Somewheres with her boyfriend."

"Who? Who's her boyfriend?" Jeannie raised her voice, feeling close to throttling them both, one with each hand.

"What's his name? Peppers?" Strawberry asked.

"Dalton Pepper," Eyeliner said.

"They're off to get married." The girls exchanged sly smiles. "They didn't say where they was going. But they come by here last night and told us goodbye, like they was going off somewhere or something."

Jeannie felt sharp prickles of anger in her veins, as if her blood were freezing. How could Patty do this to them? What had she gotten herself into? Jeannie turned without a word and started walking home. It was just like Patty to ruin everything, to show no regard for all the hard work Jeannie had put into taking them somewhere. And not just for Jeannie. For all of them. For Patty, the one who was dying to go somewhere and do something! She shook her head. "Too impatient for your own damn good," she said aloud to the squirrel who ran out in the road in front of her and then back up a maple tree.

Tree limbs sagged over the sidewalks, sometimes so low that Jeannie had to stoop or step to the side, as she walked, dreading the announcement she'd have to make to her parents. She tugged some leaves from a low-hanging oak and shredded them. From a side street up ahead, she heard a motorcycle growl. Her heart lifted, irrationally. She looked up, but it was a heavy man with a helmet. Not Wick.

# Come Home

When Patty finally showed up on the family doorstep, she was tired and cranky, and her rounded belly strained against her untucked shirt. Jeannie couldn't believe it, but it was clear. Her little sister was pregnant.

Dalton was out in his car, smoking a cigarette. "Ain't he even gonna come in and face us?" Big Jean asked.

Patty turned around and waved Dalton in. He took his time, finishing his cigarette and then flipping the butt across the yard, ambling in, letting the screen door slam behind him.

"This is Dalton," Patty said. "We got married."

Jeannie crossed her arms and scowled, unable to hide her disgust. This was what Patty had left the Gospelettes for? This backwoods runt with bad skin and bad manners? She'd rather spend her life with this little punk than travel and make music and be adored by their fans?

"We're gonna be living out in the country. Dalton's uncle has a house he's letting us stay in. Just thought I'd come by and let y'all know we're back." Patty walked from the doorway into the living room and flopped down on the couch. "I'm not feeling so hot," she said. Dalton sat next to her and clicked his silver lighter open and shut, open and shut.

Garland stomped off to the kitchen. Patty's defiance and lack of remorse for what she'd done, not to mention her choice of a husband, were more than he could stomach.

"Well," Big Jean said, at last. "Are y'all hungry? I made beans and cornbread."

"A'ight," said Dalton.

Everyone followed Big Jean into the kitchen, where she served Patty and Dalton the leftover beans and cornbread plus most of the chocolate pie she'd made for the church potluck the next day. Garland stomped back to the living room, apparently unwilling to be in the same room with them.

After they'd eaten everything on the table, Patty pushed back her chair and said, "I guess we'll go. Y'all probably have a singing tonight."

"Now how do you know we're still singing? How do you know we ain't been too tore up to ever sing again?" Big Jean demanded. She dabbed her eyes with a dish towel.

"Tore up!" Garland shouted from the living room.

"Please. Y'all love it too much to quit just because of me," Patty said. "I know Jeannie's not going to let it go that easy." She leaned her head against the back of the kitchen chair and closed her eyes.

It was true that the Gospelettes had carried on without Patty and Junior. It wasn't the same, of course, with just four of them. It hurt Jeannie to think about how they had sounded when the whole family was together, how those two additional voices made the harmonies complete, but when they'd gotten a phone call from Patty two days after her disappearance, saying that she was fine and was in St. Louis and not to come looking for her, Jeannie had convinced her parents to resume their performance schedule. They'd missed the big opportunity in Springfield, but the next week, they had gone back on the road. "We *cannot* let one person's disobedience stop us from doing the Lord's work!" Jeannie had insisted, and when she put it like that, her parents had to agree.

Later that week, Dalton brought Patty over to visit her family while he went to see some of his buddies who got on her nerves. He was late coming back to get her, and Garland and Big Jean went on to bed. Jeannie, Debbie, and Patty huddled together on the couch, covered with an old quilt, and talked in low voices. Patty told them that she and Dalton had planned to travel around, be free spirits, live here and there, and not be tied down to any one place. She wanted to go to Alaska or maybe San Francisco. Definitely west. As far away as they could go. But the car had broken down in St. Louis, so they'd stayed there, trying to scratch up enough money to fix it. St. Louis was cold, Patty complained. "And after that arch, it's all downhill," she said. Dalton got a temporary job, and after he made enough money to fix the car, he just wanted to get home before deer season was over.

"So much for freedom," Patty said, placing her hands on her bulging belly and sighing. "So! What about y'all? Did anything happen while I was gone? Anybody get a boyfriend?" She elbowed Jeannie. "What about Wick? You ever see him?"

Jeannie felt herself blushing, but fortunately they were sitting in the dark. She had seen him around town a few times, but he hadn't come back to Ogles Market to see her. He must have been going somewhere else for his Cokes, Vienna sausages, and cigarettes. "What *about* him?"

"I know a thing or two about a thing or two," Patty said. "He likes you, but he's not gonna jump through Daddy's hoops. You can forget about that." She turned to Debbie. "And *you're* spending five days a week with a bunch of men at the hardware store. You got any old men coming in and flirting with you? Coming back in the next day to buy some nails? And the next day wanting some screws?" She threw her head back and laughed.

Debbie pulled the quilt over her head.

"There is, isn't there? There's some old man coming in to see you!" Patty declared. She tried to pull the quilt from Debbie's face.

So Debbie did have a boyfriend. The realization sat on Jeannie, a leaden weight on her heart. Patty was married and pregnant. Junior was having adventures in Florida. Soon Debbie would make her escape, most likely. Jeannie was the only one staying the same, twenty years old and never had a boyfriend, married to the Gospelettes.

Dalton drove up and flashed the lights, and Patty jumped up. "Gotta go." She ran out to the car as fast as she could in her condition, her long hair flying behind her, throwing herself at the future.

# The Lost Soul

In April 1975, Jeannie, maid of honor, stood next to Debbie, clutching a bouquet of plastic daisies and wearing a pink suit dress that clashed with her groom's red-white-and-blue leisure suit, facing Brother Clarence in his living room. Brother Clarence peered through reading glasses at the black leather Bible open in his hands. Jeannie had never been in his and Sister Lucy's home before. Long, olive-green velveteen drapes kept out the sunlight. An array of carefully placed figurines, shepherd boys and girls and such, posed on every flat surface in the room, a sort of congregation of her own assembled by Sister Lucy. The green jacquard furniture looked as if it had never been sat on.

Jerry Lee Dix, the groom, was thirty-nine to Debbie's nineteen, divorced, and the father of two children, who stood to his right. Barry, the twelve-year-old, chewed a drinking straw throughout the ceremony. Christie, the ten-year-old, held Jerry Lee's hand and wouldn't let go when he was supposed to put the ring on Debbie's finger, so he ended up just handing it to her so she could put it on herself. She had met Jerry Lee at the hardware store, just as Patty had predicted.

Garland had refused to attend the ceremony, and Big Jean said, "Well, I don't guess I need to be there either, do I?" And Patty was at her home, ready to pop.

Jeannie would have gladly missed it too, but when Debbie asked her to stand up with her, she couldn't refuse. She agreed with Garland that Jerry Lee probably hadn't treated his first wife right, and now that she'd left him and the kids, he'd found a young girl to take advantage of, a slightly bigger kid to raise his kids for him. She'd tried to express as much to Debbie, but Debbie had just cried and asked,

"Where is this perfect man Daddy has in mind? We've traveled to seven states and sung at Lord knows how many churches, and I've yet to run into this perfect man he thinks we ought to wait for."

After the ceremony, standing around in Sister Lucy's spotless kitchen, the tiny wedding party had punch and coconut cake that Big Jean had made and sent over. Jeannie snapped a picture of Debbie cutting the cake, Jerry Lee's big, rough hand over hers on the knife, and in that moment Jeannie could see the way he would take control of every single thing in Debbie's life from that moment forward. Sister Lucy stood throughout the little reception holding a trash bag ready to collect their paper plates and cups, making sure not a crumb or a drop touched her shiny green-and-yellow linoleum floor. She clearly wanted them out of there, so they took her hint and swallowed fast and dumped the rest.

Across the street, Garland was parked in the Gospelettes van, ready to pick up Jeannie. She paused in the driveway, looking back at Debbie. They were all scattered now. Junior in Florida, Patty out in the country with her husband and a baby on the way, Debbie about to ride off to the little redbrick ranch house that Jerry Lee had lived in with his escaped first wife.

"Don't worry," Debbie whispered in Jeannie's ear as she hugged her goodbye. "I'm not leaving the group. I'll come over and rehearse after work, just like we do now."

Jeannie glanced at Jerry Lee, who was yanking off his tie and tossing it into the car ahead of him. His mouth was a grim line. She wondered why Debbie was whispering.

Back at their once crowded and noisy house, now echoing, cavernous, Jeannie sat at the piano, but she wasn't in the mood to play. She wandered to the kitchen, where Big Jean was making a meatloaf, half the usual size, and finally upstairs to the room that was now all hers. The evening shadows cast their gloom over the walls. There were no singing sisters, no Junior thumping on the bass. Just Garland ranting at the TV about Watergate and how the country was falling apart, Big Jean sighing and clattering pans in the kitchen, and Jeannie staring out the window at the street, never seeing Wick ride by.

The next Monday, after work, Jeannie found herself turning right instead of left in front of Ogles and walking toward the train tracks to

Wick's house. If she had planned this, she might have worn a jacket or sweater, as it had recently turned cold, a springtime flashback to winter, and the walk to his house was farther than the walk home, and maybe she would have also worn something more becoming than the brown polyester pantsuit that Big Jean had sewn for her. But this was a spontaneous visit, the only kind that she was likely to make because if she thought about it, she knew she'd talk herself out of it. There were a hundred reasons for a good Christian girl like her not to get involved with Wick Whitaker. So instead of thinking, she walked.

She found him sitting in a wooden kitchen chair on the front porch, wearing an army jacket and ragged jeans, playing "You Are My Sunshine" on guitar as if he were waiting there for her. It seemed to her that the guitar was singing, that if she hadn't known the words, she could have guessed them by the sound of it. She wondered if he'd been playing that song already or if he'd started it when he saw her coming up the road.

He ended the song and smiled, seemingly unsurprised to see her. "My lovely Miss Holliman," he said.

"Long time no see," she said and felt her face turn hot with embarrassment.

He stood the guitar next to him and held it by the neck. "I was just playing a tune for Sally."

Jeannie looked at the large golden-brown mutt next to Wick's chair. Sally rose to greet her, and Jeannie scratched behind her ears. They were silent for a while, looking at Sally, the crumbling concrete steps, the empty road in front of his house. Jeannie smelled smoke from a wood stove inside and saw through the window the blue light of a TV and the dark outline of a man in a recliner—Wick's father, she guessed.

"Did you come to sing with me? Or to invite me to a revival?" he asked, his eyes teasing.

"No." She laughed. She didn't know why she was there. "Just . . . saying hello."

"Well. Hello." He leaned the guitar against the wall, stood, and stretched. "Getting chilly. Would you like to come in?"

"No. No. I'm fine." She looked at his army jacket with the name "Whitaker" on the front. While he lit a cigarette, she looked down, lightly kicked his top step with the toe of her boot, gathering her courage to ask him a personal question. "What did you think about while you were there? In Vietnam? Did you think about coming home to Bethel? Or about a girl?"

Wick looked into the distance, toward the line of budding trees across the road. He stared at the trees a while, flicking ash over the porch railing. "You know what I'd think about? I hadn't thought about this since I got back."

Jeannie held her breath. "What?"

"I'd think about . . . how my mama used to carry me from the couch to my bed when I'd fall asleep watching TV. You know that feeling? When you're a kid and you're just asleep enough that you can't open your eyes and get up but still awake enough to know somebody is carrying you?"

She nodded. She remembered being carried from many an evening church service that way as a child.

"So when I was tired and wore out, out in the field, that would come to me . . . how I wished Mama could just carry me home and put me to bed." He turned his eyes from the trees to her and gave her a little, unbearably naked smile.

The image of him far away in a jungle, exhausted and desperate for home, longing in some fevered, half-conscious state for his mother to come get him, brought tears to her eyes.

"Are you all right?" he asked. "Hell. I didn't mean to make you sad."

She shook her head. "No, it's OK. I'm fine." She wanted to tell him, *I love you. I can't stand the thought of you dying unsaved. I want us to be together in this life and forever.* She took a deep breath. She suddenly knew why she had come there. "Can I ask you another personal question?"

He smiled. "Shoot."

She hated to ruin the mood, but she had to hear it from him. She lifted her chin and locked eyes with him. "Are you a drug dealer?"

He jerked his head back and made a surprised noise. "Mmm!" He ran one hand through his hair, exhaled long, gave a half laugh. "Are you a drug buyer?"

She gazed at him, unblinking. "No."

He looked back at her, solemn. "Well." He leaned, one hand on the front porch post. "We have a family business that involves . . . a lot of different activities. I've been known to sell used cars, car parts, motorcycles, ice, bait, beer, liquor, grass, pills. . . . If I've got it and somebody wants it, I'll sell it to them. So. Yeah."

She nodded. She knew she should turn around and walk home, but she felt as if her legs wouldn't move.

Wick reached out and pulled her to his chest, wrapped his arms around her, and kissed her hair. "I'm sorry," he said. "I know that's not what you wanted to hear."

Nobody in the family ever said the word "pregnant"—a vulgarity to Garland and Big Jean—or even "baby" in connection with Patty, but the next week, a baby boy appeared, as if Patty had found him in the weed patch by her mailbox, and the whole family showed up at her and Dalton's tiny, gray cinder-block house with the leaky roof and exposed electrical wires. There was one concrete block for a front step, and they had to hitch themselves up from there to the doorway. Jeannie wondered how Patty had managed this in her condition.

While Garland drove off in search of sturdier blocks for steps, Jeannie, Debbie, and Big Jean hauled in diapers, baby clothes, and the crib that all four Holliman kids had slept in as babies. Patty accepted the gifts indifferently and, as soon as Big Jean picked up the baby, turned her attention to a rerun of *Here's Lucy* on the old black-and-white TV that had been at the Holliman home for as long as Jeannie could remember. The kids had begged for a color TV for years, and Garland had finally bought one, now that they were all gone, except for Jeannie.

"Hello, John Paul!" Jeannie cooed at her nephew. "Hello!" Thin-faced and somewhat rodent-like, he looked peeved, ready to squall any second.

"JP for short," Patty reminded her, with impatience.

"Did you name him after the Beatles?" Debbie asked.

Patty walked over to the TV and turned up the volume.

"How's my little grandson?" Big Jean asked the baby. "Say hi-dee to Mamaw! Say hi-dee to Mamaw! Hi-dee! Hi-dee!"

Jeannie looked around the room, crammed with hand-me-down mismatched furniture and not a single picture hanging on the dirty off-white walls. The TV was Patty's only contact with the outside world. She didn't have a phone or a car of her own. She had quit school when she eloped, didn't have a job or even a driver's license. All she had was a squalling newborn, a shiftless husband, and an old black-and-white TV that showed one snowy channel. So why did Jeannie feel ever so slightly envious, just a tiny bit left behind?

# Satisfied

A few weeks after JP was born, Garland allowed Patty to return to the group. She was just happy to get out of the house. Some of the ladies from church took turns babysitting during rehearsals and singings, which gave her a break from the never-ending drudgery of caring for a newborn. Jeannie thought her attitude toward motherhood was deplorable, but on the other hand, the group sounded so much better with all three sisters. They performed at a Sunday night service at their church, and the harmonies seemed to levitate the stage. She wished Junior would come back, too, but having Patty back made a big difference. The congregation kept requesting more songs, and they ended up staying an hour past time for the service to end.

After they packed everything into the van and Jerry Lee picked up Debbie and Patty, Jeannie stood alone in the moonlit church parking lot, waiting for Garland and Big Jean to finish their conversation inside with Brother Clarence, Sister Lucy, Brother Roy, Sister Katherine—all the old people hanging on to the last minutes of the evening, like teenagers at the end of a party. Now that the Gospelettes were mostly all together again, she wanted to cut another album. Garland had given his stamp of approval to eight new songs that Jeannie had written. She was arranging one of them in her head when she saw a spark and a movement across the street.

She shaded her eyes from the glare of the streetlight and peered into the darkness. Wick was sitting on his motorcycle, lighting a cigarette as he watched her.

She glanced over at the church door. They might come out at any moment, but then again, you never knew with Garland. He could stand and talk for hours, and complaints from the rest of the family did absolutely no good.

She crossed the street, holding the skirt of her ruffled granny gown above her ankles. "Hey," she said.

"Hey," Wick replied. She could see his white teeth shining at her in the dark.

"What's so funny?" she asked, glancing back at the church door.

"Nothing," he said. "You look sweet as can be."

"Thank you." She wanted to feel his body against hers, like she had on his bike and on his porch that day that he'd hugged her. She wanted more than that.

"So . . ." He took a long drag and squinted at the church. "Are you satisfied?"

She looked at him, brows knitted. An odd question. Then she remembered that they had finished their performance with an encore of the gospel song "Satisfied." She looked back at the church door again and then at Wick. "You heard us?"

"I did." He smiled. "I could hear *you*. You could sing paint off the walls, girl. You had the hair on the back of my neck standing up." He rubbed the back of his neck and shivered.

She smiled at the pavement. "You could come in and have a seat, you know. We've got these things called *pews*. They're like benches. You can sit down on them and listen."

"I know what a pew is, Miss Smarty, even if my ass ain't personally acquainted with any. I could hear you just fine outside. Y'all were rocking the whole street."

"You ought to come in sometime. I think you'd like it." She looked back at the church door. "And Daddy couldn't argue that you're a bad influence if he saw you sitting at church, trying to do right."

"Quit looking over there and look at me," Wick said. He tossed his cigarette, got off the motorcycle, and held his hand out to her. She took it, and he pulled her to him. She could feel his heart pounding and his erection and then his lips on hers. "I asked you a question," he whispered.

She tried to catch her breath, tried to turn and look at the church again, but she didn't want him to let go. "What question?" she whispered.

He buried his face in her hair and breathed into her ear. "Are you satisfied?"

She could hear voices coming from the church. Garland might walk up at any moment and make a scene. But she wanted to be in Wick's arms too much to walk away.

"Are you?" he asked. "Because I'm not. I can't think about anything but you. I can't even listen to the radio without thinking how I'd rather hear your voice. And if you need me to quit dealing, that's fine. I'll just run the cars and motorcycles side of the business. And if I have to marry you, then I'll marry you. If that's what you're waiting for, then let's do it."

Her heart felt as if it had lurched from her body. "What?" She looked back again and saw her parents emerging from the church door.

Wick took her hands in his and pulled her behind a tree, out of Garland's view. "Will you marry me?"

Wick and Jeannie went down to the courthouse and got married, without family or friends. She wore a short cream dress with an empire-style waistline and lacy sleeves, from Sears, and carried a handful of irises—what Big Jean called flags—that she'd secretly picked in the yard and tied with a white yarn hair ribbon. She was so breathless she could barely say her vows. Wick was scrubbed but still rugged with his long, curly hair and beard, and his eyes suggested that he'd put up with this ceremony another five minutes, tops, before he carried her off to the apartment he'd rented for them downtown, right on the square. It was a combination living room and kitchen, one bedroom, and a bathroom, over a men's clothing store that the owner opened only when he felt like it. Inside the apartment, after the ceremony, Wick covered her eyes with his hands. "I have a surprise for you," he said, and he led her into the bedroom. "OK. Open."

She gasped. "A waterbed!" It took up nearly the whole room and had an elaborate mirrored and shelved headboard.

Wick fell back on it, riding the wave. It gurgled and sloshed. "Hop in. It's warm." He grinned and patted the bed.

"What if I get seasick?" she asked, crawling on. It felt crazy and unsteady, but so did she.

Wick was unzipping her dress before she could get good and settled in.

"Honey—hey—slow down," she said, reaching for the sheet to cover herself.

Wick's mouth was on her neck, just below her left ear. "How long have we known each other?" he whispered.

She sighed. "Two years."

"Seems pretty slow to me." He smiled.

"Are you all right?" he asked afterward.

"Yeah, I'm OK." Her voice and hands were shaky from shock or embarrassment or excitement or some combination of these. She pulled the sheet up to her chin.

"My God, Jeannie. You're shaking like a damn leaf. What can I do for you? Can I get you something?"

"A Coke, please."

"You need a toke, not a Coke." They had no groceries in the apartment yet, so Wick put on his pants and rushed downstairs to find a Coke machine. He brought the cold bottle to her, lay down, and lit a cigarette.

Jeannie drank the Coke and felt her strength return. She felt shy but almost unbearably happy.

"Better?" he asked.

She nodded. They looked at each other and laughed.

"Well, you did it, didn't you? You held out till your wedding day. Almost twenty-one and never got laid. That must be a record."

"Oh, come on! You're making me sound like some kind of freak." She laughed. "Surely I'm not the only girl around who believes in waiting until marriage to have sex."

"The only girl *I* know."

She shoved him, but he didn't move. The bed just rolled beneath him. She didn't mind his teasing. It felt too good to be there, lying beside him. The only thing that she could remember that felt as good as being with him was singing—when it was really right, when the spirit was moving. It felt wrong to think that, to make a comparison between being in bed with Wick and singing in church, but she couldn't deny it.

"Wick, you know what I believe," she said. "You know that I try to do God's will."

He crushed out his cigarette in a folded piece of paper on the headboard shelf and turned toward her. "Do you think it was God's will for you to marry me?" He smiled at her, sexy and sleepy-eyed.

She smiled back at him. "I sure hope so."

Everybody else—her family, the people at church—might wonder why she married Wick, but for her it was simple. There was the fact that her younger sisters had both beaten her to the altar and left her to suffer Garland and Big Jean alone. But it was more than that. Wick was so purely himself, as easy and natural as anybody she'd ever met. Not the least bit worried about anybody else's rules and expectations. Of course she ran to him. Why Wick married *her* was the mystery. He had plenty of girls who were interested in him. She wondered what made him choose her, but she didn't ask. She knew he'd probably make a joke about this being the only way he could get her in bed, and she knew that wasn't the real reason. She wondered if it might actually have something to do with the Gospelettes. There was something enchanting about their music, about her voice in particular. That night he'd sat on his motorcycle outside the church and heard her singing, he'd asked her to marry him on the spot.

She closed her eyes and imagined Wick as part of the Gospelettes. He was an even better guitar player than Garland. Or he could take over the bass guitar. Before she could get Wick in the group, of course, she had to get him in church. She sighed and turned toward him. "Will you ever go to church with me?"

He was silent a while, thinking. He shook out another cigarette but didn't light it, just held it between his fingers. "I quit the business for you," he said.

She nodded.

"I don't need somebody to tell me what's what."

"Brother Clarence, our preacher, isn't like that," she said. "I promise. He's good as gold, not judgmental at all."

"This is what I am, Jeannie. I didn't lead you on. Do you want me to be like Junior, pretending I'm holy at church and then getting wired with my friends?" His eyes were turned to the high ceiling, which was cracked and aged to a brownish yellow.

"No. I sure don't want you to be like Junior. I'd just like for you to come hear us sing sometime." She stroked his beard, his chest.

Wick nodded. "Sometime."

They lay on the waterbed the rest of the afternoon, naked, listening to each other's heartbeat, like two babies floating in the womb.

# THE 1980S

# I've Got Confidence

The Gospelettes met Brother Oren Alford at a tent revival on the old Holliman family farm in July 1983. Brother Clarence had heard about this dynamic preacher—originally from Tulsa, Oklahoma, and now an assistant pastor at a growing church in Nashville—and invited him to lead the one-week revival. It was what every church, including the Bethel Independent Church of the Pentecost, needed from time to time, Brother Clarence had told Garland and the family, a different preacher to wake people up. Garland let the church set up a tent under the stars in a field next to the old homeplace. The house was dark and weathered. Garland had boarded it up long ago. No one on two legs had been inside for years. In the distance, the trees along the river trembled. Ordinarily, you could have heard the crickets and frogs and maybe a hoot owl and the river's soft conversation as it turned the bend, but this was a shouting revival.

Jeannie, like the rest of the congregation, was mesmerized by Brother Alford. (She wasn't sure why he was referred to by his last name rather than his first, as were most preachers she knew.) From their folding chairs in the front row, the Gospelettes watched him shed his suit jacket and loosen his tie. He wiped his glistening face with a spotless white handkerchief. Beyond the bright tent lights, the darkness of the outside world threatened to swallow them up, but inside, it was as if he held them all safe with his confidence and kept the evil at bay.

At the end of the week, Brother Alford said, "Right here in Bethel, Kentucky, the spirit is moving stronger than I've ever witnessed, and I've been everywhere, brothers and sisters. I've been all over the United States and five foreign countries preaching the gospel. Yes, the spirit is moving stronger than I've ever witnessed—anywhere, *anywhere*, right here, brothers and sisters, *right here*—and God has mighty works to perform yet!"

Everybody said amen.

Already, dozens had been baptized in the Holy Ghost, speaking in tongues, dancing, rolling, and getting slain in the spirit, including one girl Jeannie had known from school who was a Baptist.

"God is just getting warmed up, brothers and sisters," Brother Alford declared, holding his fat Bible over his head. "God is just getting warmed up for an unprecedented, miraculous healing dispensation, and Satan's demonic forces are already working hard to destroy it."

His ice-blue eyes were fixed straight ahead. He refused to look very long at anyone. No friendly banter. He was listening to a voice only he could hear. He would sit before the service in his wooden folding chair on the plywood platform, his lips moving in prayer. Jeannie could almost see a force field around him, shimmering like heat above pavement. People—mostly women—screamed and fell at his feet on the sawdust floor, crying out in tongues. His wife, Sister Diane, in her bright, shoulder-padded dress suits, zipped around them, covering the slain women's legs with baby blanket–sized cloths that had been sewn for this very purpose. He walked past them or over them, pointing a finger and making a swooshing noise that sounded like Jeannie's nephews playing with toy spaceships, and down more of them went.

"Let me tell you how the Lord will bless you if you're walking in the Word and claiming the promises," Brother Alford began. He rarely raised his voice. He carried a small microphone and expected everyone to listen when he spoke. When people started shouting, overtaken by the Holy Ghost, he paused and let them, and sometimes he'd just swoosh.

He positioned himself in the center of the platform and held the microphone in both hands, lowering his voice to nearly a whisper. The crowd hushed and leaned forward to listen. "A few years ago, not long after the Lord called me into the ministry, I went to the Lord and told him, 'I need a car.' I was driving this old clunker that would die on me every time I stopped at a stop sign, and I was preaching a revival about a hundred miles from home. I was staying with the minister and his family, and the next morning, a member of his congregation came over and told me to come outside, that he wanted me to have something for my ministry, so I go out, and there in the driveway is this beautiful $52,000 import car. Now, this was a few years ago, so today it would be a $65,000 car. And I said, 'Lord, I told you I needed a car, but this wasn't what I meant!' I said, 'Do you want me to take it and sell it and put the money in the ministry?' And God said, 'No, I want you to drive it. I promised that I'd take care of you. What makes you think I wouldn't want the best for my faithful servant?'"

He paused and cocked his head, perfectly still, smiling. "I drove it for many years, and then I sold it to some people. One day, God said, 'I want those people to have it.' And I said, 'OK. Do you want me to give it to them?' He said, 'No, I want them to buy it. I have blessed them with the money, and I want them to learn how to spend their money responsibly.' You see, God will bless you beyond how you would bless yourself. And if you're walking in the Word and you make a request known to God, you'd better be ready to receive it."

Jeannie was skeptical, not a familiar place for her to be. Faith had always been easy for her. Their little church was an extension of her family, and Brother Clarence was the kindly father figure who never let them down. Being a gospel singer had cemented her place in that comforting world. But so much had happened in the eleven years since the Gospelettes had gotten started and in the eight years since she'd married Wick. So many disappointments. Gospel music wasn't as popular as it used to be, and she had been struggling with what to do with the group. Their full schedule those first few years had decreased to a couple singings a month and then to just one every now and then. This loss of favor hurt her more than she was willing to admit. Debbie and Patty had never cared as much. They would have quit long ago if Jeannie hadn't begged them to stay with it. Patty's son, JP, was eight, and Debbie, besides raising Jerry Lee's kids from his first marriage to adulthood, had two children under six, Randall and Lee Ann. They had their hands full, and their marriages were unstable. Meanwhile, Junior was who knew where doing who knew what. He had come back home a few times over the years, after hitting bottom with drugs and alcohol and running out of money and luck, and each time, he'd left again for a longer period, leaving Garland and Big Jean desolate and wracked with worry. He had married three times and had a child with each wife, one in Tennessee, one in Florida, and one in Texas. The family had only seen one of his kids, Heather in Tennessee. It had been nearly three years since they last heard from him.

And the years had been hard on Jeannie and Wick. She'd had two ectopic pregnancies early on and had gradually accepted her infertility. Time had eased that pain, but she remembered the shame of finding out from her doctor that it was a disease that had caused this, something Wick had given her, something she hadn't realized was as serious as it was and hadn't treated. Wick had been broken by the news, not because he'd wanted children but because it had made her distrust him. He'd had no idea, he assured her, no symptoms he could recall, and he swore it had to have been something he'd caught before they married and didn't know about, that he had never cheated on her. She believed him. Her anger at Wick dissolved into a sadness they shared, a kind of bond.

After his daddy died of a heart attack, they had moved out of the apartment downtown and back into the house Wick had grown up in. It only made sense. His salvage yard and mechanic shop were there on the property, and his older brothers had their own places to live, one in a house he shared with his wife, the other in prison for selling weed. Jeannie had deep cleaned and redecorated, hoping to make a fresh start, but it was still the bootlegger's house in her mind and probably everybody else's.

Lately, it felt like life was just one sorrow on top of another. She had lost count of the number of friends and buddies, many from the war, that Wick had lost since they married—drug overdoses, car accidents, suicides. He wasn't surprised anymore to get the call. He'd shake his head, shrug. He had started drinking more, alone, in recent years. She suspected, judging by the recent increase in traffic to his shop behind the house, that he might be selling drugs again.

Now Brother Alford was telling them that they only needed to "name it and claim it" to have all the desires of their hearts. Had she been doing it wrong all this time?

At the end of what was supposed to be the last night of the revival, Brother Alford said the Lord wasn't finished with Bethel yet. Afterward, he asked the Gospelettes to stay and talk. They stood in a huddle beside the platform, watching him shake hands and talk with dozens of people as they filed out.

"What do you reckon he wants?" Garland asked.

"He wants you to say he can keep the tent here longer," Jeannie said. "And he probably wants us to keep singing for him." Patty groaned and rolled her eyes. Debbie sighed. Big Jean tended to the grandchildren, unwrapping suckers for JP and Randall while she held Lee Ann, who had somehow slept through the second half of the service, passed to and from helpers each time the Gospelettes performed.

"I don't know what in the world Clarence was thinking, bringing that rotten doctrine over here," Garland grumbled. "He thinks you can just order up what you want from the almighty God like that? The Lord is a sovereign God! You don't tell him what to do. He tells you!"

Jeannie was surprised that Brother Clarence had invited him, too. What Brother Alford was preaching didn't sound a thing like what Brother Clarence preached, nor did it sound like anything she had ever heard from Garland. Brother Clarence preached about love and forgiveness. Garland mostly talked about judgment and tribulation. Brother Alford was all about health and wealth. The crazy thing was, they were all quoting the same book.

When everyone else had left, Brother Alford came over to the Gospelettes and draped an arm across Garland's shoulders. Jeannie thought they looked like old pals who had grown up together, with their similar hairstyles and clothes. "Brother, the Lord has told me he's doing a mighty work here, and he wants me to stay here longer," Brother Alford said.

"Is that right?" Garland stood still as a stone, looking askance at Brother Alford.

"The anointing on you all is so strong, Brother Garland, that God wants you to come sing every night."

"Well, we'll have to look at our schedule and whatnot," Garland mumbled.

Jeannie raised her eyebrows. The schedule, as he knew, was clear.

"The Lord has told me he wants to bless you with part of the offering," Brother Alford added.

"Well." Garland cleared his throat.

Brother Alford clapped Garland's shoulder. "Your testimony between songs tonight was powerful, Brother Garland. Powerful!"

"Well, I just let God do the talking," Garland said.

"Amen!" Brother Alford pivoted to stand facing Garland and placed one hand on his shoulder. "I have a prophetic word for you, brother." The family formed a circle and watched Brother Alford, who nodded, eyes closed, as if listening. "Brother Garland, your son has the hand of God upon him and angels standing guard all around him. 'Fear not,' saith the Lord! He is bringing him back. He has work for him to do right here. He is bringing him back, with a league of angels."

"Aaaaa-men," Garland breathed.

Jeannie watched her father's face change and knew the Gospelettes would be back the next week.

# Get in Line, Brother

The one-week revival turned into two weeks, then three, then four. This was a problem for Brother Clarence and, in turn, the Gospelettes. Brother Clarence had canceled Wednesday night and Sunday night church services the first week of the revival so that the congregation could attend the revival. When Brother Alford declared the Lord wanted them to continue into the second week and then the third, Brother Clarence had obliged him and canceled services again. But by the fourth week, Brother Clarence was ready for things to get back to normal, and, taking the microphone at the end of the service that Saturday night, he let everyone know that he would be resuming services at the church the next evening.

"We sure do appreciate Brother Alford coming up here from Nashville every night for these past four weeks," he said, as mildly as anyone in his situation possibly could. "Praise God? And we want to keep coming as long as the spirit is moving. But we're going to get back on our regular schedule at the church tomorrow night."

At first, the revival had been mainly for the church, but word spread in the community, and people from other churches—and, Jeannie presumed, no church—had started attending. Then, Brother Alford began taking out full-page ads in the newspaper every week, featuring photographs of people laid out drunk in the spirit and inviting everyone to come and experience revival miracles. When the Gospelettes got up on the platform to sing, Jeannie saw the crowd grow each night, more chairs getting squeezed in and even spreading out beyond the tent.

Brother Alford took back the microphone from Brother Clarence and stood gazing into the distance, as if listening to something.

Everyone got so quiet that they could hear the crickets and cicadas and frogs beyond the tent. "When God says *go*, I go. When God says *stay*, I stay," he said finally, striding across the platform. Amens scattered from around the tent. "I don't ask God why. Noah didn't ask why. He just built the ark."

"That's right!" a man's voice called out from the back.

"Abraham didn't ask why. He just picked up the knife and his little boy and walked up the mountain." Brother Alford bent over, reenacting the scene.

"Amen!"

"I don't say, 'But we only have the tent reserved for one week, Lord.'" He said this in a small, whiny voice. "I don't ask, 'But aren't people going to get tired of it, Lord? Aren't they going to want to be home watching *Dallas*?'"

There were more amens and a few chuckles.

"No. I say, 'Whatever you *say*, Jesus! You are the *boss*, Jesus!' And that's why the Lord blesses me. I say *yes* to him, and he says *yes* to me! That's why you won't see me sick, brothers and sister," he said. "You won't hear me say, 'Oh, I can't preach tonight. I've got a sore throat. I can't preach tonight. I've got laryngitis. I can't preach tonight. I'm down in my back.' You won't hear those words coming out of my mouth, brothers and sisters. I've already been given the victory, and what I speak is what I get."

Jeannie looked over at Brother Clarence. His head was bowed as if in prayer. Next to him, Sister Lucy's head had taken on an enraged, palsy-like shake, and her lips were set into an uncomfortable-looking pucker.

The volume of shouting increased. Brother Alford paused to let the noise die down. Then he began speaking softly: "Jesus said, 'Whosoever shall say unto this mountain, Be thou removed, and be thou cast into the sea; and shall not doubt in his heart, but shall believe that those things which he saith shall come to pass; he shall have whatsoever he saith.' I didn't say that. Jesus did! I'm just standing on the promises!" He hopped up on a folding chair. "I'm just standing on the promises! He said, 'What things soever ye desire'!" Brother Alford turned and looked at the people to his right. "Do you desire a new car? Do you? I did, and I got one." He turned toward the people in the middle. "Do you desire a house? If you already got one, do you desire a better one?" He turned and asked the people to his left, "Do you desire for your children to live holy lives? Do you desire to be free of cancer or diabetes or arthritis?" He waited.

A few people called out, "Yes, yes!"

"Well, do you believe it?"

"Yes!"

"Well, Jesus said to believe that you will receive them and you shall have them. Does Jesus lie?"

"No!"

"Well, if Jesus don't lie and you don't have the desires of your heart, it must be one of two things. Either you haven't told that mountain to be removed or you haven't believed. Because Jesus is always faithful, my brothers and sisters."

In the midst of the commotion in the crowd, Jeannie saw Sister Lucy march away, followed by Brother Clarence. Out in the darkness, their car, parked near the tent, lit up as they got inside. She could see Brother Clarence peering at his dashboard and Sister Lucy talking angrily, her head bobbing. She was watching them drive away when Brother Alford said, "Gospelettes, would you sing us off to victory?" They rose and took their places on the platform. Jeannie looked over at Garland and saw that he'd seen Brother Clarence and Sister Lucy leave too and that he was just as unsure as she was of what to do next, other than sing.

# Only Believe

The family had discussed where their loyalties should lie on Wednesday and Sunday nights—with Brother Clarence at the church or with Brother Alford at the tent—but, ultimately, it had been Garland's decision, of course.

"Brother Clarence had us singing at church twice a week when everybody else had stopped calling," Jeannie pointed out.

"Our home church ought to come first," Big Jean suggested.

"Maybe we don't need to be *anywhere* every single night of the week," Patty complained.

But after two months of revival, Brother Alford had decided to take off Monday nights for prayer and meditation, and he asked Garland to be the guest preacher on those nights, which settled it for him. "I've been right there in the church since the day it started, and Clarence never once asked me to be a guest preacher. 'A prophet is not without honor, but in his own country, and among his own kin, and in his own house,'" Garland declared.

With that invitation, he seemed to have forgotten about his theological differences with Brother Alford. Jeannie still couldn't help but wonder about Alford's prosperity gospel. She'd always considered herself a mature Christian, not a baby Christian, but he seemed to suggest that if she didn't have all the desires of her heart, she wasn't as strong in her faith as she liked to think she was. If she focused her mind on only the good things that she wanted and spoke only blessings on her life, if she could just *think positive*, maybe everything would change. Wick would stop drinking and dabbling in drugs and would start going to church with her. The Gospelettes would get back on track and have the success she longed for. She hardly dared to think about the possibility of having a baby—it was too painful to consider—but, yes, maybe God would make a way. And she did try positive thinking, sometimes for days at a time, before reality intruded on her thoughts. It was hard. Garland and Big Jean had raised them on doom and gloom, not speaking the victory. Every other sentence they uttered was a warning.

After Garland had dropped off the sisters and their kids following another night at the revival, Jeannie's phone rang, unusual at such a late hour when she had to go to work the next morning. She picked up and immediately recognized Debbie's sniffling and gasping. "Debbie? What's wrong?"

"I don't—I guess I just don't know how to . . . *believe,*" Debbie sobbed.

Jeannie took a deep breath and exhaled. "What do you mean?" she asked, even though she knew exactly what Debbie meant.

"When I'm there, at the tent, and we're singing, and everybody's shouting and praying, I do believe. I really do! But then, as soon as we step out into the dark, and then I walk in this house and—" She paused to sob, caught her breath, and continued in a low voice. "I don't even know where Jerry Lee is right now. I think he's seeing somebody. I can feel him slipping away."

"Debbie, that's not your fault." Jeannie watched Wick walk in from his garage. She smelled weed when he paused to kiss her forehead and walked toward the bedroom. She closed her eyes and sighed. "That has nothing do with you or who you are as a wife or with your faith."

"I felt like I was seeing the Lord move on some situations at home when I started making seed faith donations," Debbie said. This was one of Brother Alford's major points, the need to make weekly donations, planting the seeds that would grow the blessings you were praying for. "But then I had to buy Randall some school clothes and didn't make my donations the last two weeks." She took a long, gasping breath. "And Barry and Christie aren't speaking to me anymore because I stopped giving him money for college when I found out he'd dropped out."

Jeannie shook her head. "Debbie. Please. Listen to me."

"I'd been sending Barry a check every month, and turns out, he hasn't been enrolled for over a year. And Christie has turned her back on me since she graduated and moved in with her mama." Debbie sobbed. "I was just nineteen when we got married, but I tried to raise his kids like they were my own. I guess I don't mean anything to them. Or to Jerry Lee."

"Oh, Debbie."

"He doesn't love me. He never did. I raised his kids for him, and now he's probably found somebody new, just like Daddy warned me."

Jeannie held the phone a few inches from her ear and slumped into a kitchen chair. What could she say to help? It was all true, and it was terrible. She listened to Debbie cry for a while, so tired that she felt like she would fall asleep if she put her head down on the table. She had the first shift at Ogles Market in the morning, and she knew Debbie had to go in to work in the morning too. "Debbie? Do you think you can go to sleep?" she asked hopefully. "Or do you need me to come over?"

Debbie's voice was airless and faraway. "Can you come over?"

Jeannie made a grim face. "OK. I'll be right there." She hung up and walked to the bedroom. Wick was under the covers, arms bent behind his head, watching her. "Gotta go check on Debbie," she said.

He reached out one hand, and she walked over and took it, sitting on the side of the bed. He was familiar with Debbie's issues and didn't have to ask for more information. "Wish I could at least see you in bed since you're gone every evening," he said. "How the hell long is that revival gonna go on?"

This was something Jeannie had wondered herself. The answer seemed to be as long as Brother Alford wanted it to. The crowds kept coming, mesmerized by the show, the likes of which Jeannie had never seen before, despite growing up in a charismatic church. Many of them, she was sure, were intrigued by the idea that they could be as successful as Brother Alford seemed to be and promised they could be. Who didn't want a happier marriage, a better job, more money in the bank, a healing? How many parents, just like Garland and Big Jean, came to the revival, night after night, praying for their children to come home and get off drugs? Jeannie wondered about the thin, sad-eyed woman who brought her young, disabled daughter in a wheelchair almost every night. Jeannie had watched the woman struggle to push the wheelchair over the bumpy ground to reach the tent, stepping high in her scuffed shoes through the rough grass that had once fed the Holliman cows. Was she naming and claiming a healing that never seemed to come? Jeannie had seen the woman's deep-shadowed face in the crowd and, next to her, the girl's pained eyes, looking up at the Gospelettes as they sang. Their lips moved along with the words.

"You look sad," Wick whispered, squeezing her hand.

Jeannie wanted to tell him about the woman and her daughter and how Brother Alford was telling everybody that all they had to do was speak the victory and they could have everything they ever wanted. But she knew exactly what Wick would say. If she was ever going to get him to church, get him saved and heaven-bound, she needed to make sure everything he saw and heard about it was positive. Wick could sniff out a polecat a mile away.

She pulled her fingers from his grasp and sighed. "Don't wait up for me."

# On Our Way

The revival carried on into October, when nights were cool enough that people started to wear sweaters and Brother Alford had heaters set up on the edges of the tent. "How long are we going to keep this up?" Patty demanded, as they rode to the farm in the Gospelettes van. "I ain't singing out there in the snow."

"What if your butt gets froze to the seat?" JP asked, and he and Randall and Lee Ann erupted into wild laughter.

"Don't say ugly words, JP," Big Jean said.

Brother Alford seemed unusually happy that evening, and when the service ended, he told the Gospelettes that he had a special word from the Lord and would be at Garland and Big Jean's house the next morning, a Saturday, to tell them. He was full of messages from the Lord, so the sisters might not have shown up except that he assured them they'd want to be there for this one.

Jeannie woke up early, piddled around the house, went out in the yard, and pulled some weeds. Wick's old dog, Sally, walked alongside her, stopping now and then to rest and sniff the air. The vet said she had arthritis, and that made Jeannie want to cry. She heard Wick open his garage. She looked over and saw him there, communing with his motorcycles, head bowed. He seemed weighed down with sadness, but it was possible that she was just seeing in him what she felt in herself.

Who knew what Alford might have to say that day? He'd already told Garland and Big Jean that Junior would be back. Well, Jeannie figured you didn't have to be a prophet to guess that Junior might come crawling back when he ran out of money and luck. Alford had prayed with Debbie for the restoration of her marriage, but Jeannie had her doubts about that happening. The main thing that Jeannie wanted, the one thing she couldn't let go of, was success for the Gospelettes. *Real* success. She couldn't say exactly what that meant, but she would know it when it happened. It wasn't that she wanted money or fame or accolades. It was just that she wanted her music to touch lots of people—and usually when music touched lots of people, money and fame and accolades followed.

She walked over to Wick. "I left you some breakfast on the stove. Did you see it?"

"Yeah. Not too hungry today." He looked up, saw the keys in her hand. "Where you headed?"

"Over to Mama and Daddy's for a little bit." She wasn't going to tell him why, get into all that. Early in the revival, she had described Brother Alford and what he was preaching, and Wick had said he sounded like a con man. Well, how would he know? He'd never set foot inside a revival or a church service of any kind. He'd just decided they were all out for something, usually money. It depressed her and felt like the greatest failure of her life, that she'd never been able to change Wick's mind about religion.

The sisters sat in their parents' living room, while the kids ran around in the front yard, throwing acorns and pretending to shoot at each other with sticks.

"I hope the Lord's message is that he needs to fold up the tent and head back to Nashville," Patty said. She was stretched out so that she took up most of the couch while Jeannie and Debbie squeezed onto the other end.

"I don't think he'd call a special meeting with the Gospelettes to say that," Jeannie said.

"I said 'I *hope*!'" Patty poked Jeannie's leg with her toe.

"Why? Do you have something else to do?" Jeannie asked, with some venom, knowing that Patty didn't have a job or much of anything else going on.

"Yes. Live my life," Patty replied.

"Y'all hush. Here he is," Garland announced as Oren Alford's Mercedes pulled into the gravel driveway. Through the picture window, they all watched him approach, dressed in his suit, as usual, ignoring the children as he walked by them.

Inside, he declined to sit, standing for a long time with his eyes closed, palms together in front of his mouth. They all watched, waiting for him to speak. He was a master at making people wait. He opened his eyes finally and spoke. "Since I was a child, I've answered God's call to be a prayer warrior. I spend hours each day in prayer. That's what it takes to hear God's voice. You don't have to have any highfalutin degrees from fancy universities. You don't have to have a doctorate from Harvard Divinity School. You get to hear God's voice when you spend hours and hours in prayer and practice faith!"

"Amen!" Garland was nodding. Brother Alford was speaking his language.

"It's been coming up in my spirit, 'Speak the Victory. Speak the Victory.' The Lord is calling me to start a new ministry," Brother Alford continued. "There's a TV program that operates out of Tulsa, where I'm from, *The John Percy Power Hour*, that I used to preach on from time to time."

Jeannie nodded. She had heard of this TV evangelist, though she had never watched his program.

"The Lord is working mightily through them," Brother Alford said. "And he's been telling me that I need to expand that work. I talked to a brother in Nashville, and he's made arrangements for us to do it from there—"

"Do what?" Jeannie asked.

Brother Alford spread the fingers of both hands wide as if casting light from his fingertips. "A daily television program, *Speak the Victory!*, featuring Brother Oren Alford and the Gospelettes. To be distributed nationwide!"

They all stared at him, speechless.

He went on to explain his plans. He would pay them for their appearances, and, eventually, when—*when*, not if—the show took off, he planned to bring them on full time as the resident band. He wanted Jeannie to work for him part-time at first, to plan the music portion of the program, arrange for musical guests, and so on.

"The song you all sang Monday night, the one about God being present—did you write that one, Sister?" Brother Alford asked Jeannie.

Jeannie nodded. "'Always Present.' I wrote that one just a couple weeks ago."

He smiled. "It was inspired. Deep! Very deep for such a young woman." He looked at her for a few seconds. His eyes had a certain electricity to them, something compelling but dangerous that she couldn't quite identify. "Later that night," he continued, "I was in prayer, and the Lord told me that he wants your songs to be heard more widely. He has big plans for you. I had a vision of people watching televisions all over America, and it was your voice coming out."

Jeannie hadn't known what to expect from Brother Alford's visit, and she certainly would never have guessed all this was about to transpire. "Oh," she said at last. "OK." It was as if he knew her prayers, though she'd never shared them with him.

He answered a few more questions, then put his hand on Garland's shoulder. "Go to God in prayer, and then we'll talk more."

The family stood at the window and watched him walk to his Mercedes, back out, and drive away before they said anything.

"I can't believe it," Jeannie said. She had been knocking herself out for over a decade to get the Gospelettes somewhere, and now it was happening—*something* was happening—and she didn't even know what she felt. "Is this real?"

"This is wild," Patty agreed. "A TV show is definitely better than a tent."

"Are we going to do it, Daddy?" Debbie asked.

Garland had gone to sit in his chair and was staring straight ahead. Big Jean hovered nearby. They all held their breath, watching his face.

# Sinner, You'd Better Get Ready

By November, the tent had come down and the revival had ended, but Jeannie was busier than ever, helping Brother Alford launch *Speak the Victory!* He'd located a studio in Nashville that they would be using. His wife, Sister Diane, was set designer and wardrobe supervisor. And Jeannie was planning the music, writing songs, and working with the sound and camera guys on how to handle the musical numbers. She was introduced to some contemporary Christian singers in the area and attended some of their performances. When she brought cassettes to Garland and Big Jean's for the family to listen to at a rehearsal, her father had made a face of confused disgust. "What kind of instruments are they playing?" he asked. "What's that tinkling noise?"

"Maybe it's a zither," Patty said, smirking.

"I don't know, Daddy. It's just an example," Jeannie said, punching the stop button on her boom box. "I'm not saying we have to imitate them." Getting him on board to update the Gospelettes' sound was going to be more difficult than she'd realized. She wished Junior were still around. He would have had an easier time convincing Garland to try new things, she was sure.

After a day working at Ogles Market and an evening watching a Christian rock band at an enormous church in Nashville, Jeannie drove the hour up Interstate 65 toward home, singing a song she was composing. She often did this, since Wick had taught her to drive and purchased a car for her. She'd turn the radio off, and songs would come to her as she flew past billboards and barns. By the time she got home, she'd have a new song or two to add to the

Gospelettes' repertoire. Brother Alford wanted all original songs for the show, none of the old gospel standards they'd been singing for years.

When she got home, it was close to midnight, dark and moonless. She thought Wick might already be in bed, but she saw the light of the TV shining in the living room as she pulled into the driveway. She went inside and found his guitar, which she hadn't seen him pick up in a couple of years. She wanted to play him the song she'd just written before it left her head. Maybe he would play something for her too. Lately, when he was home, he was drinking. He was making a dent in the seat of the recliner they bought the second year they were married and a water circle on the wood side table where he set his beer. He barely moved his eyes from the TV—a *M*A*S*H* rerun with the volume turned down—when she carried the guitar to the living room and sat on the couch, tuning it.

She strummed a couple of times and then looked over at him. "Do you ever play anymore? You used to play songs for me all the time."

He lit a cigarette and took a drag.

"Why don't you, Wick? I was listening to this Christian rock band at a church in Nashville tonight, and they were so good—the kids were going crazy—but I was thinking, *Wick can outplay anybody on that stage.*"

He lifted his beer can and finished it off.

"We need to do things together," she said. "Couples need to have *something* in common. Like music. You could join the Gospelettes."

He cut his eyes at her and scoffed. "What the hell, Jeannie?"

She set the guitar on the couch and stood up. "Never mind. Just . . . never mind."

She walked to the bedroom. The waterbed Wick had bought when they married was in the shed—he had developed a bad back and couldn't sleep on it—so they used the antique bedroom suite his mother had brought with her when she married and had left behind when she ran off. The room felt crowded with the dark, heavy furniture and with the musty, sad memories Jeannie thought she'd emptied from the dresser drawers when they moved in. She slipped off her dress and pantyhose and lay on the bed, staring up at the motionless ceiling fan in the dark.

Wick appeared in the doorway. "I got a call while you were out," he said quietly. "Headlight—"

She rolled her eyes. "What about him?"

"He's dead."

She sat up. "What?"

"Yep. Another one bites the dust."

She couldn't see his face, just the outline of his body, the slump of resignation in his posture. "What happened?" she asked.

"Russian roulette and Early Times."

"Oh, my God." She covered her eyes.

"Yeah. Ol' Headlight. Son of a bitch." He undressed, got in the bed, and sighed. "Son of a bitch."

Wick had lost many friends over the years, but this was the first one that truly made Jeannie sad. Headlight was a decent guy, despite his obvious flaws. The kind of guy who never hurt anybody but himself. He'd always been nice to her. Jeannie felt suddenly ashamed that she'd never invited him to church or talked to him about salvation, but at the same time, she felt silly for thinking that would have made a difference. Maybe if Junior had tried, Headlight might have been interested. Maybe if she could have gotten Wick to church, he could have gotten Headlight to church. She was surrounded by lost people, and she realized she wasn't doing them a bit of good. She started crying there in the dark, tears burning her eyes as she tried not to gasp or otherwise let on that she, who barely knew Headlight, was having such an over-the-top reaction. It didn't do any good.

"Jeannie? Why are you crying?" Wick asked.

Jeannie swallowed and said, "I'm not," but it was obvious in her choked voice. "OK. I'm just . . . wondering about his soul and . . . thinking about what I should have done. I've been singing gospel music all these years, but I haven't really been witnessing to the people in my life that I should have been witnessing to."

Wick sat up and looked at her. "Are you serious?"

"Yes. Why wouldn't I be?"

Wick uttered a short, derisive laugh. "All right, Jeannie." He sat leaning over the edge of the bed and ran one hand through his hair.

"I don't think it's very funny! Do you think spending eternity in hell is funny?"

"I don't know, Jeannie." He got up and pulled on his jeans.

She sat up and wiped her eyes. "You don't know? I think we need to talk about this, Wick. I don't want something like this to happen to you, with you being unsaved just like Headlight."

Wick closed his eyes and took a long breath. "Look, Jeannie. I get that you have all these beliefs, and I'm not trying to change your mind about anything. But Headlight's soul isn't what I'm worried about, OK? My friend got shit-faced and shot himself. That's what upsets me."

"It upsets me too. But—"

"But the magical guy in the sky is making a list. I know. Just—" He threw up his hands. "Just spare me for a while, OK? Let me get through this before you start reeling off the Bible verses."

She watched him walk to the window and look out into the darkness, staring at nothing. Part of her wanted to wrap her arms around him and rest her cheek against his smooth, bare back. The other part wanted to scream and beg for him to see the light before it was too late. "Wick, I love you. That's why I'm saying this. I'm worried about you. I think you're selling again. You are, aren't you? You're selling drugs again."

He turned to face her. "Do you really believe that me selling some marijuana is worse than your daddy growing and selling tobacco all those years? I mean, aside from the fact that it's against the law. Yeah, I get that. Somebody decided that one plant—tobacco—is legal and another plant—marijuana—is not. But, just from your God's eye view, do you think he's OK with all these churchgoing farmers around here selling something that people smoke that causes cancer and emphysema and whatever, but he draws the line at marijuana? Is that what you're telling me?"

"I don't want you going to prison! OK? Let's just leave aside what God thinks about it. It's illegal, and you could go to prison like your brother!"

"I'm not going to piss off the wrong people like Clayton did."

"You won't even try. You won't even go to church just *one time*. For me, your wife. Just to see if you like it. Just to listen to me sing. You're too stubborn to do that one thing for me."

"All right—so let's talk about what *they're* selling. How much are these churches taking in their collection plates from good, hardworking people living hand-to-mouth? Do you know, Jeannie? How much is that revival preacher raking in every night from people desperate for a miracle? Huh? Did he ever let you count it? It must be a pretty good haul if he's starting a TV show now."

Jeannie got out of bed and stood in front of him. "Is that what you think of us? That we're out here trying to rob people? We've been singing gospel for eleven years, and we've probably spent more to keep it going than we've *ever* taken in from fees and collection plates."

"I'm not talking about you, Jeannie. Or your family. I'm talking about these religious salesmen. That's what they are. Selling promises." He waved his hands above his head. "Selling something in the clouds, in the sweet by and by." He shook his head, and she felt his words point right at her heart. "At least when I sell a product, I can guarantee it."

# Your First Day in Heaven

Over the years, the Gospelettes had stood on stages, platforms, and bandstands of various types, large and small, carpeted, scarred wooden planks, sawdust, in a few grand churches and a lot of not-so-grand ones, lit through stained glass and by bare hanging bulbs, looking out at congregations in wooden pews, folding chairs, and even at people seated on the floor and standing up, leaning against walls, in overflow crowds. But the Nashville studio where they taped the first episode of *Speak the Victory!* was something entirely new.

"Lord o' mercy," Big Jean breathed as they walked onto the stage for their first rehearsal.

Even Garland was frozen, staring out at the black walls and floors, the lights shining up from the front of the stage and hanging down from the ceiling.

"Are we gonna be on TV?" Randall asked. Debbie held him and Lee Ann by their hands tightly.

JP ran to the edge of the stage and jumped off, landing on a cameraman's foot.

Then Brother Alford was beside them, fully suited as always. "Praise God, the day is here!" he announced. He strode over and shook Garland's hand. "This is it, Brother Garland. This is where we will be taping *Speak the Victory!* and transmitting the Word all over the world!" He waved his arm in a wide arc.

Garland was speechless, for once, so Jeannie spoke up. "All over the world?"

Brother Alford gave her a rare smile. "It's a smaller TV market right now, but with satellite, our program is going to be seen by churches all over the United States and seven other countries. This is the future of evangelism." He turned back toward Garland. "Think about it. All those years on the road, Brother Garland. Traveling from place to place. The hours and hours of driving." He shook his head. "I was a traveling evangelist for years myself. I know what it's like." He put an arm around Garland and grasped his shoulder. "Brother Garland, we've been in the vineyards together many years." He turned back toward the camera crew. "But now we can reach them from right where we are. It's a miracle. I spoke the victory, and I knew it was coming. If you speak it and you believe it, the devil better just get out of the way. Amen?"

"Amen," Garland murmured.

Big Jean settled at a black grand piano on the side of the stage, patted her hair (a smaller version of the beehive she'd worn for years), and began warming up with the high plinking introduction to "When Morning Sweeps the Eastern Sky."

"Sister Jeannie," Brother Alford said, "I want to hear this song you were telling me about."

Jeannie nodded. She'd written a song especially for the show, its own theme song to play at the beginning and end of every episode. They had performed it at home several times. She looked at her sisters. "Are y'all ready?" she asked.

They took their positions. Garland tuned up his guitar, Jeannie strapped on the bass, Big Jean played the opening riff, and they let it loose.

*When I have a need, I just speak the victory!*
*When I have a need, I'm just gonna speak the victory!*
*When I go to God, I just speak the victory!*
*I'm gonna tell him what I need right now!*
*Good measure, pressed down, I just speak the victory!*
*Shaken together and running over, I'm gonna speak the victory!*
*Whatsoever I desire, I just speak the victory!*
*I'm gonna tell him what I need right now!*
*When I see that mountain, I just speak the victory!*
*I say unto that mountain, I'm gonna speak the victory!*
*Be thou removed, mountain, I just speak the victory!*
*I'm gonna tell him what I need right now!*

Brother Alford sat listening in one of the upholstered seats in the darkened theater. When they finished, they squinted out into the seats, looking for him. Finally, he appeared under the lights in front of them, looking down, his hands clasped in front of his lips. They waited, holding their breath.

"Amen," he said, quietly. "Amen! That's why God is blessing us, brothers and sisters!" He nodded at the Gospelettes, at the crew, at the men in jeans, boots, and aviator glasses who stood on the side of the stage, arms crossed, surveying the scene. Who were they? Jeannie counted fifteen different men. Patty had called them Oren Alford's mafia.

"You got it, Sister Jeannie." He pointed at her. "You got it."

Their first taping was that Saturday. They would do five half-hour shows, with short breaks in between, to be aired Monday through Friday the following week. Most of the congregation from the tent revival rode down to Nashville on buses to see them. Sister Katherine, who kept a supply of Juicy Fruit gum, funeral home fans, and assorted dime-store toys in her purse, sat with JP, Randall, and Lee Ann out in the audience. Backstage, the family could hear the audience's excited chatter as they filled the seats. The crew set up. Sister Diane arranged silk ferns on the stage, adjusted the position of two high-backed wicker chairs that looked like thrones (in which she and Brother Alford would be seated at the beginning of the show), gave orders, and paused for the makeup girl to touch up her triangular blush application.

The sisters huddled backstage, waiting to be told what to do. Jeannie caught Sister Diane by the arm as she flew by. "Where's Brother Alford?" she asked.

Sister Diane cocked her head and gave her an open-mouthed smile. "Oh, he's in his prayer closet! That's where he always is before he preaches."

"What do we do?" Jeannie asked.

"Go to the dressing room. I'll send Karen over." She lifted one hand, snapped her fingers, and pointed them toward the dressing room.

The peach, poufy-sleeved dresses that Sister Diane had selected for them were hanging on a rack, along with matching heels. They dressed and then sat in the makeup chairs, looking at each other in the mirror with comical expressions. Karen applied makeup to all of them, even Garland.

"I wish Junior were here to see this," Jeannie said to her sisters in a low voice.

"I wish Junior was here to get his nose powdered!" Patty said.

Debbie laughed behind her hand.

Back in the wings, they peeked out at the audience. The lights were too bright for them to make out any faces, but they could hear the audience murmuring. Even after the hundreds of times they'd performed, they were nervous. They'd never been on TV before.

"I just can't believe this is happening," Jeannie whispered. "How many thousands of miles did we drive, playing at little churches in the middle of nowhere? How many hours upon hours did we practice?"

"Oh, God," Patty said, closing her eyes. "Don't remind me."

Don, the stage manager, broke in. "You're on. Ignore the lights, and pretend like your very best friend is behind the camera."

They walked onto the stage, blinded by the lights, and got into place. Jeannie strapped on the bass and looked into the camera, taking Don's advice and pretending that Wick was behind the enormous glass eye. They sang "Speak the Victory!" and after the last note, the crowd jumped to their feet and cheered.

# I'm Gonna Walk Them Golden Stairs

Living her dream was fairly exhausting, Jeannie learned within a couple of months. She worked at Ogles Monday through Friday and made a couple of afternoon runs to Nashville each week to take care of music business for the show. The family still practiced at least one night a week at Garland and Big Jean's house. On Saturday mornings, they drove down to the studio to rehearse on stage, then taped shows after lunch. They had to do makeup and change outfits between shows so that it looked like each one was on a different day. Doing five in one day had proved to be too much, so they split them into three on Saturday and two on Sunday. Between their full-time jobs and their weekend tapings, she, Debbie, and Garland were all working seven days a week, and even though Patty didn't have a job outside of doing the show, she had a lot to say about the schedule.

"When do we get a weekend off?" Patty wanted to know, as they walked from the studio to the van at dusk.

"You're off Monday through Friday. Looks like you'd be glad to get out of the house on Saturdays and Sundays," Jeannie snapped.

"I can't sing that damn theme song one more time," Patty said. "Can't you just play a recording?"

"Singing it for each show gives us more airtime," Jeannie said.

"What a crock," Patty said. "Were you taking down every word that fell out of his lying mouth and writing it into a song?"

Jeannie crossed her arms and glared at her. "To what are you referring? The biblical references in the song? That would be Luke, Mark, and—"

"Whatever!"

"What do you mean 'whatever'?"

"I mean, whatever you want to believe!" Patty stood between Jeannie and the van door, hands on her hips. "Do you really think that if you believe, God will give you whatever you want?" She spread out her arms in a rainbow gesture.

JP, hopping around her, yelled, "I want a shotgun!"

"Well, you're not getting one," she said. Then she cocked her head at Jeannie. "See how that works?"

"Yeah, I am!" JP insisted. "Daddy said—"

"Daddy said, Daddy said," Patty mocked him.

Jeannie cast a glance back at Garland and Big Jean, who were still standing at the studio door, talking to Brother Alford and Sister Diane. She turned back to Patty and Debbie, who stood holding her children's hands. It bothered her quite a bit that Patty didn't seem to believe what Brother Alford was preaching. But why should it? What Patty believed was her own problem, when it came right down to it. As the oldest, Jeannie had always tried to keep the others in line, even Junior, who was just minutes younger, but she couldn't very well control their thoughts and beliefs. She supposed that it worried her because if Patty wasn't buying into it, she might leave at any moment. Maybe it also worried her because it brought up her own doubts, and this was no time for doubting. "But look at what's happening!" she said.

"What?" Patty demanded.

"This!" Jeannie waved her arms at the studio, at the lights of Nashville, at the busloads of people leaving the parking lot, honking and waving at them. "Everything we've been dreaming about and working for is happening! That's what!"

"I for one have not been dreaming about spending my entire weekend working for free," Patty said. "Do you know how much those cameramen get paid?"

"No," Jeannie said. "How much?"

"I don't know, but if they get anything, it's more than what we get!" Patty opened the van door and threw herself onto the back seat.

"I am *too* getting a shotgun," JP said, climbing in behind her.

"Whatever!"

The rest of them piled in and waited for Garland and Big Jean to finish their conversation with the Alfords. The kids, especially JP, were nearly crazy from having to sit for so long. "Quit wallowing all over me!" Patty told him. She rummaged in her purse and pulled out some toy cars. "Here. Take these Hot Wheels and roll them around out there in the parking lot until Papaw gets here."

JP, Randall, and Lee Ann scrambled out of the van and ran around in the nearly empty parking lot.

Jeannie took a deep breath. "Patty, I know it's a lot of work, and it might seem like it's for nothing, but things are really coming together. Brother Alford said he'll start paying us soon. We just need to hold on. We're finally making it, after all these years. You've got to believe in that! We don't want to lose you. We can't depend on Junior, but at least the three of us can stick together." She reached out one hand to grasp Debbie's and the other for Patty, who ignored her.

Already, Lee Ann and Randall were fighting over the toy Camaro, and JP was yelling, "Shut up! Shut up or you're both gonna get your ass kicked!"

Jeannie opened her mouth to correct him but stopped herself.

"Listen, the Gospelettes and the TV show ain't even half of my trouble." Patty took off her shoes and then reached under her dress and pulled off her pantyhose.

"What's wrong?" Jeannie asked.

Patty threw the wadded-up hose at her purse. "Dalton's a big shit. I don't know why I ever married him. Well, I *married* him because I was knocked up, of course. But I don't know why I've *stayed* with him all these years. Anybody can make one mistake when they're fifteen years old, but it's all these years since . . ." She propped her feet on the seat in front of her and stared at the ceiling of the van. "He just doesn't care. He really doesn't give a shit. That's the God's honest truth. He's got his truck, his guns, and his liquor. What does it matter whether I live or die?"

They ignored the yells from the parking lot until they heard a thud against the van and a cry that could only be Randall hitting the asphalt. Debbie went to check it out.

"Believe me, Patty, you're not alone," Jeannie said. "I love Wick, but it's not easy living with his . . . ways. I guess that's what Paul was talking about when he said not to be unequally yoked together with unbelievers—"

"I'd rather be on my own than living this bullshit life," Patty said, cutting her off before she could launch into a full sermon. Jeannie realized how haggard Patty looked, despite the stage makeup, years older than her actual age of twenty-five, her face already beginning to set in the disappointment of middle age.

Debbie climbed back into the van. "You know," she said softly, turning to place her hand on Patty's knee, "what you speak is what you get. Just say to yourself every day, 'God has blessed me with a loving and caring husband,' and 'I am blessed with a wonderful marriage,' and it'll be so."

Patty scowled at Debbie's hand until she drew it back to her own lap.

"It's working for me. I'm just speaking the victory every day," Debbie continued. "I'm just saying, 'Thank you, Lord, for blessing me with a wonderful marriage!' I'm saying, 'Thank you, Lord, for giving me a Spirit-filled husband to be my head!' And I can already see the difference it's making in my life. The other day, Jerry Lee came in and, out of the blue, goes, 'Have you ever read the Book of Job?' and I said, 'Yes,' and we talked about it for a while. First time in almost nine years of marriage he's ever so much as mentioned the Bible. Now you tell me God doesn't give you what you claim."

Jeannie rested her forehead in one hand and closed her eyes, overwhelmed with the feeling that this was all going wrong. Wrong, wrong, wrong.

"You know what?" Patty kicked the seat in front of her and turned toward Debbie. "I haven't said a word about Brother Alford and his name-it-and-claim-it bullcrap. I figured I'd just go with the flow. I'm a flow-goer! But now you're telling me I'm supposed to say the sky is green and the grass is blue, and it'll be so. I can claim Dalton is freaking Robert Redford all day long, but he's still going to be Dalton Pepper."

The sisters watched the shadows lead Garland, Big Jean, Sister Diane, and Brother Alford to them. The men walked ahead, the women tapped along behind them in their heels. Alford was telling a story. They couldn't hear the words, but the tone said it all. He was right, and somebody else was so wrong.

Garland opened his door and said, "Brother Alford has something for y'all."

Then, Brother Alford reached into the inside pocket of his suit jacket and handed each of them—Jeannie, Debbie, and Patty—an envelope. "The Lord is blessing our ministry," he said, "and he wants the Gospelettes to continue to be a part of *Speak the Victory!* We'll be adding you to the payroll as soon as we get some things paid for, but he wants you to have this small offering in the meantime."

As he walked away, the sisters opened their envelopes and each found ten crisp hundred-dollar bills, the most money any of them had ever held in their lives.

# Take My Hand, Precious Lord

Jeannie videotaped the show every day and had all the videocassettes lined up, in order, in a bookcase in the living room. She didn't have much time to watch them, but every and now then, if she had a free evening, she would pop in a tape and try to watch it as if she were someone else, to get a sense of how it might come across. On one such Monday night in the spring, while Wick was out fiddling with his motorcycle in the garage, she poured herself a Coke and rewound that day's show in the VCR. She sat on the couch, the fading light of the day seeping in through the sheer curtains, and looked at the blank screen, hoping that what she was about to see wouldn't disappoint. They had gotten so much positive feedback over the past few months. Lots of people—church friends, neighbors, even a few old schoolmates—had called or bumped into them out and about and told them how much they enjoyed the show. They were even getting fan mail from all over. Jeannie kept one letter in her Bible, from an elderly woman in Alabama who said hearing the Gospelettes sing was the highlight of her day, Monday through Friday, and that she dreaded the weekends because they weren't on.

She pressed play, and there they were, bigger and better than life, the Gospelettes. She and her sisters—dressed in matching silky pale-violet dresses with shoulder pads and peplums (selected, as usual, by Sister Diane), their hair teased, fluffed, and sprayed—held microphones and sang from artfully glossed lips. Garland, looking awestruck in a gray pin-striped suit, sang and played guitar on one side of them, and Big Jean, in a dress that matched her daughters', played piano on the other. The bass player, one of the Alford mafia, was further to the side, off-camera, as Garland and Brother Alford had agreed that Jeannie would look more "angelic" just singing rather than singing while thumping on the bass.

And, truly, with the blurry pastel nature backdrop and the beautiful lighting on their made-up faces, they did look otherworldly. As Jeannie listened to her family sing the song she'd written, she felt Wick's presence in the doorway to her right.

"Damn." His voice was soft, admiring. "Is that my wife?"

She had wondered if he'd ever watched the show, and she guessed now that he hadn't. She smiled at him and turned her eyes back to the screen. "Go on, Wick. Let me watch it by myself." She felt embarrassed, for some reason. She knew they sounded good, but she wasn't sure what Wick would make of Brother Alford's preaching. To be honest, she rarely listened to him anymore. When they were taping, she was focused on the songs they would be performing, giving reminders to the rest of the family or to the sound and lighting guys. The music portion of each show was her responsibility, and there were many details to manage. Brother Alford's messages, his prophecies, his prayers, his requests for money, all had become background noise as she did her job.

Wick leaned against the doorframe. "Nope. I ain't going nowhere."

"Shhh!" She waved the air, her eyes on Sister Diane. She considered pushing pause, but part of her wanted Wick to see it, to be proud of her.

"We speak the victory for health, wealth, and all the desires of our heart," Sister Diane said into the microphone she held in her fuchsia-lacquered, ring-covered fingers. "Thirty-two years ago, Brother Oren Alford answered God's call to lead a life of prayer and to preach the Word mightily."

The screen cut to Brother Alford on one knee in his dressing room praying, his jacket off, eyes closed, his hands like claws pointing toward heaven.

"He has spent thousands of hours in prayer," Sister Diane's voice-over continued, "claiming the victory in all areas of life, and God has been true to his word in blessing him. He has a great gift for interceding for others and speaking the victory on their behalf."

Brother Alford rose and put on his suit jacket, looked off in the distance as if surveying an Old Testament battlefield.

"The key to a more abundant life is to speak the victory!" Sister Diane declared.

Brother Alford walked from his dressing room to the stage, past the Gospelettes as they played their instruments and hummed softly in the background. He joined Sister Diane in front of their throne-like white wicker chairs, gave her a kiss on the cheek, and took the microphone she held out for him.

"Hallelujah!" Brother Alford peered at the studio audience and then straight into the camera. "Your victory is at hand."

Jeannie looked over at the doorway, but Wick had disappeared. She wasn't sure whether she was relieved or disappointed. She could hear him in the kitchen, getting something out of the refrigerator.

Brother Alford gave his message. He really had only one message, as far as she'd been able to determine, with one subsidiary that he occasionally added to it. The main message was "speak the victory"— that Christians who claim God's promises can have whatever they desire. The subsidiary message was that Satan and his forces will try to keep Christians from believing and claiming the promises and will do whatever they can to destroy Brother Alford and his ministry in order to achieve that goal. Brother Alford seemed to be focused on the main message in this episode.

"Let me tell you, brothers and sisters, God is always with us. Amen?" He walked across the stage and made a sweeping gesture with his left arm to indicate the whole studio audience. "We know that God's always with us. But let me tell you something that I've learned, that God has revealed to me in prayer. There are *special* anointings at times. I've believed God's promises and named them and claimed them for many, many years, but at times I've asked, 'Jesus? Where are you? I'm standing on your promises, and I'm not seeing the results I want.' And Jesus said, 'Beloved, just wait. Just hang on. There is a special anointing coming.' And, sure enough, that anointing comes."

He looked into the camera and smiled, narrowing his unsettling blue eyes. "A special anointing is here, brothers and sisters," he said in a low voice, almost a whisper. "I'm talking about Jesus being right here." He extended his right hand with the microphone to his side. "Right here." He nodded, cocked his head to the side, moving only his eyes, as if scanning the air around him and listening, and nodded again.

"This guy's a freak," Wick said, settling in beside Jeannie on the couch and popping the top on a can of beer.

She pursed her lips in disapproval.

"There's going to be a special working of miracles here," Brother Alford said. "I felt that special anointing as soon as I walked into this building. I felt it in my spirit. After all these years of spending hours in prayer every day, I've developed a spiritual radar, and it tells me when a special anointing is nigh." He paused, spoke in tongues, pulled out a handkerchief, and wiped his face. "Will you sing, Gospelettes?"

They took over and sang while he prowled across the stage, pointing at people in the audience. People came down the aisles to the stage—two, three, then a dozen, and more.

Brother Alford stood at the front of the stage, both hands on the head of a middle-aged man with stooped shoulders and graying hair. The Gospelettes sang softly in the background, and Brother Alford prayed, eyes pressed shut, occasionally giving the man a shake.

At the bottom of the screen was a phone number, address, and message: "Become a Speak the Victory! partner today." Sister Diane's voice-over said, "Call now with your prayer request. Someone will take your call and pray with you. Or send a letter telling us your needs. And if you send a seed faith donation of twenty dollars or more, you'll receive the Speak the Victory! newsletter and a personal message from Brother Oren Alford specifically addressing your needs."

Brother Alford moved down the line, praying for an elderly woman, a teenage boy, continuing to pray and shake people, speaking in tongues, ordering devils out until the program came to a close with the Gospelettes singing "Speak the Victory!" again.

The recording ended, and the screen turned blue. "Well, you were on fire," Wick said, finishing his beer and heading to the kitchen for another. He returned and lifted his can to Jeannie in salute.

She smiled. "You liked it?"

He pulled her close and gazed into her eyes. "I liked you. That's for damn sure. Did you write those songs?"

"Yeah." She felt herself blushing under his praise. It was funny how she still wanted to impress him. "We're doing all songs that I wrote on the show. And we're getting all kinds of requests for an album, so we're going to start recording in a couple of weeks."

Wick nodded and took a drink. "That preacher, though—he's a snake oil salesman if I've ever seen one."

She stiffened and pulled away from him. "I don't know about that. He seems to believe what he preaches."

"Take it from a salesman, honey. I know one when I see one. He may be selling Jesus, but he's selling Jesus for a profit."

She jumped up from the couch and grabbed her empty Coke glass. Sharp waves of anger traveled up her neck and down her arms. She felt an urge to throw her glass at him, but she just rattled the ice instead. "All right. He's selling Jesus. I agree with that. But at least he's selling hope, not destruction! At least he's getting people hooked on Jesus, not drugs!" She raised her eyebrows at him and stalked over to program the VCR for the next day.

"I don't know that anything I do is any worse than the racket he's in." Wick put down his beer. "Matter of fact, I'd say we're in the same business. Having a party, having a revival. Smoking dope, speaking in tongues. It's all the same thing. It's just people trying to get through the best they can. That preacher's got his party, and I've got mine."

Jeannie squinted at him. "Are you serious?" Did he really think her ministry was on the same moral level as selling dope? After almost a decade of marriage, that was the extent of her influence on him? "I don't believe this."

"I'm not criticizing *you*, honey," he said. "That show would be the best thing on TV if it was just y'all singing."

"No, you're just criticizing what I believe."

"That's what you believe? Really? 'Cause I've heard you talk about your Bible and your Jesus all these years, and I've never heard anything like that coming out of your mouth." He reached out to grasp her arm, but she jerked loose from his grip. He sat back and studied her for a moment. "Something's going on, isn't it?"

"Yes! The Gospelettes are actually getting somewhere, and people are watching and wanting to buy our albums and wanting us to do concerts—"

Wick cocked his head. "Has that old preacher tried to get you to sleep with him yet?"

She felt herself soften a little. She sat beside him again and took his hand. "Oh, Wick. Please." It bothered her that that's where his mind went immediately. She just knew that if she could get him to church, he'd see how wrong he was. She leaned in, snuggled close to him, reminded of how much she loved him, how he was always there for her.

# Where Could I Go?

Jeannie thought they ought to be used to it by now, after twelve years as the Gospelettes and nine months of doing *Speak the Victory!* But Debbie would still get anxious, almost to the point of having a panic attack, before going on stage. Fortunately, Debbie admitted that the actual singing part was fine. She even felt powerful once she started. It was everything that came before that nearly broke her—thinking about it, walking onto the stage, taking the microphone in her hand, taking a breath before the first note. And then, afterward, she worried about how she had performed. But *during* the singing, she felt free. When she sang, the thoughts sat down and shut up, like the people in the audience, utterly transfixed for the length of the song.

"You know how the apostle Paul said to pray without ceasing?" Jeannie whispered to her as they stood onstage, waiting for their cue. "You need to sing without ceasing. Just sing to yourself."

Debbie nodded and swallowed.

As usual, Brother Alford was preaching on the importance of making seed faith donations that day. "God didn't ask if you wanted to give ten percent," he said. "He *told* you to. That's what 'tithe' means. So after you give your ten percent, then go before God and ask, 'What else can I give, Lord?' Because when you give something to the Lord, he always pays you back with interest. Amen? He said he would open the windows of heaven and pour out a blessing! Does our God lie?"

"No!" the audience shouted.

"And when you bring that money in, you tell God what you want! Then get out your umbrella and let it rain, Lord!"

The Gospelettes took the cue and began singing a song Jeannie had written called "Let It Rain, Lord." Below them, dozens of people made their way to the altar and lifted up their faces and hands, as if showers were actually falling from heaven, washing them clean, refreshing them inside and out. They were showering in the music, letting the Gospelettes' voices rain down on them. A man in front of them shook his head in ecstasy, eyes closed, as if he were shaking off water being poured on his head. The woman with the daughter in a wheelchair that Jeannie remembered from the tent revival had her eyes closed, too. Tears dripped off her face, and her small, nail-bitten hands trembled as she held them up, as if to catch any blessing she could get a hold of.

"Are you ready to receive your miracle?" Brother Alford asked. "God's not going to stop until every one of you is blessed to overflowing!" It had worked for him, he said. He'd been a struggling evangelist, driving an old clunker that kept breaking down on him, problems at home, physical ailments of various sorts. He knew the Word, but he wasn't *applying* it. But then he made the shift. He put his money where his mouth was. He committed to what he claimed to believe. And everything turned around.

Jeannie was headed out to Ogles Market for her Friday morning shift when the phone rang.

"Hey." It was Patty. "Have you talked to Debbie?"

Jeannie sighed loudly and checked her watch. "Not since rehearsal Tuesday. Why?"

"Well. Maybe you should go see about her." Patty sounded annoyed. "I don't know what to tell her."

"What's wrong?"

"Jerry Lee. As usual."

Jeannie rolled her head back and closed her eyes. "All right. I'll go by there after work."

That afternoon, she drove to Debbie's little redbrick house. Jerry Lee's truck wasn't there. From the porch she could hear "Seasons in the Sun" coming from Debbie's bedroom, even with the windows shut against the autumn chill.

She walked in without knocking. Lee Ann was sitting on the couch in the living room watching Randall play Donkey Kong. Empty bags of potato chips and cookies and several Coke cans covered the coffee table. Toys and random items—a potholder, a few pink sponge hair rollers, an overturned potted philodendron, a high-heeled burgundy pump—were scattered around the room.

"Hey, kids!" Jeannie said as cheerfully as she could. "Give me sugar!"

"Aunt Jeannie!" Lee Ann ran over, and Jeannie picked her up, light and wiry as a little monkey, and kissed her. Randall mumbled and continued with his game.

"Where's your mama?" Jeannie asked, glancing toward the bedroom from where the music came.

"In her room," Lee Ann said. "Listening to *that song*."

"She has that stupid record player set on replay," Randall said, his eyes still on the screen. "She's played that song about three hundred times today."

"She played it about five hundred million thousand times yesterday," Lee Ann added.

Jeannie set Lee Ann down and looked her over. Her hair was a tangled mess, and she was wearing a summer dress, both too light for the weather and too tight for her body, and no socks. Randall was wearing food-stained pajamas and had cookie crumbs in the corners of his mouth. "Did y'all go to school today?" Jeannie worried that the debris on the coffee table was the remains of both breakfast and lunch.

Randall looked up for the first time. "What day is it?"

"Friday," Jeannie said, frowning.

"Oops." He grinned at Lee Ann.

"Oops," she repeated.

Jeannie walked to Debbie's bedroom and tapped on the door. She could hear her sobbing and gasping inside. "Debbie?" She let herself in. There was a staleness in the room, like Debbie had worn her nightgown for days without changing or bathing. She lay on a tear-dampened pillow, her hair matted, face blotchy. Jeannie pushed aside the jumble of faded blue-green bedspread and sat next to her on the bed. She waited, stroking Debbie's hair and squeezing her hand.

Finally, Debbie sobbed, "He left two days ago."

The song started up again, more of that infernal backup wailing, and Jeannie walked over, lifted the needle, and turned it off. It was the old record player they'd had in their bedroom growing up, a relic from their girlhood.

"What happened, Debbie?"

"He's seeing some woman," she gasped. Her voice had a nasal sound, like someone with a bad cold. "He's never coming back. I know because he took everything he had in our closet. Look!" She turned her head toward the open closet, half empty now. "He's gone. He took the underwear from the drawers and the guns his grandfather left him."

"Do the kids know what's going on?" Jeannie asked.

Debbie turned face down into the pillow. "He didn't even say goodbye to them," she said, her voice muffled. "It doesn't matter. He was never home anyway. It's not any different for them."

Jeannie pulled a shirt and jeans from Debbie's closet and found a bra and underwear in her dresser drawers. "Come on. Get a shower."

"My head hurts so bad."

"I imagine it does."

Debbie hoo-hoo-hooed so loudly that Lee Ann peeked in, then scampered away when Jeannie winked at her. "What if I have a brain tumor?" Debbie said. "Maybe then he'll be sorry for how he's treated me."

Jeannie sighed. "I doubt it."

"I've been praying," Debbie cried. "I've been speaking the victory every day. Every single day."

Jeannie draped the clothes over a chair in the corner and sat at the foot of the bed. "I know."

"What am I doing wrong?" Debbie sobbed. "Why don't I have enough faith?"

Jeannie fell back on Debbie's bed, as if pushed down by the weight of the question. How many people, how many lonely wives, how many men bent by hard work and debt, how many heartbroken mothers, how many fans of *Speak the Victory!* were asking that very question? Alford seemed to think that faith meant believing you would get what you want and then getting it. She didn't know what to say. She wanted to tell Debbie she'd be better off without Jerry Lee, but she kept that to herself.

"Maybe you can talk to Brother Alford about it tomorrow," Jeannie said at last.

The next morning, Debbie sat in a swivel chair in the dressing room of the *Speak the Victory!* studio while Karen worked on her face. Karen had a deep tanning-bed tan, and her honey-brown hair was curled, teased, and sprayed crispy. She looked like someone in a music video, and when she finished working on the sisters, they did too. Jeannie was relieved that Debbie had pulled herself together enough to make it to the studio. Any family member's absence would throw off all her careful plans for the next week's shows.

From the backstage area, they could hear Brother Alford greeting the crew. Jeannie, who drove herself to the studio most of the time, had talked to him about Debbie's situation before the rest of her family arrived.

"He's out of his prayer closet," Patty said, twirling in the chair to Debbie's right. "I wonder what's up."

Karen powdered Debbie's face, then stepped back and examined her in the mirror, cocking her head. "Girl, what is going on with you?"

Jeannie watched Debbie look at herself in the mirror. Her slumped posture and red eyes gave her away. "My husband left this week." Her face reddened, and tears welled up. "I'm going to mess up your work."

"Oh, sugar, I am so sorry," Karen said, placing her hands on Debbie's shoulders. "Well, he is just a piece of shit, that's all. Can I say that here?" She looked around. "He's a piece of *poop*, OK?"

"That's exactly right," Jeannie said. "She's better off without him. She doesn't know it yet, but it's true."

"Lord, I wish Dalton was that easy to get rid of," Patty said.

Karen laughed. "Y'all are a hoot. *A hoot!* My grandma watches you every day. *Every day!*" She dabbed at some lipstick with a tiny brush. "She is so excited that I work with y'all. She tells everybody she knows. *Every body!*"

"Aw—that's so sweet." Jeannie smiled. "You should bring her to watch us live."

"I should," Karen agreed. "*I should!*"

She removed the smock that covered Debbie's rose-patterned dress. Sister Diane had arranged for the female Gospelettes to have new matching dresses for every show, loaned to them by various shops in Nashville in exchange for mentions in the credits. Jeannie was amazed at all the details that Sister Diane managed. She was a woman who got what she wanted. She wore a diamond the size of a small acorn, and she also wore a different dress for every show, although hers didn't match the Gospelettes'.

"Sister Debbie?" Brother Alford stood at the dressing room door, already made up and coifed. "The Lord has a word for you."

Debbie rose from her chair and looked over at Jeannie as if asking what she should do. Jeannie made a motion toward the door with her head. Debbie teetered out of the dressing room on the high heels Sister Diane had picked out and followed Brother Alford to his private dressing room—what he called his prayer closet—at the end of a dark corridor. Jeannie hoped he could lift her out of her doldrums, give her one of his inspiring prophecies.

"Poor Debbie," Karen said, shaking her head.

As Karen finished spraying Patty's hair, which she had curled on enormous hot rollers, Sister Diane popped her head in the dressing room. "Everything good here?"

"We're just looking beautiful!" Karen said. "*Beauty full!*"

"Where's Debbie?" Sister Diane asked.

Karen rummaged in her makeup case, silent for once.

Jeannie turned toward the door. "Brother Alford said the Lord had a word for her," she said.

Sister Diane raised her eyebrows, just slightly—being a bit possessive, Jeannie thought. "Glory to God!" She turned and clicked away, giving orders to a crew member.

Karen held up a pocket camera. "I want a picture of me with you girls to show Granny. We'll have to wait for Debbie, though. I can't take a picture with just two of the Gospelettes."

Jeannie checked herself in the mirror. Posing for pictures and signing autographs were not uncommon for them now. These requests came mostly from older people, usually middle-aged or elderly women, so the Gospelettes weren't exactly like rock stars, but it was flattering anyway. More than that, it gave her such joy knowing that people enjoyed their music and that it meant something to them. Just the week before, an old man came into the store, recognized her, and sang a song she had written that they'd performed a couple of times on the show—almost the whole thing, word for word. She'd felt like crying, right there at the cash register at Ogles. Instead, she'd just stood with her hand over her mouth, smiling with secret pleasure.

Debbie floated wordlessly into the dressing room, as if she'd just been lowered from the heavens back into the studio, and Karen grabbed her. "Come on, girl! I want to get a picture with y'all." She stepped outside and pulled in a crew member, handing him the camera. She ran around the makeup chair and put her arms around Jeannie and Debbie, with Patty sitting in the chair in front of them. "She is going to freak out," Karen said. "*Freak out!*"

After the first taping, the Gospelettes went back to their dressing room to change into their next outfits and get touch-ups on their makeup. "That hair's not going anywhere," Karen assured Jeannie, patting her shellacked hairdo.

Jeannie zipped Debbie's dress and examined her face in the mirror. "So—what was the word Brother Alford had for you?"

Debbie made a sad half smile. "He said the Lord told him he has special plans for me."

Patty crossed her arms. "Could he be a little more vague?"

Debbie touched the top of her head. "He anointed me with oil." She locked eyes with Jeannie in the mirror. "And he said the Lord has special plans for me, something I cannot even imagine."

# Higher Ground

Brother Alford asked the Gospelettes and members of the crew to come to the studio early so he could share a word from the Lord. They gathered on the stage and waited for him. Sister Diane had decorated the set with artificial pine trees, fake snow, and sparkly ornaments for their Christmas shows. Jeannie looked out at the empty seats that would soon fill with audience members. At first, Brother Alford had sent buses to Bethel to bring people in, but the show was so popular now that tickets were reserved weeks in advance, and fans came from all over. The Gospelettes had recorded a new album, and they were selling hundreds of copies every week through *Speak the Victory!* This didn't mean they were rolling in money, but it was exciting nonetheless. Just knowing that people all over the country were listening to their music made Jeannie happy.

Finally, Brother Alford appeared in the wings and walked to the center of the stage. Everyone formed a circle around him. They were all in their street clothes, but he was in his suit, as always. He looked solemn, hands clasped in front of his chest. Jeannie wondered if something was wrong. She knew the costs of keeping the show running were high, and the financial burden was something he carried alone. Was he going to tell them that the Lord was calling for an end to the show? She couldn't tell from his face if the message was good or bad.

He spread out his arms and looked around at everyone. "The Lord wants us to go bigger."

The Gospelettes and the crew stared at him, all holding their breath. The show was moving to a major satellite network that would bring them into every home in America, he informed them. They would be doing live hour-long shows every weekday instead of taping five half-hour shows on weekends. They would be operating with a bigger budget, and he would be sharing salary offers individually in the coming days.

Jeannie released the breath she'd been holding. She wasn't sure exactly what this meant, but it seemed positive. One by one, the others started clapping and then shouting praises to God. "We spoke the victory, brothers and sisters!" Brother Alford declared. Then he released the crew and asked the Gospelettes to join him in his prayer closet. Stunned, they followed him backstage and down the hall, squeezing onto the small sofa and upholstered chairs in his dressing room. They sat and exchanged glances, waiting for more information.

"You've been my faithful partners in this journey," he said. "The Lord has instructed me to employ all of you full time starting in the new year if you want to come on board. Sister Jeannie, the Lord is calling you to continue to be the musical director of the show, bringing in additional acts alongside the regular performances by the Gospelettes, so I'll be offering you a thousand a week. Each of the rest of you I can offer five hundred a week, and you will all need to be here Monday through Friday to do live shows."

Jeannie stared at him, unable to speak. She was making a fourth of that at Ogles. This offer was more than what Garland was making at the sewing factory and what Debbie was making at the hardware store. Big Jean and Patty didn't have paying jobs at all. They looked at each other and back at Brother Alford.

"So we'd have to quit our jobs?" Garland asked.

"That's right," Brother Alford said. "You will be full-time employees of *Speak the Victory!*" He stood. "You can pray about it."

"It does sound . . . incredible," Jeannie said. "Like a dream come true."

"I'm in!" Patty said.

Debbie smiled at Brother Alford and nodded.

Everyone looked at Garland. "We'll pray on it," he said.

The Gospelettes had all ridden together to Nashville in the van, so they discussed the matter at length on the drive home that evening. "I just don't know," Garland said, both hands gripping the steering wheel as he inched up the interstate. Jeannie could see his furrowed brow in the rearview mirror. "How do we know how long this show is gonna last?"

"We don't," Patty agreed, shrugging.

"That's right," Garland said. "We don't. It's been on the air for—"

"Almost a year," Jeannie said.

"Not yet a year. These TV stations could decide next month they don't want to run it no more." He glared at Big Jean as if she were arguing with him about it, which she wasn't. "The hosiery mill has been in business for over forty years. He can't expect me to leave a steady job for a TV show that's been around for less than a year."

"It's up to you, Daddy," Jeannie said. She hoped the family group would stay together, but it didn't worry her like it used to. She knew she could replace anyone who quit, now that they had reached this level of success.

"He's just offering it to you," Patty said. "If you don't want to do it, we could get a couple of Brother Alford's mafia guys to play guitar and piano for us. They're not bad." She'd heard them playing around occasionally before taping. "Not bad-looking either," she said under her breath to Jeannie.

The very idea seemed to set Garland ablaze. Jeannie could see his face redden, and he had to loosen his tie and unbutton his collar.

"Garland, watch the transfer trucks!" Big Jean grasped her door.

"I'm watching!" He huffed and shook his head. "Between the two of us, though, we'd make about twice as much doing the show than if I kept working at the hosiery mill," he told Big Jean.

"You don't think God would bring us this far and just leave us in the desert, do you, Daddy?" Debbie asked. "I have faith that Brother Alford is looking out for us."

"I mean, we've been doing this *for free* for more than ten years," Patty said. "I'd say it's about time we got paid."

The next day, Jeannie walked into Ogles Market to quit her job. She told Mr. Ogles, apologetically, about the new full-time opportunity with the TV show she'd been doing on weekends.

"Why, that's good news, young lady!" He patted her hand in a sweet, fatherly way that made her eyes tear up.

She smiled. "Yes, it is. I'm excited, but I sure will miss this place." She looked around at the dim little grocery store, which looked exactly as it had for the past several decades. She cast a sideways glance at the Coke cooler that Wick had set her on and kissed her once when he came to pick her up and take her riding on his motorcycle, her heart pounding with excitement and fear of getting caught. "But I'll be back as a customer, you know."

"Yes, indeed!" Mr. Ogles said, busying himself with opening a box of Wrigley's Doublemint gum packs.

Jeannie said her goodbyes and stumbled out to her car, half-mad at herself for being sentimental over such a nowhere job. She couldn't help it, though. It was the site of so much of her innocence and maturing, where she met Wick, where she wrote her first gospel song, where she yearned for the success that finally found her.

"Hey, Jeannie! From the Gospelettes!" a woman's voice called out. Jeannie looked over and saw the thin, raggedy woman, the mother of the girl in the wheelchair that had gone to the tent revival and then followed them to *Speak the Victory!* She sat behind the wheel of a paint-stripped old Buick, waving her thin arms out the window.

Jeannie walked over. "Well, hello," she said, and gave a little wave. The girl was in the back seat, slumped in a homemade car seat, her wheelchair collapsed in the floorboard beside her. She lifted her head as best she could and smiled at Jeannie.

"We just had to say hi," the mother said. "We used to ride the bus down to Nashville to see y'all when they used to run the buses."

"I know! I recognized you!" Jeannie said.

"We are your biggest fans," the woman said. "Carolyn knows every single one of your songs. We've got every album y'all have made. Well, we don't have that new one, but I'm gonna get it as soon as I can save up the money."

Jeannie looked at the woman's car, which appeared to be held together with duct tape. It grumbled like the ancient beast it was and died.

"Oh, shoot," the woman said. She turned the key and tried to start the engine again, but it refused. "Well, shoot. I better go in and tell Mr. Ogles my car's gonna be here until I get the money to get it fixed." She turned and looked at the girl. "Looks like we're walking home, sweet pea." She got out of the car and opened the door to the back seat.

"Hey—I can take y'all home," Jeannie said. "My car's right here."

The woman, who appeared to be barely over five feet tall and not an ounce over a hundred pounds, looked up at her. "I don't want to put you to no trouble."

"It's no trouble! Where do y'all live?"

"Out Morristown Road."

"Oh! That's too far to walk!"

"We done it before."

"No, no, no! Get in my car. I don't mind it one bit."

"Well, I needed to get some things at the store," the woman said.

"Go ahead!" Jeannie said. "I'll sit here with your daughter. What's your name? Carolyn?"

The girl raised her head and seemed to nod.

"Is that OK, if I sit here while you go shop?"

The woman grabbed her purse. "I'll be right back. You don't have to do this. You're probably busy."

"Go on!" Jeannie said, waving her away.

The woman ran into Ogles Market, and Jeannie sat in the passenger seat of the car and turned around to face the girl. "How old are you, Carolyn?"

The girl raised her head slightly and made eye contact.

"I'm going to guess . . ." Jeannie paused. She thought twelve might be a reasonable place to start. "Twelve. Are you twelve?"

Carolyn made a sound, whether agreement, disagreement, or pain, Jeannie couldn't be sure.

"OK. Well." Jeannie looked at the door to Ogles. "Um . . ."

The girl made a noise then, a sort of humming sound. Jeannie turned back around. It was a long note, a perfect D sharp. Then an E and another D sharp. Jeannie couldn't understand the words, but she knew the tune. It was a song she'd written for the Gospelettes' fourth album. She sang the first verse, with Carolyn groaning along behind her:

*I am here with you*
*Even when you feel alone*
*I am with you always*
*I will walk you home*

Jeannie felt like her heart might crack wide open. This was the reason she'd been singing and working to keep the Gospelettes going all these years. Not for money, fame, or glory. Just for this moment.

They were in the middle of the third song from the album when the mother came out with two paper bags of groceries. "Is she singing for you?" she asked Jeannie.

"Yes, she is." Jeannie jumped out of the car and put the bags in the backseat of her Trans Am while the woman transferred the folded-up wheelchair and carried Carolyn over.

The woman told Jeannie her name was Gail Taylor. Jeannie wondered how old she was. "Did you go to Bethel High School?" she asked, thinking she might be able to figure out if Gail were younger or older or about her own age.

"No," Gail said. "I went to Morristown until eighth grade."

"Oh." Jeannie nodded.

"I didn't get to go to high school. I had her. I had to take care of her."

"Ah. Yes."

Gail got in the passenger seat. "So you'll go straight out Morristown Road and turn down there by the Stricklers' barn. Then you veer left by the tree that got hit by lightning."

Jeannie turned toward her own house. "I need to do something first." When she pulled up, Wick was in his garage with a couple of guys she'd seen around before. She got out of the car and walked over to him, eyeing them warily. Customers. And not the kind she wanted Wick to have.

"Hey, baby."

"Hey." She turned back to Wick. "Listen. This lady's car broke down at Ogles. Do you have something you can loan her?"

Wick looked over at Gail and Carolyn. "Yeah." He went behind the garage and drove around with an old green Pontiac GTO. He handed the keys to Gail.

"What in the world?" She stared at the car, mouth open.

"Take it," he said. "I'll take a look at yours and see if I can fix it."

"I appreciate it, but I can't afford to pay you right now." She tried to hand back the keys.

Wick stepped back and shook his head. "Naw. Don't worry about it. Let me do you a little favor."

Gail covered her mouth with her hand. "I can't believe it." She shook her head and looked back at Jeannie. "You're not gonna believe this. I sent Brother Alford a check last month, and now look! He's right, isn't he? Just speak the victory!"

Jeannie didn't know what to say to that. Wick raised his eyebrows at her and walked back to the garage.

# Welcome Table

The new hour-long show had taken off, even better than Brother Alford had promised. Jeannie hadn't seen the viewership or financial reports, but she knew from the fan mail and calls that came in for the Gospelettes that a lot more people were watching.

Brother Alford told the audience during one show, "Brothers and sisters, when a prophet of God tells you what the Lord has in store, you better listen. Amen?" He looked into the camera. "Let me tell you what the Lord was telling me last year. He said, 'I want this program to be on the air every weekday for a *full hour*.' Praise God! Some people said, 'Now, Brother Alford, do you think you can stand to praise God for a whole hour Monday through Friday?'"

The audience stood and cheered.

"I said, 'I can!' That's why the Lord blesses me! I speak the victory!"

"Amen!"

The Gospelettes watched him from their corner of the stage as he paced and then looked into the camera again. "He wants you to be *Speak the Victory!* partners and plant a seed right here." He pointed at his feet. "Can you handle that much glory, brothers and sisters? Can you stand it if the heavens open up and rain down the blessings on you?" He walked to the right side of the stage. "Can you handle being healed?" He walked to the left side. "Can you handle your bank account being so full that you can't even think of anything to spend all that money on? Hallelujah!"

He sauntered to the center of the stage. "God told me he doesn't want us to leave here today until we've planted a seed. He wants you to build a Speak the Victory theater here in Nashville. He showed me the exact spot. He said, 'I don't want you coming to this studio to do my work. There was a season for that, but now we are entering a new season and a new place.' He said, 'This will be a place where you can come and be renewed. You're going to be able to see it on a hill, and everyone who drives by is going to see *Speak the Victory!* shining there!' Praise God!"

He opened his arms. "We're gonna let you bring your seed faith donations right up here. Just lay it on the altar. I think there ought to be a stampede! If God says to plant a seed and he's gonna bless you, you oughta run up here and do it. And brothers and sisters who are watching at home, you can see our phone number and address at the bottom of your screen. You can claim that blessing just like everybody here! You can be a Speak the Victory partner too."

Jeannie watched as lines of people rushed to the stage and dropped bills. Men and women. Old and young. Most well-dressed, some slightly shabby. The Gospelettes played a song while piles of money grew at Brother Alford's feet like flowers blooming.

A few days later, Junior came home. He sat at the picnic table in Jeannie and Wick's backyard while Wick grilled steaks and listened to "Voodoo Chile" on the stereo playing full blast from his garage. After a moment of hesitation, Junior turned down the beer Wick offered from his cooler. "Nah. I told the Lord if he'd get me back home in one piece, I'd quit all that."

"Do what you gotta do," Wick said, tipping up his beer can.

Jeannie set the sides she'd prepared, potato salad and corn on the cob, on the table. "We're glad you made it back. We've been worried about you."

"How long has it been since anybody heard from you?" Wick asked.

"I don't even know," Junior said.

"Four years," Jeannie said, laying out their napkins, forks, and knives. Wick whistled.

"Is that right?" Junior stared into the distance, seeming to do math in his head.

"Yep," Jeannie said. "You missed a few things."

"I don't know. Bethel looks about the same." Junior smirked.

"Did you hear about Headlight?" Wick asked, lighting up a cigarette.

Junior laughed. "No, what's that little dumbass gotten himself into this time?"

Wick took a drag, studying a wasp hovering under the eave of his garage. "Shot himself."

Junior's face dropped. "To death?"

Jeannie nodded.

"When?"

"About a year and a half ago," Wick said.

They sat in silence for a while. Jeannie watched Junior's face change from shock to sadness to acceptance in less than five minutes. She didn't judge him for it. That was just Junior.

Wick broke the silence. "So you saw the Gospelettes on the TV?"

Junior smiled. "Yeah! I was outside of Houston, sitting there in Angela's trailer—"

"Angela?" Jeannie asked.

"Yeah. My girlfriend, wife, whatever. She claims to be my wife, but I haven't seen nothing to prove it."

Jeannie sat across from him at the table and put her head in her hands. "Oh, Lord."

"I'm pretty sure she's lying. I said, 'Show me the marriage certificate.' If you can't produce a marriage certificate, that's just wishful thinking. Anyway, I was just sitting there, and I looked up, and there y'all were on the TV in living color. There was Jeannie, front and center, hair all teased up, face all made up, singing the roof off the building like she always did."

Wick laughed and turned the steaks.

"And there were Debbie and Patty, all grown up. Then there was Mama banging on the piano and Daddy in a shiny new suit playing a new Gibson. And I go, 'That's my family!' I don't know if I'm tripping or what. And Angela goes, 'What are you talking about?'" Junior leaned forward and squinted like he was looking into a TV. "And I go, 'Wait a minute. Who's on bass?' And I see there was some skinny dude on bass, kind of off to the side in the shadows like he was hiding." He slapped the table with both hands. "I said, 'All right, Lord. I hear you loud and clear.' I said, 'That skinny dude is in my spot. I'm coming home!'" Junior rubbed his hands on his jeans and smiled at Jeannie. "Mama said, 'We knew God would bring you back. Brother Alford told us he would.'"

"How did you like that slick preacher and his fake-ass wife?" Wick asked. "How much time out of every hour would you say they spend asking for money, Jeannie? About half?"

Junior and Jeannie ignored him. "So you're going to live with Mama and Daddy?" she asked.

"For the time being," Junior said. "Till I can raise some funds." He looked over at Wick. "Unless y'all want to take me in."

"Nope," Wick said, putting a steak on Junior's plate.

"All right. I guess I can make it over there for a while." Junior spooned potato salad on his plate. "I'm just glad to be back in Kentucky." He nodded at Jeannie. "With my twin." He nodded at Wick, who sat next to him and cut into his own steak. "And I didn't have a friend in the whole state of Texas that was half the friend Wick is. That's the truth."

"I don't doubt it," Wick said.

"So—" Junior looked at Jeannie. "When can I start?"

Jeannie buttered her corn, reflecting. He had admitted he'd been drinking a lot, and she felt sure he'd been using drugs. Maybe he was clean now. It felt wrong to pass judgment on him. She didn't like being in the position of deciding whether he was worthy or not. "When was the last time you played?" she asked.

"Aah—it's like falling off a log," Junior said.

"I hate to hurt Jimmy's feelings," she said.

"That skinny dude?"

"Yeah."

"You know I'm better than he is." Junior ate across his corn cob. "And I was one of the original Gospelettes."

Wick chuckled, and Jeannie sighed. "Well, I guess I could offer Jimmy some guest appearances with the band he's starting," she said. "That might smooth it over."

"There you go!" Junior took a bite of steak. "Mmmm! Best steak I've ever eaten," he said to Wick. Then, to Jeannie: "How much do y'all get paid?"

Jeannie smiled at him. She couldn't help but love him. They'd been together since the beginning. The very beginning. Garland's angel had spoken. All was forgiven. And the circle was unbroken. Jimmy couldn't sing a lick, and she could already hear Junior's harmonies blending in with the family.

# I Just Feel Like Something Good Is about to Happen

*Speak the Victory!* changed everything. Jeannie went from working in a small grocery store in Bethel, seeing the same old people each week—she could even tell you what time on Thursday that Mr. Rippy would walk through the door and exactly what he would buy—to working with some of the most creative and interesting musicians and producers and songwriters in Nashville. She went from just getting by, living paycheck to paycheck, to making enough that she had a savings account for the first time ever. Now people recognized them almost everywhere they went. They were stopped for autographs at Rivergate Mall. People wrote them letters from faraway states, places they'd never been in all their travels, and told them that they had played the Gospelettes' music at their weddings, in hospital rooms, at deathbeds and funerals.

Many days, the air felt electric. When the Gospelettes walked on stage at the beginning of the show, the audience, the whole place, the whole world, seemed to vibrate, the Gospelettes' voices and instruments vibrating along with everything.

Something was happening that Jeannie didn't know how to identify or categorize. It was exciting. Bigger than she knew how to manage. It felt almost dangerous. That's what she was thinking as the Gospelettes, now complete again with Junior back on board, finished the opening song and Brother Alford came out and stood center stage, silent, arms raised, until the audience got quiet.

"This has only happened to me a couple of times in more than three decades of ministry," he said. He stood completely still, eyes narrowed on some spot in the audience. Everyone hushed. Only Big Jean's piano tinkled softly in the background. "I'm talking about Jesus walking right alongside me. Right here. Ready to work miracles!" He walked toward the right side of the audience and pointed at someone. "Come down here."

A balding man with a mustache came forward, and Brother Alford put his hands on his head and spoke in tongues. He shook his hands, and the man jumped as if he'd been struck by lightning.

"Can you handle the glory, brothers and sisters? Can you stand it if the heavens open up and rain down the blessings on you?" He walked to the left side of the stage. "Can you handle your bank account being so full that you can't even think of anything to spend all that money on?"

Soon, the front of the stage and the aisles were filled with people coming down to ask for prayer. Brother Alford put his hands on the head of each person in line. He shook one woman. "Don't argue with me, devil! You come out!" He turned to Sister Diane. "Did you see that?"

Sister Diane nodded and lifted her microphone to her glossy fuchsia lips. "Yes, I did," she said. "Her chest and neck and face just turned bright red."

"Feel that." He moved Sister Diane's hand to touch the woman's neck.

"It's hot," she said.

"I want you to witness that heat because the devil's gonna tell her later that didn't happen," Brother Alford said. "But you see it. That's cancer leaving her body right there."

It crossed Jeannie's mind what Wick might say if he saw this episode. She hoped he wasn't watching. He rarely did. And why did she care anyway? Not everybody believed in faith healing or the other fruits of the spirit, and what they thought about her and the Gospelettes being on the show was their business. She couldn't very well change what the Bible said to suit other people and their doubts. Sometimes she found herself having arguments with Wick in her head about things that happened on the show, claims Brother Alford made, the phone number that scrolled across the bottom of the screen telling viewers how to donate money to make a prayer request. But they rarely talked about their different opinions in reality. Wick wasn't easy to argue with.

After the day's taping, they all stood in the Gospelettes' dressing room, outfitted with a long mirror and makeup chairs and partitions to separate the men's and women's changing areas. "Where's Debbie?" Garland asked, ready to go. They looked around.

"Probably asking for prayer again," Patty said, rolling her eyes. Debbie and Jerry Lee were still legally married, but he came and went, depending on how his latest fling was going. She had worn out the entire family with her marital strife and despair, and they were somewhat relieved to have all that fretting transferred to Brother Alford.

Garland shifted from foot to foot. "I ain't waiting around no longer. Can you bring her home, Jeannie?"

"No problem." Jeannie usually came early and stayed late anyway, setting up and checking on the sound for the next musical performance. They now had at least one musical guest for each show, so she did the scheduling and took care of their needs. That day their guest had been a teenage girl from Georgia who sang "El-Shaddai" exactly like Amy Grant, and Jeannie had had to make sure they had their permissions lined up. There was always a lot to do, so many details to take care of. She had learned so much about the music business, the good and the bad, and she loved it. Honestly, it was beyond anything she'd dreamed of back when they started the Gospelettes, more interesting, more challenging, more exciting than she could have imagined. "If you speak the victory, God is bound to give you the desires of your heart," Brother Alford always said, and Jeannie thought he must be right because it was happening for her.

Debbie appeared in the doorway. "Everybody's gone?" She went behind the partition and changed clothes, walked over to the mirror, pulled her hair back in a ponytail, and examined her face. She looked blotchy, Jeannie noticed. Had she been crying? What more could Jerry Lee do to her? Jeannie had told her she should go ahead and get divorced, that it was perfectly OK, no one would judge her. But Debbie said she and Brother Alford were praying about it, and God had told her to wait.

# Heaven's Jubilee

The new Speak the Victory Theater was perched on a ridge north of Nashville. It was much larger than the studio they'd been using downtown, seating more than five hundred people, with spacious dressing rooms and offices for Brother Alford, Sister Diane, and members of the *STV!* team. The Gospelettes and other members of the team had gone to see the piece of land Brother Alford had chosen, a rocky patch of weeds and dust, overlooking the interstate. Standing there looking out at the gray city in the distance, gas stations and rumbling semitrucks below, the air scented with exhaust fumes and filled with the sound of never-ceasing traffic, Jeannie hadn't seen anything promising about this move. The studio in town had seemed more than adequate. But now, as Garland drove as slowly up I-65 as the traffic would allow, she gazed up at the theater, the words *Speak the Victory!* lit with bluish spotlights that matched the deep watery blue that rimmed the evening sky, and she marveled at what Brother Alford had manifested. They would be taping there the next day.

She carried a box of supplies into her new office, across the hall from Sister Diane's. Her name was on a brass plate on the door. The office was painted dusty blue with a wallpaper border of blue-ribboned geese (Sister Diane's choice).

"Whoa! Look at that!" Patty said, following her into the room. "Jeannie's got a computer!"

"Guess I'd better learn to use it," Jeannie said. She sat at her desk and spun around in her rolling chair. Behind her was a Roland keyboard she'd picked out for songwriting.

Junior lifted the receiver on her phone and said, "Hello? Yes, this is Jeannie Whitaker of *Speak the Victory!* . . . Why, yes, Mr. Cash, we would love to have you and June sing on our show. Let me see if we can fit you in."

Debbie stood at the door and looked across the hall into the French doors of Sister Diane's luxurious, all white, brass, and glass office.

The Gospelettes walked around and saw the stage, the sound room, the kitchen, and the dressing rooms, ending up outside the closed door of Brother Alford's office, on the opposite side of the building from the other rooms. They all jumped when he opened the door and said, "Come in and pray with me!"

Jeannie stepped into his office first, sank into it, really. The carpet was thick and soft. The walls were covered with a dark purple-green swirled wallpaper, and the gold-leaf ceiling glowed. He had an enormous, dark-wood desk, ornate built-in bookshelves, and several brass-framed photos of himself and Sister Diane with various suited men and dressed-up women, as well as some of him and Sister Diane with their daughter, who was now grown and lived in Oklahoma. Attached to the office was a sitting area with upholstered chairs, a coffee table that matched the dark wood of the desk, and a large, overstuffed sofa. Heavy velvet curtains covered the windows. He had his own bathroom. The Gospelettes stood and looked around, not touching anything. Finally, Debbie stroked a throw pillow on the sofa. "It's beautiful," she murmured.

"God has seen our faithfulness and rewarded it," Brother Alford said. "I understand that you have a new song prepared for our celebration tomorrow?"

"Yes, we're ready," Jeannie said.

"Wonderful! I know it will be special," Brother Alford said. He put one arm across Garland's shoulders. "When you've got an apostle and a prophet on stage at the same time, you better watch out. Amen, Brother Garland?"

"Amen," Garland said.

Brother Alford held out his arms to the group. "Let's pray."

They prayed together, and then the family filed across the lobby and back to their side of the building, gathering in the Gospelettes' dressing room, already stocked with next week's clothes.

Junior whistled and raised his eyebrows. "That was fa-a-an-cy!"

"I could *live* in Brother Alford's office," Patty said.

"You wouldn't need a bed," Junior said. "You could sleep on that humongous couch."

Patty sat in a makeup chair. "You ain't lying."

"Kind of makes Jeannie's office look like it's supposed to be the broom closet," Junior said, slapping Jeannie on the back. She laughed.

"Yeah. And Sister Diane's office is pretty swanky, but it ain't nothing compared to his," Patty added.

Debbie closed the door. "Y'all act like you don't understand what he has on him," she said, barely above a whisper. She seemed to be almost in tears. "All the people whose livelihoods depend on him, all the expenses of the show, all those little things that none of us can even *imagine* that he has to worry about."

Everyone looked at her for a moment. Then Garland nodded. "That's right. We can't hold nothing against him. God has ordained him, and it ain't for anybody to judge."

Jeannie had recorded their "New Foundation Celebration" on her VCR, as she did all episodes of *Speak the Victory!* That evening, when she got home from Nashville, she took her bowl of potato soup and glass of Coke to the living room and ate at the coffee table as she watched the show. They'd added special effects to the opening, lots of confetti and twirling ribbons and fireworks, and shots of joyous people clapping, jumping, waving their arms, and singing along in the five-hundred-seat theater. The Gospelettes sang an especially rousing version of "Speak the Victory," and then Sister Diane announced, "Today, God has chosen *you* to be a part of the New Foundation Celebration at the new Speak the Victory Theater! This is no ordinary day, brothers and sisters. This is the day you've been waiting for!" The camera cut back to the Gospelettes. On the left side of the screen, Big Jean played a rolling introduction on the piano. On the right, Garland and Junior, in matching tan suits, joined in on their guitars. In the middle stood Jeannie, with Patty to the left and Debbie to the right, in matching long, hot pink dresses, microphones in hand. They sang the song Jeannie had written for the occasion:

> *This is the day, the celebration day,*
> *The day of Holy Ghost fire!*

*This is the day, the celebration day,*
*And the Lord will give whatever you desire!*

In the middle of their song, Wick walked in and watched, standing in the doorway, until they sang the last, long note of the song, hands and eyes upraised, and Sister Diane introduced Brother Alford.

"We speak the victory for health, wealth, and all the desires of our heart," Sister Diane said into her microphone. "Thirty-four years ago, Brother Oren Alford answered God's call to lead a life of prayer and to preach the word mightily." The next shot was Brother Alford on one knee praying in his new office.

Wick turned, grabbed his guitar from the corner, and went out on the front porch, Sally at his heels. Jeannie heard him tune up and play "The Long and Winding Road." She pressed pause on the VCR and walked to the screen door and watched him as he played. The weather was warm, and he was in jeans and his undershirt. She hoped none of his old girlfriends came riding by at that moment to see how gorgeous he was.

"Hey—I have a band that could use you. Want to join?" she asked through the screen.

"Do I have to sell my soul to the devil?" He grinned at her and struck a nasty blues lick.

She made a disapproving face, careful not to laugh. He started up "Cross Road Blues" as she closed the storm door.

# When I Lay My Burden Down

At ten years old, Heather, Junior's daughter by his Tennessee ex-wife Rita, came to visit her grandparents for the first time. Rita had seen Junior on *Speak the Victory!* and tracked him down for child-support payments. Junior brought Heather over to Garland and Big Jean's house when the whole family—except Jerry Lee, who was separated from Debbie—was gathered on Christmas Day.

"I told Rita, I said, 'All right. If I'm gonna have to pay you all this money, I'd dang well better get to see my kid at Christmas!'" Junior told his family as they sat in the living room after the kids—Heather, JP, Randall, and Lee Ann—had opened presents and run upstairs to play games.

"Well, I would think that you'd *want* to see her, not just do it for spite," Jeannie said, scowling. She made eye contact with Wick across the room where he sat next to Dalton, in-laws on the outskirts of the room in chairs they'd brought in from the kitchen, and he grimaced and just barely shook his head so that no one would notice but her. They had already discussed Junior's waywardness and agreed that it was despicable. He had spent years running from his parental responsibilities and had even avoided calling the family so that they couldn't give his ex-wives information on his whereabouts. The fact that Wick and Jeannie had never been able to have a child compounded their distaste for Junior's behavior. Jeannie imagined the kind of father Wick would have been, the way he would have taught their child to play a guitar and fix a flat tire on a bike. She could see him sitting in his recliner watching TV with a little one on his shoulders holding him by his curls. But no. Junior got the blessing. Junior got two kids, maybe three, no one was quite sure. Just like he got the angel prophecy when he and Jeannie were born. She had hustled and made phone calls and visited radio stations and written songs and prayed and read the Bible all those years, and then, when the work was all done and they had arrived, Junior came swooping in to rejoin the Gospelettes.

"Well, we sure are proud to have little Heather," Big Jean said. "Better late than never." Still hot from a full day of cooking, she fanned her red face with a folded piece of Christmas wrapping paper.

"God has blessed you," Garland said.

"That's for sure true," Junior agreed.

Jeannie jumped up from the couch, where she sat between Patty and Debbie, and headed to the kitchen. "I've got the dishes, Mama!" she said in a tone that she hoped was breezy and didn't give away how she felt about what her father had said. If God had blessed Junior by giving him a child that he didn't want, what did that mean for Jeannie? Had God cursed her by not giving her one that she did want? Had she failed to "speak the victory"? Or was it his punishment for her marrying a drug dealer? Never mind that Junior had been far less faithful. She filled the sink with soapy water and began scraping off plates into the trash. Bits of ham fat. Crumbs of biscuit. Dollop of mashed potatoes. All that was left of Big Jean's jam cake were smudges of icing. She dropped the glasses in the sink first, stared through the frosted window into black night.

Junior had moved out of Garland and Big Jean's house after a few weeks back home, as soon as he got a paycheck from *Speak the Victory!*, and into a new apartment building that had recently been built on Nashville Road. Then, claiming the rent was too high, he moved in with his new girlfriend, Connie, and her small children, Ginger and Pepper. This prompted a family discussion in the dressing room at the Speak the Victory Theater when Garland found out.

"What in the world are you doing, Junie?" Garland demanded. "How do you think that looks for a gospel singer to be living like that?"

Junior gave his sisters a weary look and turned to Garland. "I understand, Daddy, but I'm a grown man. This ain't open for discussion."

"Well, I reckon it is!" Garland swiped his forehead with a handkerchief and loosened his tie. "You ain't working for yourself. You're part of a family band and employed by a gospel ministry."

"We don't need to get Brother Alford involved," Junior said, dropping into a makeup chair. "I'm sure he's got more to worry about than my living arrangements."

"Brother Alford don't need to get involved," Garland said. "Jeannie's your boss. She's the musical director for *Speak the Victory!*"

All eyes turned to Jeannie, who was hanging that day's performance dress on the rack. She turned and raised her eyebrows. "I don't know that judging the morality of our performers is in my job description."

"Why, it most certainly is!" Garland said. "You wouldn't let just anybody sing on the show, would you? If a fella killed somebody but he could sing like a bird, you wouldn't let him on the show, would you?"

"If you kill somebody, I'll kick you off the show, Junior," she said, putting her heels back into their box.

"I'll try not to." Junior made a face and cut his eyes toward Garland.

Jeannie didn't feel comfortable in this conversation at all. She could say she had a clear conscience herself. She prayed and read the Bible every day, pretty much followed all the commandments, sang for the Lord Monday through Friday, and went to church most Sundays, even though things had been a bit tense between Garland and Brother Clarence since Brother Alford had come in and torn up the church with the revival. She considered her own faults. Maybe she coveted now and then, wished for certain things that apparently weren't hers to have, but that was about it. Still, she was married to a former and maybe current outlaw. Wick had told her when they married that he wouldn't do any of the illegal stuff in his family business. His daddy had continued bootlegging until he died, and his brother Clayton had sold drugs until he got busted, but supposedly Wick had stayed out of it. But now that his daddy was dead and Clayton was in the pen, Jeannie suspected that Wick had picked up where they left off. She didn't ask, and he didn't tell, but, yes, she was pretty sure. And she didn't say anything to him about it because she couldn't deal with it. There was too much on her plate already, and, honestly, she didn't want to know. If she knew, she would have to do something, and what would she have to do?

"Anyway, me and Connie might be getting married before long," Junior said. "Ginger and Pepper need a daddy."

Nobody said, "So do your own kids," but Jeannie knew they were all thinking it.

Since Headlight's death, Wick had reconnected with some of his old buddies. Jeannie had seen a few of them skulking around Wick's garage on the weekends and in the evenings when she got home from Nashville. One of them, Tony, had invited her and Wick to a party in his new hot tub, for which she had given Wick a *look*. Now that Junior was back, he was hanging out with Wick and their old buddies again. Jeannie watched from a distance, not quite sure what was up but sure that it was nothing good.

Her suspicions were confirmed one Saturday night—actually early on a Sunday morning—when she woke up to the sounds of banging and knocking, retching and gibberish, coming from her bathroom. She jumped out of bed and found Wick in the doorway of the bathroom, leaning over a man in soiled clothes lying on the floor, in vomit. She covered her nose and mouth with one hand and peered around Wick. Junior sprawled on her bathroom floor, passed out.

"Oh, my God! What happened?"

Wick squatted and wiped Junior's face with a towel. "I don't know, but I can guess."

"Is he breathing? Do we need to take him to the hospital?" Jeannie felt panic flood her body, a thousand prickles on her skin from her face to her neck to her chest to her arms.

"He's breathing," Wick said. "Let's clean him up and put him in the bed. See what we need to do from there."

They pulled off his soiled clothes and cleaned him up as best they could. Wick half dragged, half carried him to one of the spare bedrooms, and Jeannie pulled back the sheets and helped hoist him onto the bed. She wiped his face with a cold washcloth while Wick cleaned the bathroom. Junior came to for a while and talked to her in some wild, incoherent language, looking at her with frustration and anger that she wouldn't act on whatever it was he was telling her, then fell back into a deep sleep.

Wick came in. "Go back to sleep if you can. I'll sit with him."

She glared at him. "I can't sleep with him like this. What happened? Were you with him?"

Wick shook his head. "I was with him at Tony's last night, but I got in hours ago. I was in bed and heard him banging on the door. Closed our bedroom door hoping we wouldn't wake you."

Jeannie looked back and forth between Junior, mouth open, reeking, and Wick, sitting on the floor beside the bed, defeated. "What were y'all doing over there?"

Wick looked at her and then down at his hands, hanging between his knees. "Partying."

"What were you taking?"

"I don't know what *he* was doing. I'd guess a speedball. I don't do that shit."

They sat with him until the sky turned light gray through the window blinds. Jeannie got up from the rocking chair in the corner. "I guess I'll go to bed."

Wick nodded. "I got him."

Later, Jeannie checked in and found them both asleep, Wick on his side on the hardwood floor, using his bent arm as a pillow, Junior snoring loudly in the bed. She went to church, even though she was exhausted. She suddenly longed for that sweetness she remembered in their little white-painted-wood church, the people she'd known all her life, mild Brother Clarence up front smiling at everyone, his face as pale and pure as a bar of Ivory soap. But it wasn't the same, not really. Some of the people she remembered were gone now, and others had come in that she didn't know. She and the rest of her family had stepped back somewhat, busy with *Speak the Victory!* and all their new responsibilities.

At the end of the service, when Brother Clarence invited the congregation to come down if they had prayer requests, Jeannie walked to the altar and whispered in his ear, "Junior." He nodded, put his hands on her shoulders, and prayed.

Junior was still in bed, in the same position, that night when she checked on him. She had washed his clothes and draped them over the rocker.

Wick, on his way to bed, paused at the door and looked in.

"How long will he be like this?" she asked.

He shrugged. "He was halfway making sense for a few minutes today."

"You act like this is normal," she said. "Look at him! How could you be involved in this? How could you let him get in this kind of shape?" She felt disgusted by both of them, wanted them out of her sight.

"I didn't let him do anything." Wick leaned against the doorframe. "Like I said, I wasn't there—"

"You were at the same party!"

"I saw him there earlier, and I left by ten o'clock."

"You act like that makes it all right. Like you're completely blameless."

He lifted his hands. "I—" He threw his hands down as if closing something and walked to their bedroom.

The next morning, Jeannie got up, wondering if Junior would be awake or if she'd have to make an excuse for his absence at the taping that day. Wick was already up. She crept across the hall and looked into Junior's room. The bed was empty and unmade. He and his clothes were gone.

She walked to the kitchen and found Wick sitting with his coffee. "Where's Junior?" she asked.

"No idea," he said, taking a sip.

"You haven't seen him this morning?"

"Nope." He drained his cup and took it to the sink. "He was gone when I got up. His truck's gone too."

"Maybe he went home," she said.

"Maybe."

She dialed his phone number, and Connie answered. "This is Jeannie. Have you seen Junior?"

"No. Have you? He hasn't been home in—what?—three days now? And I'm just about ready to kick him out. If you see him, tell him his shit is gonna be in trash bags out in the yard."

"All right." Jeannie hung up the phone and went to shower and get ready for the show. She felt burdened with him, with everything, as if she were carrying Junior and her sisters and her parents and the show, all of it, on her back.

She drove herself that day, not feeling up to riding an hour each way in the van with her parents. Junior would probably be there already, she figured, hee-hawing with the crew. He liked to tell them corny jokes and pull pranks on them. Just like a kid. Or maybe he'd be in Brother Alford's swanky office, praying for his delivery from this relapse. That's what she hoped. But he wasn't there, and he didn't come in later. They had to do the taping without him that day and the next and so on, and eventually, they had to admit that he was gone.

# When I Wake Up to
# Sleep No More

Garland and Big Jean had worried over Junior to the point that Jeannie was afraid she'd have to replace three group members rather than just one. She had finally asked Brother Alford to pray with them, and when he did, he assured them that Junior's backsliding was all part of God's plan, that God has his hand on Junior, wherever he was, and would be calling him back. Somehow it worked. Her parents came out of his office looking better than they had in months, reassured that this was just a test of Junior's faith and would lead him to greater spiritual heights.

Jeannie watched them in the mirror as Karen got them camera-ready and wondered how Brother Alford did it. It seemed like a power he had over people's minds. He could tell them . . . anything, really, and they would believe it was so. She'd seen it over and over again. At the tent revival. At their *Speak the Victory!* tapings. With her parents and, especially, with Debbie. Debbie and Jerry Lee were still separated, he rarely saw the kids or paid child support, and yet she seemed to have spoken the victory to such a degree that none of that bothered her in the least. It was strange, almost spooky, but Jeannie decided not to go looking for trouble. She had plenty.

Since Junior had disappeared, Wick seemed to be on a downward slide. Did he feel responsible? Jeannie had certainly tried to pin the blame on him after that disastrous night at Tony's, but she realized, in the light of reason, that none of it was Wick's fault. Junior was a grown man, in theory. He had made his own decisions. Wick wasn't some high schooler exerting peer pressure to get Junior to mix drugs.

Junior may have been a sorry excuse for a man, but he was a man nonetheless.

She hadn't expressed this realization to Wick or apologized for implying that Junior's problems were his fault. But he knew, didn't he? She'd let it go, gone back to loving Wick as she always had.

And yet, things were different. It was still light out when she got home from taping in Nashville one night, and the summer air reminded her of the rides she used to take with Wick on his motorcycle when they first started seeing each other and of that first summer together after they married, when they would come home from work to their apartment above the men's clothing store and immediately go to bed and lie together with the windows open, feeling the breeze on their naked skin. But now Wick was out somewhere. Another buddy from way back had died of an overdose, and since the funeral, he was spending more time with old friends that she'd hoped were part of the past. He was drinking more at home, and she wondered what else he might be using with them.

In the early years of their marriage, he used to have nightmares about Vietnam that shook him out of their bed. He'd leave in the night on his motorcycle and ride until his head was clear and he felt like he could go back to sleep. She would lie in bed, wide awake, listening for the hum of his motorcycle coming back. Then, after a couple of years of marriage, it happened less often. Maybe once or twice a year. Lately, though, the night terrors had resumed. He got up in the night and didn't come back until morning, or he didn't bother to come to bed at all. Something was different.

She was gone a lot with her job. There was always so much to do, and the theater was an hour away, so she spent a lot of time driving. Even when she was home, she was working on songs or making plans for the show. So, now, it was a surprise to see that he was struggling.

She changed into shorts and a T-shirt and sat on the porch with Sally, stroking her ears. Poor old girl was hanging in there. "What do you think he's up to?" Jeannie asked. Sally sighed, shifted her weight, made an almost imperceptible whine deep in her throat.

# Hold On

The sisters sat around Patty's kitchen table on a Saturday morning. Things hadn't changed much in the years she and Dalton had lived in the cinder-block house in the country. Patty had tried to hold down the ripped-up linoleum on the kitchen floor with strips of duct tape. The cabinet doors that were still intact hung open, refusing to latch. The window over the sink was cracked. Flies buzzed past the sisters' heads in their path through the house and back to the kitchen.

"So what brings y'all here? Ha ha!" Patty got up to make coffee.

Jeannie looked into the living room and saw that Randall and Lee Ann were deep into a video game. JP was fishing with Dalton. "Well, you know we're worried." She looked at Debbie and back at Patty. "After what you said yesterday." They had been standing backstage, about to walk on, when Patty had casually mentioned that she was going to be leaving Dalton soon—and JP along with him.

Patty set three mugs beside the coffee maker and sat down again. "And?"

Debbie scratched away a spot of dried food on the table. "Patty, are you speaking the victory over the situation? Because it really works. I am living proof that it works!"

Patty closed her eyes for about thirty seconds and then opened them on Jeannie. "You see that car out there? I saved up the money I made on the show and bought it so I can leave any time I want to. Victory!" She walked to the coffee maker and brought back mugs for the three of them. She stirred in her Sweet'N Low. "I'll find me an apartment. I'll drive out here on Saturdays and do JP's laundry and cook something for him. He'll be fine."

Jeannie couldn't believe her ears. How could Patty think that was fine? "JP is twelve years old. Twelve years old! He needs his mother. If you have to leave Dalton, fine, but take JP with you!" Tears sprang to her eyes. It felt like everything was falling apart, the whole family just flung hither and yon.

"He doesn't want to go!" Patty yelled. "He likes it here with his daddy, hunting and fishing and mud racing. He doesn't want to move with me and be away from everything he loves."

Jeannie wanted to pick up the coffee mug and slam it on the table, wake her up from her stupidity. It had always astonished her, baffled her—honestly, infuriated her—that God had given children to her brother and sisters and not to her, the only mature, responsible one in the bunch. "If I had a twelve-year-old, you'd better believe—"

Patty leaned forward and narrowed her eyes at her. "Don't tell me what you'd do if you had a child. I don't live in your fantasy world," Patty said. She ticked off on her fingers: "I lived with his son-of-a-bitch daddy for almost thirteen years for him. I cooked for him. I waited on him. I went through agony bringing him into this world. I can't do no more." She pushed her mug away, sloshing coffee on the table. "I was the one who always wanted to go places. I never wanted any of this. None of it. Not this marriage. Not this cracker box of a house. Not that stupid TV show. None of it."

Debbie sat in stunned silence. Jeannie covered her face with her hands, rubbed her temples. She felt a headache coming on. "You're not going to leave the show too, are you?" Jeannie lowered her hands. "First Junior and now you?"

Patty got up and grabbed Dalton's Marlboros from the counter. She lit one, took a long, thoughtful drag. "No. It's good money, and I'm gonna need it." She blew a stream of smoke at the ceiling. "And I might wait a while to leave Dalton. Maybe when JP turns sixteen and can drive wherever he needs to go." She nodded to herself. "That's long enough. When I was that age, I was a wife and mother, cooking meals and changing diapers."

Jeannie exhaled and exchanged relieved glances with Debbie. Crisis averted, for now.

# Build My Mansion

*Speak the Victory!* took a two-week vacation in August 1987 and showed reruns. Brother Alford invited the Gospelettes and some key members of the Speak the Victory team to his lake house for a retreat the first weekend of vacation. Jeannie looked at the map and read the directions to Garland as he drove the family in the Gospelettes van. They all stared in disbelief when they reached the address they'd been given.

"Is this it?" Debbie squeaked out. "Are you sure?"

Jeannie checked the address again. "That's it."

"It looks like a hotel," Patty said. "A *fancy* hotel."

"Well, he said there would be plenty of room for everybody," Jeannie said. She was amazed. It was unlike any house she'd ever seen in Bethel or on any of her travels with the Gospelettes. It was like five or six large houses built onto each other, each with its own roof but all seamlessly attached. It was somehow lake-casual and elegant at the same time. They had passed several other magnificent houses on the lakeside road, but this one was the most impressive.

Truly, when she slowed down her busy showbiz life enough to think about what was going on, she was amazed by all of it. The show was gaining stations and viewers and paying partners every day. Brother Alford had recently given them all a raise. They were selling albums faster than they could make them. She no longer had to go looking for talent to appear on the show; many of the most popular contemporary Christian performers were now calling her. The Gospelettes were even invited to sing on a country Christmas TV special that would be taped at the Grand Ole Opry. She'd heard that the musical guests would include the Judds, Dolly Parton, and Ricky Skaggs.

"Do just the two of them live there?" Big Jean asked.

"I reckon so," Garland said, parking the van in one spot in a long, covered carport, with roofing and details that matched the rambling house.

They got out and stood together, stretching their legs and staring at the house, until two of Brother Alford's team members, Brother Jim and Brother Lloyd, came over and took their bags, guiding them to their assigned rooms. They walked across a lawn so manicured it looked to Jeannie as if someone had measured each blade of grass to make sure they were all exactly the same height.

The team members and the Gospelettes were given bedrooms in the main house, with the kids taking an upstairs bunk room that featured a slide, a big-screen TV, games, and enormous bean-bag chairs.

Then they all gathered out back at tables under the trees, overlooking the sparkling lake. Sister Diane had hired a caterer who made just-like-homemade fried fish, hush puppies, white beans and cornbread, coleslaw, creamy potato salad, baked beans, banana pudding, peach cobbler, and iced tea. After lunch, some of the team members' wives put life jackets on all the kids and took them down to the Alfords' own boat dock and onto the boat, letting the kids take turns being pulled on inner tubes. Garland and Big Jean were nervous about this, watching the water worriedly throughout the team meeting.

"Remember all the times we drove past lakes and rivers on our way to singings?" Patty asked Jeannie. "I'd look down and see all those people in boats, water-skiing, swimming, floating in inner tubes, and think, 'Huh, must be nice.'"

Jeannie nodded. She expected Garland to scramble down the bluff to the boat dock and wave them back in any time.

Brother Alford started their first meeting of the weekend with a prayer. Then he announced the new initiatives the Lord had called them to. A monthly magazine. A jewelry line that Sister Diane was launching. Quarterly men's fellowship retreats at various golf courses, fishing camps, and hunting lodges. A music telethon, which Jeannie would need to arrange guests for.

They had another catered meal for supper, took twilight boat rides, played horseshoes, and talked late into the night, listening to frogs and insects and lonesome birds call out to one another across the water.

After most of the team had turned in for the night, Jeannie lay in a hammock near a trail into the woods, thinking about how far they'd come. Was it ordained? Was it luck? Had she created it through hard work and perseverance? Had she named it and claimed it? She could convince herself that any one of these possibilities was true if she tried.

She heard footsteps on the trail to her left and a whispered voice. Debbie? Or Patty? The sounds stopped abruptly, and Jeannie waited, peering into the dark trees, swaying in the hammock. There was a pause, a watchful silence, steps on the trail again, and then Debbie appeared.

Jeannie sat up, dangling her legs over the side of the hammock. "Hey."

"Hey." Debbie wore a sundress and sandals and an azalea from the Alfords' landscaping above one ear.

"What are you doing?"

"Just walking." Debbie turned toward the lake, which was dark but reflected the half-moon and scattered lights from houses along the shore. "It's so peaceful here."

"Yeah." Jeannie watched Debbie's back. She didn't talk much about Jerry Lee anymore. Maybe she was relieved he was gone. Maybe, now that she was making a good living at *Speak the Victory!*, she didn't feel so desperate. "I think the kids are having a blast."

"Definitely." Debbie looked back at her. "Going to bed now?"

"I'll be right there," Jeannie said. She watched Debbie stroll to the house. Then she looked back at the trail and listened, waiting. When she heard the last of the team members talking and entering the house, she finally followed them.

After the lake retreat, the Gospelettes rode back to Bethel, where most of the houses and buildings seemed small, tipped to one side, about to fall down, and the lawns were weedy and overgrown, with an occasional snowball bush or crepe myrtle likely planted by some grandmother. Jeannie had left her car at her parents' house during the retreat, so she started up her engine, then waved goodbye and backed out of their driveway. The sky drizzled, and the streetlights made eerie reflections on the wet streets. No one else seemed to be out in town. She passed only two other cars on her way home.

The lights were off when she got there, and Wick's car was gone. She didn't even want to go inside and see if he'd left a note. She drove on by, toward Morristown Road. She had been thinking about Gail and Carolyn. She was worried about them, though she couldn't say why. She hadn't thought much about them since that day Wick had given them one of his old cars to drive.

She drove to their house, hoping she was taking the right roads in the dark. Finally, she saw the little house some distance off the road, a pale yellow lamp glowing through the front window. She eased down the long, bumpy driveway, the holes overflowing with water turning to mud. Gail came out on the porch and peered at her as she got out of the car. Jeannie dashed through the rain to the porch.

"Sister Jeannie?" Gail wore what looked like an elderly woman's house dress, a grayish cotton thing with tiny flowers.

"Hey! Sorry to surprise you. Just checking in. I was driving through town and remembered I hadn't seen you in a while."

Gail looked embarrassed. "I'm so sorry. I meant to return that car. We couldn't get my old car going, and—"

"No, no, no!" Jeannie waved her hands in front of her. "We're not worried about that at all. Wick has a dozen cars behind our house that he's tinkering on at all times. I promise. Not an issue!"

Gail opened the screen door. "Well. Come on in. It's kind of a mess, but—"

"It's fine," Jeannie said. "How is Carolyn?" She stepped into the cramped living room. The walls were covered with a rose-patterned wallpaper that was falling off in faded strips. A small coal fire sputtered in an iron stove, and an old black-and-white movie played on a snowy TV screen in the corner. Jeannie was startled when she saw an old woman on the couch, silent and unmoving. "Oh! Is she OK?"

"Oh, yeah. Mama, this is Jeannie from the Gospelettes. You know? From *Speak the Victory!*"

The woman lifted the corners of her mouth and nodded. "Hi-dee."

Jeannie smiled back. "Hello, there."

Gail wheeled Carolyn into the room. "Look who's here! It's Sister Jeannie!"

Jeannie bent over and gave Carolyn a gentle hug. "Hey, sweetheart! How have y'all been?"

Gail pretended to scratch under her eye, and Jeannie saw that she was crying. She stood up straight and walked over to her. "Are you all right, Gail?"

Gail wiped her eyes with the back of her hand.

"What is it?" Jeannie couldn't imagine what other bad luck could have befallen them.

Gail looked away. "Can I show you something?"

Jeannie followed her to a bedroom and sat on the edge of a chenille-covered bed while she rummaged through a dresser drawer and pulled out an envelope. Gail drew a long, ragged breath. "I thought I could keep up my pledge. I have every intention of doing it," she said. "But I was saving up to get my car fixed, and then Carolyn had to go to the dentist and get some fillings, and—"

"What are you talking about?" Jeannie felt like everything inside her, all the excitement and pride and hope that had been building up since she joined Brother Alford's ministry, was being hollowed out.

Gail sat on the bed and handed over an envelope, and Jeannie pulled out the letter.

*Dear STV! Partner,*

*We are deeply troubled by your failure to make the last two payments on your seed faith pledge. We know that God spoke to your heart and instructed you to make this pledge and He promised to be faithful and bless you a hundred fold. God is true to his word!!!!!! Will you be true to your's???????*

*God has said that if you bring your tithes into the storehouse, "I will rebuke the devourer for your sakes, and he shall not destroy the fruits of your ground; neither shall your vine cast her fruit before the time in the field, saith the Lord of hosts". That is if you are obedient Sister Gail. Doesn't it follow that if you don't honor your promise to God, that he will NOT rebuke the devourer for your sake and he WILL destroy the fruits of your ground????? What are the fruits of your ground? The things that are most precious to you!!!!! The fruits of your labor in this life—your finances, your house, your family, your child!!!!!*

*We are praying feverently for you to honor your pledge to God and resume your seed faith payments including the two you missed. We do not want to see all the blessings that you have believed for and spoken*

*into excistance to be lost. God is a loving God but also a just God. He
will reward and punish justly.*

*Do you want to take the risk of dis-pleasing God????? We are fear-
ful for your home, your family, and even your life!!!!! We are praying
for your obedience. Follow the leading of God!!!! We are praying for
you to . . .*

*Speak the Victory!*
*Brother Oren and Sister Diane Alford*
*& The Speak the Victory! Team*

Jeannie felt as if she might not breathe again. Like everyone else
in the country, she'd been following the *PTL Club* scandal. She'd
been wishing it would go away, hoping the disgust and ridicule
that had been directed at the Bakkers for their greed and sin didn't
get transferred to *Speak the Victory!* How unfair that would be!
The unsaved and the ungodly always gloated at these unfortunate
cases. They didn't see all the good preachers and gospel singers and
religious leaders devoting their whole lives to God's work! But now,
the finger was pointing to her, not by Gail or by anyone else, but
by her own conscience. She took a breath at last, folded the letter,
and put it back in the envelope. They both stared at it there on the
bed between them.

"I'm believing that the Lord is going to provide a way for me to
make up those payments I missed," Gail said. "It's been three now."
Jeannie saw now that her eyes were red and swollen, as if she had
been crying for days. "Do you think it could really happen?" she whispered. "Do you think I could be in danger, or Mama or Carolyn, because of what I've done?" Her voice broke, and she sobbed. "I've been
believing for Carolyn's healing, and now I'm worried about whether
she'll even make it to her next birthday."

Once Jeannie might have cried along with her, thinking about
all the prayers that were answered and the ones that weren't, about
how the people who didn't get what they were claiming must feel,
like they weren't doing it right, like they just didn't believe enough,
really believe. She might have followed her questions to the abyss,
this feeling that there was nothing there to hold her up, and fall-
en in. But what she felt about Brother Alford wouldn't let her cry.

What she felt was fury but not the kind that led to hot tears. It was cold. If he were in front of her now . . . If she were back at his lake house, and he was standing at the back of his property, on the edge of that bluff . . .

Jeannie picked up the letter and looked at it. "Do you mind if I take this?"

# Blessed Assurance

Jeannie drove the backroads around Bethel, sunglasses on, radio off, thinking. Wick had come home late—early that morning—acting strange and restless. She wondered if he was having nightmares about Vietnam again or if he was doing drugs with his old buddies. Or both. She wanted to talk to him, probably argue with him, about it, but he had disappeared into his garage, and she decided a drive out to the old Holliman homeplace might clear her head.

She turned onto the road that led to the river. The old bridge had been replaced with a new, safer one. It seemed like just a continuation of the road, with higher sides that kept her from being able to see into the river, all business, none of the drama of the tall steel beams that had announced she was headed somewhere special. On the other side, she drove to the homeplace, overgrown with weeds now, and parked in the grass and gravel driveway.

Everything had changed inside her, and, yet, nothing was different. For three days, she had kept the letter the Alfords had sent to Gail tucked in her purse, waiting for . . . something? Perhaps waiting for a crack to appear so that she wouldn't have to be the one to break the whole thing. Just a word of dissatisfaction from Garland would have been enough for her to swoop in and say, "That's right! And look at this!" But Garland seemed perfectly content. In fact, she'd never heard him complain less. For years he had complained about the Gospelettes' struggles and about Brother Clarence not appreciating him, not inviting him to participate in church leadership enough, not asking him to preach on those rare occasions when Brother Clarence was sick or on vacation. But Brother Alford had validated him, given him a very public pedestal, and paid him—paid them all—well.

And that was the problem. He and Debbie and Jeannie had all quit their jobs to work for Brother Alford. Now they made more than they had before, doing the Lord's work. Was Jeannie supposed to jerk the rug out from under them all, leave the whole family without income, make them all have to go looking for new jobs, because she didn't like how someone at *Speak the Victory!* had worded a letter?

She wanted to walk around the old farm, but she wasn't dressed for chiggers. She got out of the car and stood under the big oak in front of the house, then leaned against it. Strange that she could feel that it was alive. It wasn't like leaning on a post or against a car. It seemed to hum, low, like the bass part of a gospel harmony.

She looked at the front porch and remembered sitting there with her daddy and her papaw, listening to them talk in that unhurried way people used to have but didn't seem to have anymore. Words weaving in and out of subjects: neighbors, weather, crops, church, politics, funny stories of people long gone. Then, Papaw Virgil would get out his harmonica and play a happy tune. She wondered what they'd say about Brother Alford if she could go back in time and tell them about him. Or if she could walk over to them and show them that letter right then.

Of course, she *could* tell her father. He was just a short drive away. And she felt that was just what she *should* do. He was the one that started it all, really. Yes, she was the lead singer, the voice of the group, and she was the leader of the group when it came to getting their names out there, cutting records, marketing and sales, writing new material. But the group was his idea to begin with, and they'd all done it to please him.

She drove back to town in a light rain, to her parents' house, and sat in the driveway, looking at the front door, thinking about how to tell them, listing the points of her argument in her head—how Oren Alford had come in and run roughshod over Brother Clarence, how he'd made himself rich off the donations of struggling people, how his "prosperity gospel" bore no resemblance to anything Jeannie had ever heard Garland preach in all her years. She opened the car door and dashed across the soggy yard and up the porch steps. She could see Garland through the window, reading his Bible in his favorite chair.

She opened the front door and stuck her head in. "Daddy?"

"What are you doing?" He was startled and set the Bible on the side table.

She cleared her throat and stepped inside. "I need to talk to you about something."

Big Jean entered from the kitchen, frowning. "What's wrong, Jeannie? You look awful."

Jeannie wished she could be anywhere else. Anywhere in the world but there in her parents' living room telling them they needed to give up the show, their livelihood, *her* dream. "I'm just—I guess I'm just having some doubts," she said. "About Brother Alford." She exhaled and sat in the rocking chair near the door.

Garland squinted at her. "Doubts? What are you talking about?"

She locked eyes with him. "Daddy, you know what I'm talking about."

He stood, hands on his hips, and glared at her, then stalked across the room and back. "Is it the money he's bringing in? Is that the problem? Because you know how much money we made singing all these years."

"I know. Daddy. I was the one handling the business, if you recall."

"None," he interrupted. "I'll bet we didn't even break even."

"I know, Daddy."

"Nobody wants people in the ministry to make any money. I reckon we're supposed to eat air. Like we ain't human beings that have to pay for our food and clothing and shelter like everybody else. 'Cause soon as we start making a little money, they come after us. They start accusing us of this, that, and the other."

Jeannie took a deep breath and sighed.

"Am I lying?" he demanded.

"I don't know."

"What do you mean you don't know? Do you know how much money it takes for him to pay us and his crew and to build that theater and keep it running, electricity, water, and whatnot? You think all that's free?"

She shook her head. "No."

"No, it ain't." He picked up his Bible and held it aloft. "The Bible says anybody that don't provide for his own is worse than an infidel. And I don't want to hear no more about it! This is supposed to be our vacation."

Jeannie sat in silence for a minute, listening to the rain make music on the porch roof and in the trees. She felt unbearably sad. "Do you remember that little raggedy woman who used to come to the revival and bring her little girl in a wheelchair?"

Garland didn't answer, but Big Jean said, "Yes, I remember."

"Her name is Gail." Jeannie pulled the envelope out of her purse and handed it to Garland. "What do you think about this?"

He took out the letter and read it, with Big Jean reading along over his shoulder. Jeannie watched his face turn from pink to red. He folded the letter and put it back in the envelope, then rolled it to fit in one hand and held it tightly as he spoke. "She shouldn't have done it."

Jeannie knitted her eyebrows. "Done what?"

"Pledged that money if she couldn't pay it." He paced across the room and back again, squeezing and releasing the letter.

Jeannie sat in disbelief. She'd known he would be unhappy, but this wasn't what she'd expected to hear. "So you think it's all right what he's doing to that poor woman, taking her money and then scaring her to death when she can't make the payments?"

Garland wheeled around and pointed at her with the rolled-up envelope. "When you've got a ministry to run, you've got to know you can count on people to support you," he said in a low voice. "We ought to understand that better than anybody, with the ministry we've kept going all these years. Look at all the money we had to put into it ourselves when other people didn't, when they wouldn't follow God's leading their hearts."

Jeannie's mouth was set in a tight line. "Daddy, that woman has nothing. He's robbing poor, desperate people, and we're helping him!"

"That's enough! Enough!" he shouted.

Jeannie stood face-to-face with him. "He's a con man," she said. The realization had taken too long, but now that it was here, she couldn't ignore it any longer. "It's time we all faced the truth. He's a *crook* and a *thief* and a *con man*."

Garland jabbed a finger at her. "Do you think you know better than the almighty God? Do you think God only uses perfect people? Peter betrayed Jesus, and he still used him! Abraham had concubines! Samson kept a harlot! David was a murderer!"

Jeannie looked over at Big Jean, who stood nearby, one hand covering her mouth.

Garland slapped the letter against his leg in a threatening way that made Jeannie flinch. "I been going out there to Clarence's church for forty-some-odd years and I never once got asked to teach. And I go out to that tent a few weeks, and Brother Alford opens his arms to me and then hires me—pays me—to perform on his TV show! You think Clarence would have ever done all that for us? He was too busy running off to hospitals and funerals of people he don't know from Adam, and all the while he had a prophet in his midst that he didn't recognize. God made a promise to me when that angel—"

Jeannie put up her hands to stop him. "What does Brother Clarence not inviting you to preach have to do with this? We're talking about Brother Alford. Do you believe in him? Do you believe he really is a man of God?"

Garland was so angry that his breathing was labored. He wasn't used to being questioned by his own daughter. "Don't you remember how I prayed before I quit my job?" he asked. "Do you think I would make a decision like that without going to the Lord about it?"

"So you couldn't have made a mistake?" she asked. "We couldn't have made a mistake? Is that it? If you're a good enough Christian, you can't ever make a mistake?"

He blinked a few times, as if clearing his vision. "You will not talk to me that way," he said through gritted teeth and showed her the door.

Jeannie stared at him, not quite believing what she was seeing. Her father was telling her to leave his house? She looked over at Big Jean, who looked stricken but remained silent. Always silent. Nothing made sense anymore. Everything she had thought was true, everything they had claimed to believe about God, about the poor and the humble and meek, about what was right, it seemed, had been turned upside down.

She walked out to her car in rain that battered her, accusing her of wasting all those years.

# Are You Washed in the Blood?

The whole world, or at least the world between Bethel, Kentucky, and Nashville, Tennessee, was lit up, decked out, ho-ho-hoed to the max for Christmas. It was inescapable, as much as Jeannie might want to escape it. She pondered this new mood on the way to work. Something that had always been fun and joyful and sweet now filled her with dread and distaste. She took her exit and drove toward the Speak the Victory Theater, the sign and light posts all trimmed with greenery and red bows, and her stomach turned.

The whole thing had dimmed for her. Singing with her family. Listening to sermons. The holy facade. The ministry, for sure. She could hardly bear to stand on that stage while Sister Diane read the number for viewers to call to make their seed faith donations. Every single day since she and Garland had argued about the letter, she had thought of quitting the show.

The thing was it wasn't that simple. Just like with all the Christmas crap. She could choose not to celebrate, no tree, no gifts, none of the traditional foods and songs, because it was all so fake and crass and overdone, but she would miss it. She would miss the goodness at its core. She'd miss her mama's Christmas dinner and singing "Silent Night" at church and reading the nativity story and watching her nieces and nephews go nuts over their presents. And that was the dilemma she faced with *Speak the Victory!* She couldn't walk away and keep the good.

She parked and stared at the back of the building. Took a deep breath and walked in. Before she made it to her office, she was bombarded with questions and requests. Sister Susanne had Zeal (where did they get these names?) on the phone, wanting to know if they could be on the show next month. She also handed her a request from an up-and-coming contemporary Christian singer for permission to record two of Jeannie's songs. Brother Lloyd wanted to know how to set up for today's musical guests. One of the sound techs wanted her opinion about a new piece of equipment. Sister Lauren teetered toward her with an enormous holiday floral arrangement, a thank-you gift from the previous day's musical guest. She was important here. She had everything—no, she had more than everything—she had dreamed of. And yet. But still.

She walked down the hall to her office and set the floral arrangement, an assemblage of red poinsettias and pine boughs and glittery gold ribbons and silver ornaments, on her desk. Across from her office door, Sister Diane's French doors, covered with flouncy balloon shades, were closed, but she could hear strange sounds. A scuffle, as if someone had tripped or was being knocked around. Muffled cries. She moved closer to the doors and listened. She heard what sounded like slaps, sobs, growled threats. She jiggled the locked doorknob and knocked. "Hey! Sister Diane? Is everything OK in—" The sounds stopped for a moment, then started up again, a hard smack and a loud cry.

It sounded like Debbie.

Jeannie knocked again. "Hey! What's going on? Let me in!" She put her ear against the crack between the doors. She could hear Debbie crying in pain, pleading with someone to stop. "Debbie? What's wrong?" Jeannie backed up and slammed herself against the doors twice, and then someone opened the door on the right.

Debbie crouched face down in the middle of the white carpeted floor, in front of Sister Diane's glass and brass desk. Her hair was in disarray. She didn't move, just knelt, curled with her chest over her knees and arms over her head. Sister Diane stood over her, wearing a pink jogging suit, hands on her hips. One of the *STV!* team members, Sister Wilma, stood near the door, which she had apparently opened.

Jeannie looked from one to the other, her heart racing. "What the hell is going on?"

Sister Diane turned her head toward Debbie, lip curled. "Why don't you ask *her*?" Debbie sobbed into her knees but didn't move.

"Debbie?" Jeannie knelt beside her, trying to get a look at her face. "What's going on?" Debbie winced when Jeannie took her arm and tried to pull her up. Her face was red and wet with tears, and red scratches on her arms were starting to ooze blood. Jeannie looked up at Sister Diane. "Why did you do this?" she demanded. "What's wrong with you?"

Sister Diane narrowed her eyes. "Oh, my dear, the question is what's wrong with your whore of a sister?" If it weren't for Sister Diane's voice, Jeannie might not have recognized her. She looked completely different without her makeup, poufy hairdo, and power suit, sort of like a shaved cat. She looked down at her right hand, scowling. "I broke a nail." Sister Wilma hurried over to the desk and found an emery board.

"What are you talking about? Are you crazy?" Jeannie examined Debbie's face. A red mark around her eye would soon be turning black.

"No, I'm not crazy, but *she* must be if she thinks that she can walk into *my* program and *my* marriage and mess around with *my* husband," Sister Diane said, filing her broken nail vigorously. "I don't think she knows who I am and who she's not."

"You—" Jeannie shook her head. "I think you're confused. This is Debbie. She's—" If someone was messing around with Brother Alford, it was surely one of the other *STV!* team members. She could even imagine Patty doing it, given the right motivation. But never Debbie. She looked at her hunched over, peering out beneath a curtain of frizzed hair, and immediately Jeannie saw it in her eyes. She remembered the night at the lake house, hearing voices on the trail and then seeing Debbie alone. Debbie's sudden acceptance of Jerry Lee's walking out on her. It was true.

"There is always some little piece of backwoods trash that thinks she can turn my husband's eyes from me and from the Lord, and they always learn different. Always." Sister Diane smiled, arms crossed.

Jeannie helped Debbie up and held on to her as she stumbled across the hall to her office, depositing her in the desk chair. In the kitchen, she got a damp dish towel and a glass of ice. She checked the parking lot as she walked past the back doors, but no one else in the family had arrived yet. Back in her office, she closed and locked the door behind her. Debbie had collapsed onto the desk, sobbing. Of all the men in the world, of all the men right there in Speak the Victory Theater, running cameras and sound and whatnot, she had to get involved with Oren Alford? Jeannie wrapped some ice in the towel and gently touched it to Debbie's eye. "Tell me how this happened."

Debbie could barely get any words out between sobs. "I don't know!" She was curled into a fetal position in the desk chair, one arm wrapped around her legs, one hand holding the ice pack on her eye, chin resting on her knees. "It just . . . happened. It started out . . . He was praying for me and Jerry Lee, and—" She sobbed again. "I don't even know what happened. He was under so much stress, trying to pay for the theater and keep up with all the expenses. He prayed and asked God to forgive us."

Jeannie put her hands up. "Stop. Stop telling me about his stress. I can't—" She walked toward the closed door. "That's it. I'm done." She turned to face Debbie. "I'm going down there and telling him the Gospelettes are out of here."

"No, Jeannie! I don't want to leave!"

Jeannie shook her head and looked up at the ceiling. "You're sitting here covered with bruises and scratches, with chunks of your hair pulled out, and you don't want to leave? How do you think this is going to continue? Number one, do you think Sister Diane is going to let you stay? And number two, do you think Daddy is going to be OK with Brother Alford pulling this with you?"

"Don't tell Mama and Daddy!" Debbie cried, falling to her knees and grabbing Jeannie's arm. "It's my own fault, Jeannie! Don't tell Daddy. He'll just get mad at me, and we'll have to leave the show. I don't want to be the one that messes this up for us."

Jeannie pulled her up, took her by the shoulders, and shook her. "You haven't messed it up, Debbie. Oren Alford messed it up."

"Please, Jeannie, please don't tell them! Promise! Promise me!" The desperation in her high-pitched voice grated on Jeannie's nerves. She wanted to push her away, beat some sense into her just like Sister Diane had tried to do. How could they even be sisters, just a year and a half apart, and yet so different?

Jeannie gritted her teeth. "I won't tell them what happened. I'll tell them you're sick." She leaned against the wall and closed her eyes, completely drained. She hated everything in that room. The country-blue walls, the framed photos of the Gospelettes on stage, the damn geese. What was it going to be like to get on that stage after this? She couldn't even bear to look at that sleazy con man again. "Does he know she did this to you?"

"Brother Alford?"

"Yes. Him. Does he know?"

"I was . . ." Debbie gasped.

"What? You were what?"

"I was in his office, and Sister Diane came in."

"Oh, my God." Jeannie dropped into the other chair. "And?"

"And she and Wilma dragged me all the way down here."

"And he just let them? He didn't even try to stop them?"

Debbie shook her head and cried silently, mouth open, until one croak came out. "Don't tell Mama and Daddy, and don't quit the show. Everybody will hate me."

"What am I supposed to do about *you*, Debbie?"

"I'll drive home. You can tell them I'm sick. And then, maybe Brother Alford will . . . work everything out."

"How am I supposed to get on that stage now?" Jeannie felt sick to her stomach. "I don't ever want to see him again."

"Please, Jeannie." Debbie grabbed her hands and squeezed. "I don't want us to leave. This show means everything to me. It means everything to you and to Daddy and to everybody. I just know that Brother Alford will work it out. He has a way of . . . always getting his way."

"Oh, yeah," Jeannie said. "That's great."

"You know what I mean." Debbie wiped her tears with the dish towel. "He's learned how to speak the victory. He really has! Every time something goes wrong, he makes it go right."

Jeannie went down the hall to see if the coast was clear, then waved Debbie, wearing sunglasses and wrapped in a scarf and coat, out of the office. She followed her out to her car. "Are you sure you're OK to drive?" she asked. Debbie nodded, her face splotched red and blue and green, and Jeannie watched her drive away.

# I Saw the Light

In the dressing room, Karen asked about Debbie while she powdered Big Jean's face.

Big Jean sighed. "She's having female troubles." This was the story Debbie had instructed Jeannie to give the rest of the family. "I hope she don't have to have an operation."

"Well, tell her I love her, and Granny loves her, and thousands of Gospelettes fans love her and are gonna miss her today," Karen said.

"I sure will," Big Jean said.

"You ready?" Karen asked Jeannie.

Jeannie's nerves were still jangled from the events of the morning. She could feel her heart pounding, even hear the blood pumping in her ears. She sat in the makeup chair, and Karen dipped a sponge in foundation. "Should I give you a little extra Christmas sparkle?"

"Whatever you think." Jeannie smiled. "I trust you."

"Not that you need it," Karen said, dabbing the sponge on her face. "You're already a shining star."

Jeannie laughed.

"No, I mean it!" Karen stopped and cocked her head. "Look at all those people who watch you on TV and buy your albums and stand outside the theater hoping to get a look at you. Don't you try to downplay it. Let that little light shine!"

Jeannie held these words in her heart and fondled them. She thought this was true. Yes, there was a light there. A fire in her. Something that made her the leader of the group, something even Oren Alford had recognized and harnessed when he made her musical director of his show. Maybe it was even hers to use as she chose. Karen put the finishing touches on her stage mask, but Jeannie knew it was still under there, burning.

The remaining Gospelettes stood backstage, waiting for their cue. Jeannie watched Sister Diane click-clack rapidly toward the stage in a teal skirt and jacket with enormous shoulder pads, looking not the least bit flustered. Even her broken fingernail had miraculously been restored. If she was concerned that Jeannie might tell anyone what she'd done to Debbie or call the police on her, it didn't show.

The stage manager pointed at them to walk onstage. Jeannie felt like she was in a dream, couldn't feel her legs moving to her place, couldn't feel the microphone in her hand. She *could* feel a stream of sweat trickling down her back. The stage lights felt hotter than they ever had. In front of her was a sea of people applauding, smiling, cheering. The black eyes of the cameras stared at them.

Big Jean played the opening to their "Speak the Victory" theme song, but when it was time for Jeannie to sing her part, the lead, the words wouldn't come. She couldn't remember them, couldn't get her mouth to make the right shape, couldn't even figure out what she was supposed to be doing. Patty sang her harmony part and nudged her.

Garland stopped playing and told Big Jean, "From the top." She played the opening again. Jeannie looked at the microphone in her hand, but nothing came out. The guitars fumbled to a stop.

Then, Jeannie, as if she were a star looking down at the earth, watched herself walk to the front of the stage. She watched the faces in the audience look up at her with anticipation of her testimony. She watched one of the cameramen come out from behind his camera to look at her directly, confused. She heard her voice speak into the microphone: "Y'all need to know something." The piano background music stopped, and the crowd grew quiet. "Y'all need to know what's going on before you send another dollar to this ministry." She looked around the studio audience. "I know you want to believe in Brother Alford. I did too." Someone turned her microphone off, so she shouted the rest. "But then I found out some things!" Four crew members rushed toward her, and Jeannie spoke quickly: "He's been taking money from the poor and handicapped and then sending them threatening letters when they can't keep up their pledges! He's got a six-car garage full of high-priced cars! He's talking about buying a plane!" Two of the men grabbed her by the arms and pulled her across the stage, past her family, who stood frozen and open-mouthed, and backstage, past Brother Alford, who had emerged from his prayer closet to see what the commotion was about.

"Let me go!" she yelled at the men. "Do not touch me!" She turned her head toward Brother Alford as they dragged her toward the back hallway. "Taking money from poor single mothers with disabled children and the elderly. Are you proud of yourself?" His expression of cool distance didn't change.

When they turned Jeannie loose, she ran to her office, came out with her purse and keys and her notebook of songs, and marched past the crowd of team members who stood blocking the stage entrance. "Are y'all proud of what you're doing? What do you think Jesus would say? Huh?" She saw Patty standing there, microphone still in hand, and asked, "Are you coming or not?"

Patty dropped the microphone and followed her. They pushed through the back doors, took off their heels, ran through the parking lot in their pantyhose to Jeannie's Trans Am, and jumped in. They peeled out just as Garland burst through the back door and ran out to the parking lot, too late to stop them.

# I Believe He's Coming Back

In the backyard, under the willow tree, Wick hacked at the frozen ground with a shovel, stomped the shovel blade down with the full force of his body, threw clods onto a distressingly small pile. His heavy breathing made a white cloud around his head.

Jeannie sat in a lawn chair holding Sally's body, which was wrapped in the old blanket she'd slept on her entire sixteen years. The air was icy, and Jeannie wore a puffy coat, wool scarf, and gloves. She bounced her legs up and down to keep warm. "I could go borrow another shovel and help you," she said.

Wick shook his head. "I got it. You need to go in." He paused to catch his breath, propped one foot on the top of the shovel blade. "No sense in both of us freezing our asses off." He resumed digging.

"Are you sure it's not too frozen? It's gonna need to be a pretty big hole." Jeannie looked down at the body in the blanket.

"Gotta be done," he said. That wasn't entirely true. Jeannie imagined they could fit poor Sally in the big freezer at Patty's house where Dalton and JP kept their deer meat and then bury her later, when the ground warmed up, but she didn't want to suggest this. She and Wick had both cried inconsolably that morning, something she'd never seen him do before, even when his father died. Storing Sally with deer steaks and delaying the burial didn't seem like a great alternative.

It occurred to Jeannie that her life would make a good (or bad) country song: she'd lost (well, quit) her job, her family was mad at her, her husband was drinking too much, and her dog had died. She could have written that song, but she wouldn't want to subject anybody else to all that misery.

Garland had taken her decision to walk out on the show hard. "That should have been a family decision! That affected *all* of us, not just you. It should have been discussed and taken through the proper channels and planned, not just *flit flit flit*—" He made motions with his hands like aimless butterflies. "'I'll just do whatever I want! It's my life!'"

She understood his point—her decision *had* affected them all—but she knew what he really meant when he said it should have been "discussed" and "taken through the proper channels" was that it should have been decided by him, not her. She had tried to discuss it the day she showed him the letter to Gail, and he had shut her down.

What it had really come down to, though, was an impulse, something out of her control, something that felt outside of her but that was maybe so deep inside of her that she hadn't known it was there. She hadn't planned anything. She just knew. Something in her finally saw through what she wanted *Speak the Victory!* to be to what it really was. She had felt like she was in a dream when she made that announcement on the stage, but maybe she'd been in a dream before and was just then waking up. Of course, she didn't tell Garland or anybody else that. They wouldn't get it.

Big Jean had been shocked for a day or two, but now she seemed glad to have her old housewife life back. She and Garland had been able to save most of their earnings, as they had been used to far less. Garland had gone back to the sewing factory, though at a lower-level position. Patty was enjoying her freedom. She'd joined a bowling league and started going out with a group of friends. She said she'd look for a job later. Debbie, on the other hand, was not taking the breakup well. For her, it was more about losing Brother Alford than about losing the show.

Jeannie held her gloved hands in front of her face and breathed into them. Wick planted the shovel in the ground. "Be back," he said and headed to his garage. Jeannie decided to help out while he was gone, but she didn't get far. Shoveled up enough dirt to fill a gallon jug, maybe. Hard work.

When Wick came back a few minutes later, he had quite a bit more energy, and that worried her.

After a month of sleepless nights, Debbie was a wreck. Jeannie came to check on her and the kids on a Saturday and found Randall and Lee

Ann sitting on the couch with a bag of Doritos between them, arguing about which cartoons to watch. "You'll just have to take turns," Jeannie told them, setting plates of fried chicken, mashed potatoes, and macaroni and cheese that she'd made for their lunch on the coffee table.

"He won't!" Lee Ann insisted. "He already watched *ALF* when *Pee-wee's Playhouse* was on, and then he watched *Ghostbusters*, and I said I want to watch *Mighty Mouse*, but he wouldn't let me, and now he's watching *Popeye*, and I want to watch *Fraggle Rock*!"

"Hmm. That's a lot of TV watching. Maybe you two could read a book or draw for a while," Jeannie said. They looked at her suspiciously and continued their argument.

Jeannie walked to Debbie's bedroom, calling her name.

"In the bathroom!" Debbie's muffled voice came from down the hall.

Jeannie looked at Debbie's unmade bed and cluttered nightstand. She picked up a medicine bottle and read the label: Valium. She picked up another: Flurazepam, for sleeplessness. She put the bottles back in their places and sat on Debbie's bed, waiting, wondering what she could say that might work this time.

Debbie shuffled in, wearing a graying white flannel nightgown with pink rosebuds, looking worse than she had weeks before, when Sister Diane had slapped her silly. Dark circles had developed under her eyes. Depression seemed to weigh down every feature of her face and every part of her body. Jeannie had taken to coming by her house every day, to make sure the kids were eating and going to school and that Debbie was getting some kind of adult interaction.

"How are you?" Jeannie asked. She knew the answer but thought Debbie should have the chance to say for herself.

Debbie sat beside her. "I don't know." She turned to look out the window. "Is it cold out there? It feels like it's cold."

"Yeah, it's cold."

"I should go check on the kids."

Jeannie followed Debbie to the living room. "Mama!" Lee Ann leaped from the couch and ran to Debbie, grasped her hands, and jumped up and down. "Randall is watching all his shows, so I get to watch what I want next Saturday. OK? Remember that, OK?"

"OK," Debbie said, bending to kiss the top of her head. "I'll remember." She went to the kitchen and started the coffee maker.

"Have you applied for any jobs?" Jeannie asked. She filled the sink with soapy water and started washing dishes that must have been sitting on the counter for a few days.

Debbie let out a quivering sigh and sat at the table. "No. I don't think we should give up on *Speak the Victory!* After everybody cools down, Brother Alford might want us back."

Jeannie turned her head around to look at her. "That's not happening, Debbie. I don't want to be a part of it anymore. I don't believe in it."

"Wha—how can you say that? What does that mean? You don't believe in the Word?"

Jeannie attacked a crusty plate. "I don't know. I don't believe in *his* version anyway. And even if I was willing, he's not taking us back. He's got Grace & Mercy as his house band now." She had brought them in as musical guests four or five times. The band had two attractive young women singers. She was sure Alford had moved on. She looked back at Debbie's stricken face, wiped her hands on a towel, and sat next to her. "We have other options, you know. People still love the Gospelettes. We can perform elsewhere. I've been thinking you, me, and Patty should form kind of a country-folky-poppy trio like Dolly and Emmylou and Linda. I've been writing some songs in that kind of style, you know? 'Oh, the pain of loving you . . .'"

"No, Jeannie! No! He needs us. He needs you to handle all the music stuff for the show, and—"

"I watched part of the show yesterday. They're doing just fine. Still raking in the dough, I'm sure."

"He needs me!" Debbie looked embarrassed that she had said it out loud. They locked eyes for a few seconds, and then she looked down. "I know you don't understand that, but she's awful to him. He's carrying it all on his shoulders, and she just keeps demanding more and more and more money before she'll give him a divorce."

"Debbie." Jeannie leaned toward her.

"It's just a marriage of appearances. That's all. As soon as they can come to a financial agreement, she's going back to Oklahoma where their daughter and grandchildren live, and we can be together." Debbie reached across the table to clasp Jeannie's hand. "We love each other."

Jeannie slapped the table. "He's a con man, Debbie. He's a charlatan. He says whatever he needs to say to get what he wants, whether from you or from Daddy or from little old ladies and their Social Security checks. That's all. That's it."

Debbie shook her head. "No, Jeannie. He has a powerful connection. I've seen it, and so have you. Look at where he took us!"

"Exactly. Look at you. Look at you!" Jeannie held out her hands. "Look at what he's done to you."

She went back to the sink to finish the dishes. The worst part wasn't what he'd done, she thought. It was what she felt *she'd* done to them all.

# God Walks the Dark Hills

The family was gathered at Garland and Big Jean's for Sunday dinner, except for Debbie, who said she was sick again. Jeannie had picked up Randall and Lee Ann for church that morning, not even bothering to talk to Debbie. The kids were solemn. "I miss the birds," Lee Ann said, looking out at the bare trees on the ride.

"There are birds around in winter," Jeannie said, scanning the fields as she drove. No birds anywhere. "I've seen redbirds in the snow before. They're so pretty! And there's sparrows and blackbirds and a bunch of others."

"I think they all died," Randall said. "I heard it on the news."

Jeannie frowned and looked at him in the rearview mirror. "Huh. I didn't know you watched the news."

"He doesn't watch the news," Lee Ann said.

"Yes, I do."

"No, you don't."

"I watched it with Dad!"

"We haven't seen Dad in a hundred years."

Big Jean made a big pot of vegetable soup and a pan of cornbread. "No matter how I try, I can't make soup like yours, Mama," Jeannie told her as they sat around the table and started eating.

"What's different about it?" Big Jean asked.

"I have no idea. I use the exact recipe you gave me. Yours is just more flavorful."

"Do you drain the hamburger grease?"

"Yeah."

"I don't drain the grease."

Jeannie looked at her bowl. "Really?"

"You ain't hunting today?" Garland asked JP.

"Naw. Yesterday."

"What did you hunt?" Randall asked.

"Rabbits," JP said.

Lee Ann dropped her spoon in her soup bowl and wailed. "Nooo!"

"Hush, now," Garland said. "God put plenty of rabbits on this earth."

"Do you need a haircut, honey?" Big Jean asked JP. His hair was long in the back and short in the front, and he looked exactly like Dalton.

"That's the style, Mama," Patty said, rolling her eyes.

"Well." Big Jean looked doubtful.

When the kids finished eating, they went to the living room to play with JP's electronic Karate King game, their heads all together over the tiny screen. Big Jean turned to Jeannie. "Did you see Debbie this morning?"

Jeannie shook her head. "I just went in and got the kids. I think she was still in bed."

"Oh, Lord." Big Jean buried her head in her hands.

"What's her deal anyway?" Patty asked.

"She's upset about the show," Big Jean said.

Jeannie pressed her lips together. None of them knew about Debbie and Brother Alford. Not even Patty, apparently. And Jeannie had promised not to tell. She knew that, if she did, the rest of the family would understand her blowup that last day onstage, but it was important to Debbie that they never know she'd committed adultery, and Jeannie intended to keep her promise. Besides, what they *did* know about Alford ought to have been enough.

"We could at least perform at church if she'd get out of bed," Garland grumbled.

"She might still be having female troubles," Big Jean said.

"Maybe," Jeannie said. She got up and started clearing the table.

"Will you go in and see her when you take the kids home?" Big Jean asked. "And take her some soup?"

"OK, Mama."

"I think she's still depressed about Jerry Lee too," Big Jean added. "Does he ever even see those children?"

"I don't think so." Jeannie sighed.

"Too many troubles on her mind," Big Jean said. "I'm gonna have to lay down, y'all. I've got the headache." She took off her apron, wiped her eyes with it, and went to her bedroom.

"She's just trying to get attention," Garland said.

"Who?" Jeannie and Patty said in unison.

"Debbie! Just whining." He stood up from the table. Jeannie recalled that he had done quite a bit of whining himself when she blew up their *Speak the Victory!* deal, but she kept her mouth shut.

Jeannie went in the house with the kids that evening and brought a bright yellow Tupperware bowl of soup and foil-wrapped cornbread for Debbie. Darkness had fallen, and all the lights were off in and outside the house. She tripped on the sidewalk, almost falling down, wishing she had a flashlight. The front door was unlocked, and the house was so quiet she could hear the wall clock ticking. Lee Ann flicked on the lights, and Randall ran to the TV to stake his claim.

"Debbie? Are you up?" Jeannie took the food to the kitchen, then walked back to Debbie's bedroom and turned on the little lamp on the dresser.

Debbie rolled over, blinking and groaning.

"Have you been sleeping all day?"

Debbie turned toward the alarm clock on her nightstand. "What time is it?"

"Almost six."

"Six p.m.?"

"Yes. I brought Mama's soup and cornbread. Have you eaten today?"

Debbie moved her tongue around in her mouth and licked her lips. "No. I'm not hungry."

Jeannie looked her over, frowning. "How much weight have you lost? You're like a stick."

"I had a dream. It was so real." Debbie closed her eyes again, concentrating.

"What was it about?"

Debbie lay there, brow furrowed, remembering. "We were standing on a platform, about to sing. The lights. There were lights." She lifted one hand like she was reaching for them. "All these people jumping, like clambering for something out of reach. And I was holding a microphone close to my lips."

Jeannie nodded. "Sounds familiar."

"And then I was walking between the aisles of chairs. So many empty chairs, on and on. But nobody noticed I'd left the stage. I thought Daddy was gonna run after me and drag me back for leaving in the middle of a song. I just kept walking. I saw these kids in the back row playing hangman on scraps of paper." She laughed once softly. "The light was harsh, and there was this buzzing noise. We were under the tent. And then I just stepped out into the cool, peaceful twilight."

Jeannie smiled. "Remember how good it felt to step out into the open air after being in that tent with all those people?"

"And then there were all these other people in the field," Debbie said. "They were walking with me in the furrows. And then the tent was gone. I looked up at the sky, and the sun was setting, a color I'd never seen before. I was thinking, *Is that even a color?*"

"Wow." Jeannie tried to imagine a color that she'd never seen before, but it didn't seem possible.

"I didn't know where I was anymore, but I looked at everything around me: a barn, a fencerow, a gravel road, a little hill. And I knew exactly where I was and how to get home."

"That sounds nice," Jeannie whispered.

"All the people in the field were singing but not with their mouths. It was kind of like humming that came from—" Debbie touched her heart. "And I could smell sweet hay from a field. I started walking faster, and then I ran with my arms out, and then it was like . . . my feet were just skimming over the earth."

"That's quite a dream," Jeannie said.

Debbie nodded, eyes still closed.

The sounds of the TV and the children laughing floated from the living room. "The kids need to see you," Jeannie said.

"I know," Debbie murmured. "Poor babies. They don't have any parents."

Just being in the same room with her was making Jeannie tired. "They do have parents," she said. "Just not very good ones." It was an ugly thing to say, but she wasn't feeling generous.

# Too Late

Jeannie sat in the living room strumming Wick's guitar and jotting down lyrics in her notebook. She had written at least a dozen top-notch songs since she'd left *Speak the Victory!* These weren't gospel songs though. They were angry, defiant songs about leaving and quiet, reflective songs about making peace with the past. One was about getting on a plane (something Jeannie had never done) and flying away from a bad relationship. They weren't Gospelettes songs, but they would be good for *somebody*. Maybe a trio of sisters pivoting to a new genre?

Wick was still in bed, sleeping off something. She didn't know what and didn't think she wanted to know. She was tired of caretaking. Tired of asking him where he'd been, what he'd consumed, and why. Tired of worrying about him driving home impaired and killing himself or someone else. Tired, tired, tired. She'd taken a chance on him when everybody in her life thought she was making a big mistake, and she was, frankly, pissed that they might have been right.

She was tired of taking care of her family too. If she got a call from one of them, she knew for damn sure it wasn't going to be them checking on *her*, asking how *she* was doing. They needed her to do something, take care of something, fix something for them. Garland needed her to come over and set his VCR. Big Jean wanted her to listen to her cry about Junior. Where was he, and why didn't he just let them know that he was OK? Patty called to complain about Dalton. And then there was Debbie. Jeannie came by every day to check on Randall and Lee Ann. She and Big Jean alternated taking home-cooked meals to them, but she was the one who checked on their schoolwork and events, made sure they had clean clothes and toilet paper and were taking baths. She'd been working on Debbie every day, trying to get her to get up and out. *Take a shower. Let's go shopping. Maybe get a part-time job? File for divorce from Jerry Lee and start dating again?* None of her suggestions, encouragements, or gifts of time, money, and energy were appreciated.

She set the guitar on the couch and went to the kitchen, glanced at the corner where Sally used to sleep. Not a single person in her family had expressed sympathy for her loss. She sighed. She hated feeling sorry for herself, but she felt sorry for herself anyway.

She had bought a nice-looking pineapple at the grocery store the day before. She set it on the chopping block and got her big knife, hacked off the ends, sliced down the prickly sides, cut four long pieces around the core, then cut the long pieces into small chunks. There was something satisfying about using a big, sharp knife, cutting away what you don't need. Seemed like a good metaphor. Maybe she would write a song about it.

She put the edible chunks in a pretty glass bowl. So much of the pineapple was a waste. She scraped those parts into the trash, remembering how Papaw Virgil used to throw food scraps in a big, stinking pile a few yards from the house and turn them over from time to time, letting them go back to the earth. Another good metaphor, but she wasn't sure she could get a song out of it.

She ate a bite of the pineapple. Fresh and sweet. It made her think of having a frothy drink at the beach, something she'd seen pictures of but never done. Maybe she would. Maybe she would stop taking care of everybody else and think about herself for a change.

For the next four days, she didn't take any calls from her family. She'd check the caller ID and walk on by. She didn't go to Debbie's house. Their parents could see to her. She couldn't listen to any more of her whining.

Jeannie wasn't sure what made her answer the phone the morning she finally did. Maybe intuition? Maybe the time of day? No one usually called that early. She dashed from the bathroom to answer it on the third ring.

"Aunt Jeannie?" Lee Ann's voice sounded small and faraway, as if she were calling from overseas.

"Hey, sugar! What's going on?" Jeannie gripped the phone tightly and pressed it hard against her ear.

"Mama won't wake up."

She felt the chill of death, as if it had seeped through the phone lines. A hard freeze in her veins, that knowing that something can't be reversed, that it is, it is, it is. And you can't. Can't go back, can't fix it, can't do a single thing. She called an ambulance but made it to the house before they did. She ran to the bedroom and saw immediately that it was too late. Debbie had been gone a while, several hours.

Jeannie fell to her knees beside the bed. Behind her, in the hallway, Lee Ann and Randall were asking questions. She could tell by their tone that they were asking something, but she couldn't put their words together in her mind. "Stay there, babies. Stay over there," she said. When had she talked to Debbie last? Four days ago. "Hold on, kids. It's OK." It really wasn't, and they knew that. She could hear Lee Ann crying, calling for her mama.

She had failed. She had cut Debbie off. And now Lee Ann and Randall had seen her that way, and she couldn't erase it for them, couldn't go back and check on Debbie sooner, couldn't go back and leave Oren Alford when she had that first doubt—and save them all.

# THE 1990S

# This World Is Not My Home

When Jeannie was young, she had thought things never changed in a town like Bethel. But this wasn't true. The weather had become hotter and drier in recent years, although only the farmers and a few town people who had grown up close to the land noticed the difference and wondered aloud whether it was a sign of the end times. Walmart had come in, and stores she'd seen all her life that had seemed as permanent as the sun that greeted her every morning disappeared one by one. The strong and vital adults, the giants of her childhood, slowly caved in on themselves, their bones crumbling and their backs bending, and then they disappeared, replaced by young people who didn't know her, even though she knew them because she knew their parents and grandparents.

She was beginning to realize that even the things she believed to be true and right and everlasting, what she thought were the laws of the universe, could loosen from their fixed positions and burn away like stars falling from the heavens.

She drove past the apartment where she and Wick had lived when they were first married, past the decaying feedstore. Did anyone buy feed anymore? She supposed someone did, but she didn't know any of those people. She drove past the boarded-up windows of former downtown businesses. Meyers' had closed, and so had the Commonwealth Shoppe and Charlie's Dime Store. Past Percy's Drug Store, where she, Debbie, and Patty used to sit in a green vinyl booth and drink cherry Cokes after school. It was closed now too, the windows covered with black plastic inside.

Sweet Debbie. It had been three years since her overdose, and it still broke Jeannie's heart every time she thought of her. And she thought of her every day. She had no choice. She'd taken Randall and Lee Ann to raise, living reminders of Debbie and all she was missing, whether intentionally or unintentionally. They were living reminders, too, of what Jeannie would have, should have, could have done if she'd only known how bad off Debbie was or if she hadn't been so selfish and fed up with Debbie's neediness. Jeannie had taken on the big sister mantle willingly and meddled in her siblings' business freely her whole life, and then, when one of them needed her most, she had cast it aside. Sometimes she thought the only thing that kept her from disintegrating from the shame of it was the fact that the kids needed her. But then Randall had decided, when he turned thirteen the previous year, to move in with Jerry Lee. She understood why he might want to live with his father. Maybe she should have been happy that they were rebuilding their broken relationship. But it hurt to watch him go. She felt like she was letting Debbie down again.

Lee Ann was a joy in her life, though: the child she'd never had. Lee Ann had grown attached to Wick too, always following him around in his garage, wanting him to build her something—a clubhouse, a pedal car, a bicycle with a wide seat and canopy—and he seemed happy to oblige.

He still drank too much, was still using (Jeannie wasn't sure what). He was (she had determined from her reading) a high-functioning substance abuser. He still worked and maintained their vehicles and mowed the lawn. If there was a problem, he'd hinted, maybe it was with her.

Jeannie passed the Copper Kettle, now a church with its name and preacher's name and worship service hours crudely hand-lettered on the front window in white paint. She'd never heard of the preacher and didn't care to meet him. There had been a time when she knew every preacher in the county by name, when the Gospelettes were performing at churches all around. They hadn't sung together since they left the show. People at church asked them to sing from time to time, but when the family lost Debbie, the Gospelettes died too. Jeannie couldn't even imagine it, and she knew Garland and Big Jean couldn't either. They had been devastated. Big Jean had gone to bed, and Jeannie had feared she might never get up, just like Garland's mother had done when his brother had died in the war. But then

Garland had injured his hand at work, and Big Jean snapped out of it, got up, and took care of him.

Jeannie drove past the Bethel Dipper, where she expected to see Wick from a couple of decades ago, bell-bottom jeans and sandaled feet, his hair brushing his sunbrowned shoulders.

And then she arrived at work. Mr. Ogles had sold his store to the Handi-Mart corporation, and now it was a fluorescent-bright square of perfectly aligned aisles filled with junk food. The ancient wooden cash register and the old Coca-Cola cooler and the sagging shelves, all the familiar things, were gone. But she was back.

# Whispering Hope

The day after JP turned sixteen, Patty moved out of the house and filed for a divorce from Dalton. As soon as Garland and Big Jean got the news, they called Jeannie to get her on the case.

"Lord have mercy, what is that girl thinking?" Big Jean cried. "I couldn't have no more left my kids than cut off my own arm."

Jeannie could hear Garland in the background, ranting. "Worldly influences! Ever' one of them . . . won't listen . . . weren't raised that way . . ." Jeannie rolled her eyes at the phone. Of course, they weren't raised "that way." They—the girls, at least—were raised to be taken care of by their husbands, just like Garland took care of Big Jean, but none of the men in their world seemed willing to cooperate. Wick, the unchurched outlaw, had actually come closest, though Garland would never have acknowledged that.

"She's living in a bowling alley!" Big Jean declared.

Jeannie thought she must have misunderstood. "She's living what?"

"She got a job at the—let me see. I wrote it down." Big Jean rattled around and came back on the phone. "She got a job at the Bowl-o-Rama, and she's living in a room in the back."

"Are you sure she's living there?"

"That's what she said."

"Oh." Jeannie squinched up her face. "OK."

"Maybe you can talk some sense into her," Big Jean said.

"I don't think Patty wants to hear anything I have to say about it," Jeannie said.

"Well, we've talked till we're blue in the face," Big Jean said. Garland was still talking at the same time, so Jeannie had trouble understanding the rest.

"All right," she said finally. "I'll try."

That evening, she stopped by the Bowl-o-Rama and found Patty eating an early dinner—french fries and a chili dog—at the snack bar. Patty looked up and threw down her napkin. "Oh, look who's suddenly taken up bowling!"

"Ha ha," Jeannie said, smiling sadly.

"Have a seat. Can I get you something? I'm the snack bar manager."

Jeannie sat across from her in the booth. "I see! How did this happen?"

Patty gave her the full rundown. She and Dalton had been going bowling every Thursday night with some of his buddies and their wives and girlfriends ever since the family left *Speak the Victory!* They were terrible bowlers, but it was right around the time that alcohol sales were voted in for their county, so they would all have a few beers and laugh and act crazy. She was actually enjoying herself for the first time in a *long* time, despite the fact that Dalton was there. Then one night she saw a Help Wanted sign on the door of the bowling alley. She went up to the snack bar and talked to Bill, the owner, and landed a job. "I told him, 'I'm getting a divorce, so I'll have to find an apartment I can afford,' and he looked over at Dalton and shook his head, and then he showed me an office in the back with a couch I could sleep on and told me I could stay there as long as I needed to for free."

Jeannie thought her face must have revealed too much, because Patty added, "It's *fine*, Jeannie. I have my own bathroom, and I can eat whatever I want from the snack bar for free, and Bill is the absolute best. He said, 'I don't even use that office. You stay as long as you want.' And not once has he 'just happened to walk in' or expected anything from me beyond my job as snack bar manager."

*Unlike Oren Alford*, Jeannie thought. *A bowling alley owner with better morals than a preacher. Imagine that!* "Well, that's great," she said. "I just don't understand why you need to stay here for free. Didn't you save most of your money from doing the show?"

Patty took a sip from an enormous cup of Coke and raised her eyebrows. "I did. I put most of it in a savings account, but Dalton got a hold of it and bought new trucks for him and JP and a boat and some guns and I don't know what all."

Jeannie groaned and covered her eyes.

"But I had enough sense to hide some of it, and it's gonna stay hid till this divorce is final."

Jeannie nodded. "All right. I'm not here to argue with you about leaving Dalton, even though I think that's what Mama and Daddy want me to do."

"Good."

"But what about JP? He needs his mother."

Patty had that all worked out, she said. She'd kept a key, and she'd go to the house every Thursday evening when Dalton came to bowl. She would check on JP, do his laundry, look around his room and make sure she didn't see any drugs, and visit with him for a couple of hours. "That's more than I saw him when I was living at home," she insisted. "He doesn't need me! He's just like Dalton. They're always hunting or fishing or cleaning their guns or sorting through their tackle or whatever it is they do."

"You could at least *try* to get him to come with you," Jeannie said. "Y'all could move in with us for as long as you want."

Patty shook her head. "It won't do no good, Jeannie. He likes his life the way it is. He doesn't want to live with us. He'd just leave and go back home. Then what am I supposed to do? Call the police every day to haul him back?" She took another sip of Coke. "He's fine. I'm fine. Everything is fine."

Three men came in, needing to rent shoes, and Patty patted the table twice. "Back to work. I'm kicking you out now."

"All right, I'm going." Jeannie walked to the door, then turned to wave goodbye. When she looked back, Patty was talking to her customers and laughing like she was having the time of her life. Well. She and Jeannie had always been different. Jeannie was the one who had a dream. In fact, she was different from all her siblings in that way. And now she had to learn to live with the disappointment. Patty could leave the past behind her—Debbie, the Gospelettes, her marriage, even her kid—and live and work in a bowling alley, eating chili dogs and flirting with the narrow variety of men who came in, and be perfectly content. Meanwhile, Jeannie felt the sharp pang of regret over Debbie every single day, the shame of failure every time someone recognized her at Handi-Mart and asked if she used to be on that TV show, sorrow and self-pity in a roiling ball, and then that stupid, relentless ambition beating its wings against her rib cage.

# Going Home

Summer was Jeannie's favorite season at the homeplace. Sitting in the shade in the front yard, feeling a little breeze now and then, looking out at the fields, just green upon green as far as she could see and a perfect blue sky and golden sun filtering through the tree canopy. She felt peaceful there. All the bitter memories seemed to dry up in the sun.

Since early spring, she had been working on the house, cleaning it out, clearing out critters, and painting. She'd hired a plumber and an electrician to get everything working. Just in case it came to this.

The house had sat empty for nearly thirty years, since her grandfather, Papaw Virgil, died, and now the thirteen-year-old great-granddaughter he never met would bring life back into it. Jeannie had fixed up the biggest bedroom for her, brightened up the walls with Lee Ann's favorite color (pale lavender), and painted the dark wooden furniture a glossy white.

Lee Ann had cried when Jeannie told her she was divorcing Wick. He was more like a father to her than Jerry Lee had ever been. Jeannie didn't know how much she should tell her about her reasons. There were probably books that could inform her about what was recommended in these situations—what to tell or not tell a child about the many expectations and disappointments of a marriage or about the fact that a parent or guardian is an addict or is breaking the law—but Lee Ann had been living with them for four years by that point, so she knew enough. After her tears stopped, she shrugged and started packing. Once, she'd had a mother and a father and a brother all in one house, and then things had changed, and now they were changing again.

Wick and some friends or customers, or whatever they were, were sitting on stools and lawn chairs around his garage when Jeannie and Lee Ann came out of the house with their boxes. Jeannie had cleaned up the old furniture and cookware and dishes that had been at the homeplace when her grandfather lived there, and she had bought and already taken over a few new things—mattresses, a TV, a phone—so all they needed to take from her and Wick's house were their clothes and personal items. Wick followed them and helped Lee Ann fit her boxes into the trunk of Jeannie's Honda Accord (her choice to replace the Trans Am that had been his choice).

He pulled Lee Ann to his chest and hugged her tightly. "I'm right here when you need me."

"I know, Uncle Wick."

When Jeannie got in the car, he knelt beside the driver's side door.

"Damn it, don't do this, Jeannie," he said, so low she wasn't sure she'd heard him. "Don't leave me alone like this."

She scoffed. "You're never alone, Wick. You've got your customers." She looked over at the group assembled at the garage, all of them pretending not to watch. "They're your real family, aren't they?" Maybe that was harsh. She didn't know anymore. She started the car and studied the gauges, trying to distract herself from the tears that were building up and from Lee Ann's sniffling beside her.

"You've changed," he said. It was a realization, not an accusation. The change had taken such a long time to happen that Jeannie supposed he hadn't noticed until now.

# Softly and Tenderly

Jeannie was sleeping on her couch on a Saturday night, wrapped in an afghan that Big Jean had made, a book by Reinhold Niebuhr still in her hands, when she awoke to a knock at the door. She looked at the wall clock—after midnight. Her first thought was of Lee Ann, who was at a sleepover with a group of friends. Might something have gone wrong? Lee Ann was staying at the Woodwards', and Jeannie had known them to be good people all her life, but of course, there were a million things that could go wrong, as Garland and Big Jean had drummed into her since she was a child. She'd already watched Randall go back and forth between her and Jerry Lee, wanting to be with his dad and then arguing with him and running away half a dozen times (each time to her house, thankfully). She had talked him into going to college and hoped that he would make it through this first year. He was majoring in music, which reminded her of herself at his age, when she turned down that music scholarship. Garland had tried to talk Randall out of going, as he had Jeannie, but she had cut him off. "He's going," she had said. "This is not a debate. We're just telling you what's already been decided."

Lee Ann would soon be sixteen. She was a great kid, smart, more studious than Randall. Each time Jeannie met with Lee Ann's teachers, they poured on the praise. She was proud of Lee Ann, of course, and of her own role in raising her and encouraging her academic abilities, but she was always worried too. She worried that she would let Lee Ann and Randall down just as she felt she had let down their mother. It was a failure she was sure she'd never get over.

Another knock, louder. Jeannie got up, tangled in her afghan, and tripped over to the front window to look out. She didn't recognize the car. She combed her hair with her fingers and turned on the porch light. Peering through the tiny window in the front door, she saw him standing huddled against the cold without a coat or hat or gloves—Wick.

They hadn't seen each other in nearly three years, since the divorce was finalized. Maybe they had passed on the street, but she didn't know what kind of car he was driving now, so she couldn't tell. He had disappeared from her life. That was what she wanted. She didn't want to expose the kids to any more than they'd already seen and gone through. They'd lost their mother to a drug overdose. Wick had said he understood that and claimed he would do better, but she couldn't press pause on the kids and wait for him to live up to his promises. Still, when she saw the sweet curve of his familiar face and his pained eyes, she knew some part of her heart still belonged to him.

She opened the door. He was bigger, heavier than when she'd left, and there were tiny lines radiating from the outer corners of his eyes and deep grooves on either side of his mouth, a little silver in his three-day beard. "What are you doing?" she asked. "It's forty degrees, and you don't even have on a coat."

"I might need your help, Jeannie." His voice sounded gravelly. "I've got Junior in the car."

Heart pounding, she slipped on her shoes and ran out to the car. Junior was completely reclined in the passenger seat, seemingly unconscious. She opened the door and saw in the overhead light that his face was older, lined, and, unlike Wick, he was thinner than he'd been when she'd last seen him, eight years before.

She turned to Wick, who stood beside her, looking worried. "What happened?"

"He just showed up at the house like this. He was asking for you." Wick lifted Junior. "Just get the doors for me," he grunted, carrying him up the porch steps and into the house. Jeannie led him to the spare bedroom she'd fixed up for Randall, helped undress Junior, and tucked him in, just as they'd done years ago when she and Wick were still together. He lay curled up in bed, shivering, whimpering in his sleep, occasionally waking up and saying something they couldn't understand. Wick looked even more anxious than he had the last time Junior had come to them messed up. He patted his pockets looking for cigarettes and, coming up with nothing, paced the hallway outside Junior's room. He speculated that it was crystal meth this time. "Give him a couple of days. Maybe three," he said.

Jeannie sighed. "I don't want Lee Ann to see him like this. I wish you had taken him to Patty's."

Wick shrugged. "He was asking for you."

The next evening, Wick came back to check on Junior, who was still sleeping. He felt his pulse, then stopped at Lee Ann's door to say hello. She ran over and hugged him. "Uncle Junior is back!" she said.

"I saw that," Wick said, planting a kiss on the top of her head.

"Aunt Jeannie said he's not feeling well and needs to rest a while." She gave Junior's closed door a dark look. "I just wanted to say hello to him."

"I guess you're gonna have to say hello to ol' Uncle Wick instead."

"Hello, ol' Uncle Wick." Lee Ann grinned.

"How's school? Aunt Jeannie said you're getting straight Fs."

"Right."

"Yep. She's trouble." Jeannie smiled. It was sweet seeing them together again.

"Do I need to come over here and sit on the porch with a shotgun and keep the boys away?" Wick asked.

"Yeah. See 'em over there sneaking through the cow pasture?" Lee Ann pointed out the window.

Wick squinted. "Yep. I see 'em." He kissed her head again. "I've got a car ready for you as soon as you get your permit."

Her face brightened. "Are you serious?"

He followed Jeannie to the living room. "Thank you for checking in," she said. She sat on the couch. "Is this normal?"

He shrugged. "From what I hear." He sat beside her, closer than necessary. They were silent for a while, staring out the front window at the fallow field across the road, watching the light fade. The only sound was Lee Ann's stereo playing Tom Petty's "You Don't Know How It Feels." Then Wick leaned over and lay his curly head, now run through with strands of silver, on her lap. "Do you ever think about me?" he whispered into the leg of her jeans. Jeannie could smell alcohol on his breath. She wanted to get up and leave the room. She didn't want Lee Ann to walk in and think they might be getting back together. But his sorrow was so deep that she couldn't move.

"I thought she'd come back when I was grown," he mumbled.

Jeannie could barely make out his words. He was silent for a while, and she thought he must have fallen asleep. "Wick?"

"Once I was grown and wasn't no trouble anymore, I thought she'd come back. When I got back from 'Nam, she could've come to see me. I wouldn't have asked anything of her."

Jeannie realized he was talking about his mother, and she felt her throat close up. She placed one hand on his head, awkwardly, and then stroked his soft, familiar hair. "Do you even know if she's still alive?" she asked softly. "Maybe something happened to her."

He was quiet for a minute. "My aunt Lula in Springfield calls me now and then. Says she hears from her." He drew a long, ragged breath. "She's alive."

Through the window she saw headlights on the road in front of her house and then in her driveway. "Somebody's here," she said, pushing him gently off her lap and walking to the door. She didn't want to worry her parents, so she hadn't told them about Junior yet, but she had told Patty. She opened the door to her.

Patty walked in and sat beside Wick on the couch. "So you rescued him again," she said.

Wick stood. "Let me know if y'all need anything."

Jeannie saw him out, then led Patty to where Junior was still sleeping.

"There he is, in the flesh," Patty said, standing over his snoring body. "Did you talk to him last night?"

"Not really. He was just mumbling nonsense."

"I'll bet he doesn't even know Debbie is dead," Patty said.

Jeannie groaned. Another job for her.

Late winter sun poured through the kitchen windows as Junior sat with Jeannie, Patty, and Wick, regaling them with the story of his awakening. "I sat up and looked around, thinking, *Where the hell am I?* I see these clean clothes all folded up and ready for me, so I put them on and step out into the hall and look around. Hell if it didn't look like Papaw Virgil's house! How did I get to his house? And I hear

Gram Parsons singing on the stereo. And then I go, *Oh, shit, am I dead?*"

They all laughed a little.

"Not this time," Wick said.

They all looked down and sipped their coffee then, except Junior, who sipped from the large glass of orange juice that Jeannie had set in front of him. His face was haggard, and he looked like he was in desperate need of vitamin C.

"Everything has changed," Junior said. "I feel like Rip Van Winkle." He shook his head. "Debbie's gone. Jeannie's out here at Papaw Virgil's house. Y'all left the show. Y'all are all divorced." He looked at Jeannie and then Wick. "Why'd y'all get divorced anyway? That's some bullshit right there."

Jeannie cleared the breakfast plates from the table, avoiding Wick's gaze.

"Listen to *you* talk," Patty said. "How many times have you been married and divorced? Do you even know?"

Junior wagged his head back and forth like he wasn't sure.

"People have their reasons," Patty said.

"People do, but I'm not talking about 'people.' I'm talking about Jeannie and Wick," Junior said.

Wick stood and drained his cup. "All right. I'm gonna go work on your bike, brother."

"I appreciate you," Junior said, standing and giving Wick a handshake-backslap-hug.

Patty stood. "I've gotta go too."

"Aren't you working nights?" Jeannie asked.

"Yes, but I've also got a life," Patty snapped.

"All righty." Jeannie raised her eyebrows and turned back to the sink.

After Junior saw them out, he came back to the kitchen and stood next to Jeannie, not drying the dishes as she washed, just sharing the view out the window of the field and the trees along the river, some now starting to bud. "Nice," he said.

"Yeah." Jeannie smiled. "I love it out here."

"You don't miss being a town girl?"

"Nah. Not really." She drained the sink and wiped her hands, then leaned one hip against the counter and crossed her arms. "What's next?"

Junior exhaled hard and turned to face her. "First thing: Can you call Mama and Daddy and Brother Clarence? I need to talk to them."

After Jeannie made the calls, she and Junior sat in the living room and waited quietly. They heard a car pull in, and Jeannie looked out the front window and saw Garland and Big Jean trotting across the yard as if they were in a race. They hugged and cried over Junior so much that Jeannie had to walk out the back door and stand on the porch in the cold and just breathe. Then Brother Clarence arrived, and they prayed over Junior. Jeannie stayed outside, waiting until their voices, all raised in simultaneous prayer, died down.

When she walked back in, Junior asked her to sit down. He had an announcement to make. He stood in front of the TV, looking slightly deranged with his sunken cheeks and unruly beard and oversized clothes (borrowed from Wick). He clapped his hands once and glanced around the room at them all. "I'm answering the call to preach," he said. "The Lord told me it's time to fulfill Daddy's prophecy."

Garland said, "Praise the Lord!" Big Jean gasped and covered her mouth with both hands. Brother Clarence smiled. Jeannie remained silent.

"I can't run from it no more," Junior said. "The Lord won't let me."

# King's Highway

Seventeen motorcycles (she counted them), mostly Harley-Davidsons, were parked in a row in front of the Bethel Independent Church of the Pentecost when Jeannie walked through the parking lot and into the church, at the last possible moment. She hadn't been to church in months, but Junior had called her earlier in the week and asked her to please change her work schedule for that Sunday so she could be there. Something big was happening.

She stepped inside the vestibule and saw a packed house. Lined up across the back row were the motorcycle riders, mostly middle-aged men, in leather, jeans, and bandanas, some bearded, some graying, most of them sporting a paunch. A few women, also mostly middle-aged, in leather jackets, tight jeans, and black T-shirts, with sunglasses perched on their heads and long, frizzy hair. She saw Junior walk by them, shaking and slapping hands along the way, and sit in the middle of them. She walked down to where her family sat in their usual pew.

DeWayne Deaton, the minister of music, and his praise team were singing a fast number, something apparently chosen especially for the guests on the back row, with the phrase "I'm a soldier for God!" repeating in the chorus. Jeannie wondered if the electronic keyboard DeWayne was playing was set on "screeching guitars." Whatever it was, the riders seemed to like it.

When they finished the song, Brother Jenks, a stooped old man now, said, "Praise God!" and handed the program over to Brother Clarence, who began by welcoming the visitors. "And I hope I can stop calling you visitors soon and call you members of our church family," he said. "I want to start today by saying Jesus wants all of you, whoever you are, wherever you've been. Jesus wants all of you, and so do we." Somebody said amen.

"This week, Brother Junior Holliman and I have been going to the Lord in prayer about something the Lord is calling him to do," he continued. "Come on up here, Brother Junior, and tell us. Praise the Lord." Brother Clarence held out one arm toward the back of the church. Jeannie looked back and saw Junior stand up, smiling. He was wearing jeans and leather like the rest of the guys on his row, and she could see the startled looks on some of the old-timers' faces.

In the pulpit, Junior told a story of being lost somewhere—"I couldn't even tell you what state I was in, much less what city"—nearly out of money and "coming down off a three-day toot," when he got into a conversation with another biker in the parking lot of a truck stop. "He said, 'You're riding with guys who ain't on the same path as you are, am I right?' And I said, 'Now how did you know that?' And he goes, 'I see it on you, like the mark of God.' I tell you what, I got chills all up and down my body. Then he goes, 'I got a group I want you to ride with. We're doing a ride Saturday and having a big lunch and then riding back, but it ain't for the faint of butt so don't go with us if you can't handle it.' I said, 'I can handle it.' I figured maybe I'd get a free meal, right? So I go, and it turns out they were Christian bikers, and they had a riding ministry. Now I don't know what made me start talking to this man, you know? And this place where I ran into him, I hadn't ever been there before. I didn't even know there *was* a truck stop out that road. I just rode out there like somebody was leading me there. And it *was* somebody leading me there, amen?"

Jeannie cut her eyes at Garland and Big Jean, who stared straight ahead at Junior, barely blinking.

"So I went, and it was like nothing I'd ever experienced before," Junior declared. "So then I said, 'All right, Lord, what do you want me to do?' And the Lord said, 'I want you to go home where you know people and have friends that you know are looking for me. They might be riding with a bad group. They might be going the wrong way on this highway called Life. But I want you to bring them in. They ain't pew warmers; they're highway warriors!' And he gave me our name—King's Highway Warriors—and he said, 'Put it on your right arm as a seal.'"

Junior pulled up the right sleeve of his T-shirt and showed a tattoo on his bicep. "If you can't see it back there, it's a cross and a motorcycle, and it says, 'King's Highway Warriors.'" The row of bikers erupted in applause and shouts.

"I came home and talked to Brother Clarence about it, and we worked out this arrangement. So those of y'all that want the traditional service, it'll still be here at 10:00 a.m. Those of y'all that want the casual service and want to ride with us, you can meet us at Shoney's breakfast bar in Springfield at that time and then we'll all ride in for our service at 12:30. Now that means Brother Clarence is going to have to wrap it up on time." Junior turned to him, and Brother Clarence smiled and nodded. "But it's all right if you run a little over, Brother Clarence. We'll just ride around and around the church revving our bikes till you come out!" The bikers cheered again.

"And, listen, all you cagers are welcome too. That's people in cars, if you don't know. You can pick one service or go to both. It don't matter. The Lord wants you either way."

After church, the family gathered for Sunday dinner at Garland and Big Jean's, without the grandchildren, who all had things to do. Jeannie ate and left early, saying she needed to get home and change clothes for the night shift at the store. A few minutes after she got home, she heard the sound of a motorcycle and looked out the window. Junior.

"Hey," she said, stepping down from the porch.

"Hey." He walked over to the fence separating the yard from the field beside it, and she followed him. "Lord, how many hours did I spend over there in the tobacco patch?" He rested one arm on a fence post and looked out at the empty field. "So. What do you think?"

"About . . ."

"About my motorcycle ministry."

"Well." She took a deep breath. "It seems like you've already got a following. That's—" She nodded toward the trees in the distance, thinking about how to say something that was both positive and true. "That's encouraging."

He paused. "But you think I'm biting off more than I can chew, don't you? You think I'm not going to be able to do it."

She shook her head. "I didn't say that."

"I'm talking about what you think, not what you said. You think I'm not ready, that I haven't studied the Bible enough to be a preacher."

She shrugged. She once would have had an opinion about it, but it didn't matter to her anymore. He just wasn't aware that she had changed. "I don't know, Junior. What do *you* think?"

He leaned back against the post and crossed his arms. "You always knew the Bible backwards and forwards. Daddy used to get so mad at me because I couldn't quote scripture like you or find verses as soon as he called them out. I'd be flipping through the Bible for ten minutes after you'd done found it. Remember that time he made me stay up half the night trying to get me to memorize the verses he was calling out?"

Jeannie shook her head. "No."

"No, *you* don't remember because *you* got to go to bed." He laughed. "He goes, 'You ain't going to bed until you can quote ever' one of these I call out.' But I never could get them all, and he was wore out, so he let me go—I don't know—somewhere around midnight, I reckon."

"Wow. That sounds rough."

They watched two squirrels skitter up the oak tree and chase each other back down.

"How come you've been playing hooky from church?" he asked. "I mean, I'm not judging you about it. I'm just curious."

She felt there was something she needed to tell him about herself, but it wasn't fully formed yet. She didn't have the words. Her faith had changed in the years since Debbie died, but she didn't know how to explain the change or what the dimensions were. It felt like something enormous but invisible that she carried around everywhere, all the time. She'd lost her sister, and she couldn't blame anybody but herself for backing away from her at the end, when she most needed help. Somehow, all the promises of eternity with her loved ones didn't assuage that guilt and sorrow one bit. She'd lost her dream of the Gospelettes too, her ambition for all those years. Over time, she'd gone to church less and less. It wasn't that she didn't believe, exactly. She believed *something*. She just wasn't sure what. She'd even asked to work Sundays at Handi-Mart so that she could use work as an excuse to her parents for her absence from church.

A few years ago, when Brother Henry Morris, the church's former song leader, died, Brother Clarence asked Jeannie to take his place. "No one in our congregation is more qualified than you, Jeannie," he had said kindly. "I believe the Lord would be pleased to have you in that position." It was painful to tell him no, but she knew her heart wasn't in it. In fact, she hadn't sung at all since the day Debbie died. Eight years.

They heard a motorcycle coming up the road and watched it turn in her driveway. "Somebody's here to see you," Junior said, smiling.

They watched Wick amble over to the fencerow and stop in front of them. "What's shaking, Gospelettes?"

Junior gave him a thumb-lock handshake. "Hey, brother! Where were you today?"

Wick looked at Jeannie as he answered. "Here and there."

"I was hoping you'd come out," Junior said. "We had a bunch of the guys at church and then went riding. Had a good time."

"So I heard," Wick said.

"All right. I've got to get back and—do some stuff. Come out and ride with us, brother," Junior said, winking at Jeannie as he swaggered to his motorcycle.

Jeannie cleared her throat, waiting for Wick to say why he was there.

"Well." Wick squinted up at the sky and was quiet for a minute. "I just came here to tell you that I'm . . . you know . . . I'm working on getting myself straight. Me and Junior are going to AA meetings. He's kind of staying on my ass about it, so . . . I just thought you should know that. Since I'm doing it for you."

Jeannie was touched and yet, somehow, annoyed. Of course, she was glad Wick was getting clean, but the time for him to do it for her had long since passed. She'd finally started dating. DeWayne Deaton from church had invited her over for dinner at his house a couple of times, asking for her input on some songs he had written. There was no chemistry there, she had to acknowledge, but it had been three years since she'd divorced Wick, and she figured she had to start somewhere.

"I'm glad, Wick. I really am." She sighed. "But you need to do it for you. Not for me."

He ran a hand through his hair and rubbed his neck. "It ain't easy, Jeannie. I'd like it if you'd be proud of me."

She smiled a little. "I *am* proud of you, Wick." She couldn't deny what she felt every time she saw him. But she knew what to expect from him. More of the same.

"I'm walking through hell right now," he said. He patted his pockets, found one cigarette in a pack, and tapped it out. His hands shook a little as he lit up. "Do you believe in me?"

She rolled that word—believe—around in her mind, examining it. She told Wick what she hadn't been able to tell Junior. "I don't know what I believe anymore, Wick. About anything." Belief seemed like a relic from her ancient past.

# Working on a Building

Jeannie drove home from work on a Sunday afternoon, car windows down so she could smell the spring rain in the fields. When she got home, Lee Ann was back from Garland and Big Jean's, where she'd had Sunday dinner after church.

"How was your visit?" Jeannie sat on the couch, where Lee Ann had camped with her textbook and notes, studying for an exam.

Lee Ann shrugged. "It was cool." She lay her head on Jeannie's shoulder, and Jeannie put her arms around her and rested her cheek on top of Lee Ann's head. Jeannie thought of how proud Debbie would be of her daughter if she could see her now, so mature and responsible, heading into her senior year of high school. Sometimes Jeannie had angry conversations in her head with Debbie over the fact that she had left the kids. At some point, she had migrated from guilt to anger over Debbie's death and found that anger felt better. She didn't know if her overdose was on purpose or not, and it didn't matter. Either way, she made her choice. She valued belonging to a man more than her own life and her own children, Jeannie had decided.

"Cool." Jeannie laughed. "Not a word I normally use when referring to Mamaw and Papaw, but OK."

"Mamaw made some killer friend chicken."

"Better than mine?" Jeannie pretended to take offense.

"She made me take some leftovers in aluminum foil. They're in the fridge."

"Was it used pieces of foil that she had folded up in a drawer?"

"Well, duh."

"I swear, she's been reusing some of those same pieces since the seventies."

"That's cool. She's, like, an environmentalist."

Jeannie hooted. "Right. Not on purpose, but I guess the effect is the same."

Lee Ann tilted her head back to look up at Jeannie. "You aren't super close to Mamaw, are you?" The kid knew how to cut to the chase.

Jeannie sighed. "No. I guess I'm not super close to Mamaw or Papaw either one."

"But you used to be close to Papaw, didn't you? Back when y'all had the group? Like, the two of you kind of got your heads together and ran the show, right?"

"Yeah." Jeannie smiled to herself and nodded. "I guess you could say that."

"Were you the favorite?"

"Nah. I'd say Junior is the once and future king of the Holliman children."

"So . . ." Lee Ann sat up and faced Jeannie. "Uncle Junior made an announcement at church today. About the new church? Do you know about it?" She cocked her head, brows knitted.

"No. What did he say?"

Lee Ann grimaced. "So, like, they're outgrowing the old church, with all of Uncle Junior's motorcycle dudes and other new people coming in, and they've raised a bunch of money, and he says they're building a new church out here at the farm."

Jeannie turned toward her, startled. "Out here?" She pointed at the floor.

"Yeah. He said at the old Holliman farm. I asked him where exactly it was going up, and he said over there as you come across the bridge." She pointed northward.

"Huh." Jeannie stared into space, imagining the field beside her house covered with a parking lot, her peace and tranquility shattered.

"He didn't even tell you?" Lee Ann asked. "I mean, you're gonna have, like, a thousand people next door."

"Yeah, it would have been nice. But Junior's not one for keeping people updated on his plans." Jeannie rolled her eyes. "What am I talking about? Junior never has plans. He just flies by the seat of his pants." She imagined that Garland worked it all out for him, donating the land to the church for a new building. Well, it was his to give. Jeannie was just living there.

"Evidently it's going to be gi-freaking-normous," Lee Ann said. "Papaw was like, 'People are coming from all over the country!'" She did a perfect imitation of Garland's old-timer's country accent. "But I think he's exaggerating."

"Maybe a little," Jeannie snorted, propping her sock feet on the coffee table.

"I guess it's gonna be harder for you to pretend you're at work every Sunday morning with the church next door." Lee Ann smirked.

Jeannie closed her eyes and laughed. She hadn't realized that Lee Ann saw through her, but of course she did. "I tried to get away from the church," she said, "and now it's following me."

For the next several months, Jeannie watched the new church—beige metal trimmed by brown brick with long windows and connecting annexes, angled like a giant book standing half open, pages down— grow out of the field that once grew cheerful yellow butterweed next to her house. It was huge and otherworldly, like a spaceship that had landed just outside Bethel, sending the wildlife skittering away. When it was finished, she walked around the front of the building with the family while Junior pointed out its impressive details. It lacked the quaint charm of their old church building and the stately dignity of the big churches downtown, and she wondered who was on the building committee that let this thing be constructed.

Still, it was impressive in size and ambition. Over thirty thousand square feet. The glass doors in front opened into a wide, airy vestibule with a ceiling higher than she could guess, an echoing tile floor, and a gurgling fountain in the center. Sets of wooden doors opened into the sanctuary, and hallways on either side led to offices for the pastors and other church leaders, Sunday school rooms, the fellowship hall, the youth center with its own coffeehouse, theater, and gym with a walking track and basketball court.

"We're aiming to have church members in here all the time, not just on Sundays but every day," Junior said, leading the family down a long, carpeted hallway, past room after freshly painted new room. He strutted, filled out now and packed tightly in jeans and a T-shirt, chains jangling. "It's going to be a way of life, not just a place people get dressed up and go to on Sundays and then forget about. We're going to have classes all during the week. Aerobics, country line dancing, singles get-togethers—"

"Line dancing?" Jeannie peered into a large, mirrored room, perhaps designed for just that.

"Yeah!" Junior grinned. "And scrapbooking, investing—"

"Wow." She didn't know what else to say.

"And get this. I asked for this meeting room just for the King's Highway Warriors." He opened a door and turned on the light, revealing a room featuring a four-wall mural of riders on Harley-Davidson motorcycles cruising through a landscape of hills, trees, a bridge, a river, and the sprawling new Church at Holliman Farms—or "the compound," as Jeannie liked to call it.

"Shoot, me and Brian should just move in here," Patty said. "It's so big, nobody would even notice." Brian was a member of the King's Highway Warriors and her fiancé.

They walked through the rest of the church, gasping and cooing over each new room. Jeannie noticed that Garland was uncharacteristically quiet, though. He walked around, arms crossed, lips pressed in a thin line, a grim realization seeming to dawn on his face.

To think Junior's first unpromising sermon (Jeannie had been there, so she knew) had evolved into all of this! He'd acquired a following, no doubt about it. Word got out among bikers about laidback services with gospel-rock music and casual attire, and soon other people—"cagers"—were attending. Junior had started a program just for single parents and their kids, an undisguised Christian dating service, really. Youth attendance went way up, followed by more and more families. JP had even started attending occasionally, to the family's astonishment. And Randall, who was studying music in college, came home on Sundays to sing in DeWayne Deaton's worship team.

"I'm all turned around," Big Jean said at the end of the tour. "I feel like I'm at the mall. Garland always has to lead me to the right door or else I'd just wander around all night."

"You could definitely get lost in here," Jeannie said, raising her eyebrows at Patty, who was too impressed by it all to appreciate her irony.

Junior led them back to the front entry, Garland by his side, Patty beside Big Jean, who limped along behind them in her Sunday shoes (she wouldn't wear her sneakers into the church, country line dancing or not), Jeannie trailing in back.

At the first Sunday service in the new building, Jeannie walked through a crowd of strangers, so many people she didn't recognize. The vestibule rang with their high laughter. She could see no way out of being there for Junior's big day, as he took the helm and Brother Clarence scaled back and became assistant pastor.

Inside the sanctuary, she finally saw some familiar old faces. Sister Nannie, Brother Jenks, Sister Katherine. And her parents, near the front in the center set of theater-style seats approximately where they sat in pews in the old church, with Patty, Brian, JP, and Lee Ann. She walked down the aisle and scooted in beside them.

And there, on the stage, illuminated by the recessed lights, was Junior. *Brother* Junior, in his olive-green T-shirt, black leather vest, well-worn blue jeans, and black boots. He sat in the pastor's chair, holding a big Bible open in his lap. She tried to see him as the others in the church might rather than as the twin who knew him too well, but it was impossible.

DeWayne and the praise team were firing up the crowd with their electrified instruments, flashing colored lights and projecting song lyrics onto the walls. It was excruciating, but she still smiled at Randall, a member of the praise team, holding a microphone and leading the congregation in song, even though there was no way he could see her with all that was going on in the sanctuary. *He's turned out all right too*, she said to Debbie, as if her spirit were floating above them.

As for DeWayne, she had let that relationship die a natural death, not even sure who had made the last call. It was a relief to let it go. She thought they could remain friends, though he was pretty entrenched in the church world that she'd been drifting away from, so maybe not.

She suddenly missed performing. Brother Clarence had wanted her to take over as song leader, and she had turned it down. If what she was hearing from the speakers was the direction the church was going in, it was just as well. She was forty-two, and she knew every generation thought their music was better than the next generation's music, but this truly was garbage. Absolute garbage. Sugary ballads to Jesus, crowing anthems, trance-inducing chorus repetitions. And why exactly did DeWayne need a ten-person praise team on stage all singing the melody? Of course, she had to acknowledge that her worst composition, "Speak the Victory," had been every bit as bad as these, but overall, the Gospelettes' music had been real, heartfelt, none of this faux emotion. She flashed back to moments singing with the Gospelettes when she'd felt the music lift her from her body. She remembered hearing Marcella Benton at that showcase back in 1973, her voice like a physical force, removing everyone's defenses. Like it was peeling Jeannie's skin off and leaving her at God's mercy.

Junior's meandering sermon came to a close in a pleasant enough way. "God loves us all," he told the congregation. "He loves you." He pointed toward the bikers. "And he loves you." He pointed to Sister Lucy, who looked sour as ever, sitting on the stage next to Brother Clarence. "And he loves you." He pointed toward a row of teenagers. "He loves you all the same. Young. Old. Fat. Skinny. Short. Tall. Black. White. Red. Yellow. Jew. Greek. I-talian. He is always fair and just. You think God has ever been unfair and unjust and unloving?" He walked back to the podium and lifted his Bible above his head. "Read every verse in the Bible. You won't find it in here!"

Jeannie sat counting up all the places in the Bible she could think of where God did play favorites, beginning with favoring Abel over Cain, moving on to Jacob and Esau, and so forth. Of course, that contrasted with the New Testament welcoming message from Jesus, which she supposed Junior was trying to get at here. But who were they *really* willing to welcome to the table? The young, old, fat, skinny, short, tall people in that room, yes. Throw in a few other races plus Jews and Italians, maybe, up to a point. But gay folks or Muslims? Or anybody who didn't line up exactly with their way of thinking—on anything? What about somebody like her, who wasn't even sure what she believed anymore? No, not acceptable. She sighed, ran a thumbnail along the grooves in her Bible's leather cover. It seemed like there was a sweet spot of knowledge that fostered good church citizenship, and maybe she had passed it.

The sermon was over, and everyone was standing, embracing, all talking at once, heading toward the potluck feast in the fellowship hall, which was practically in Jeannie's backyard. She turned toward the doors, eager to get out. She had already told Lee Ann she was going to skip the potluck, go home and put on her sweats and read.

She was in the vestibule, almost to the door, when someone bumped into her. She looked up.

"Wick!" She was surprised to see him there. He wore jeans and a new-looking black T-shirt. She felt an odd relief that he was dressed like himself, not in "church clothes." Even now, after all that had happened, she wanted him to retain the essence of who he was, the Wick she remembered walking into Ogles, fully in his flesh and aware of his effect on her. He was heavier now, though, and his face looked fleshy and tired, the playfulness gone.

"Look who's here," he said, locking eyes with her. "A few years too late."

She smiled sadly. "Well. It's never too late to get sober, right?" She hoped she sounded neutral, that she wasn't giving him any false hopes about them getting back together.

He said something, but she couldn't hear him. Chattering church-goers clogged the vestibule, so many people who seemed to have so much to say. "What?" she asked, squeezing through the crowd toward the door.

He followed her outside. "I said, 'I was hoping I'd see you here.'"

She didn't say anything, kept her face blank, polite.

"I guess I waited too late to hear the Gospelettes," he added.

They stood in front of the church, aswarm with people. She looked up at him. "Yeah. A little late for that."

They walked through the back parking lot that stood between the church and Jeannie's house. At the end of the pavement was a gap in the fence that she slipped through when going back and forth. She stopped and cleared her throat.

"You aren't going to the potluck?" he asked.

"No—" She started to make an excuse but let it drop. It was Wick. No excuses necessary. "No."

"I'd like to eat with you," he said. "I miss that. We could go out to Floyd's Barbecue if you don't want to eat here."

"No, thank you, Wick." She walked through the fence gap and lifted one hand to wave goodbye and hold him there. She missed him. But not enough to go back to what used to be.

# Through It All

Mostly, the family accepted that, between her work schedule and the fact that she was a grown woman, Jeannie didn't come to church as much as they might think she should, but sometimes Big Jean talked her into coming for a special event. In the spring of 1999, DeWayne left his position as minister of music, and Junior appointed Randall to take over. "You don't want to miss his first day leading the music," Big Jean told Jeannie over the phone.

"I'll be there," Jeannie said. Her parents were getting old, and she hated to disappoint them. They'd had so many disappointments in life. Besides, Lee Ann was coming home for a weekend visit from college too, so she'd get to see both the kids. They weren't really kids anymore, but they always would be to her, the closest she ever got to having her own.

"Did Junior tell you he hired Wick to be the groundskeeper at the church?" Big Jean asked.

"No, he didn't." Jeannie looked out her kitchen window at the church. "Not too worried about nepotism, is he?"

Wick had started out riding with the King's Highway Warriors, then began coming to church regularly, and had even gotten baptized. "It was you that planted the seeds, Jeannie," Big Jean said. "You were a good witness to him when y'all were married, and it might've taken twenty-some years, but they finally growed."

Jeannie figured that leaving him had done more to set Wick on the straight path than any witnessing she had done over the years, but it didn't matter. He could move into the church for all she cared.

"He wasn't over here much when y'all were married, but he must've heard enough," Garland was saying in the background. "He's bound to have heard something I said about the Lord and let it into his heart."

"Daddy said, 'He wasn't over here much—'" Big Jean began.

"I heard him," Jeannie said, rolling her eyes.

She had heard that Wick had been clean for quite a while, no drugs or alcohol. "He asks me about you every time I see him," Junior had told her recently. "And I see him almost every day."

"Well," Jeannie had replied.

"Somebody said he had him a woman in Tennessee, but ain't nobody seen her with him," Junior had added, though Jeannie hadn't asked. "I think he doesn't want to have anybody around in case you decide to come back."

"Well."

A few months before, Junior had married a woman named Rosie who had four kids, and Patty had been married to Highway Warrior Brian for a few years. Jeannie had recently started dating someone. Working at Handi-Mart one afternoon, she had waited on Lee Ann's former biology teacher, Tom Becker. They had had some friendly conversations at school functions in the past, and he remembered her and asked about Lee Ann. "She's majoring in biology and wants to be a researcher," Jeannie told him. "You must have really inspired her."

"Well, you did a great job raising her," he said, smiling. "She was every teacher's dream student."

He stood in the store and talked with her for a while, stepping aside to let other people make their purchases, then resuming the conversation. He was forty-one (four years younger than Jeannie), divorced, no kids. He was an amateur musician and self-declared "music nerd" and had been intrigued—and, she thought, possibly amused—by her gospel music background. He had lived all over, played in bands, worked in labs, started a PhD program but dropped out, and then went back to school and got a teaching certificate. Now he lived in Bowling Green and drove back and forth to Bethel to work.

"You mean you don't want to live here in Bethel?" she teased. "Not enough excitement for you?"

He laughed. "I get plenty of excitement teaching high school. I just want to live where there's a bookstore and a coffee shop and a couple of movie theaters."

"That's reasonable." She smiled.

He smiled back and ran his hand over his bleached buzz cut. Lee Ann had told her that the kids used to call him Mr. Sting because he resembled the singer. He did have the look of an aging, pleasantly mellowed rock star. Maybe it wasn't quite the level of excitement she'd felt for Wick all those years ago, but she was definitely attracted.

"Do you have any plans for Saturday night?" he asked.

So Jeannie had gone with him to eat out and see *The Matrix* in Bowling Green that weekend and then to see a bluegrass band at Station Inn in Nashville the next weekend, and soon they were seeing each other every weekend and throughout the week as well.

Lee Ann said he was a really nice man. "I mean, if you and Uncle Wick aren't going to get back together, I guess Mr. Becker would be my next choice for you," she had said.

Jeannie invited Tom over for dinner that Saturday night. Lee Ann and her new boyfriend, Nate, were visiting from college. She made a full Italian meal from her new cookbook, and Tom brought two bottles of Chianti. "Ooh la la," Lee Ann giggled when she saw Jeannie set out her new wine glasses. "Oh, wait. That's what the French say. What do the Italians say?"

"No idea," Jeannie whispered, grinning, "but don't let Tom know that I'm a rube who's never owned wine glasses before."

Lee Ann put a forefinger in front of her lips. "No rubes here."

Over dinner, they talked about Lee Ann and Nate's college experience, some of the highlights of Tom's teaching career at Bethel High School, and, finally, Jeannie's years of performing with the Gospelettes.

"You were on an actual TV show?" Tom asked Jeannie.

"She wasn't just *on* the show," Lee Ann said. "She was, like, a big deal."

"What did you do?" Nate asked.

"Oh, I was musical director for the show," Jeannie said. "I planned all the music. We performed in every show. I wrote some of the songs. Booked acts. Produced albums. Handled all the music business." She smiled into the distance. Now that she was eleven years away from Oren Alford, she could remember fondly all the interesting things she'd done in her Nashville days.

"So why did you leave?" Tom asked.

Jeannie sighed. "It's a long story." She waved it away. "I'll tell you about it sometime."

"OK, but . . . you left there and just went to work at Handi-Mart?" he prodded. "Why? Why didn't you use some of those contacts? Keep your foot in the door in Nashville?"

Jeannie shrugged. "I don't know. I was . . . kind of stressed out."

"My mom had just died," Lee Ann said. Everyone got quiet and looked at her. "My mom died, and Aunt Jeannie was taking care of me and Randall, and she dropped everything else." She looked at Jeannie. "Right?"

Jeannie put her arm around Lee Ann's shoulders. "Honey. It's not *your* fault. I made my own decisions."

"I know." Lee Ann smiled. "But that's why."

# Ain't Got Time for You Devil

Jeannie and Lee Ann walked across the yard, surrounded on three sides by the golden splendor of the farm in autumn, all yellowed fields and orange-rusted trees and distant faded-red barns, and on one side, ahead of them, by the beige metal and brown brick monster that haunted Jeannie's peace. They walked through the gap in the fence into the mostly empty parking lot, just starting to fill up. They had decided to walk over early to wish Randall the best on his first day as minister of music.

"Here they come," Lee Ann said, as they darted around and side-stepped the lines of cars, trucks, and motorcycles beginning to fill in the spaces.

Jeannie could think of only one change from the old Bethel Independent Church of the Pentecost to the new Church at Holliman Farms that she liked, and that was the fact that she and Lee Ann were wearing jeans and boots instead of dresses and pantyhose. Mostly just the older churchgoers still wore suits and dresses.

Inside, they found Randall in the vestibule surrounded by a group of men and women in motorcycle garb. "Hoo boy," Lee Ann said, cutting her eyes at Jeannie. Jeannie waved at him, and he excused himself and walked over.

"So good to see you two!" He gave each of them a hug.

"Hey, bub!" Lee Ann said, patting his back. "Nice goatee."

"Congratulations, Randall!" Jeannie smiled. "Your mama would be so proud."

"Thanks, Aunt Jeannie." Randall smiled at the floor. "I can't believe you actually came. You've really been hiding out over there."

Jeannie felt the condemnation behind the words but chose to ignore it. Undoubtedly he had been talking to Garland and Big Jean and Junior and Patty and had joined the family project to bring her back into the fold that she had quietly left. "Hiding in plain sight," she said. "Are you excited?" She could hear loud, frenetic, recorded music playing in the sanctuary.

"I'm excited by all that God has in store for us!" Randall declared, lifting his fists and shaking them. "He has some great plans for the church that Uncle Junior is going to announce today."

"Awesome," Lee Ann said with a clear lack of enthusiasm.

Jeannie hoped to steer the conversation in a better direction. "So where did DeWayne go? Did he get hired at another church?"

Randall twisted his mouth and looked away. "No, I don't think so. I hope not, anyway."

"Why? What happened?"

Randall drew a deep breath. "Someone saw him in Nashville in some . . . not very Christian activities, so Uncle Junior let him go."

Jeannie frowned. "Oh? Like what activities?"

Randall made a grim face. "He was walking around with a group of gay men, and he was wearing . . ." He waved his hands in the air. "Some kind of necklace. I don't know exactly. A necklace made of big wooden beads or coconut shells. I don't know what. But clearly . . . gay."

Jeannie stood completely still, letting it all sink in. "DeWayne is gay?" she asked finally.

"Afraid so." Randall nodded. "Did you not pick up on that when you were dating?"

Jeannie tried to home in on one of the many emotions battling within her. Surprise, confusion, sadness, anger. She looked at Lee Ann and saw the same reflected there. "I didn't know. I just . . . thought we weren't a good match."

Randall raised his eyebrows. "Well, now you know why."

"So Uncle Junior heard some gossip about him and just dumped him?" Lee Ann asked, her face reddening.

Randall made an exaggerated blink of contempt. "It wasn't just gossip. He asked him if he was gay, and he said yes."

"So?" Lee Ann demanded.

"So DeWayne made a decision to do what he did, and Uncle Junior had to make a decision that was best for the church." Randall frowned and took a step back. "I have to go get started now."

"OK, honey." Jeannie felt like her voice was coming from outside her body and that there were layers of cotton between her and everyone else.

"I'm not going in there." Jeannie heard a voice and realized it was Lee Ann. "I'm going home."

"Yeah." Jeannie grabbed Lee Ann's hand and squeezed. "Yeah. I get it." She watched Lee Ann stalk out the front door, passing several people who were greeting her, without reply. She didn't know if Debbie would be proud of her daughter in that moment, but Jeannie knew for sure that *she* was. Lee Ann had the gumption and moral bearings she only wished she'd had at that age.

Jeannie walked into the sanctuary, down to where her family always sat. She would ask Junior about DeWayne. Maybe there were things she didn't know. Maybe he wanted out anyway. Garland and Big Jean joined her, making a big to-do about her being there, and then Patty and Brian sat on her other side. Patty lifted her hair off her back to show her the top of her new tattoo, an enormous pair of Harley-Davidson wings with "Heavenly-Debbie" in the patch in the middle where the company name would normally be.

"Wow," Jeannie said, figuring that was the most appropriate thing she could say.

After the music, Junior took the stage. The next several minutes were a confusing mash-up, something about the year 2000 approaching, a series of sermons they were going to do on the Last Days. Pre-tribulation. Post-tribulation. The rapture of the church. The Arabs. The Russians. The Chinese. The United States. The European Union. The euro and the dollar. The Book of Revelation. Angels with golden candlesticks. A pale horse with a rider named Death. Beasts and seals and scrolls. Earthquakes, fire, plagues. Dragons and harlots. Blood up to the horses' bridles.

When Junior announced the upcoming series, "The Countdown to Armageddon," the King's Highway Warriors cheered, seemingly looking forward to some relief from the kind, gentle, and somewhat boring Jesus they usually heard about.

"We been knowing a long time there's gonna be a war, with the UN coming against the US," Brian was saying to Patty as the cheers subsided. "About time somebody's talking about it."

Jeannie watched Junior preen before the cheering crowd, nodding and shouting, "Amen!" She was sorry she came. She wished she had left with Lee Ann.

"I want to introduce to you our special guest preacher who's going to be delivering these sermons over the next nine weeks until we hit the new millennium," Junior went on. "And then who knows what? The Lord only knows! But I know y'all are going to be excited because a lot of you have seen this warrior for God in action before." He reached out his arm, and a man in an expensive-looking navy suit walked to him. "Brother Oren Alford!"

And there was Jeannie in the middle of it all. In the middle of the church, in the middle of the row of seats, in the middle of her family. And Brother Alford looked out into the crowd and spotted her right away and smiled.

# THE NEW MILLENNIUM

# If That Isn't Love

On the first day of the year 2000, Jeannie stood out on her back porch and watched the parking lot next door fill up with vehicles, overflowing into the field behind her house. The Church at Holliman Farms was holding a "New Millennium Day of Prayer and Praise," a full day of prayers for Christ's return, sermons by Oren Alford and Junior, and music by the church praise team and guest performers.

Brother Alford's idea was to have a special reunion performance by the Gospelettes. Junior had been crazy enough to propose it to Jeannie in the middle of Thanksgiving dinner at their parents' house, the first time she had been around her family since he had brought Brother Alford to the church.

She had looked at Garland, then Big Jean, then Patty, all of whom were avoiding her eyes. "Are you kidding me? A Gospelettes reunion without Debbie?"

"Jeannie. Come on." Junior plopped more mashed potatoes on his plate. "Is that what Debbie would want? For us to stop singing together?"

"Of course not," Randall said.

Lee Ann stared down at her plate.

"I would love to hear you all sing live," Junior's wife, Rosie, said. "I've heard so many great things about the Gospelettes."

"I'd say if the Lord tells you to sing, you'd better sing," Patty's husband, Brian, said in an almost threatening tone.

Jeannie glared at him. Why were they even in the conversation? If Junior wanted to propose such a thing, he should have done it privately or at least with just the remaining members of the Gospelettes, not with these *strangers* who knew nothing about their history with

*Speak the Victory!* She stood up from the table. "My family knows how I feel about Oren Alford. If a Gospelettes reunion ever happened, it would *not* be at an event that included that man." She dropped her napkin in her chair and turned to go.

"Sit down!" Garland barked, apparently unaware of how frail he was now, no longer as threatening as he'd once seemed.

"Honey, finish your plate," Big Jean pleaded. "We won't talk about it right now."

"What do you mean by 'that man'?" Junior asked. "That man is helping me save the church! That church had one foot in the grave when Brother Clarence was in charge, and we're bringing it back to life! The offerings are double what they were before he came in."

"Amen!" Brian said.

"What did he do?" Lee Ann asked.

"Jeannie didn't like how he raised money," Garland said.

"Jeannie don't know how much money it takes to keep up a building and pay employees," Junior said.

"Women don't know where money comes from, but they're real good at spending it," Brian said.

Jeannie resisted the overpowering urge to throw the gravy boat at Brian's head but not the urge to point her finger at him and yell, "You! Don't! Know! Shit!" punctuating each word with a finger jab.

The room went completely silent. She looked around the table at her whole family. None of them knew the truth. If they knew—at least, if Garland and Big Jean knew—how Oren Alford had manipulated Debbie, luring her in under the pretense of praying for her failing marriage, having sex with her right there in his so-called prayer closet, allowing his wife to slap her around, surely they would wake up from this spell he seemed to have them under. The problem was the promise she'd made to Debbie that she would never tell them. It would be disrespectful to her memory to tell her secret now, when she wasn't there to give her own version of events. Debbie wouldn't want her children to know that she'd had an affair while she was married either, even though Jerry Lee had left her and was having his own affairs for years by that point. Debbie had asked one thing of Jeannie before she died, to keep this secret. Jeannie couldn't just decide to tell Debbie's story, no matter how good her reason was. She shouldn't have to. What they already knew about him ought to have been enough.

"I can't do this," she said. She grabbed her coat and purse on the way out the door, stopping only to say, "Sorry, Mama!"

Out on her back porch, getting some fresh air and gazing at the horizon, Jeannie was startled by a voice saying, "That ground's soft, and I ain't pulling them out of the mud when they get stuck." She turned and saw Wick a few feet away, looking at the vehicles in the field.

"I don't blame you," she said.

He put one foot on the bottom step and looked up at her. "I guess you've seen me over at the church a lot. Did anybody tell you about my new career?"

"They did." She nodded. "How's that going?"

He looked toward the trees in the distance and squinted in the bright sunlight. "It's all right. I just keep everything clean and running. Mow the grass. Do repairs. Shit like that. I figured that would keep me busy and away from, you know . . . old habits." He turned back toward her. "You know I've been clean for almost three years now?"

Jeannie gave him a tight smile. "That's great. I'm really glad, Wick."

He seemed disappointed by her response. He had a heaviness about him that was more than the weight he'd gained in recent years. She realized he was about to turn fifty. She could almost see the young man she'd fallen for all those years ago, encased in excess flesh.

"Isn't that what you always wanted, Jeannie? A man with an honest job. A man in the church." He waved his arm at the church building. "I've made a life out of this."

She couldn't even look at the church, enormous and hideous, demanding attention. The old homeplace had been so quiet and lovely, and now every time she looked out her window or sat out on the porch, she saw *that thing*. "It *was* what I wanted, a long time ago," she said.

"But not anymore?" He looked stricken. She could see him trying to make sense of what she was saying. "What happened?"

She didn't have the time or the inclination to go into all that. She wasn't even sure she knew the answer. "It's hard to explain."

He was quiet for a long moment. "Well, can you try?"

She shrugged. "Just the years, Wick. Years and years of little changes. Grief. Disappointments. Lost dreams. Seeing things with older eyes." She looked back at the wide expanse of beige metal that made up the back of the church and the rows of shiny pickup trucks and SUVs. She saw two middle-aged couples walking through the field behind her house toward the building, the women wearing identical angled blond bobs and the men wearing identical cowboy boots. Even from fifty yards away, she could see an attitude about them that she didn't like, a confidence in their rightness that they wore along with their similar outfits. She knew she was judging them, but she also knew that if she walked over and asked them what they believed about anything, they'd give the same answers they'd heard from Brother Alford and Junior.

"I think that son-of-a-bitch preacher is trying to take over," Wick said, scowling. "I've been trying to tell Junior, but he won't listen."

"Me too," Jeannie said.

"I guess his TV show went off the air?"

"Oh, yeah. A few years ago."

"Mm-hm. He came sniffing around when he heard about the new church," Wick said. "Smelled money from all the way down in Nashville. Next thing I heard was Brother Clarence is retiring. That made me real suspicious. Now Junior and Alford are calling themselves co-pastors, and the King's Highway Warriors are eating it with a spoon."

"It's sickening," Jeannie agreed. She tapped the porch railing. "OK. Gotta go to work." She turned to go in the house.

"Jeannie?"

She turned to face him. "Yeah?"

"Just so you know, I'm on your side," he said. "Not theirs."

She smiled. It was good to know.

# In the Garden

Spring at the old homeplace was a festival for the senses, with every green thing bursting, the sky full of birdsong, dew-fresh morning air. Jeannie felt as if she'd only been *acquainted* with the seasons when she lived in town. Now, after living on Papaw Virgil's farm for eight years, they were kinfolks whose habits she'd come to know well.

Tom had come to love spending time there too. When they had first started dating, he always wanted her to come to his apartment in Bowling Green on weekends, or he'd suggest they get a hotel room in Nashville and go to some music shows. But the peace and beauty of the farm won him over, and they started splitting their weekends between her place and his. She no longer worried about whether Garland and Big Jean might see his car parked in her driveway early on Sunday mornings when they came to church. As close as she was getting to fifty, it was about time she lived her life her own way.

They sat out on the back porch drinking coffee on a Sunday morning, reading the *New York Times*, which Tom had driven fifteen miles, over the state line, to purchase. He read aloud parts of an opinion piece on corporate farming replacing family farms and shook his head.

"Yeah," Jeannie said. "Daddy left the farm to work in a factory, and now the factory's leaving." He had just found out three weeks before, and within a week, it would be gone. "I don't know what people are supposed to do for a living."

"Hmm." Tom looked up. "Maybe the megachurch next door is hiring."

Jeannie sat with her back toward the church, doing her best to forget it was there. "I think I need to plant a tree right there." She pointed at the space between her porch and the fence that separated her yard from the church parking lot. "Something low and wide." That reminded her of Sally's grave under the weeping willow tree in Wick's yard. An unbearable sadness washed over her, and she stood quickly and picked up her mug. "Need a refill?"

"Not yet."

She went into the kitchen, wiped her eyes, and finished her coffee standing over the sink, looking out the window at Tom. Sometimes she couldn't believe she had found him—right there in Bethel. Someone smart and open minded. Someone who read newspapers and books and thought deeply about things and enjoyed talking to her about them. He wasn't arrogant about the fact that he had college degrees and she didn't. He recognized her intelligence and praised her for encouraging Randall and Lee Ann to go to college even though that hadn't worked out for her.

They both enjoyed music too. He played his guitar and had even wheedled her into singing with him a few times. "You've got a fucking amazing voice, Jeannie! I can't believe you don't use it anymore," he had said. She had shaken her head and fluttered her eyelashes, dismissing him. She didn't tell him that she didn't feel worthy of singing since Debbie died. How could she explain it? It didn't even make sense. She refilled her mug and went back outside.

Tom was peering over at the churchgoers as they started filling up the parking lot, his eyes narrowed, chin in hand.

"You look like you're formulating a theory," Jeannie said, sitting next to him.

"Did I tell you my parents are Baptist?" he asked.

"Yep."

"I used to argue with Dad about his literal interpretations of the Bible," he said. "I can't understand how, in the face of so many contradictory passages in the Bible and libraries of scientific data, he can state with absolute conviction that every word, every single word, in the Bible is literally true."

"Yeah. I've definitely changed my thinking on that," Jeannie said. She stretched out her legs and breathed deeply. "I mean, Jesus told parables all the time. Clearly, he saw the value of telling truths in metaphorical form. So why don't they get that?" She waved her hand at the church. "Can't there be larger spiritual truths in the Bible even if it's not all literally true?"

Tom swirled the coffee in his mug. "Spiritual? I don't know. What people think of as 'the spirit' or 'the soul' is really just a set of neural connections in the brain that generates spiritual perceptions, right?"

Jeannie eyed him over her mug. "I don't know." He looked handsome and slightly rumpled in a faded oxford shirt and wrinkled khakis. She wasn't sure if she wanted to kiss him or argue with him. She went for friendly argument. "I mean, maybe we have spiritual perceptions because there's a spirit to perceive."

"All right. Look at it this way." He tossed the front section of the newspaper on the table between them. "Humans evolved and developed the capacity for foresight. Which might have something to do with our capacity to enumerate. No other animal can count up to a hundred or a million or a billion, and then add one more, and so we became aware of the concept of infinity, of eternity. And of an eternity that will go on and on without us."

"It's all math's fault!" Jeannie joked.

Tom was in full science teacher mode. "We became aware of how brief life is," he went on. "Suddenly, we're staring death in the face, and we have a reaction very much like any prey has in the face of a predator: absolute terror." He paused. "So how did humans cope with this terror? They developed the concept of life after death! Then we began burying our dead and placing objects with them for the afterlife. And we developed religions to explain where we came from and where we're going. And this helped us because it eased that terror. It enabled us to feel protected. It stopped the dangerous physical reactions. So humans who had this mechanism for overcoming anxiety were able to survive."

She nodded. Anxiety. Fear. She couldn't help but think of her parents and their multitude of fears and the faith they relied on to keep moving through them.

"Now," Tom said, "the question is, Do we still need religion? I say, we've found a better way of explaining things, a more accurate way, with science, which is why I'm an atheist. So now we're in this transition period where we're learning to replace the old system with the new one." He looked over at the church again. "It might take a while."

Jeannie gazed up at the elm behind the house and listened to the cardinal perched on high. She often wondered how birds felt when they sang. It seemed to her like more than a utilitarian exercise.

"I've bored the hell out of you," he said. "I'm sorry."

She laughed. "You're kind of a geek, but I'm not bored. Just thinking."

"Tell me what you're thinking."

"Well, not really thinking. Remembering." She watched the cardinal fly to the feeder she'd set out in the yard. "I'm remembering how I used to feel when I would sing onstage."

"Yeah?"

She rubbed her fingertips across her lips. How to explain it? "It was like . . . certain songs had a . . ." She wanted to say "spirit," but it would be like speaking a foreign language with him. "Certain songs had an *energy* to them. And certain harmonies that we would do were just . . . *different*. Like, you could feel them in your body. My whole body would sort of vibrate, and I could feel . . ." She moved her hands to her neck and slid her fingers up the sides of her face. "I could feel this energy kind of move through me and out into the audience, and sometimes I would feel like . . . like I was actually floating? Like I wasn't even standing on the stage anymore. I was somewhere . . ." She wiggled her fingers above her head. "Somewhere up there."

He raised his eyebrows. "Wow. That sounds intense."

"So I guess I'm saying I'm not an atheist." She smiled and shrugged.

"Wild." He looked back at the church and squinted.

Jeannie turned around and saw Wick look at them and then walk the perimeter of the parking lot as if guarding something, or someone.

# Where No One Stands Alone

For months, Jeannie felt that she had been in a standoff with her family. They didn't talk about Oren Alford, who, with Junior's help, had moved himself into the church leadership right next door. She didn't go to church anymore or even step her foot across the fence line onto the property. She still called and checked on them all and occasionally stopped by for a short visit with her parents, but if the conversation turned toward church, she made a quick exit. It might have been terribly isolating if it weren't for the fact that she and Tom had been spending so much time in Nashville. He knew about the best hole-in-the-wall clubs, the most exciting up-and-comers, and where to find those underappreciated old-timers and songwriters that were the backbone of the city's music scene. They went to the Ryman and the Bluebird Cafe, open-mic nights and song-writers' showcases, honky-tonks and nightclubs and gospel brunches featuring Black singers (the kind of gospel music Tom could appreciate). He was always impressed when someone came over to say hello to Jeannie, remembering her from the show, often from working with her.

One Sunday, coming out of the bathroom after a gospel brunch at a restaurant in Nashville, Jeannie saw a woman going in and knew who it was immediately, despite the nearly three decades that had passed. She stopped and reached out to her. "Marcella? From the Benton Family Singers?"

The woman smiled and cocked her head. "Yes! And you're a Gospelette! From that show!"

They moved to the side of the hallway, out of the way of waiters carrying their platters of food, and grasped one another's arms. "Yes. Jeannie Holliman."

"Jeannie! That's right, that's right."

"You look just like you did when I saw you at that music festival back in the seventies!" Jeannie said.

Marcella fell against the wall and laughed. "I don't remember all this back in the seventies." She posed with her hands on her hips.

Jeannie felt overcome with joy. "Marcella! I was looking for you for years! When I did the music scheduling for the show, I wanted to have your family on as guests, but I couldn't seem to track you down." She was glad now that she hadn't dragged Marcella and her family into that cesspool, but at that time, she'd been bitterly disappointed.

"Oh, we had stopped performing together by then. I got married and had five kids." She laughed. "I was too busy for all that. Now I just sing at our church now and then."

"Five kids! That's great!"

"Well. Sometimes." Marcella laughed again. "What about you? Do you have kids? Are you still singing?"

Jeannie looked away and sighed. "No. And no. I mean, I raised my niece and nephew after my sister died, so they're mine, more or less. Well, my niece is anyway."

Marcella nodded. "And you don't sing? Not even at your church?" Her forehead wrinkled with concern.

Jeannie shook her head. "No. Our family group broke up after we left the show, and . . . my brother is the preacher at our church now, and . . . I don't go anymore." She groaned. "There's been a lot of drama. It's . . . complicated."

Marcella closed her eyes and shook her head. "I don't know what you're talking about. Family and church drama? What is that?" She gave Jeannie a pointed look, and they both laughed. She grasped Jeannie's forearms again. "You are always welcome to come to my church. I can't promise no drama, but I promise we will love you."

"I appreciate that," Jeannie said. "I'm not sure I want to go at all anymore, but, if I did, I'd want to go to yours and hear you sing."

"That's all right, sweetie," Marcella said, her eyes full of warm understanding. "Didn't you write songs too?"

"Yeah." Jeannie had a chest of drawers full of notebooks with songs scribbled in them. Sometimes songs came to her even now, like angels whispering in her ear. Sometimes she even pulled out a notebook and wrote one down. "Not so many gospel songs anymore, though. Other stuff has been coming to me lately. Not sure what it is or where it fits, you know?"

"Listen. I used to love to sing Aretha Franklin and Nina Simone and this, that, and the other, and you know what my mama and daddy would say? 'That's devil's music!'" Marcella shook her head. "I said, 'No. If God gave me this gift, it don't matter whether I'm singing at church or on the radio or rocking a baby to sleep. It don't matter if it's gospel or pop or opera.'"

Jeannie nodded. "You're right."

"I say it's all for God! Whether you know it or not!"

Somehow this felt true to Jeannie, despite all her doubts. "Absolutely."

"So you need to take some of them songs you've been writing and get out there and sing."

From the dining room came a woman's voice stretching the first note of "I Know I've Been Changed," a long jubilation, followed by shouts from the crowd. Jeannie and Marcella turned their heads toward the racket and back at each other, smiling, remembering the feeling when they brought forth that kind of reaction. "I'd better get in this restroom before they have to bring a mop," Marcella laughed, and they hugged goodbye.

Jeannie's encounter with Marcella stayed with her for days afterward. Maybe she was right. She *did* need to sing. And she needed to write and perform her own songs. The next week, she got out her notebooks and some old cassette tapes she had recorded. She was surprised the tapes still worked. She found a handful of songs that she still liked well enough to play and worked them up into a set. When Tom came over that weekend, she sat him down on the couch and asked him to listen.

After her first song, he fell back and covered his face with his hands. "Shit, Jeannie! Why have you been hiding this?"

She suppressed her smile, eyes wide. "What do you mean?"

He raised his hands in the air. "I mean you're blowing me away! I mean I'm jealous as hell because I wrote about a hundred songs for my college band, and not a one of them comes close to that." After she played her second song, he pointed at her. "You're doing an open mic in Nashville next weekend. No arguments."

The following weekend, at an open mic at a bar on the south side of Nashville, she was sitting at a table with Tom, nervously sipping a beer, afraid that it would make her have to pee as soon as she got on stage, when she heard someone say, "Jeannie?"

She looked up. It took a moment for her brain to register that the person in front of her, in a rhinestone cowboy suit and artfully drawn makeup, was DeWayne Deaton. "Hiiii." The word was just a long exhale.

"Hiiii," he said back.

She introduced him to Tom, and he sat at their table and accepted a drink. He was helping to run the open mic, serving as an emcee. "Really using my minister of music skills," he said.

"Definitely." Jeannie nodded. As hard as it had been for her to separate herself from her family and church, she imagined it must have been a hundred times harder for him. "DeWayne? Can I tell you something?"

"Of course."

"I don't agree with how Junior treated you. It's awful and narrow-minded and self-righteous, and I told him so. In fact, I still live next door to the church, but I haven't been back since I found out what happened. Between what he did to you and then bringing that snake oil salesman Oren Alford in, I just couldn't." She said all this in a rush, then paused. "I just wanted you to know that."

DeWayne smiled, looking down so that she saw the glitter on his eyelids. Then he looked her in the eye. "Oh, I can tell you some things."

He knew people who knew Oren Alford before and after the Gospelettes were with him. He'd been kicked out of the church where he was assistant pastor before the show. He'd had an inappropriate relationship with the pastor's daughter. And then, after the Gospelettes left *Speak the Victory!*, he had had an affair with the new music director and had made overtures to other young women and girls. DeWayne didn't know the specifics, but he'd heard enough stories from different sources to know there was a problem. "The father of one of the girls told him he'd better get out of town before he killed him," DeWayne added.

Jeannie didn't tell him about Debbie. She just nodded and repeated, "Wow."

"*And . . .*" DeWayne checked his watch. "One more minute before I go on. *And* did you hear about why the show went off the air?"

"No," Jeannie said, leaning forward.

"Because somebody higher up in the network got wind of what was going on, and they were like we don't need any more of this Jim and Tammy Faye and Jimmy Swaggart shit, and *then* his wife finally divorced him and took most of his assets. So he's been living in a rat hole in Hendersonville. No lie. I drove by there and saw it myself. His ratty Caddy was sitting there in the driveway. He's broke. Flat-ass broke. But I guess he still has all his expensive suits, so people at the Church at Holliman Farms think he's still 'manifesting.'" He wiggled his fingers in the air.

"Wow," Jeannie said again. She was delighted to hear that he'd gotten what he deserved but newly disgusted to realize how gullible they all were at the Church at Holliman Farms—Garland, Junior, all of them, still fooled by his posing.

DeWayne leaned toward her and whispered, "I'm moving you to the best slot. Knock 'em dead, girlfriend." She watched him sashay up to the stage, marveling at the change in him. In both of them. She smiled. Maybe they'd survived the people who had tried to take what was wonderful in them and press it down until it couldn't breathe. After all, here they were, living their own lives, still making their music.

"Are you nervous?" Tom asked before she went on.

She considered her body, her powerful and steady heart, her fingers that were starting to remember their old moves. "No," she said. When DeWayne introduced her, she walked up on stage, greeted the crowd, and played the opening chords on her guitar. When she sang that first note, she felt right at home, like she'd joined in again on a song the universe had been humming forever.

# Love Lifted Me

Jeannie had recently taken up gardening, returning to the plot her parents had worked on weekends at the farm when she was a kid. Summer had been a mess of vegetables growing faster than she could pick them and weeds growing faster than she could hoe them. She was relieved to be down to some squash and a pumpkin vine in the fall. She found the perfect one to pick for Lee Ann to carve when she came home from college, and she cut it with an old knife that she had found in Papaw Virgil's shed and sharpened. It made her ridiculously happy to hoist the pumpkin onto her hip, something solid she'd grown from the land she'd learned to love. These were the most satisfying achievements, she thought: raising her niece, writing and singing songs, growing things.

"Let me get that for you." Wick had come from the church and was walking across her yard to the garden. He took the pumpkin and balanced it on one shoulder, holding the stem.

"Thanks." Jeannie turned toward the house. She never knew how to be with Wick since their divorce. It felt natural to be their old familiar selves, but they weren't those selves anymore, really. What were they now, then? She wasn't sure. "It's not that heavy," she said.

"I know. I just had to get away from there for a few minutes." He followed her, set the pumpkin on the front porch, and sat beside it.

She sat on the edge of the porch a few feet away. "Why? What's going on?"

Wick lit up a cigarette and looked out at the sun setting orange over the fields. "I ain't cut out for this shit." He blew a stream of smoke at the sky. "I took this job to get me away from my old habits because I knew I needed to get clean to—" He glanced at Jeannie. "To have a chance at getting you back." He shook his head. "But I can't be around these clowns, acting like Jesus talked to them from their Special K this morning." He propped one booted foot on the edge of the porch and rested his forearm on his knee, cigarette dangling between his fingers. "If they want to go buy a new Road King, they can't just say they want to go buy it. They've got to say Jesus told them to. They turned on the radio and heard Jesus say go to Clarksville and there's gonna be the exact bike that he wants them to get." He looked thoroughly disgusted. "Now Jesus is telling them to vote for George W. Bush."

Jeannie laughed, and Wick shook his head.

"They all love to talk about how they used to be addicted to drugs or alcohol and now they're 'addicted to Jesus.'" He scoffed. "You know what I think? I think they're addicted to their cult. They can't handle life unless they're all marching together. They've gotta be over there all the time, having their meetings, riding with the Warriors, going to their potlucks, listening to Junior or that asshole Alford, who's leading them all over a cliff."

"And yet you're still there," Jeannie said, brushing the dirt off her pumpkin.

"I'm just keeping my eye on Junior," he said. "He doesn't know what he's getting into with that Alford joker."

"No, he doesn't. He doesn't know what he did to Debbie." It came out before Jeannie realized what she was saying. She'd kept Debbie's secret for so many years, and now it was out, at least to Wick. She felt better, somehow.

Wick's face turned serious. He crushed the butt of his cigarette and turned to her. "What did he do to Debbie?"

Jeannie sighed. She didn't feel like telling the whole story, but she could see in Wick's eyes that she didn't have to.

"It's not just Debbie either," she said. "I saw DeWayne Deaton a while back, and he told me all the dirt on Alford. Lots of young girls. He got kicked out of a couple of churches and lost his show for it." She made a sour face. "And comes out smelling like a rose every time."

"Somebody needs to kill the son of a bitch."

Jeannie caught her breath. She could see Wick doing it, just because somebody needed to. "Wick. Don't you dare get yourself in trouble over him. He's not worth it."

He looked into her eyes, and she felt the intensity of his devotion to her, so strong it almost scared her. "I'm gonna be there, keeping my eye on things, as long as you're here," he said. "And I'll do whatever I have to do."

Tom's Honda rounded the curve and pulled into her driveway then. Jeannie wanted to know more about what was on Wick's mind, but now wasn't the time. They watched Tom get out of the car and walk over, arm lifted. "Hey!"

"Hey!" Jeannie called back.

Wick stared at him, straight-faced.

Tom approached and kissed Jeannie on the mouth, which some-how felt wrong. She didn't want Wick to see. "Tom Becker," he said, extending his hand to Wick.

"Ah, this is Wick Whitaker, my ex-husband," Jeannie said. She cleared her throat.

"Oh." Tom looked at her and back at Wick, who gave him an al-most imperceptible nod of greeting.

"He's the caretaker at the church," Jeannie explained. "I think I told you that before? And he was just telling me . . . some things that have been going on."

"Anything good?" Tom asked, putting his arm around Jeannie's waist. Was he signaling his place to Wick? Or just being affectionate? She wasn't quite sure. Wick's face was hard as stone.

"Not really," she said.

"That's a shame," Tom said, kissing the top of her head. "I know it's hard to watch your whole family fall for that guy again."

Wick twitched and tapped another cigarette from his pack.

"I wish I could just . . . wake them up," Jeannie said, moving away from them both, back to the porch to brush off the pumpkin again. She felt like she had been trying all her life, trying to take care of her family, trying to help them, trying to *save* them. She didn't know if she had any fight left in her.

"All you can do is try," Tom said.

"If you can't, nobody can," Wick said. Then he waved and saun-tered back to the church.

# Sorry I Never Knew You

Jeannie dialed the number. She wasn't sure why her hand was shaking as she held the phone. It made no sense. What could this Sharon Alford Shelton do to her? Hang up? Yell at her? Jeannie had done some digging and found the name and number of Oren Alford's daughter in Oklahoma. Maybe the woman could tell her something that she could use to convince her family that Alford was a fraud, even dangerous.

When Sharon answered, Jeannie swallowed hard and said, "Hello! My name is Jeannie Holliman. Is this Sharon Shelton?"

"Yes, it is." The voice was familiar, saccharine. A replica of Sister Diane's.

"Oren and Diane Alford's daughter?"

A pause. "Yes?"

Jeannie had written out a statement, but she knew it would sound wooden if she read it. Instead, she stumbled through her history with the Alfords on *Speak the Victory!*

"Yes. I'm familiar with the show." The woman's voice was stiff. "Can I help you?"

"Sharon, your father has recently come back into our lives. My brother has a church on our family land, and he has let your father come in as an assistant or copreacher, I guess? He basically pushed out our old preacher."

"Hmmm."

"And I have some concerns. About his past behavior toward my sister . . . and rumors I've heard about other women and girls . . . not to mention all the money. I'm just wondering if you have anything you can tell me that might help me persuade my family that they don't need to let him back into our lives."

There was a long silence, and Jeannie was afraid that she might hang up. Finally, Sharon said, "You're right to be concerned."

"Why do you say that? What can you tell me?" Jeannie let out a long breath she had been holding since she picked up the phone. "Can you confirm any of these rumors? Surely your mother has told you some things."

"My mother—" Her breathing was heavy now. "There are things that happened that should not have happened." Jeannie had the sense from the change in Sharon's voice that she might be crying. "But I've forgiven him."

Jeannie waited, listening to her breathe. "Forgiven him for what?"

"That's all I can say."

"Please, Sharon. I need your help."

"He's too old now anyway. Those days are gone."

"I don't know about that. He's still able to lead people where he wants them to go. It may not be for sex now, but he still wants power and money."

"That's all I can say."

The phone clicked off, and Jeannie was left more worried than she'd been before.

After her phone call, Jeannie looked through her old Gospelettes albums, caressing the covers, peering at the pictures of herself and her sisters, in particular. What would her relationship with them have been like if Debbie hadn't died? Would they have been united, the three of them against the world? She missed their sisterly bond. She'd always taken care of them, looked out for them, bossed them around because, of course, as the oldest, she knew best. They had loved each other anyway. But now all that was gone.

She wondered if she had underestimated Patty. Hadn't Patty always been the rebel? From the beginning of the Gospelettes, when Jeannie was trying to whip her siblings into line, Patty had been the irreverent one, the one to roll her eyes and question what she was told. When Jeannie decided to leave *Speak the Victory!*, hadn't Patty jumped in the car with her, riding shotgun as Jeannie peeled out of the lot?

The next day, after work, Jeannie decided to stop by Patty's house. Patty and Brian had recently moved into a new, modest-sized house with white siding and black shutters—cookie-cutter but still a far cry from the concrete-block box she'd lived in with Dalton or the back room of the bowling alley. They had just finished getting everything in place, so Patty showed Jeannie around. Plaques and framed pictures with Bible verses and inspirational sayings covered the walls. Jeannie counted three different wall hangings of the "Footprints" poem: in the bathroom, in the living room, and in the hall. Patty had also hung some framed pictures of Brian's sons from his previous marriage and a few of JP when he was small.

"Looking good!" Jeannie lied.

Brian sat in his recliner watching TV. When Jeannie spoke to him, he grunted and eyed her suspiciously. She *had* told him he didn't know shit the previous Thanksgiving, but he had been weird around her even before then. It seemed that he liked to keep tabs on Patty. She said he wanted to go everywhere with her. He even hovered over her as she talked on the phone, always asking, "Who was that?" when she hung up. She had told Jeannie this almost proudly. Here was a man who cared, she seemed to be saying.

"Can you stay for supper?" Patty lifted a pan from her shiny new cabinets with pull-out shelves. Everything in her kitchen was new: the matching white mixer, blender, and toaster; the throw rugs, dish towels, and pot holders with a fruit-and-vegetable design.

"No. I just wanted to stop by." Jeannie tried to make eye contact, but Patty wasn't interested. "I haven't been seeing family much lately, you know."

Patty dumped a package of ground beef from the refrigerator into the pan. "Yeah."

"So I'm curious: Do Mama and Daddy and Junior talk about me not going to church anymore? And why?" Jeannie leaned against the kitchen island.

"Well, yeah. They're always talking about what in the world is wrong with you. Daddy blames it on Tom Becker."

Jeannie closed her eyes and chuckled. "Of course."

Brian walked into the kitchen, peered into the pan, and strolled back out, without a word, just checking in. Patty broke up the meat, pushed it around, stirred. "You were on the prayer list yesterday," she said.

"Are you kidding? What for?" Jeannie asked.

Patty shrugged. "To call you into your divine purposes?"

"Well, great!" Jeannie tried to sound unbothered. "It might not help, but it can't hurt." She waited for her to say something Patty-like, something sarcastic about the prayer warriors or a blistering Oren Alford imitation, but it seemed that Patty had gotten her rebellion out of her system early, as most reasonable people do, and was settled into a life of ease now.

"OK. Well. Just wanted to see your new house," Jeannie said, taking out her car keys. "It's really nice."

Patty moved her wooden spoon around and around, set it on a ceramic spoon rest shaped like an eggplant. "Thanks." She followed Jeannie to the door.

Like everyone and everything else, Patty had changed. It was obvious that she wasn't going with Jeannie on this journey. It was almost as if they'd switched positions when Jeannie wasn't looking. She wondered why it hurt so much to realize this.

# Beulah Land

Out of the blue, Junior showed up on Jeannie's doorstep a few days later. *My twin*, she thought, with a rueful laugh. Now, if she imagined them together in the womb, she saw them as the yin and yang symbols, opposites in every way.

"Come on in, stranger," she said, holding the door open.

"I reckon I will," Junior said, easing himself into the room and sitting on the couch, arms stretched out to each side, one boot propped sideways on the other knee, mirrored sunglasses folded onto the neck of his T-shirt. He looked around the room. "Still can't believe this is Papaw Virgil's house. You really spruced it up."

"Yep." She sat in the chair beside the couch. "How have you been?"

"Never been better!" He grinned. "How about you?"

"Pretty good."

"We miss you at church."

She nodded. "Well."

"That's a deep subject." He jiggled his boot and tapped out a beat on the top of the couch.

"So . . . what's up?"

"So . . . Wick told me I ought to come tell you personally since you weren't at church for the big announcement."

"What big announcement?" She couldn't imagine what it might be and wouldn't be surprised by anything.

Junior put his foot down and leaned forward. "Something really exciting!" He paused, grinning wider. "We're building a Christian theme park. Creation Park! Right here on the farm."

Jeannie closed her eyes and shook her head, as if to clear out the fog. "What?"

"We're building a theme park! Brother Alford had the vision for it and thought he'd build it outside of Nashville, but then God just kept leading him right back here where the revival had been. It's gonna be a place for Christian families to come together and have fun!" He clapped his hands once. "It's gonna tell the creation story. We're gonna recreate the Garden of Eden right here on the farm and have a little zoo, some rides, a water park, a campground. Maybe a hotel later. And I suggested a motor track." His face lit up like he was ten years old and it was Christmas Eve.

Jeannie jumped up from her chair and walked across the room, just needing to put some space between herself and his ridiculous words. "What the hell are you talking about, Junior?"

He smiled. "A theme park. Creation Park or something like that. We might come up with a better name."

"Where?" She looked through the doorway to the kitchen at the window overlooking the rolling hills between her house and the river. "Here? All around me? You're going to build a goddam theme park around this house and all over Papaw Virgil's land? Is that what you're telling me?"

Junior's face fell, and he knitted his brows. "What's your problem, Jeannie? Nobody is farming this land anymore. You use about one acre for the house and your little garden patch. Rent-free, by the way. Are you that selfish that you can't share the rest of this with kids and families from our church? And other churches all over the country? Something that could teach them about God's creation and give them a place to be with other Christians?" He stood, hands on his hips. "I don't get it!"

She paced the living room, alternating between fury and sorrow. How could Garland, especially, have allowed this? He must have given his OK since he owned the land. Alford had figured out a way to slither right back into their lives and onto their farm. The farm, which had always been quietly there in the background of her life, was suddenly more precious than she'd realized. The acres of fields gone wild, the trees gathering their heads together like old friends, the muddy river she crossed to get to work and then back home each night, and the homeplace that she'd worked so hard to bring back to life. She had been completely wrong to think she wouldn't be surprised by anything Junior had to say. She was too shocked to speak.

"We don't operate by the limitations of this world but in the pro-phetic flow of the Holy Spirit," Junior said. She knew he'd taken those words verbatim from Oren Alford. "We don't look at this farm and say, 'Well, I guess this is all it can ever be. Just a piece of land that nobody farms anymore.'" He pointed toward town. "When I came back to Bethel, I didn't look at Brother Clarence's cute little church and say, 'Aww, isn't that sweet? I guess this is good enough.' I saw what God wanted us to build!"

Jeannie narrowed her eyes at him. "When you came back to Bethel, you didn't see anything but the floor of my spare bedroom that you were puking on after your latest binge!"

"Well, I guess Wick was right. You're not gonna be happy about any of it. Not one single thing."

"Why would I be happy that that . . . disgusting, vile man is taking over my family, my church, and now my farm?"

"It's not *your* farm, Jeannie."

"Our farm! Papaw Virgil's farm! This beautiful, quiet, peaceful place!" She motioned toward the window. "That crook just wants to use our family to make money! Again!" she yelled. She wished there was a dish close at hand so she could throw it, shatter it at Junior's feet. "Oren Alford doesn't do anything unless there's something in it for him."

Junior, red-faced, walked over to the front door and pounded it with his fist, startling her, then he whirled around. "I didn't bring in all these new members by preaching funerals and sitting in the hos-pital every time some old lady had her gallbladder out." He glared at her. "That ain't how I'm gonna run things. Excitement. That's how I operate. That's how I bring two thousand people through those doors every week. Brother Alford understands that. Apparently, you don't." He flung open the door and stomped out to his motorcycle, revved up. Jeannie watched out the front window as he rode away, leaving a cloud of white dust to sift through the twilight.

Jeannie sat on the back porch, listening to the night sounds of the farm, the last of the crickets, an owl, coyotes in the distance, and thinking about how soon the peace would be ruptured and the pas-tures and woods replaced by roller coasters and water slides, when the cordless phone rang.

"Did you see your brother on the Bowling Green news just now?" Tom asked, sounding out of breath.

"No . . ." Jeannie wondered if her blood pressure might be rising. She didn't know what that felt like but thought this tightening in her head might be it.

He told her about a news segment announcing the Creation Park. "They said it's going to be at the Church at Holliman Farms in Bethel. What the hell?"

"I just heard about it this evening," she said. "What did they say?"

"That asshole preacher, Alford, was on there saying it's going to be 'a counter to the secular humanism that's taking over the country.'" Tom hooted. "They showed an architect's rendering of the park. It's in your fucking backyard. It's going to have a damn water park, Jeannie. With freaking sea monster slides! And they're re-creating the Garden of Eden, with Adam and Eve statues. I *assume* they'll have their private parts camouflaged. And then they'll have exhibits explaining how everything was created and, quote, 'exposing the lies of evolution'! They said it's going to be the answer to the evolutionist left-wing takeover of the educational system or some shit. I can't even—this is unreal."

Jeannie leaned her head on one hand and closed her eyes. "Of course."

"Jesus, Jeannie. Your brother didn't tell you about any of this before now?"

"No, he didn't." And neither had Garland.

"You know, as a science teacher, I'm going to be protesting this, right?"

She leaned against the porch railing and stared a hole through the back of the church, straight to Junior's study. "You know I will be too, right?"

# Breaking Bread

The weekend before Christmas, Tom stayed at Jeannie's house before heading up to Indiana to visit his parents and his sister's family. They made a rare appearance at Floyd's Barbecue rather than join the preholiday madness in Nashville as they usually did on weekends. Walking in, Jeannie scanned the dining room for hostile faces, but no one seemed to be staring at them.

"We could just order takeout," she whispered to Tom.

He put his hand on her shoulder. "It's OK, Jeannie. It's just Bethel. Sweet little Bethel."

"Right." She tipped her head forward and cast her eyes up at him. He'd already had several run-ins with parents and random others around town over his evolution stance in the classroom. He'd made it clear to his classes that the Creation Park would be not only an environmental disaster but an embarrassment to the community for its literal and simplistic interpretation of the biblical creation story.

A waitress pointed them to an empty table in the half-full dining room, and they scanned the menus. "Oh, did I show you this?" Tom pulled a pamphlet from his pocket and laid it on the table. On the front were the words "Evolution Exposed!" Jeannie picked it up. "Look on the inside," he said.

She opened it and read to herself: "Tell your parents and church family what you are being forced to hear about every day at school, where they think you are safe from harm! Tell Mr. Becker and Mr. Duggin (Principal) that you are against the indoctrination program of evolution at Bethel High School! Finally, PRAY that he will see the light and repent before any souls are lost to this evil doctrine!"

Jeannie felt her heartbeat accelerate. She looked up at him. "This is getting serious."

"This kid in Advanced Biology—*Advanced* Biology!—named Kristin Crenshaw was passing these out in my classroom on the last day before winter break. I said, 'Hello! Don't I get one?'" He laughed and shook his head. "She said, 'My Bible says God created everything. That's a fact. Evolution is a theory, not a fact. I don't understand why you won't talk about creationism. Aren't you supposed to be exposing us to different ideas and theories?'"

The waitress stopped at their table and took their orders. Jeannie felt the people at the table next to them, three older men in billed caps, listening to them.

"Anyway," Tom continued, "I said, 'Well, not exactly, Kristin. I teach science, and in science, we teach theories about the natural world that have been proven by the scientific method. Creationism hasn't been proven by the scientific method, so it would be irresponsible for me, as a scientist, to teach that. Whether or not you believe that God created everything is a matter of faith. It has to do with the supernatural, not the natural, and so it is not in the realm of science.'"

"Oh, boy." Jeannie sipped her Coke and rolled the straw's paper into a swirl. She was uncomfortable with having this discussion in public, but she couldn't have explained why. She agreed with Tom, at least about his role as a science teacher. Where she personally came down on the controversy was hard to articulate. It seemed like the creationists were denying science and the evolutionists were denying the possibility of anything spiritual. She felt there was a truth getting lost in there.

"So then she said, 'You're telling us that some amoeba somehow turned into a fish, and then a fish grew legs and just up and walked out of the water—like that could happen! And then it turned into a dinosaur or whatever and then some kind of mammal and then a monkey and then a human. And you weren't there to see all that happening, so how can you prove it? The Bible says God created everything in seven days, and that's what I believe.'" Tom lifted one eyebrow and smiled.

"Six days," Jeannie said.

"Exactly! That's what I told her. Six days. The Bible says God rested on the seventh day."

"I'll bet she loved that." Jeannie laughed.

"She said, 'Whatever! You know what I mean!'"

"You're doing all you can do, Tom." Jeannie had noticed his grow-ing frustration. Every day there was a new comment or a definite chill in a previously warm relationship with a colleague. The other sci-ence teachers were backing away from the controversy, preferring to dance around it rather than address it head-on.

"I'm not going to back down," he said. "I'll take it to the school board. I'll take it to the courts if necessary."

The waitress brought their food—shredded barbecue chicken, cornbread cakes, baked beans, and slaw—and they dug in, not talking for a while. The past couple of months had been exhausting for them both. Everyone who knew that Jeannie's brother was the preacher planning Creation Park and that her boyfriend was the biology teach-er at Bethel High wanted to know where she stood. And she had told them. She didn't want the park. She knew her brother meant well, but she agreed with Tom.

One of the men at the next table, the one with the loudest voice and an enormous belly hanging over his belt, started telling a joke: "Did you hear about the atheist that went on a walk in the woods?"

The other two at his table said they hadn't.

"This atheist goes walking in the woods, admiring all the nature. Looks over and there's a seven-foot grizzly coming at him. Well, he takes off running, and then he trips over a branch and falls down. He rolls over and sees that bear with his big old paw up about to swipe him. So the atheist cries out, 'Oh, my God!'"

The other men laughed. "Yeah, *now* he does," one said.

"All of a sudden, the bear just freezes. Then this bright light shines down on the atheist, and this voice in the sky says, 'You deny my existence all these years. You teach others that I don't exist and that everything I created is just a accident. And now you call on me? You expect me to help you now?' And the atheist says, 'Naw. I'd be a hyp-ocrite if I asked you to treat me like a Christian now, but maybe you could make that *bear* a Christian?'"

His friends leaned back in their chairs and laughed.

He went on. "The voice says, 'All right.' The light goes out, and the bear bows his head and says, 'Lord, bless this food which I am about to receive and for which I am truly thankful.'"

The man's friends and people at some of the other tables nearby laughed. The waitress slapped the joke-teller playfully on the back with a menu. Jeannie felt her face heating up. She looked over and saw that he was looking right at her.

"I'm going to the ladies' room," she told Tom, who was staring back at the comedian with a smirk. She was having some trouble breathing. She wished she and Tom had taken their food home and eaten in her own peaceful kitchen, with its view of the hills and trees, while it was still peaceful and not surrounded by fake dinosaurs frolicking in the Garden of Eden with Adam and Eve.

# Family Reunion

On Christmas morning, Lee Ann and her boyfriend, Nate, sat at the kitchen table but turned down Jeannie's offer to make pancakes. "We've got lunch at Mamaw and Papaw's—or dinner, as they call it—and then we have to drive to Nate's family's house in Paducah for dinner," Lee Ann said.

"Supper, as your grandparents call it," Nate said.

"We're gonna be full as a tick," Lee Ann said.

"True." Jeannie sipped her coffee, wearing the fuzzy robe and slippers they had given her that morning. Claiming a headache, she had stuffed presents for the whole family in three large shopping bags for Lee Ann to take to her grandparents' house.

"I know you don't want to go over there," Lee Ann said. "You don't have to fake a headache."

"It's a . . . complicated situation," Jeannie said.

"Are y'all speaking?" Lee Ann asked.

Jeannie shrugged. "I call Mama once a week to check on everybody."

"Does Papaw talk over her in the background the whole time?"

Jeannie raised one eyebrow. "What do you think?"

They were silent for a while. Nate went to the living room to watch TV. Lee Ann said, "So we had Christmas Eve with Dad and his new wife yesterday."

Jeannie nodded. "Yeah?"

"Yeah." Lee Ann looked sad.

"Was Randall there?"

"Yeah. And Dad's wife's kids and some other relatives I don't know."

Jeannie nodded and waited.

"And so . . . something came up about how I didn't live with Dad growing up, and he got all defensive even though I wasn't the one that brought it up, so then he pulls me aside and goes, 'I never did tell you about the coroner's report on your mom because you were too little to understand, but now I think you ought to know.'" Lee Ann's eyes were wet, and she swallowed hard. "So I go, 'OK. Lay it on me.' And he goes, 'Well, your mama was pregnant when she OD'd, and it wasn't my baby because we'd been separated for about a year and I hadn't even slept with her.'"

Jeannie put her hand on her heart. It was as if those nearly thirteen years had been just a day. All the grieving and healing still ahead of her instead of behind her. Had Debbie known? Did Oren Alford know? She felt a flash of hot anger at the thought of that man next door at that church, claiming their land after all he'd already taken from them. She could see Debbie's dead body in her bed. She wondered if Lee Ann remembered, hoped that she'd blocked it out. She'd never asked her. She couldn't.

Lee Ann continued: "And I was, like, 'Yeah, because you'd left her for another woman, right?' And I just got Nate and walked out."

"Oh, I'm sorry, baby."

"It's all right. I'm not losing a thing, believe me." She looked down at her hands. "What do you think Uncle Wick is doing today?"

Jeannie kissed her cheek. "I don't know, but I'll bet if he's home, he'd love for you to drop by."

Lee Ann wiped her eyes with the back of her hand. "I wish Tom had stayed in town. I don't want you to be alone on Christmas."

"It's OK, sweetie. I'm a big girl." Jeannie smiled.

Lee Ann shook her head. "I'm just going to stay here with you."

"No, honey. Mamaw and Papaw want to see you."

"They want to see you too. You're their daughter. And they've already lost one."

Jeannie closed her eyes and sighed. She was right, of course. Jeannie always felt caught between being part of them and being herself. She stood and took a deep breath. "All right. I'll go get ready. But only because it's Christmas."

Garland and Big Jean's house was full when Jeannie arrived. Lee Ann and Nate had gone ahead and stopped by to see Wick before coming over. Patty and Brian were there in matching Harley-Davidson T-shirts. JP was there with his girlfriend, Selena, and their baby, Cole. Junior and Rosie were surrounded by her four kids, who were mad because they'd had to leave their new Christmas toys to come to dinner. His daughters, Jeannie assumed, were with their mothers.

"Where's Tom?" Patty asked. Both her arms were wound around one of Brian's as they sat on the couch.

"Visiting his family in Indiana," Jeannie said.

"Too bad," Patty said. "That would've been a fun time."

Brian grunted.

"Sorry about your fun time," Jeannie said, perching on the arm of the couch where Lee Ann and Nate were seated.

"There's Randall and—" Lee Ann stared out the picture window, mouth open. Jeannie followed her gaze. Randall had gotten out of his car and was walking toward the house with Oren Alford.

Jeannie felt an instinct to run for the back door, as if she were an animal watching the approach of a predator. What was he doing at her parents' home at their family celebration? It felt like a betrayal.

Garland jumped up and opened the front door. "Come on in here!"

"Merry Christmas, Brother Garland," Brother Alford said.

"Merry Christmas to you," Garland said, opening the door wide and shaking his hand.

Jeannie felt every muscle in her body tense up. She watched Randall and Garland fuss over Brother Alford, as if he were a visiting dignitary. Then Junior joined them, shaking Alford's hand and welcoming him. She exchanged loaded glances with Lee Ann.

"Who's ready to eat?" Big Jean called from the kitchen. Everyone walked in that direction and gathered in a ragged circle. Jeannie kept slightly outside and behind Brother Alford, keeping him in sight but avoiding eye contact. "Garland, will you say the blessing?" Big Jean asked. This was only a formality. Of course, he would always say the blessing.

They all bowed their heads and got quiet, except for Rosie's two boys, who were kicking each other and had to be separated, grasped by the napes of their necks, by Junior. Garland gave thanks for the food and the family gathered there and summarized the nativity story. "And, Lord, we thank you for the guest at our table today. We thank you for sending him to help Junior in the church, and we ask you to guide their new venture, as they lead people in this community and in this country back to you."

"Amen!" Junior shouted.

They all went through the buffet line Big Jean had set up at the kitchen counter and stove, then found their places, with card tables set up in the living room to accommodate the younger members of the family. Jeannie hoped she'd be able to squeeze in with Lee Ann, Nate, JP, and Selena at their card table, but by the time she had filled her plate, she realized she would be at the kitchen table with the grown-ups, including Brother Alford.

Conversation soon turned to the Creation Park. Junior described it, with his mouth full of ham and biscuit. "The back of the church is going to be sort of the gateway to the park. We'll run a little road to the side of the church and add another parking area back there. And then behind the house is the park entrance with a little train station where you can hop on board and ride through the days of creation. First there's darkness, which is a tunnel with no lights. Then the second day is light, which is a tunnel with bright lights. Then the third day is the earth, which is outside on the actual farm. And then there's the sea, which is going to be a water park with sea monster slides. Then to the Garden of Eden Petting Zoo, which is going to have Adam and Eve statues, kind of hidden in the bushes and vines, and some live friendly animals. The dangerous ones will be fake and made for kids to climb on. And then the train will take you to the banks of the river, where the campground will be."

"There's water moccasins down there," Garland said.

"The kids can't wait," Rosie said.

"We can't either," Patty said. Brian nodded.

Jeannie pushed the food around on her plate, unable to eat. "Where is all this money coming from?" she asked.

"Brother Alford found some investors," Junior said. "He's taking care of all the funding. I've got enough to deal with."

Jeannie and Alford looked at each other. He smiled. She glared.

"And Daddy is donating the land for this fiasco," Jeannie grumbled. She looked at Garland. She felt as if they were all caught in a bad dream, and she desperately wanted to wake them. What had happened to them all? Especially Garland. He may have been uneducated, but he wasn't a fool. Couldn't he see the serpent that was right in front of his eyes, sitting at his own table?

"It was mine to give!" Garland said.

"I get it," Junior said. "It's going to be right behind Papaw Virgil's house, and you live there now, and I should have talked to you first. My bad! We're not going to tear down the house if that's what you're worried about."

"That's not what I'm worried about," Jeannie said, putting down her fork. She was so furious she didn't trust herself to hold it in her hand. "There's so much wrong with this idea that I don't even know where to start."

"Here she goes, ruining another holiday," Brian muttered.

"It's just something fun for families, for all the kids we're getting at the church now," Junior said, his voice rising an octave. "A petting zoo! A water park! I mean, what can you have against a water park?"

"She's always been the boss of us, and she can't stand it that she's not anymore," Patty said.

"Hush, children," Big Jean said. "It's Christmas."

"First of all, there's all the environmental issues and what this is going to do to the farm," Jeannie said, ticking off one finger. "Do you know how many trees are going to be cut down? Do you remember how Papaw Virgil used to take us fishing at the river and how we used to pick blackberries along the fencerow?"

"Oh, Lord, now she's some kind of tree hugger," Junior said.

"Then there's the antiscience aspect—which, I know, it's pointless for me to even go into that." Jeannie touched her next finger.

"You've gotten in with that Becker fellow and gotten ungodly ideas about God's creation," Garland said, brow furrowed.

"Sure," Jeannie said. "And then there's the money." She looked from Garland to Big Jean to Junior to Patty. "Y'all remember how he raises money and what he does with it, right? He's a con man. You know that." She looked directly at Oren Alford, but she didn't just see him. She saw Debbie coming to his office at Speak the Victory Theater with her prayer requests. She saw Debbie crying in her bed, grieving over the end of their affair. She saw Debbie's lifeless body. She couldn't understand how he always got away with everything. Every time. "He's a con man and a phony and a crook," she said.

"You will not sit at my table and speak to me and my guest that way!" Garland declared, gripping his fork upright like a weapon and pounding the table.

Jeannie stood and pushed her chair back.

"Yep. Here we go again," Brian said.

"If none of that matters to you, if you're willing to give him your property and your money and your mind, where's the line?" Jeannie faced Garland. "What about your children? Are you willing to give him your children? Do you know what he did to Debbie?" She saw Garland flinch and Big Jean's eyes widen. "Do I have to tell you?" Her voice broke. She imagined Debbie at the table, in her chair, where Brian was sitting now, looking at her accusingly, saying, *You promised.* "I swore I wouldn't," Jeannie said. Everyone was completely silent, even behind her, in the living room. "But he knows what I'm talking about." She pointed at Brother Alford. "He knows, and his wife knows, and his daughter knows—well, I won't even mention what she implied—and people at every church he's been in know how he finds the sweetest, meekest, most vulnerable girl in the group, the one least likely to make a fuss, the one most willing to keep the peace for everybody else, and then he goes in for the kill."

Jeannie stood there trembling. For just a second, she thought she might have gotten through. There was the slightest disruption, as if they'd been flushed from their hiding place and were momentarily out in the light. But then she saw them all scramble back to where they felt comfortable. They'd been watching and waiting for him all their lives.

"I thought you were above strifes, backbitings, and whisperings, Sister Jeannie." Brother Alford wore an expression of deep disappointment.

Garland's face was red, and Big Jean looked stricken. "The very idea, bringing Debbie's name into such a discussion!" Garland said, slamming his fork onto the table.

Lee Ann, standing in the doorway, spoke quietly. "Mamaw, we're going to Nate's parents' house now. I love you."

Jeannie, Lee Ann, and Nate gathered their coats and keys and headed to the door. Big Jean followed them, wringing her hands. "Y'all didn't open your presents yet!"

Lee Ann stopped and hugged her. "I'll come back and get them later, Mamaw."

Jeannie kept walking to her car. She didn't look back.

She drove toward home, passing all the houses lit up with Christmas lights, driveways lined with vehicles. The sky was overcast, threatening weeks of gloom ahead. She crossed the bridge. Floodlights shone on the front of the church. In the back parking lot, she saw Wick's motorcycle. It was just like him to ride his motorcycle in this weather. Anything short of a blizzard or a tornado, he'd get out and ride. She turned in, drove past the bike, cruising behind the building. She saw him there, leaning against the wall, smoking a cigarette.

She stopped and rolled down the window. "Hey."

"Hey, you. My one last addiction," he said, holding the butt up to view.

She nodded. "Maybe I need to start."

He crushed the butt on the bottom of his boot and held it between his thumb and forefinger. "Naw. Don't you do that. I need to know one thing in this world is good."

She lifted one corner of her mouth in a half smile. "That's a lot of pressure on me, Wick."

He surveyed the courtyard, the back of the building, and the parking lot. "Isn't life crazy? Look at us. I'm hanging around the church all the time, and you're staying away."

She gave a bitter laugh. "It is pretty funny. You got faith right when I lost mine."

"Says who?"

She shrugged. "Says everybody."

He shook his head. "They don't have a clue what faith is, Jeannie. They think it's believing what everybody else believes. Following the leader."

"And what do you think it is?"

His face was turned up toward the church steeple or perhaps toward the sky. "I think it's believing something good can come out of the bad." He smiled at her. "You did that for me for years."

She smiled a little. "Did I?"

"Yeah. You did."

"Until I didn't."

"Hey—how about if I take you for a ride?" The lines around his eyes creased into a look of mischief he used to give her years ago.

"In December? Are you crazy?"

"Come on. It's about fifty degrees. Just a little nip in the air."

She thought about Tom. He'd called her that morning, complaining that he shouldn't have gone to Indiana to visit his family. They should have gone away somewhere for the holidays, just the two of them, he said. Maybe to California. He couldn't wait to get back and see her the next day.

"Merry Christmas." She pushed the button to roll up the window and drove away.

# Move That Mountain

In the spring, the fields and woods around Jeannie's house were overrun with backhoes, ram hoes, bulldozers, and gravel and cement trucks. After work, Tom came over and walked out with Jeannie to inspect the damage, piles of gravel and dirt and uprooted trees everywhere. It felt like a violation of her own body. They walked toward the river. A red-winged blackbird flew in front of them, but other than that, all the animals watched from their hiding places. They reached the line of trees that still stood along the river and stepped under them, immediately feeling the temperature drop. Jeannie hoped Junior and Alford at least planned to leave them standing as shade for the campground. She couldn't bear it if they knocked them all down.

Tom took her hand in his and smiled at her. "Are you sure you want to do this?"

She looked out at the river, brown and gleaming green in the light that filtered through the canopy of new leaves. She nodded. "Yes."

She hadn't seen or spoken to her family (other than Lee Ann, of course) since Christmas. Big Jean mailed her cards or clippings, articles from *Guideposts*, a page torn from a devotional book ("When You're Troubled"). She wrote at the top, "For Jeannie" and "Saw this and thought of you." Her elderly handwriting made Jeannie feel like crying. Jeannie knew her mother was more trapped than she was. What else could Big Jean do but what she'd always done, follow? Jeannie mailed cards with short messages back to her mother: "I'm fine. Hope everyone's doing OK. Love you."

"What an absolute nightmare," Tom said as they walked back to the house through what Jeannie thought the earth might look like after the apocalypse. Lee Ann didn't even want to come home anymore.

She couldn't stand to see it. She and Nate had an apartment in Bowling Green, where she was in her last semester of college, and Jeannie visited her there instead.

They walked around to the front of the house and sat on the porch, where the view was better. They could see the Wilsons' farm across the road, corn coming up.

"Here they come," Tom said, looking up the road. Jeannie watched the Channel 5 News van from Nashville turn into her driveway.

Jeannie and Tom watched the news segment the next night.

*Welcome to the town of Bethel, Kentucky, population 7,300, where there's a church on nearly every downtown street, sometimes more than one . . .*

They watched the streets of Bethel flash across the TV screen, shots with First Baptist, Second Baptist, Bethel Church of Christ, Hillview Methodist, the Church at Holliman Farms.

*. . . and where gospel music can be heard drifting through the air . . .*

Gray-haired members of the Second Baptist choir sang a hymn. Jeannie shook her head. It wasn't exactly gospel music, but how would that reporter know the difference?

*In fact, one gospel-singing family in Bethel was so popular through the 1970s and 1980s that they sang in hundreds of churches and other venues during those years, cut several albums, and for a while, even had a TV program . . .*

Video of the Gospelettes performing on *Speak the Victory!* and pictures of their album covers flashed across the screen. One of the Gospelettes' songs—a song Jeannie had written—played in the background.

*Now the lead singer and songwriter of that group, Jeannie Holliman, is singing a different tune, and this time Bethel residents are not saying "Hallelujah!"*

A close-up of Jeannie's picture from their first album, circa 1974, appeared, growing larger and darker as if it were a cloud covering the sun over Bethel.

*It all started when her brother, Junior Holliman, pastor of the Church at Holliman Farms, decided to build a Christian theme park celebrating creationism.*

Film of the church appeared, followed by Brother Alford's architect's drawings of Creation Park.

*In response, Bethel High School biology teacher Tom Becker spoke out about his views of a theme park that denies evolution, breaking the school's unspoken rule not to address the issue of evolution in the classroom.*

Tom spoke on camera then, standing behind Jeannie's house, surrounded by machinery and uprooted trees.

*"We cannot allow people who don't know anything about science and don't want to know anything about science to determine what we can and cannot teach kids in a science class."*

*Not many in the community have supported Becker in his quest, but one person who has might surprise you: pastor Junior Holliman's twin sister and former gospel singer Jeannie Holliman, who also happens to be Becker's girlfriend.*

A shot of Jeannie standing on her back porch, looking mournfully at the destroyed farm, flashed across the screen.

*"I hate to see them destroy this beautiful land that belonged to my family for generations. I don't think they've thought through the environmental damage they're doing. If they wanted to bring kids out here to camp on the land and be closer to nature, I'd be all for it. But not this."*

Jeannie swept her hand across the view behind her house. Then the reporter appeared on the screen and asked a question.

*"Can religion and science coexist in Bethel?"*

The shot returned to Jeannie, looking over at the church.

*"If you read the Bible and take every word literally—then, no. But if you interpret stories in the Bible—like the creation story—as metaphors for how human beings have developed, stories that are true in that they teach us how to live, how to interact with others, how to take care of the earth, how to see our place in the world, then yes, religion and science can coexist."*

*But many people disagree, including the assistant pastor at the Church of Holliman Farms and former pastor at Nashville's Speak the Victory Fellowship, Reverend Oren Alford.*

Oren Alford, standing in the middle of the church, appeared on the screen.

*"We want to reach out to all the churches across America and around the world and ask them to support the Creation Park with their prayers and donations so that we can teach the truth about God's creation. I don't know what authority Mr. Becker and Ms. Holliman answer to, but we answer to the authority of the Bible, and we want to have twenty thousand other believers standing with us in this park to say to these evolutionists, 'No. We do not believe your lies. Evolution may be endorsed by the government; it may be endorsed by universities; it may be endorsed by our public school system. But creationism is endorsed by the almighty God!'"*

*And how do the people in this community feel about one of their own taking the opposing side in this fight?*

A woman standing in downtown Bethel, cars on the square cruising slowly behind her, spoke.

*"We don't know what to make of it. She used to come to our church and sing real often, and I thought, 'Now that's a voice blessed by God.' And then for her to go and do something like this . . . it's just unbelievable."*

The segment ended, and the newscasters cut to a commercial. Jeannie lay back on the couch and gazed at the ceiling.

"When I invited them here to interview us, I wasn't expecting them to make *you* the story," Tom said.

She cut her eyes at him. "Yeah. Me neither."

"I'm sorry if it makes you uncomfortable."

"It's fine," she said. She wondered if Garland and Big Jean had watched. Brother Alford had probably told them it would be on. "I guess Daddy will never get over this."

Tom leaned forward, looking at the floor, deep in thought. "Jeannie?"

"Yeah?"

He was so quiet she could hear his breathing. "I've been thinking about moving."

She sat up. "Moving where?"

He looked at her. "Maybe Oregon? Or Washington?"

"Oh." She knew he'd been upset about the election and the way the Supreme Court had intervened to put Bush in office, the general direction the country was going in. Now, dealing with school politics and living in a place that supported the Creation Park were just too much for him. He was always pissed about something that he couldn't control. This was one of the things she liked about him, actually. He cared about more than himself.

"I just—" He ran his hand over the top of his head as if to clear the angry thoughts gathered there. "I think I need to be . . . not in the Bible Belt."

"I understand." She hoped the shock and hurt that were washing over her didn't show on her face.

"You know," he said, "you could come with me. They need convenience store clerks and kick-ass singer-songwriters in the Northwest too."

She smiled at him, and they kissed. She'd never thought of leaving Kentucky, except maybe to go as far as Nashville. He liked living out west and assured her she would too.

But, if she left, who would hold vigil for the trees as they fell, one by one? Who would stand watch as the farm died?

A few days later, early in the morning, Big Jean called. When Jeannie saw her number on the caller ID, she was immediately alarmed. They hadn't talked on the phone in months.

"Jeannie! Garland won't get up," Big Jean said, out of breath. "He's acting strange. He always gets up by six. He's just laying there. Won't even talk."

Jeannie told her to call 911 and that she'd be right there. She put on the clothes she'd thrown on a chair the night before and sped to their house, not letting herself think. In the driveway, the paramedics were loading him into the ambulance. Jeannie parked her car on the grass and ran over to him. He seemed smaller on the gurney as they lifted him. Had he shrunken that much in four months? His face was drawn and ashen, and he couldn't seem to focus his eyes on her when she stood over him and cried, "Daddy!"

Big Jean stood near the ambulance, dressed in her beige Sunday best, right down to the pantyhose, clutching her matching beige purse. Jeannie led her to her car, and they followed the ambulance.

"I think it's a stroke," Jeannie told her.

Big Jean held a tissue to her mouth and nodded. "His blood pressure has been so high since—"

Jeannie's heart sank. She should have been checking on them. Even if everybody was mad at her, she should have marched right in and demanded to know how they were feeling, what their various medical stats were, when their next doctor's visit was. Even if it meant never expressing an opinion around them again. Even if it meant giving up every desire, every ounce of independence, and submitting to his expectations.

At the hospital, she sat in the waiting room tending to Big Jean, who was feeling faint. Patty and Brian came in, wearing matching Toby Keith concert T-shirts. Whoever that was. Jeannie had no idea. Then Junior came in, looking annoyed that he had to be there.

"They're allowing two at a time back there," Jeannie told him. The first words she'd spoken to him since Christmas. "You can go ahead. I had to bring Mama out here to settle down."

Their church friends—Brother Clarence, Sister Lucy, Brother Roy, Sister Katherine, Sister Nannie, Brother Jenks—crowded in, dressed, like Big Jean, in their finest Sunday clothes, clean and perfumed.

"He's had too much on him," Big Jean cried to them. "It's about killed him."

Jeannie wandered over to the door through which they'd taken Garland. She looked back. The church members had circled Big Jean and were praying aloud.

Wick came in next. He'd heard about Garland's stroke from Junior and came to the hospital to sit with Jeannie. She walked outside with him so he could smoke. She watched him out of the corner of her eye, hidden behind her sunglasses. The curls she'd always loved were clipped short now, and his skin was leathery from years of being in the sun.

"Hey—I never wished you a happy birthday on the big five-o," she said.

"Yeah. How about that? I never thought I'd make it." He stared into the distance. "Some of those guys I was with in 'Nam have been dead over thirty years now. They just stopped, like a clock that's run out of batteries. They're frozen in time at eighteen or nineteen. But I keep going, and I don't know why."

They watched the traffic around the hospital for a while. Then Wick asked, "How was he?"

She shook her head. "Not good." Her face grew hot with backed-up tears.

He crushed his cigarette butt in the receptacle. "I didn't tell you about my mother. Aunt Lula called me back in October." He drew a deep breath. "She died."

"Oh, no." Jeannie put her hand on her heart. "I'm sorry."

"Yeah. Well, I hadn't seen her in about forty years, but, you know, as long as they're alive, you can hope that . . . something can change."

She nodded.

"Jeannie?"

She looked up at him. The sun glinted on the silver in his beard. Silver in Wick Whitaker's beard! And here they were, almost thirty years after they first met.

"I know this ain't a good time . . ." he started.

"For what?"

"For me to tell you I still love you."

She touched his arm, squeezed it, let go. She had no words that seemed right.

At Garland's bedside, Jeannie held his hand, kissed his forehead, careful to avoid the tubes attaching him to the world. He was still, moving only his eyes, and his silence was strange, unsettling. "Daddy, we're here," she said. Big Jean and Patty stood on the other side of his bed, as silent as he was. "You'll be better soon."

Suddenly, she longed to hear his voice, the sound she had been enraged at so many times in her life and had avoided for the past four months. She wanted to hear him speak to her again, giving her his blessing or even his condemnation. She felt the deep, old sorrow return, how she'd felt when they lost Debbie. The guilt. It had taken so long to get through it. And now, she'd done it again, put up a wall between herself and her family and then had to face the fallout. If she'd only been there, if she hadn't turned her back on her sister, and now on her father, perhaps she could have saved them.

# He Will Set Your Fields on Fire

In September 2001, just a few days after the Twin Towers fell, the family celebrated the first birthday of JP's baby, Cole, at Garland and Big Jean's house so Garland could be there. He didn't go out anymore, except to the doctor. He had suffered several mini-strokes after the first one, and he rarely spoke.

Jeannie gave Cole a child-sized acoustic guitar. Patty and Brian gave him a child-sized battery-operated Harley-Davidson motorcycle. He wasn't quite big enough to play with either one, but he enjoyed banging on Big Jean's kitchen pots with a wooden spoon.

"I wish Cole would go ahead and take off. How old was JP when he started walking?" Selena asked Patty.

"I don't remember," Patty said. "Maybe a year old?"

"Randall started walking at eleven months," Jeannie reported. "And Lee Ann started the week after her first birthday." She had read these facts in their baby books, written in Debbie's careful penmanship.

"He started crawling late too," Selena said, looking worriedly at Cole.

"My children never did crawl," Big Jean said.

Everyone turned to her with puzzled looks.

"Seriously?" Jeannie asked.

"Garland wouldn't let you all down on the floor. Said it was too dirty." Big Jean sat, ankles crossed, in a Sunday dress, panty hose, and low heels. Jeannie had tried all summer, to no avail, to get her to wear long shorts or capris, comfortable sandals or tennis shoes. Her beehive, partly gray but still mostly black, was not quite as tall as it had been in its 1970s heyday. "Jeannie and Junior stayed in the crib or a playpen and played together. Then one day Junior just climbed out and took off running, and Jeannie took off after him."

Jeannie looked over at her father, crumpled in his wheelchair. He had operated from fear his whole life, and it had saved him, all of them, from nothing. The Bible said perfect love casts out fear. Garland's love wasn't perfect, but it was love nonetheless, she knew.

Since Garland's stroke, they had come back together, as best they could. It was uncomfortable for Jeannie, and she was sure it was for them as well. But they were family, so they tried. They didn't talk about Oren Alford or the church or the Creation Park or the stripped and flattened land around the homeplace. They didn't talk about Debbie. This was how Jeannie was able to come around and check on Garland's health and celebrate Cole's birthday.

On TV, the film clip of the falling tower was showing again. They watched the plane sail into the building, watched the smoke fill the sky, watched people fall to their deaths. It was like watching a movie, not quite real, and yet, at the same time, exactly what they'd all been expecting their whole lives.

Brian shouted, "What do you say about it, Brother Garland?" He seemed to think Garland was hard of hearing.

Garland trembled slightly, gathering his words in his head, collecting them on his tongue. They all waited quietly, not wanting to interfere with the process. "The end," he said at last.

"We've gotten too soft!" Junior declared. "Should've been on those Muslims' tails all these years instead of letting them come right in and destroy us. You watch. They'll be going after Israel next."

"Amen!" Brian said. "Thank the Lord that Bush is president for this instead of Al Gore. He'd be handing them terrorists the keys to the White House."

"Isn't that the truth," Junior said.

"We're gonna have to go over there and kick some ass to get our country back," Brian said. He turned to Big Jean and added, "Sorry, Miss Jean."

"That's exactly right." Patty nodded.

"I'd sign up myself if I was twenty years younger," Brian said.

"Oh, me. Don't be giving JP any ideas," Big Jean said. She patted JP's leg. "You need to stay home with that baby."

"We're planning a Patriot Night at the church," Junior said. "We've got the praise team working on some patriotic songs, and I'm putting together a fireworks show. We need to get everybody saying 'God bless America' again."

"Amen!" Brian said.

Jeannie checked her watch and said, "I need to get going." She picked up Cole and gave him a kiss. "Happy birthday, Coco." Junior had already pinned him with this nickname. Then she kissed her mother and squeezed Garland's good hand, the one that hadn't curled and shriveled, and drove home.

Patriot Night was the next Saturday. Tom had come to spend the weekend with her, and they were sitting on the back porch with a bottle of wine when the crowds started gathering in the new Creation Park parking lot behind their house. The church had erected a wooden platform earlier that day, prompting Tom to ask Jeannie if they were planning a hanging. But it was a stage for the praise team, led by Randall, which started with a frenzied rendition of "God Bless the U.S.A." at dusk.

"I can't believe they're leading with that," Tom said, swirling his wine. "Isn't that a finale kind of song? Where do you go from here?"

The crowds, seated in camping chairs in the parking lot or on blankets on the sparse patches of grass left behind by the bulldozers, were now standing, swaying, arms lifted. Families all dressed in red, white, and blue. Bikers in black but with flag bandanas tied on their heads.

Neither Jeannie nor Tom was exactly enjoying it, but they sat on the porch the whole time and watched from a distance, mesmerized. Junior prayed, and Alford gave a "prophetic word" between songs. Jeannie had the uneasy feeling that it really was a prophetic moment, that some unfortunate turn was coming to her family and the church and the whole country that she couldn't prevent, any more than she'd been able to prevent what Brother Alford had brought. She and Tom had talked about it a lot, this feeling that the reaction to the terrorist attack, more than the attack itself, was sending the country, especially their part of the country, down a dark road. He was still weighing options for a move. He'd visited a friend in Portland over the summer and taken a drive up to Seattle while he was there, feeling it out. He said he liked the vibe there.

At the end, sure enough, the praise team started up "God Bless the U.S.A." again, with a fireworks show. With Junior in charge of fireworks, which were being set off among the debris that the construction crews had left littered in the fields, there was a good chance that the whole thing would catch fire, including the church and the house.

The thought didn't worry Jeannie. In fact, she felt a little thrill of perverse joy, thinking about watching the church go up in flames. She even had the thought that she could do it, after everybody left. She could set it all on fire. And if her house was part of it, maybe no one would suspect her.

Well. They would just collect the insurance money and build again. Why did she think she could save people who didn't think they needed to be saved? She'd been trying and failing all her life. All she could do was save herself.

# Run On

Nearly six months had passed since Jeannie had seen any activity on Creation Park. The machinery was gone. No trucks had come rumbling up the road in front of her house lately. Piles of lumber were out there rotting. A three-foot-high concrete wall they had constructed along the road next to Jeannie's house stretched about the length of a football field and then ended abruptly. Jeannie wondered how they thought it would keep freeloaders out of the park, even if it did make it all the way around the farm. At first, she thought they must have taken the winter off from construction, but as spring woke up the remaining trees and warmed the scarred land, she began to suspect something was up.

She hadn't heard any news about the park from her family, but then she didn't see them much. She had resumed visiting her parents on a limited basis, dropping in to deliver prescriptions or taking them for doctor visits since Big Jean didn't drive and Garland no longer could. Things weren't the same between them, of course, but were things *ever* the same? No. That was the great realization of her life, the obvious truth, that everything changes.

The distance from Junior and Patty was hard to accept. Her twin and her only living sister. They had always looked to her for answers, and Patty was right about one thing: it did bother Jeannie that she wasn't their boss anymore. They needed one, and it needed to be somebody other than Oren Alford. But they didn't want to hear what she had to say. They didn't believe, as she did, that Alford always left destruction in his wake and always walked away scot-free.

She had walked across what she now called "the wasteland" to the river, just to give her eyes something to rest on, and walking back, she saw Wick repairing the fence between her yard and the church parking lot. It wasn't technically church property—she supposed it was her responsibility—but when she stopped and thanked him, he seemed more than glad to do it.

"I haven't seen any activity over here on the farm for a few months," she said.

"Mmmm-hmmm." He squinted at the razed land where the mini train station was supposed to go. "I don't think you're going to be seeing any activity anytime soon. Maybe ever."

"Really?"

Wick nodded. "They've run out of money."

"No shit?" She felt a little smile creeping up.

"Donations have dropped. A lot of people lost jobs in the recession, plus the two factories that closed in the past year." Wick bent over to put his pliers and extra wire in his toolbox, groaning a little when he stood up again. "Junior's flipping out. Trying to stay on top of everything. Plus, apparently Rosie is expecting."

Jeannie's mouth formed an O.

"Yeah. What's that, like seven, eight kids between the two of them? Anyway, he's in the shit. I told him from the beginning Alford was gonna leave him holding the bag. I think he believes me now. Alford hasn't been here in a couple of weeks. Said he was going to visit his daughter and grandchildren in Oklahoma. But nobody's heard from him, and that ain't normal."

"I doubt that his daughter lets him around his grandchildren," Jeannie said.

"Wherever he is, I doubt he's coming back."

"Well, that's good news!" Jeannie smiled.

Wick looked away.

"What?" Jeannie asked.

"Alford was taking payouts for this, that, and the other. Supposedly for architects, concept designers, blah blah blah. Now Junior owes all these contractors, and apparently your daddy mortgaged the farm to help pay for it." He looked back at her, with eyes that looked as sad as they had the day she left him.

Jeannie felt as if the wind had been knocked out of her. She put one hand on a fencepost and tried to breathe. "Probably the house too," she said.

Wick put his hand, big and rough and warm, over hers.

Late on a Monday night a couple of weeks later, Jeannie was reading in bed when she heard a motorcycle growling in her driveway. She could hear every little noise out there in the quiet of the farm. She sometimes heard vehicles pass on the road in front of the house, but she knew this one had stopped. Her first thought was that it was Wick, coming again to check on her or try to convince her to take him back. She waited, listening to the engine. Tom's car had been vandalized at the school when he spoke out about the Creation Park, and she worried that this might be someone out to get them, maybe one of the King's Highway Warriors, there to mess with her house or car, or to scare her, or worse. She picked up her phone and crept to a window at the front of the house. She peered between the curtain and the window frame. She had no lights on in front of her house, so all that illuminated the motorcycle were its own headlight and the faint security lights shining from the church parking lot. She had protested to Junior about the light pollution, so he had agreed to at least turn them down.

She couldn't make out who it was, but he sat there for a while, maybe two or three minutes, and then drove south, toward the Tennessee line.

# This May Be the Last Time

Tom resigned at the end of the school year. The furor over his statements had died down along with the Creation Park, but he was never really one of them after that, in the town or at school. This wasn't his place, he said. He stayed until his lease was up in July, reluctant to leave Jeannie but eager to make a new life in Seattle.

Jeannie drove to his apartment in Bowling Green and helped him pack his car with his few possessions. He and his neighbor in the apartment building, a college guy, carried his couch and mattress next door. He'd given his thrift shop café table and chairs to the graduate student across the hall and taken the crates he'd used as coffee table, TV stand, and nightstand to the curb.

"Thanks, man," the neighbor said, counting out two twenty-dollar bills and handing them to him. "Have fun out there."

Tom nodded. "See you, man."

Jeannie looked around the empty studio apartment, perfect for a college student. He had told her he didn't like to be tied down by possessions, and she saw that this was true. He seemed lighter, younger, already. His ties to his family, to his job, to the past—and, yes, to her—were loose in a way that she could only imagine. He reminded Jeannie of her favorite book from high school: he was like Huck Finn, lighting out for the Territory.

"I want you to come out there for a visit after I get my own place, all right?" He took both of her hands in his. "Just a visit. And then you can decide if you want to stay or come back to Kentucky."

She smiled. "All right."

He pulled her into his arms, and they held each other for a while. "I don't think I can drive away if you're standing on the sidewalk waving goodbye." He sobbed into her hair.

She kissed his cheek and pulled away. "I'll go now, so you don't have to."

Driving home, she slid her new Lucinda Williams CD into the stereo and jumped ahead to "Get Right with God." She knew if she repeated it all the way home, she'd be all right.

She stopped and got groceries for Rosie and the kids. The day after Jeannie had heard the motorcycle in her driveway late at night, Rosie had called and asked if she'd seen Junior. No one in the family or at the church had seen him that day. He'd missed his King's Highway Warriors meeting that afternoon. Rosie had last seen him the night before. His Road King was gone. They hadn't heard from him since.

When Jeannie turned into Rosie's driveway, she saw Brother Clarence pushing a mower in her front yard. He was thin and stooped, his belt looped around almost double, no cap on his bald head. Since he and Garland were about the same age, she guessed he was close to seventy-five. She got out of the car and called out, "Brother Clarence!" and waved her arms.

He stopped and turned off the mower. "Hello, little Jeannie."

She smiled, didn't remind him that she was forty-seven now. "What are you doing out here, Brother Clarence? I'm sure some of the young kids at the church could do this. Or one of Rosie's kids." The oldest one was twelve, surely old enough to push a mower.

"Well." Brother Clarence smiled. "I don't mind it a bit."

He had taken over all the pastoral duties, unpaid, since Junior and Alford had left, until the church could straighten out the financial mess of the unfinished park and hire a new pastor.

Every time Jeannie started to think it was all a scam, a hoax, a lie, everything she'd been taught about God and love and goodness, she thought about Brother Clarence, and she had to admit she just didn't know.

At the end of summer, Big Jean called Jeannie from the hospital, where Garland had been readmitted the day before, crying. "The doctor said to call the family in."

Jeannie, Patty, and Big Jean sat with him through the day and into the evening. Patty held his right hand and Big Jean held his left. Jeannie sat at the foot of the bed, face down, anointing his feet with her tears. The only sounds in the room were their sobs and his labored breathing and, from outside the room, the chatter of nurses, the beeps and whirs of medical machinery.

"Maybe we should sing something," Jeannie whispered.

"I don't know if I can," Patty said.

Big Jean caressed his hand. "I think he'd like to hear y'all sing again, one more time."

With a shaky voice Jeannie started.

*I will meet you in the morning . . .*

Patty and Big Jean joined her on the chorus, harmonizing perfectly as if they had just yesterday sung the song over and over until Garland said it was acceptable. They could hear Debbie's part and Junior's, in their heads, and Garland's line between theirs, *I will, I will.*

# Sing the Glory Down

After all the stages she'd performed on and all the TV episodes she'd appeared in, one might think that a tiny venue in a strip mall wouldn't be intimidating to Jeannie, but it was, after all, the Bluebird Cafe. Even if she'd never heard of it or been there in the audience, she would have recognized the spirit in the place. That was the only word she knew to use, *spirit*. Something not available to the usual five senses but felt in a deeper way. It was like . . . stepping on stage at the Bethel Independent Church of the Pentecost in 1972. Yes, like that.

She had been invited to do a songwriters' night in the round with three others who were better known around town than she was, so she was jittery. But it helped to know she had her people out there. Wick sat at a table with Nate and Lee Ann, who was seven months pregnant. She spotted Marcella nearby and DeWayne in the back of the room.

When it was her turn, she tuned her guitar and said, "Here's one I wrote for my ex-husband." She raised her eyebrows, and everybody chuckled. "It's a love song."

*Thank God you always walked beside me*
*Even when I closed the door behind me*
*Never once have you denied me*
*You were beside me all the way*
*Thank God we both just kept on going*
*Didn't try to stop how we were growing*
*My life's been better just for knowing*
*You were beside me all the way*

At the end of the night, flushed with hugs and compliments and a promising conversation with a music publisher, she climbed into Wick's pickup with her guitar, and he drove north to the Holliman homeplace, which they had purchased together, along with a couple of acres, from Big Jean, who had to sell the rest of the farm to pay off the mortgage that Garland and Junior had taken out. They were patching together a decent living. They had an overflowing garden, set in the ruins of what was almost Creation Park, like Adam and Eve back in paradise. Wick had built a new garage beside the house and still fixed cars and motorcycles. Sometimes they performed together at clubs, parties, weddings. Jeannie sold a few songs and did some producing and vocal coaching in Nashville.

She'd seen this life for her and Wick, created it in her mind first and said they could do it, and then they had. Maybe she'd even named it and claimed it, spoken the victory, just like Oren Alford used to say.

But, also, the doctor had just found a troubling spot on Wick's lung. That was the part Oren Alford had never included, the other side of the good, the dark spot that was always there. "Hard living," Wick had admitted. "I started smoking when I was twelve. That's forty years." Jeannie had cried all the way home, and Wick had patted her hand and joked, "No need to worry about me. I'm too stubborn to die and let Tom Becker get you back."

"Shut up, Wick."

"Puny little schoolteacher. I can take him with one lung and one hand tied behind my back."

She laughed and wiped her eyes. "Shut up, Wick."

Jeannie waited at the side door of the Bethel Senior Citizens Center. She'd talked Big Jean into attending some activities there, to get her out of the house a little. Big Jean was like a lost child since Garland passed.

Jeannie jumped out of her car when she saw Big Jean emerge and went around to open the passenger-side door.

"Lord, I'm glad I don't have to ride that senior citizens van back home," Big Jean said. "That Kevin acts like he's driving a fire truck."

"What did y'all do today?" Jeannie asked as she got back in the driver's seat.

Big Jean sighed musically, a weary bird song. "Somebody came from up at the college to teach us about writing your memoirs. I said that sounds like something a movie star would do, but she said it just means a story from your life. She said, 'You might want to give it to your children or grandchildren.'"

Jeannie stopped with the key halfway to the ignition and looked at her. "Did you do it? Did you write something?"

"I tried. I got it right here in my pocketbook."

"Can I read it?" Jeannie had realized at some point that she knew lots of Garland's stories of his childhood and family but hardly any of Big Jean's. He had filled up every room they'd been in together, and Big Jean had shrunk to fit the space that was left.

Big Jean pulled a crumpled sheet of paper from her purse. "It's just one page. I got finished and looked around, and everybody was still writing. Agnes Baugh was sitting next to me, and I looked at her paper, and she was writing about hiding in the corncrib when she was four years old. I thought, Lord, she's got a long way to go. I can barely even remember being a child. Mama died when I was six, I remember that. I remember watching her iron, and I remember being afraid to follow her into the henhouse."

Jeannie took the paper from her and read:

> In 1972 my husband Garland Holliman, Sr. started a Gospel group called "The Gospelettes" consistant of himself, our four children and myself. We travelled all over and brought the Gospel in song to people every where for many years.
>
> In February 1988 our worst fears came to pass. We lost our beloved daughter Deborah.
>
> In September 2002 the Lord called Garland home. On his tombstone we had engraved:
>
> 
>
> Garland Holliman, Sr.
>
> February 8, 1928–September 16, 2002
>
> He sings in God's angel band now.
>
> 

Jeannie handed the paper back to her. "That memoir has a lot of *we* and not much *me*."

Big Jean sighed and stuffed the paper back into her purse. "It's a long, long story, and I was getting the headache." She snapped the purse shut, ready to go home.

# GLORY LAND

Whit sings to herself, to dogs and cats that wander over, to the squirrels. She sings with the birds and the wind. She loves everything because she doesn't know not to, and she sings the gospel of love. Jeannie walks her all around the Holliman farm, under the trees behind the house, past the bulldozed earth, across the cow pasture, down to the river. Whit picks up stones on the bank and throws them in, jumps up and down and claps, and tells Jeannie, whom she calls Neenee, to clap too. She lifts her arms and sings with the rushing water. She is Lee Ann's daughter, the closest thing Jeannie and Wick will ever have to a grandbaby.

Jeannie wonders if spirits walk this place too. Out of the corner of her eye, sometimes she sees a mist or a shadow, nothing that can't be explained by science.

But she sees this: On the long, sagging porch on the back of Papaw Virgil's house, Garland sits in his mother's old rocker, reading the Sunday newspaper. Papaw Virgil is bouncing Patty on his knees and singing, "Ride a little horsie, go to town, ride a little horsie, don't fall down!" He opens his knees and drops her between them on the last line, and she squeals and laughs. Debbie and Junior are inspecting something under the porch. Jeannie sits at Garland's feet. He wears handsome brown leather shoes with pointy toes. Sometimes Jeannie plays Shoeshine Girl and cleans them for him. She pretends that he gives her money for this, which she takes to her poor, widowed mother who is too ill to work, or she uses it to buy food for her poor, orphaned brothers and sisters, for whom she is responsible. The money she makes is never enough for a complete meal, just a few vegetables to go in a pot of water to make a thin soup.

Garland is talking about de Gaulle and the Common Market and the Beast, the man Satan will send with signs and wonders. "They'll think he's from God because of the miracles he'll perform," he says, "but what they don't know is that Satan can perform miracles too." Jeannie imagines she will go off into the woods behind Papaw Virgil's house and hide when the end times come. There are trees to cover her and a river to drink from. She could catch fish and squirrels to eat. Papaw Virgil used to do that when he was a boy, so he could teach her how. But she knows there is a possibility that the Antichrist could cut down all the trees and poison all the rivers.

Papaw Virgil jumps up and starts dancing with Patty, singing:

*Froggie went a-courtin' and he did ride*
*King kong kitchee kitchee ki-me-o*
*With a sword and a pistol by his side*
*King kong kitchee kitchee ki-me-o!*

He is tall and bent and stringy, like a green bean from the garden. He pulls a harmonica out of his pocket and plays it while Patty dances. Out in the yard, Junior tries to do a Russian dance, his arms folded horizontally in front of him, alternating one leg bent and the other thrust out. "Look! I'm a commie!" Garland rattles his paper at their foolishness.

"How did Satan get the power to do miracles?" Jeannie asks Garland.

Garland pulls himself away from his paper. "He was an angel! An angel who started a rebellion."

"Why did he start a rebellion?"

"Because God gave the angels free will, just like human beings."

"Why didn't God take away his power?"

Garland doesn't answer; he's reading. Patty spins to Papaw Virgil's harmonica tune until she falls down. Junior brings a little black garden snake he's caught in some brush by the fence over to the porch and, standing behind Debbie, dangles it above her right shoulder. She screams and runs into the house to find Big Jean.

"Eh Law!" Papaw Virgil sits panting in a straight-backed chair and shakes out his harmonica. "Aunt Sary and Aunt Emmylou used to sing them old songs. One played the fiddle, and one played the banjer. They loved to play and sing and dance. They were Hollimans, my daddy's sisters. All the Hollimans could play a instrument. One day they come in—we lived with my grandparents over there at the old homeplace by the river; you can still see part of the chimney standing—and they said, 'Mammy, we're going to Texas.' They was married to two cousins, Uncle Jim and Uncle Jack, and they all wanted to go. See, everybody was going to Texas then."

"Did you cry when they left?" Jeannie asks.

"I don't recollect that I did." Papaw Virgil looks out at the trees along the road, their golden-green leafy branches moving gently in the breeze. "I followed them as far as I could down this road right here, waving goodbye. It was a dirt road then, and they rode in wagons pulled by horses. They laughed more than any two people I ever knowed. If they ever had a serious thought, they never let on."

"Do you remember them, Daddy?" Jeannie asks.

"Do what?" Garland shakes out his newspaper and looks up, frowning.

"Do you remember Aunt Sary and Aunt Emmylou?"

"Naw. That was before my time."

Papaw Virgil stands up. "Garland takes back after the McGowns, his mama's people."

"But Daddy plays a instrument," Jeannie says. She looks at Garland, but he's not listening.

Papaw Virgil steps off the porch. "You're right there. He got that from the Hollimans. You're right there."

Junior is hiding under the porch. He creeps out, holds a finger up to his lips, and tosses the garden snake a few inches from Garland's feet. Garland just kicks it off the porch and keeps on reading.

"Well, shoot," Junior says. "Won't nothing get him off that paper."

"Let's go fishing," Papaw Virgil says. He walks over to the shed and retrieves three fishing poles, with Junior and Patty following behind. "Come on, Jeannie! He ain't paying you no mind!"

Jeannie gets up, jumps off the porch, and runs after them. Debbie is looking out the window and sees them going, so she runs out and yells for them to wait for her. "You can come if you don't cry and carry on," Papaw Virgil tells her. "I ain't bringing no sugar-tit."

They walk behind the house and through the broken wooden gate. Pale yellow butterflies flutter across their dirt path to the river. They are singing the song Papaw Virgil had started on the porch:

> *Ki-mo-ke-mo ki-mo-ke*
> *Way down yonder in a hollow tree*
> *An owl and a bat and a bumblebee*
> *King kong kitchee kitchee ki-me-o!*

"McGown through and through, music or not," Virgil says under his breath when they finish the song. "I might could have saved him if I'd let him stayed in school. He'd a-been a good lawyer. But I didn't know that then. I made him quit school to help on the farm, and he was mad about it."

Jeannie is loyal. She doesn't like for Papaw Virgil to grumble about Garland. She looks back at the porch, thinking she'll run back to him, but he is absorbed. He hasn't noticed they've gone.

"He was the best student in the school. Y'all know where that schoolhouse was? Up there about a mile and a half, around that bend," Papaw Virgil points up the road. "Miss Doss said he was brilliant. She said, 'Mr. Holliman, Garland is the most brilliant student I've ever had.' But Chester was gone off to the war, and I needed his help, so I made him quit. And this is what happened. All he had was the Bible to use all that brilliance on, and so that's where he turned it. Religion ruirnt him. Made him good for nothing."

"Tell us about Chester," Junior says.

They're nearing the river. The trees are gathered there, waving them over. Patty is running ahead, sun lighting her golden hair. "Chester was a Holliman, the spit and image of my daddy," Papaw Virgil says. "Full of fun. One time, he took our old rooster to school and set him on Miss Doss's desk. She was a prissy little woman, probably never plucked a chicken in her life. I couldn't even get too mad at him about taking that old rooster because I would have paid to seen the look on her face when she seen it strutting across her desk." Papaw Virgil's laugh sounds like a rooster.

"And he died in the war?" Junior asks. He likes war stories.

"Eyah. South Pacific." Virgil seems sad now. "When they come up to the door to tell us, your grandmama said, 'Naw, Virgil. Don't let 'em in. Don't you let 'em in, you hear?' She took to the bed and never got up. Eh Law."

White clouds are floating so slowly across the pale blue sky, you'd have to sit and stare at them a long time to tell they're moving. Jeannie, Debbie, and Patty have gathered fistfuls of dandelions, fleabane, bird's-foot violets, and red clover. When they reach the shady river, they toss the flowers in and watch them float away. Sunlight glints on the water, sparkles, winks at them. Virgil takes off his hat, fans himself with it, and looks up, squinting, at a red-tailed hawk gliding overhead.

"All some people want to talk about is how they don't belong in this world and can't wait to get to the next one." He replaces his hat, puts a worm on Patty's hook, and hands her the pole. "You reckon they gonna appreciate the other side if they don't appreciate the world God's done give them?"

Whit stops and listens to every sound and asks, "What's that?" Jeannie tells her cow, bumblebee, dove, killdeer. She almost feels sad to name them for her. She knows she's taking the magic away, giving her labels to stick on everything, including herself, but she is curious, she must know. "What's that?" Whit asks, pointing to the east.

"That's a bobwhite quail," Jeannie tells her. "It says, 'Bob-*white*! Bob-*white*!'"

Whit stops and listens to the lonesome bird call. She points one wet, chubby finger to the sky, eyes wide, and says, "Listen! Listen!"

# Acknowledgments

I deeply appreciate Silas House's guidance on my writing journey. His editing and advice have been invaluable, and his generosity and willingness to lift up other writers are unmatched. What a blessing to Kentucky he is.

I'm grateful for the vision, professionalism, and enthusiasm of director Ashley Runyon, acquisitions editor Patrick O'Dowd, and the rest of the staff of the University Press of Kentucky.

A grant from the Kentucky Foundation for Women supported my attendance at the Appalachian Writers' Workshop, where Robert Morgan was the first person to read early pages of this novel. His encouragement and praise kept me going. Many years later, a Zoom writing workshop with Kristin Hanggi clarified story structure so that I could do the final revision.

I appreciate the feedback on this novel that I received from my Spalding MFA family, especially current and former faculty members Leslie Daniels, Pete Duval, Robin Lippincott, Lorraine M. López, and Mary Yukari Waters and fellow students Susan Berla and Amy Hanridge, who read and responded beyond the workshop requirements. Another writer friend, Renea Dijab, read and commented on an early complete draft and checked in to keep me accountable.

I owe everything to Barbara and Bobby Oberhausen. Mama and Daddy (who, thankfully, were not at all like the Mama and Daddy in this novel) gave me nothing but unconditional love and support from my first breath to their last.

Finally, I can never adequately thank my husband, Samir Rastoder, and my daughters, Sara and Emmy, for tolerating my occasional absences to write, encouraging me to keep going, and celebrating every little victory. Our family is my best creation.